Carl!

2/13/2013

It was a good story, and quite unique. I really enjoyed it.

Sharon P.

Great ending to a wonderful book! I would love an autographed copy! Thanks so much for this enjoyable read!

Ginger C.

Addicting.

Darren I.

It was a good book; I really enjoyed it.

Joe P.

I am so glad I got to read it as it was being born. I have enjoyed your story and loved the many twist and turns you have presented in the reading.

Donna H.

Great story sir. I want an autographed copy of this excellent adventure. So.. when's the movie coming out? LOL

Dale C.

The story is very engaging, dream inspiring, emotional and all around enjoyable. I would love an autographed copy. You could make this a very successful series, it already has a place in our favorite book shelves.

Cindy L.

Published: Hayley Publishing

Copyright © Hayley Publishing

ISBN: 978-0-615-13297-6

Many thanks to all those who helped bring this work to print.

To my cyber friends, to numerous to list here—you know who you are—for walking with me chapter by chapter guiding me through the process.

And a heartfelt thank you to Ann C. who spent hours reading and editing. Plus Ann approached Tracy F. (something I could never have done) asking her to edit.

And yes, thank you Tracy.

To Professor Craig, you got me headed in the right direction.

To Hayley, for lending her name.

To Angela—all those hours online setting me up.

Thanks Nathan, now we're head & shoulders above the rest.

Thanks to my wife, Renee, for saying, 'do it' and then performing all the home front duties giving me the endless hours necessary to accomplish this undertaking.

I'll never be able to convey here how much appreciation I have for all of you. Without everyone of your alls involvement, these pages would not exist to have and to hold.

I am truly humbled.

Enjoy

—

Chapter One

The professor's abrupt change in inflection snapped Brian out of his daze.

"This was done on a scale *never* before achieved by mankind. Today, it stands as a tribute to man's undying commitment to survive. I never said it *didn't* help."

That Brian had been half listening was something that happened more often than he would admit. As the morning progressed, this day was worse than usual for that. Earlier, although the professor did not stand in the sun, the reflection from the floor caught his white shirt. Bright, it left Brian little choice but to gaze out the windows. The view was green, rich, and earthy. It kept vying for his attention.

Brian was prone to wait on what others said and did before he was comfortable participating. He'd rather observe than contribute. When given center stage, it made him nervous.

Analogizing, hitting all the points, the professor went on for what seemed forever through his dissertation. Brian had caught something about a group of people known as Polynesians. He had missed the first half of the analogy and only caught that they were island hoppers. Once they discovered a new island, they would go fetch the rest of the clan, set up shop so to speak, and then consume what was available in order to live before moving on. At least it went something along those lines.

As Brian gazed out the windows, he heard Danny ask for clarification, "So what you're saying is we should have been planet hopping to maintain a steady supply of new resources?"

Danny was more or less the class leader or *clown*, depending on whether it was the teacher's point of view or that of a peer. It was not because he was a dominant figure; it just gravitated to him. Willing to take the initiative, Danny always cracked the first joke or brought something unusual to the attention of the others during class. Unlike Brian, Danny didn't mind the spotlight.

Almost noiselessly, a slight giggle escaped the small group at the impossibility of what he said.

"Obviously, we won't be doing any planet hopping," the professor stated. He acknowledged the groups understanding of man's ability to apply the science necessary to make it so. "But once we were committed to doing just that. Survival, kids, is a strong motivator. It needed to be done before all the earth's resources were depleted."

"So what are you saying...?" Pete asked.

Between Brian and Danny, Pete was middle of the road. He was not an instigator, but more than willing to participate in anything Danny suggested. It fell to Brian to steer them clear of anything too outrageous.

"Simply this," Ed said. "We ended up in the same position as one particular tribe of Polynesians who found an island which provided abundantly. Over the course of one hundred years their numbers grew to over ten thousand."

It was a phenomenal number. Brian tried to imagine that many people standing outside of the window.

The professor droned, explaining something to the effect that they didn't foresee the collapse of their civilization until after it had begun. By then, it was too late. There weren't enough trees on the island to make canoes. Without canoes, those left behind starved. Unfortunately, *most* were left behind.

Not able to visualize, Brian gave up trying to picture that many people.

"That's us in a nutshell," the professor said. "The Earth is just an island in space. We've consumed everything we understood how to make use of, and now, this is where we're stuck."

Brian decided that had to be the professor's analogy—the Earth was an island in space.

"So we traveled here and missed our ride out?" Pete asked. "Because we didn't recognize it was time to go island hopping through space?"

"That's a good question," the professor stated. "The answer is no." He then paused, more to draw everyone's attention to make his point rather than any reservation on what he was about to say. "Nothing in our history suggests our ancestors traveled here. What it does show, is a steady progression of our increase knowledge as we learned the sciences. And the continual improvement upon that knowledge as it was applied. I actually believe it all started right here, but so you know, there is no proof. If we travel here, then all knowledge as to how we did so has vanished, and vanished completely."

"Didn't you tell us a while ago that there were manned flights into space generated from this planet?" Danny asked. "Were any of them looking for a new place?"

"It was in its infancy," the professor said. "Those flights never ventured beyond Mars. It's an age old problem: Space. The space between us and where we need to go is far too great. The time commitment for any one individual is far too long. We wouldn't live to make even part of the trip there, let alone there and back."

"So we wasted resources on something that would never help?" Pete stated.

Brian expected the professor to say yes and wished the class were over so he could go outside and enjoy what he saw through the windows. It continued to beckon to him and finally gained a foothold completely when he saw the plane.

He began to wonder what it would be like to fly, free to be beyond the fence.

The why of what drew him to the outdoors—was elusive. There was nothing he could do except chores within the confines of the fence. Brian had lived inside it all his life. He had seen just about every square inch of accessible space.

The fence, however, represented protection. More than represented it, it actually physically provided it. The thought of truly going beyond it enticed him, but at the same time scared him. The danger was all too real.

But in the plane, he would be above the reach of any danger and free of the fence's confines.

From within the safety of the fence, he had witnessed encounters between wild animals which terrified him. Predators, were numerous, and vicious. He recalled one instance that happened so close to him while he was doing chores…it was intense when it happened, and just the thought brought on an adrenaline rush.

It was then Brian heard Ed's voice change where it caught his attention, and he quickly quieted the need to respond. The rush was slight; he was safe in the classroom with the professor.

"Those efforts produced unmanned flights which are traveling to other planets as we speak. Think about it gentleman; spaceships that were built here on earth are traveling within our galaxy."

For the first time, the professor had everybody's attention. Brian moved to the edge of his seat and leaned forward. What he heard was impossible, especially compared to their finite existence within the fence.

"What is the point of doing that if there's no one on board?" Danny asked. He looked around at the rest of the class. He had stated what should have been apparent to whoever launched the spaceships. He wanted to know why they had bothered.

"Personally, it won't do us any good," the professor admitted. "Those ships have a long way to go before they'll reach their destinations." He then bestowed upon them some incredible knowledge. "We have the capability of *manning* those flights any time we wish."

A deep silence spread within Brian's mind as he abandoned the senses of hearing and sight to digest this information.

The whole class was there; the professor took them there, as he had others before them. Brian was first to catch the professor waiting, and intuitively knew he waited on them with bemusement. Ed was an excellent professor, who over the years had taken many a student down this path of realization, and then their appreciation of man's ability to accomplish the impossible.

"How can we do that?" Brian asked.

"The science that makes this possible is the Dupe. It's what gives us hope," Ed said, starting to smile. Everyone smiled then. It lightened the atmosphere; he was making a joke.

"The time we get on is totally discretionary. We choose when." The professor still smiled at the accomplishment he was explaining, and his tone never strayed from serious.

"We're depending on a food processor to zip us through space to these ships that are hundreds of years old?" Pete yelled out, and the room erupted with laughter.

"Hey, sounds like we're toast," Danny shouted, wanting in on the act. It worked too; the professor waited, until they were silent.

"It's more than a food processor," Ed said. "That the first ships won't be arriving for a long time is also true. They'll be a lot older when they get to where they're going and none of you guys will be getting on."

"No joke?" Brian asked.

"No joke."

"Well," Brian stated, prompting for further information, "are you going to tell us how it works?"

"Well you know Dupe is slang for duplicator. What you don't know, is zero plus zero equals zero. Okay, you do know that, fine. This translates into: You can't make something from nothing." The professor paused. "Okay, I'm hoping that sunk in. When you're at the cafeteria, after you select your food, the platform holding your selection glides down to the dispensing doors just like an elevator. It has just left a chamber containing a cloud of every known element on earth. It assembled your food from that cloud."

"That basic, huh," Danny said, feigning boredom. They ate three squares a day at the cafeteria. A previous teacher had even taken them on tour of the whole Dupping facility. It was familiar stuff.

"The men who maintain the Dupe go to great lengths to ensure they keep enough of every molecule suspended in that cloud to duplicate more than just food. That's all you guys ever get to use it for. If a bearing has to be replaced on a motor, as long as the monitor on the Dupe has a selection for it, presto, it comes out from behind the same doors."

They knew that, but Danny asked, "Will it do a solar panel?"

"It's a selection."

"Will it do a computer terminal?" Pete asked, with something just as complicated but larger.

"It's in there," The professor said. "Look, you guys aren't going to keep me here all day trying to outdo each other with things that can or cannot be duped. Let me say this. When someone here dies—we use the Dupe to replace them. Every one of you came out from behind those doors."

And for the second time in one day, the room went totally silent, this time, for much longer.

***

"Food's good," Danny commented to no one in particular. Brian and Pete were seated with him around a small table. Danny was just making conversation; no one ever talked about the food.

As they ate, they now understood fully what the Dupe could do. They stared at the dispensing doors while others used it. This room for them was the cafeteria, and it was hard to fathom that they were just another item on the menu it had spat out.

They all had chosen the same lunch of gourmet fish. Spiced to perfection, fall-apart tender; it came with an array of different dips and garnishes to complement it.

For them, the cafeteria had transformed into something much more than a place to eat.

"I'll never be able to look at that thing the same way," Brian said, his mouth full. "What it is—is amazing. If we had access to more than the food menu, anything we want is ours. It's a wish come true."

"The genie is out of the bottle," Danny said, with a grin. "Go ahead, wish for something."

"Something," Pete said, taking Danny's idea a step further. "This is much better than a genie. We just call it dad and it gives us whatever we want. That's a whole lot better than the three wish thing."

"It's really too bad it didn't work like it was supposed too," Brian said.

"Yeah, but this is better," Pete interjected. "Someone's invention gone haywire that will give us anything we want."

"You heard the professor," Brian protested. "It wasn't an accident. It's just being used for something other than what it was intended. It will send anyone of us to those ships."

"Quit arguing," Danny pounded the table with his fist. "They didn't make it to produce food or anything else. So it was an accident, they wanted a transporter. But it'll dupe you instead with one of you here with us and the other on one of those ships. And there you'll soon be dead, as you starve. In case you weren't listening, there's no one on board to take care of you."

***

In the afternoon session, the professor continued. He wasn't just teaching this, he was adamant about it. He told them that Dr. Stan Swanson was the Dupe's inventor. Stan's problems began when he succeeded in transporting a live monkey from point A to point B.

Though the monkey died within minutes of transporting, Stan was elated. Clearly, the monkey was alive upon arriving at point B.

It worked!

Selecting another monkey, Stan's team put it in at point A. There, it was digitalized, vaporized, and transmitted to point B, where it was reassembled within the chamber now called the Dupe.

Autopsies showed both monkeys suffered the same fate—heart failure.

Three days later, after recalibrating and testing the equipment, the third monkey lay on the descending platform, dying, like its predecessors. A quick thinking team member, back from vacation, ran out of the room and into the hall. He grabbed a portable defibrillator, tearing open the package as he ran back. He cleared everyone and zapped the darned little thing with it. When he did, it jerked horrifically in response.

Its heart began to beat.

It lived.

Soon, the champagne was flowing.

Cameras recorded history.

Later, someone noticed the monkey. The poor thing was still lying on the platform. After the pictures, the Doctor must have set him down. Obviously, enduring the aftereffects of transporting, the monkey was gently picked up and placed back in its cage where it was left to rest.

This moved the party to an exclusive club.

By the next morning, newspapers around the world printed exclusive front-page articles with pictures taken at the lab, of the doctor—who loved to smile for the camera—with the history-making monkey. The following day their celebration continued. No one reported to work. They basked in the attention, and would do so for as long as they could. Only those who cleaned cages and fed monkeys let themselves in that day.

The morning after that, Stan was first to arrive at the lab. He went directly to see the monkey, who was now famous, and certainly had Stan destined for the history books. It was lying in its own excrement; its food and water were left untouched.

A day later, it too died.

The doctor who performed the autopsy said the cause of death was the result of dehydration.

Stan personally visited those responsible for maintaining the suspended element cloud in the chamber. He wanted to know if sufficient oxygen and hydrogen levels had been maintained. He was assured they were, and they had done so as well for the previous two monkeys.

A few days later, Stan and his team were ready. Another history-making monkey was vaporized. Its heart restarted. IVs inserted. This time, there was a medical staff. They would provide care around the clock. Stan brought in several primatologists, experts in monkey behavior. They were at his beck and call. They would observe and record everything.

He vowed to the press, "This monkey will not die."

He was correct.

Ten days later, the medical staff left. There was nothing for them to do. There never had been, except for the first day. They told Stan that the monkey was doing fine. They assured him it was just as fit physically as it had been before transporting.

The primatologists didn't draw the same conclusion. Physically fit, yes. But they told Stan it was as if the monkey was learning everything anew. Monkeys learn quickly so it was hard for the experts to say for sure how the experience affected it but to them it acted like a newborn.

This analysis led Stan to believe that the transporter project was a failure. If it transported you without your memory intact, it was useless. From the beginning, they knew this might be a possibility. The prevailing theory said it wouldn't be a problem. If the equipment worked as it was designed, and it did, it read and reassembled every atom to its correct position. The memory was there.

The primatologists suggested they could be interpreting recuperation as learning. They really didn't know and that darned monkey couldn't communicate what it had gone through.

The next morning, Stan's staff found him lying on the platform. He had rigged a timer to the defibrillator and had an empty IV bag above him. He had donned those before going in. Stan's eyes didn't quite focus on them when they talked, although it was as if he tried. His pants were wet and urine dripped onto the floor from the platform.

His brain functioned as a blank slate.

From birth, until two years of age, the brain develops to eighty percent of its adult weight. During this time, the brain generates millions of neurons; those neurons make thousands of new connections while motor and language skills develop. Unfortunately, at Stan's age, his brain was fully developed. He would be capable of learning, but neurons would not make nearly as many new connections; therefore, it would take him a lot longer.

***

The boys had finished eating and were cleaning their table off at the cafeteria.

"Can you believe what the Doc did to himself?" Pete asked. "He just invented a gold mine. Why didn't he realize he didn't have to vaporize himself to be duped?"

"He was thinking transporter all the way," Brian reminded him.

Chapter Two

The following morning Brian got out of bed, hopped into the shower, where he stayed until the sleepiness washed away. Quickly he toweled, dressed, and left the house.

At a brisk pace, he passed row after row of houses that were mostly empty. For more than four centuries, off and on, different places had served to house students in this section of the Installation. Though their colors were faded, none of them needed any major repair. Still neat and trimmed, the shrubbery, gnarled with age, matched the quaint setting. Brian's own house was just as old.

At the cafeteria, he duped a couple of gourmet sandwiches and water, items he could easily carry. The sandwiches were thick. Everything about them was exceptionally fresh, and very tasty. Brian rarely picked anything from the menu in the morning where he had to sit and use utensils.

The bottled water went into his back pocket.

Off to his next destination, he worked at devouring the sandwiches. He didn't have far to go and ate quickly. When he arrived at the storage shed, one sandwich was gone, and half of the other. He opened the door to the shed and made his way along a wall which held baggers. One-handed, Brian lifted one from its hook. A double row hung down the wall's length, all neat and symmetrically organized.

Brian stuffed the rest of his sandwich into his mouth so he could use both hands to snap the bagger onto the mower. The mowers, also in a neat row, were not far from the wall.

With the bagger in place, Brian pulled the water from his back pocket, opened it, and with several consecutive swigs, emptied over half of its contents washing down the sandwich.

With a quick jerk, he grabbed the mower by the handle and pulled it upside down. With it trailing behind him, blades rotating in the air, he left the shed.

From the time he could push one of these things, he had cut grass around the Installation.

On the way to his assigned section, he walked through an area which used to be his. As time went by, Brian had been given different sections to do. Each time, they were larger than the one before and further away from the storage shed.

Almost two miles later, well away from any houses, he began to mow. Beads of sweat already dripped from him. Brian wiped his brow as he did the work. When the bagger was full, he was done. He stood, resting for a bit, surveying what he had completed. Keeping at his chores daily, he completed close to a fifth of this section each morning. He would be back tomorrow morning to do more.

Leaving the mower, Brian made his way to a favorite spot where the grass grew right up to the base of a tree. He always looked forward to this time; it was his time. When he sat, he leaned fully into the tree. It felt coarse and rough against his back. The grass, though, thick and plush, made for a halfway comfortable seat. That morning, slightly damp from the dew, it felt cool and welcome against his skin.

He wiped his brow again, thankful he had made it out early enough to sit by the tree for a while. Few others did their chores early, and on his way out here, he had seen no one else. The Installation, however, was large, and it didn't mean no one else was out.

The fence ran alongside the tree where he sat. Electrified, it packed a powerful charge for any predator dumb enough to touch it. It successfully kept them at bay.

A lone stem of grass had grown through the fence from the other side. It was long and looked out of place against the perfectly manicured lawn and the bare ground outside of the fence. Brian leaned over and plucked it, careful not to touch the fence.

He studied the blade for a second before placing it in his mouth. The long stem began to twitch as he played his tongue over the end of it. Relaxing, he leaned back onto the trunk breathing deeply the morning air. The exercise was invigorating; the air, clean and fresh. He enjoyed getting his chores done and out of the way. This was usually the coolest part of the day to do them. And now, when class let out, the rest of the day was his.

As Brian's tongue played over the end of the tasteless stem, he began to appreciate for the first time why the clippings went to the Dupe. The Dupe would change this stem into some tasty morsel of food, or maybe something else, but more than likely food. He wasn't quite sure how it all worked, but it was impressive.

He understood the grass was a renewable resource. It did its thing because of the sun, and replenished itself after he cut it. It was the source of food for the entire Installation. If need be, it could be dried and stored indefinitely.

As he sat, looking out beyond the fence, he understood everything out there could become a source of food. The Dupe would convert it all. A green and lush variety of organic material grew fifty feet away beyond the fence. Tall, it reached toward the sky. On some level, he noted it would be another nice day. At the same time, he was still in awe of what the Dupe could offer. During all of this, the stem of grass twitched away.

Just then, a movement caught his eye. He looked where it appeared at the edge of the woods. Immediately, he recognized it was a fox, and to his wonder, behind it, out came another. Both were on a path directly toward him.

Unconsciously, Brian held his breath; the blade of grass became perfectly still.

Rarely did he catch a glimpse of these shy animals. And now, two of them at the same time, out in the open with a clear view! Much to Brian's surprise, they kept coming, though he was sure it wouldn't be long before they spotted him. Brian sat motionless, frozen in place.

They seemed very interested in one another, nipping here and there, kicking up their heels, chasing, as they romped toward him.

It didn't take long to realize that they were playing. Astonished, he was pleased to observe their behavior. Often heard, sometimes witnessed, the wide variety of animals mostly fought and killed each other on a surprisingly frequent basis.

Within fifteen feet of where he sat, still facing him they stopped. Other than rabbits and squirrels, no other animal would come this close knowing he was there. The rabbits and squirrels didn't seem to care. It was exhilarating; Brian could hardly contain his excitement. When they stopped, he thought he had been spotted, but then saw that wasn't the case when one jumped atop the other turning them both sideways.

Brian Expected a fight to ensue, but the one on bottom whimpered. This drew Brian's attention to it while it let out an elongated whine, and then yelped. Undoubtedly, they were not fighting.

This was brief.

While it went on, Brian noticed the one on the bottom didn't show any evidence of being male. He doubted this and stared, trying to confirm its maleness. In disbelief, he leapt to his feet, pulling the stem from his mouth. Instantly, the foxes bolted and disappeared, both consumed by the nearby underbrush at the edge of the woods.

Brian didn't understand how it was possible. He decided then it wasn't. But if it wasn't, what was it. This bothered him and he knew if he didn't figure it out before class, he would ask the professor. The professor would explain. If he hurried, he could catch him before class out of earshot of the other guys.

Going back to the mower, Brian again turned it over as he grabbed it; and then made haste toward the cafeteria. All the way, he thought of nothing but the foxes but any explanation as to what he saw eluded him.

At the entrance to the storage hoppers, Brian, dripping sweat, removed the bagger and took it inside. Once it was emptied, he came out and took the equipment to the storage shed.

He couldn't wait to tell the guys what he saw. But he would only tell them after he spoke with the professor. The professor would provide insight which he would then share it with them.

As he walked to the building housing the classroom, he began to feel silly; he had nothing but a dumb question about a fox. How was he going to ask? Hey, I saw a fox that didn't have one. Danny and Pete would laugh him right out of the classroom. They would take advantage of something like this and hit him up with it daily. He would never hear the end of it.

There had to be an explanation; Brian just didn't know what it was. If he asked the professor and it was something simple, he would embarrass himself. He couldn't leave himself open to that. But at the same time, he didn't know if he cared. If it didn't have one, why not?

As he entered the building, he realized he had never looked at the second fox to see if they were both the same. He wished then, he had done so.

Arriving at the classroom, Brian peeked in. The professor wasn't in yet. Danny and Pete were sitting at their desks. This was what Brian had hoped for, but while he peeked in, Pete had spotted him. Brian casually strolled in hoping his momentary hesitation and pullback went without notice. He took his usual seat and began to wait, never saying a word about the foxes.

When the professor arrived, Brian would ask for a moment in private.

The wait wasn't long. "Good morning," the professor greeted them upon entering the classroom. All three boys repeated his invocation mostly together. "At one time, gentleman, there were over seventy billion people on the Earth." Before making the desk, the professor had cranked into lecture mode without hesitation. "They generated and manipulated a phenomenal amount of information."

The professor was so quick to start; Brian knew his opportunity had slipped away. He began to reexamine what he had seen.

"Information, and man's ability to store it and control it, allowed for the development of the Dupe."

Brian had tried to imagine ten thousand before; billions couldn't be fathomed.

"The possibilities with information being manipulated on this scale truly became endless. There was nothing man could not do, and once it became clear that all they needed to do after something was digitalized was to record it into a computer memory, then that item could be duplicated as often as necessary."

Brian thought it could be an accident, like maybe another animal had bit it off; 'Ouch' ensued, because he couldn't imagine.

"A chef, for instance, could create his concoction, digitalize and store it on the web. When everyone had a Dupe appliance at home, the chef would receive credit every time someone selected his creation. Of course, the chef thought along the lines of three squares a day, extra for dessert. In a worldwide market, he would be a billionaire in no time. The beauty of all this, if what he made wasn't perfect, he would toss it and start over. He only had to get it right one time."

Brian wanted to know what a chef was. Pete raised his hand. Brian assumed he was going to ask, but the professor ignored him.

Brian wondered if it could be tucked away in some unseen pouch.

"The medical profession would benefit immensely. Any diseased organ would be vaporized and instantly replaced with one digitalized from when a person was younger. There would be no problem with organ rejection because it was yours. No surgery involved either. Vaporized in place, a new one would be duped during an office visit in the precise location it belonged. Imagine an outpatient procedure at worst to replace a heart or lung. Whatever was desired could be had, even cosmetically. Imagine putting on the face of your youth, the ultimate face lift."

Pete put his hand back down when he saw it was useless.

Following the pouch idea, Brian thought maybe it was just too small and therefore couldn't be seen.

"Manufacturers were giddy at the possibilities of what it would do for their bottom lines. They could take several of whatever they made, digitalize them, test them and only make available for duping the ones which passed their tests. Their process only had to get it right one time. Goods that were too large for the Dupe would include those notorious 'Some Assembly Required.'"

Pete raised his hand again. With his hand raised, he whispered to Danny, "I can't get the professor to stop long enough to ask him what a chef is."

"You know how he is when he's lecturing," Danny whispered back. "He'll answer questions later."

"Even counterfeiters dreamed..."

Brian wondered if maybe it never had one. That would be strange. Would that meant it could be a new species of some kind? That was practical, and he liked the idea. It fit. If the professor told him it was possible, Danny and Pete would be impressed, even envious of his theory. He had to find out.

Pete put his hand back down.

"There would never be a need to waste time shopping in buildings made of brick. No longer would click and brick be the most successful businesses; click won, hands down."

Brian raised his hand. He wanted to speak to the professor and wanted to do it now, alone, out in the hall.

"They saw a completely new science within the Dupe itself. Take the chef for instance, he would be able to take a grilled steak, digitally remaster it to remove harmful carcinogens without altering the taste. He could introduce flavorings to create new spices. Imagine, taste sensations that don't yet exist. 'New & improved,' would be labeled on everything."

Brian kept his hand raised. He surmised chef had something to do with food. Other than that, the professor lost him long ago. Everything he covered was unfamiliar.

"You might as well put your hand down," Danny whispered. "He's not going to stop until he's through."

Brian slowly lowered his hand. He wondered if there was any formal recognition for discovering a new species. He wished he would have checked the other fox to confirm they both were the same.

"There was even the possibility that the Dupe could be refined to the point where it could make all the elements it needs during the dupe process from a single material. Seemingly, we have an endless supply of saltwater."

The professor went on strong all morning long. As lunchtime approached, Brian raised his hand again.

"Yes, Brian," the professor acknowledged, surprising everyone. Brian hesitated. He hesitated so long the professor asked, "Do you have a question?"

"Yes."

Another pause, Pete and Danny both turned toward him.

Trying to recover from the sudden attention, Brian spat, "Whatever happened to Stan?"

"Ah, I have the answer to that," the professor said, pleased to light up the top of their desk with a picture of Stan. "Two and a half years after he transmitted himself, Stan's progress was good. By this time, he could crawl and sit up all on his own. Typical of any child at that age of development, he threw tantrums when forced to use a spoon to eat."

Ironically, the picture displayed of Stan showed he still loved to smile for the camera.

"A side note," the professor said. "The monkey showed no discernable difference in its development than other monkeys its own age. The goal here, gentlemen, is to solve the problem of duping man with his memory intact, or when the ships arrive at their destination, no one will be getting on board."

"I think the professor's flipped," Danny whispered to Brian. "He makes it sound as if life and death are hanging in the balance. There's more than a few centuries yet to go, someone will figure it out before then."

"He's definitely melodramatic."

"You think?"

"Well, I can see why," Brian continued at a whisper, "if the professor's like me, he can't see how anybody will ever use those ships."

Chapter Three

"Thirty-nine spacecraft launched from the Earth," the professor told them. "Their departures covered nearly thirty years. Every ship was equipped with a Dupe. The early models contained enough raw materials to dupe up to fifty men; later models, up to one hundred. Out of necessity, when they arrive at their destination, they will only stay on the ships for a brief time, then shuttle down to the planet taking the Dupe with them."

"I thought we were going to lunch," Danny said low enough that only Pete and Brian could hear him. "I'm starved."

"The professor's never missed lunch," Pete said. "He'll take a break."

"Yeah, but now it'll be later." Then he leaned toward Brian. "Thanks to you."

"Those ships were launched off platforms from the Space Station. The Space Station itself was a work in progress that had been under construction for decades. Sections of it were quite old when put into service. It was there the ships were assembled and launched."

"It's not my fault," Brian whispered.

"You got him started on the spaceships with that question about Stan," Danny said.

"Incidentally, we've lost communication with twenty-seven of the craft so far. Considering how much time there is yet to go…that's not a good thing. Think about this. Our future hinges on the outcome of the success of those ships, and only theories prevail as to why we've lost communication with so many."

"I can fix that," Brian raised his hand. With a nod, the professor acknowledged him. "Are we going to lunch anytime soon?"

"We might as well. Maybe all of you will pay attention when we get back."

***

Carrying three thin booklets, Ed looked solemn when he started the afternoon session. Brian received his copy first.

Immediately, he opened it.

"Not now." The professor said lifting one half of the cover off the desk top and pushing it closed. "These are profiles. I need you to fill in the blanks. They will be used to help determine the apprenticeship you'll be assigned."

Brian still needed to sneak in his question about the fox; but he would wait for the right moment.

"I'm Sorry, but you'll need to fill these out later on your own time," the professor said. "You gentlemen sidetracked me yesterday onto the Dupe, and now we don't have enough time to complete everything. So this afternoon, we will do an abbreviated history to catch up."

"Great," Pete blurted, sarcastically. "That'll be fun."

"Actually, I wouldn't call it fun. It's interesting, though."

Afterward, Brian believed the professor was only partially correct.

Fun it wasn't. Interesting proved an understatement; horrifying was a better descriptor.

"The analogy of the Earth being nothing more than an island in space was to have led to the collapse of civilization. It was caused by conspicuous consumption, resulting in the depletion of the Earth's resources which man used in later years on a scale that was unfathomable just to survive."

Brian listened but had a hard time perceiving the level of suffering the professor presented. He tried to imagine being in their position, having gone through what they did, and genuinely felt sorry for the people who had.

Household use of the Dupe was out of the question. The sum of all of its parts took up more space than the average size home, more like two and a half. At the time though, everyone believed it would shrink to a household appliance, just like the computer.

With the genie out of the bottle, every government vied for the attention of those in charge of the project. They all wanted a Dupe or, at a minimum, its technology, and were eager to pay.

Those in charge of the project realized the opportunity for this would only exist once. They decided to hold back on one crucial part until they had everyone on board who could afford to get on board. It was the only way to make a killing. All buyers would pay through the nose.

They started manufacturing parts using the original blueprints. This didn't go smoothly. Nothing was standard and, once made, they had to assemble each new part into the Dupe to ensure it worked. Not all of them did. Technicians had made changes under Stan's direction as he experimented.

Without Stan, they decided the best course of action was to disassemble the whole thing and then piece by piece digitalize the entire Dupe.

While that process was taking place, those who anted up astronomical sums received the designs for the structure best suited to house the Dupe.

The buildings were erected posthaste. No expense was too great, or spared.

The whole process of digitalizing the Dupe took a long time. Every step of the way, great measures were taken to ensure every original part found its way back into the Dupe. Each part was numbered and accounted for at all times. None of those in charge were sure if it would work when it came time to put it back together, but once reassembled, the Dupe did work, and it worked on its initial start up.

After that, parts began to arrive daily at the construction sites. On-site experts were made available to oversee every project. Naturally, this was at an additional cost, but no sites went without them.

Long before the invention of the transporter, now Dupe, fossil fuels had not kept pace with demand.

At first, people thought it was cool to go green. They knew their environmental impact number, and kept it updated.

Later, it became more serious and created tension; everyone became more aware of what needed to be done to reduce their impact number. Neighbors' kept track of neighbors, and called authorities to report abuse as precious resources dwindled. Some even kept reports which they showed on national news of what their neighbors' consumed.

History clearly revealed that black gold was responsible for placing seventy-billion people on the Earth at one time.

Before fossil fuels, the amount of work—a hunter-gatherer had to perform just to exist another day took up the majority of his time. It was hard on him, too. As a result, he didn't stick around long.

Fossil fuels provided freedom to people in masses. No longer did they have to hunt and gather and, as a result, the art of self-sufficiency went by the wayside. This knowledge was completely lost to subsequent generations as they too contributed toward the goal of convenience and specialization.

While fossil fuels drove the food supply, it didn't take long for man to set unprecedented numbers upon the earth. Toward the end, every second, of every day, hundreds of people died. The numbers that came into the world were stellar and far exceeded the deaths. There was a total net gain, on average, of over a million people a day.

Fossil fuels were an incredible resource, but not renewable.

If you had lived when it was abundant, it truly was a blessing for the individual.

As black gold depleted, it became increasingly expensive, and not for its name's sake. It added an enormous amount of stress to each individual with no end in sight.

Supplies continually dipped below demand. Governments at first used rationing for short periods to equal things out.

During this time, the space program approved building spacecraft with Dupes. The expectation was that someone would figure out how to make the Dupe work as a transporter, memory intact, before the ships arrived at their destinations.

The whole project took on a feverish pitch. Dupe parts were whisked away as needed to ensure launches took place when scheduled. To those in charge of the project, they represented pork belly and became priority.

As time went on, shortages of fossil fuels became more serious. Processing plants operated below capacity. The Earth no longer had the ability to give it up at the required pace. It wasn't available any longer in abundance.

Deforestation accelerated to an unimaginable scale as wood became an alternative to heat homes and drove newly built steam engines. Thousands upon thousands of businesses sprung up to cash in on alternative fuels.

Those efforts didn't stem the tide of shortages. Rationing became permanent. It stung the poor, the least influential.

These drastic measures included farmers. They plowed what they could plant and harvest, not knowing if they would receive more fuel. Some didn't bother; they sold their allotment at huge profits. This generated a scare and it became necessary to ration food immediately.

During the following years, severe shortages coupled with climate changes broadened rationing to include every aspect of consumption. Home gardening became the rage.

Dwindling reservoirs of oil had more holes punched into them, in an effort to get what was there out quickly. It was desperately needed.

Unprecedented, the space program moved. New facilities went up within eyesight of several of the Dupes. Plans to secure the Dupes with fortifications were given the go ahead.

Businesses generating alternate fuels began shutting down. The resources they needed to produce their product were reallocated as food. Home gardening proved just how inadequately people were prepared to deal with the volume needed to feed a family. They had no inkling how much land it took to feed one person for a year.

Local governments could not even feed the people they arrested, and they were arrested in droves, mostly for stealing food. Of course, incarceration didn't mean being feed. Instead, they were marched out of those jurisdictions and ordered never to return. It made matters worse wherever they ended up.

Then all at the same time, one hundred and fifty eight crucial duplicator parts shipped around the globe. Within a week, all Dupe Installations came on line.

There was a feeling of euphoria, and much rejoicing took place at each facility. Because of the Dupes, they were able to hand out food in abundance. There was pride, as people thanked those in charge for full bellies, something that had not happened to most of them in years. The Dupes began to run around the clock providing food.

Instead of helping, it only proved how desperate the situation had become. Total pandemonium broke out where the Dupes were located. As word spread, people flocked to them. At first, they came by the hundreds, then the thousands, later, literally millions showed up. This took place at every facility. All one hundred fifty nine Installations came under siege.

There was no way to make something from nothing. When the Dupes ran out of raw material, they asked those waiting for food to bring it in exchange. In no time, the vegetation for miles around was hacked to the ground and fed to the Dupe.

It was at that time Douglas Fairbanks stepped up to the plate and declared he was in charge of all Dupes.

Douglas was in on the ground floor. An associate of Stan's, he'd worked with Stan from the very beginning. The board of directors selected Douglas as Stan's replacement after Stan transmitted himself prematurely.

Desperate times require desperate measures. Douglas took matters into his own hands and made a series of bold moves.

He saw the need to unify the Dupe Installations and did so. They were overwhelmed. They quickly accepted his leadership because of his connections to the top brass at the United Nations. He provided assistance to them in the form of the military.

His first act at the helm was to declare the Installations independent. His rationale was they were unique, having the means to provide food.

Those in charge at each facility agreed to this. It gave them freedom from the constant demands of the most influential, and the selfish motivations placed on them by their previous owners. Douglas informed the Installations that his second act was to allow the dead to become raw material for the Dupes.

This act put the facilities in a position where they could continue to operate around the clock. They could not, however, provide for millions.

The rightful owners filed lawsuits in different courts around the world. These lawsuits stayed in litigation until the point was moot.

Fearful of losing control while people continued to show up in masses, Douglas ordered the military to construct a fence around each of the Dupes and appointed a council which began the process of developing a constitution to govern the Installations. He even went as far as to provide the military with the area each Installation would encompass and ordered any land seized to meet those requirements.

Labor for the project was easy to come by; work for food.

People arriving at the end of the line lost hope when they saw how futile it was. They themselves would long be dead before making it to where the food was handed out. The line was too long, if it really was a line anymore. Chaos prevailed as they began to butcher one another like a school of starving Piranha looking for the weakest member in the school. Once found, they were vanquished.

Reports of cannibalism poured into Douglas's office.

Close to the Dupe, the military kept order, beyond that, they were not as concerned. The Dupe fed them as well. They didn't need to be told what to do. They protected it by force when necessary.

There were those who joined the military, hoping to get an assignment with the United Nations. They did this because there was a chance of getting a position at one of the Dupe Installations.

Before the fences were completed, Douglas quietly increased the military presence at each Installation. Some who signed up found they beat the odds.

Eventually, Douglas himself moved into one of the facilities. Outside of the fences, food became very scarce; it was becoming hopeless. People were desperate and Douglas no longer knew who to trust.

At the Installation, it was worse than Douglas imagined. The reports had always been grave, but never conveyed the magnitude of what was going on. With so many people, it became unsanitary, and had been for some time. People died as a result and those that fed off the corpses died too.

Douglas stood inside the fence and surveyed how bad it had become. Bodies were stacked up all around the outside of the fence. New piles seemed to appear overnight faster than the Dupe could incorporate them.

The Installation reeked of death.

From within the safety of the fence, Douglas ordered all Installations to stop the feeding frenzy. It wasn't helping. He ordered the military to lock down the facilities and told them to deal with anyone attempting to enter. They complied, as every Installation came under siege.

Douglas began to view his fellow man as an infestation.

Forty-six Installations did not prevail against the on-slaught of humanity and succumbed. They were no longer under Douglas's control. Each experienced untold calamities until there were only enough people alive at each renegade Installation that the Dupe could support.

Over time, Douglas dealt with the renegades. Their survival depended on a machine. Those machines were duped from a prototype and prone to break-downs. They could not supply their own parts. Other facilities had to Dupe them. Deals were made which brought them back under Douglas's control.

Over the next year, three-quarters of the Earth's population ceased to exist.

"Seventy two years later, Douglas Fairbanks's successor announced in a celebratory ceremony that the last pocket of infestation was gone. There was no one left on the Earth who lived outside the fences," the professor concluded. "The Earth was on its way to recovery."

"Why didn't they use the Dupes to make more Dupes?" Pete asked.

"There was nothing they could do other than make food," the professor said. "Once they began, they couldn't stop. Look at what happened when they did."

"So there weren't enough Dupes, just like there weren't enough trees to keep the Polynesians from starving too," Danny surmised.

"Exactly," the professor confirmed. "It was too little, too late."

***

Several days later, the big day had arrived. Brian was excited. When the professor finished teaching for the day, he told Brian and Pete to wait in the hall.

They were going to find out which apprenticeships were best for them.

Twenty minutes later, Danny told Pete it was his turn.

"What did you get?" Brian asked as Pete went inside the classroom.

"The professor told me not to say." Then as he walked away, he added, "He wanted to be sure he was the one to tell you."

"That never stopped you before."

"He made it very clear."

"He knows you too well," Brian said louder, so he was heard down the hall.

Even though Brian was excited, he was also nervous. He was finally getting the chance to talk to the professor alone and he could ask about the foxes. Although that question wasn't as important any longer, Brian had thought of something else and had devised a nifty little plan where he would avoid embarrassment and find out if he was right.

Pete didn't take as long as Danny and when he opened the door, he said, "Your turn."

"Thanks a lot," Brian said as he got up to go in.

The professor, seated at one of the student desks motioned for Brian to sit next to him. Brian sat in the designated seat.

"I've finished reviewing your profile, Brian," the professor said. "In a quick synopsis, it shows your primary aptitude lies in child rearing. It's a good thing as they could really use your help."

"What?" Brian doubted this. The professor had it wrong. What was he thinking? Brian never dreamed...how did the professor know? Brian knew he was not suited for that.

"Yes, your profile shows you have a gift for it."

"Really?" Brian said, trying to understand. "I never gave it a thought." The professor going down this route made Brian completely forget about the fox.

"Give it a try, Brian," the professor encouraged. "You can always change to something else if it doesn't work out."

"Um, is there something else my profile shows I might be good at?"

"Maybe research. That would place you with Sandy at the Research Center. But you should only consider that if child rearing doesn't pan out. Even though research is a worthy vocation, I don't think you'll do as well if placed there and they don't have the same need for help."

Though this choice didn't sound any better, he had heard rumors of people putting in long hours there, it sounded better than taking care of a kid. He knew already he'd take research over a kid any day, even if the professor believed the Research Center was not a good fit for him.

"What else?"

"I could assign you to a maintenance crew. They'll take you, but they don't need anyone." Performing maintenance would be like doing chores all day. He didn't like the idea of that either.

"Anything besides those?" Brian asked.

"That's the end of the list."

Brian had something else in mind, even though he knew there'd be no chance of getting it.

"Do I have time to think about this?"

"No more than a day."

Brian focused on the choices given him, thought for a second, then looked at the professor. "I don't think child rearing or maintenance are things I want to do. If I had to decide right now, I'd lean toward research, but I have something I'd like to do instead."

"And that would be…?"

"Fly the plane," Brian said.

Immediately, the professor responded. "There's nothing in your profile showing you have an aptitude for that. I think it would be best if you apprenticed at child rearing."

"I really want to fly."

"Well, you don't get to fly just because you want to fly. There's a host of other responsibilities involved. Most of the time you'd be taking care of those things."

"I'm sure there is, but that doesn't matter. I will do whatever is required."

"Brian, really, I don't see it working out. That would apprentice you with the Chief and I'm sure he doesn't need anyone," the professor said this as if Henry was the worst person to be stuck with.

"Chief Henry is by himself," Brian said. "He can't stay by himself. At some point, someone will have to apprentice with him."

The Chief was the head of security and currently the only one who flew. Because of the small number of people living at the Installation, no more than five hundred, the Chief was the only one to hold the position. Henry was not that old. Brian figured it was because of Henry's age the professor discouraged him so strongly.

"Okay," the professor gave in. Brian could tell he was calling it a day. He always went tactful when he was ready to go home. He was doing it now. "I'll talk to the Chief but if he doesn't need you around, you'll choose one of the other options."

"I guess so," Brian said, feeling a glimmer of hope. "You will talk to him."

"I said I would. I'll find him after dinner." The professor then turned in his chair to get up. He was done.

"Wait," Brian said, thinking he had forgotten something.

This stopped the professor, though he stayed turned in his chair to get up. Only his head tilted back toward Brian, waiting, his posture acknowledging his annoyance at the delay.

"Brian, I already gave you all the options there's going to be and I told you I would talk to the Chief."

"That's not it. I have a question," Brian stammered. "Does the Dupe ever get it wrong?"

"What?"

"When it makes something, can it go wrong?" Brian tried to clarify, and he could see the question caught the professor off guard. "Has it ever made a mistake?"

"No."

"No! You're sure?" Brian pressed.

"Yes, I'm sure. It's a machine. It follows a program. It doesn't think for itself. It puts atoms in place, duplicating exactly what you programmed it to do."

"But we can change the program, right."

"Yes."

"Did we ever get it wrong?"

"Not that I'm aware of." The professor looked puzzled as to where Brian was going with this.

"Precisely what do you think went wrong?"

"Do we Dupe animals?"

"No," the professor answered. For Brian, all the scenarios that he'd played through his mind ended in a 'yes' here. It was the only logical explanation. Man duped the animals and either changed the program or the Dupe made an error and got it wrong. "It was done a long time ago," the professor clarified, "but we don't do it anymore."

That was all Brian needed to hear.

"Tomorrow you'll tell me what Chief Henry said?" Brian respectfully asked. He now had a chance to fly, no matter how slim, and he knew it had to be an accident or a change in the program which made the animals different.

"Sure, kid."

He would soon move on with Danny and Pete to an apprenticeship.

He wasn't sure at what yet, but he wasn't going to end up with a kid and he hoped he didn't end up working for Sandy at the Research Center.

The maintenance crew was looking better all the time. If only he could fly!

Chapter Four

The professor was working at his desk when Brian walked in.

Danny and Pete, already seated, were all waiting for him.

"Good morning, Brian," the professor said without looking up. Brian felt like he was late. He wasn't, but if he was, he wondered what the professor would say. After all, it was their last day of class.

"Morning," Brian answered.

The professor already knew whether Brian would apprentice with Henry and because of that, Brian never took his eyes off him. He wanted to catch the professor's first reaction when he looked up and made eye contact.

As Brian took his seat, the professor got up.

"No pranks today, gentlemen," he said, never looking directly at Brian. "If you go through the day without misbehaving, I'll issue passwords so you can choose an item from the snack menu." Automatically, cheers came from the group.

The boys, though, looked at each other, with Danny turning his right hand a quarter turn opening his palm to the ceiling with a slight sideways nod to the others questioning why they hadn't planned something. There was no debating it now though; they hadn't. This made it a cinch they would end up getting their passwords and Brian began thinking hot fudge sundae.

For a while, Brian studied the professor, but he never gave away what he knew. Brian resigned himself to the fact he would have to wait until the end of the day to find out. If the professor told him yes though… he began to dream of flying. What a dream come true.

Throughout the morning, the professor delivered a series of inspirational tales. In all cases, man beat the odds, and in some cases, the odds were overwhelming. As lunchtime approached, the professor was on a roll, with an exceptionally powerful delivery. As with the others, it too ended with man triumphant.

Brian could tell he enjoyed delivering the messages; the professor even had his attention during the last one.

When the professor finished, he handed out another thin booklet.

"Congratulations gentlemen," he announced. "I've written passwords for your treats inside the cover. This booklet explains where to locate your new housing. Also, you'll find passwords so you can obtain cleaning supplies to freshen the places up, and some other essentials. I know each of you will apply yourself to your apprenticeships." The professor then stood in silence, a moment to remember, and looked at each one of them. "It's been an honor to have taught you. Make me proud. There will be no afternoon session today; you're all excused, except for Brian."

"We're excused?" Danny repeated. Then, in a delayed reaction, "That's it, we're done? All right! Brian, we'll be waiting outside."

Danny and Pete immediately scurried off with their unforeseen freedom. They gave each other a high five on the way out of the door.

Usually demanding and rigid to the very end, Ed never ceased to amaze Brian. With the sudden departure of his classmates, Brian became the focus of the professor's attention. Quite aware he was about to get the news on his apprenticeship he braced himself.

After Danny and Pete made their exit, the professor came right up to the front of Brian's desk, bent over and placed both hands to either side on top of it. He bent his elbows just enough so he was eye to eye with Brian, letting the desk support his upper body weight.

This was it. Brian looked right into the professor's eyes and waited for the news.

When the door had completely shut, "Sorry, Brian," the professor said. "But you won't be flying the plane; the Chief said he doesn't need you."

"I'll do maintenance," Brian said at once as he looked away. He had tried not to let his hopes rise too high.

"Brian, Brian, Brian," the professor trailed off. "I talked to them last night too. I know yesterday I said I could place you there, but I was wrong. They won't take anyone."

This was unexpected. He had just resigned himself to the fact that maintenance was what he would end up doing, and now it was pulled out from under him too.

"No maintenance?" He asked, disappointed.

"Sorry, I misspoke myself and shouldn't have."

Brian couldn't believe how this was turning out.

"Are you sure?"

"Yes," the professor said, showing his concern. "I can guarantee you'll do well at child rearing. Your profile scored high in all aspects of it."

"Research," Brian squeaked, committing himself.

"I think you're missing out on what's best for you."

"It doesn't matter; I can't see myself doing the other."

"Do you see yourself doing research?"

Brian contemplated the question; getting his apprenticeship should be exciting and filled with anticipation. Instead, it was ruining his life.

"More so…" Then nothing. "I have to go, they're waiting for me."

"I'll let Sandy know you will be reporting to the Research Center. If you change your mind, let me know."

"Thanks," Brian answered. He got up slowly, not actually sure if he was excused. Brian then backed away from the professor and went around his chair to exit. The professor stood and watched him go.

***

Brian hurried down the hall determined to hide his discouragement from Danny and Pete.

As promised, they were waiting.

"What did you get?" Danny asked.

"Research," Brian answered.

"Me too," Danny brightened. "I can't wait to get started. We'll have fun. If we're lucky maybe we'll get to work together."

"Pete, what about you?" Brian asked.

"Pete's raising a kid," Danny answered instead. "Pete, you should have picked research, what an idiot. We could all be working together."

"Hey, come on," Pete said, defensively.

"You know that was the professor's first choice for me," Brian said. "I'm glad research was available."

"He offered me the same thing," Danny confirmed.

This was the first time they had a chance to discuss their apprenticeships. By the time he left the classroom the day before and went to the cafeteria, Danny and Pete were already gone.

"It sounds like the professor wanted all of us to do that," Brian observed. "It must be the first choice they give everyone. I don't know why they would need that much help?"

"Maybe it's because they can't convince people to apprentice at it," Danny surmised, looking at Pete.

"I doubt that's the case," Pete said. "At least I won't end up like you guys, working day after day, all day long."

"What do you mean?" Danny laughed. "When you get that kid, you'll be working day and night."

"Yeah, Pete," Brian agreed, "and you really don't know how many hours Sandy works everyone."

"You guys are going to find out real soon, but I can see it now," Pete said, defiantly. "I'll be the one having all the fun, while you guys are working, and I'll have more fun than the both of you put together."

"Sure you will," Danny said, antagonizing him. He then looked at Brian. "Shall we haul him back to the professor so he can tell him he'll be joining us at the Research Center?"

"Sorry, but that won't work," Pete said. "I'm giving this a try."

Brian couldn't tell if Pete was defensive because they were teasing him, or if it was because it was something he wanted to do. He decided Pete got talked into it by the professor. Just like he had tried to talk them all into it. Brian then realized he was projecting his own feelings onto Pete. He actually seemed okay with it.

The professor's behavior, though, since he handed out the profiles led Brian to believe someone else decided where they would apprentice.

None of it mattered anymore; Brian resolved he would make the best of it. He wasn't changing his mind and if there was a way to get onto one of those ships, the Research Center was the place to find out how.

If he figured a way to board, he would go, even if all he could to do was wander around the ship all day. He would take Danny and Pete with him.

"Suit yourself, Pete," Danny said, "Hey Brian, come by my place in the morning and we'll go house hunting together."

"Sounds like a plan."

Pete reached for the door to the cafeteria and held it open for them. Brian's mouth began to water in anticipation. He would get the large sundae. That would hit the spot. The fudge was always perfect; the ice cream, exceptionally creamy. Together, they were addictive. He could hardly wait.

It was too tempting; Pete hit Danny with the door when he entered.

Danny pointed a finger at him and made a quick move as if to light into him.

By the time the door closed behind them, all three were giggling as they headed for the Dupe.

***

In the morning, Brian went through his normal routine before he ended up at Danny's front door. He knocked tentatively, and when he did, it took Danny longer to answer the door than he anticipated.

"Why so early?" Danny asked, letting Brian in.

"It's not that early; class would have started fifteen minutes ago."

It felt strange to have awakened him.

"Whatever. The first day I get a chance to sleep in," he said, complaining all the way back to the bedroom.

"I can come back."

"Naw, I'm up now. I'll be ready in a sec. We'll get something to eat and then go." Danny yelled the last part from inside his room.

"Okay," Brian agreed. He had already eaten, but didn't tell Danny. He would get something light and eat again. They could pick up the cleaning supplies while they were there.

After they ate, they rode the shuttle seven miles to the Research Center. It was the first time either of them had ridden on it. Before this, they were not allowed and had always walked everywhere they went. They had to show the driver the booklets the professor had given them in order to get on.

The shuttle was basic. Electrically powered, it was nothing more than a cart that pulled several passenger carts behind it. They rode in the rear passenger compartment and were impressed by how little time it took to get to there. Brian had been around every part of the Installation many times and he knew how long it took to get anywhere hoofing it.

From the Research Center, they backtracked to where the housing was located. It was busier in this section of the Installation; there were a lot of people out and about.

Even though they hadn't personally met everyone living at the Installation, they recognized most on sight. They all ate at the Dupe.

Danny wanted a place close to where they would work. They turned down the first sidewalk they came to and began their search for housing.

None of the properties were locked. They had plastic tags around the front knobs or handles indicating they were vacant.

Naturally, they went into the first place that was empty.

"This place will be fine," Danny said, looking around.

"We just walked in, let's go through it and check the lay-out."

"It's a house, a place to stay; it'll work," Danny said. "Are we going to stay together in the same place or something?"

Over the next year or so, what Danny suggested would be the traditional thing to do. It was expected they would find a partner, pair up and move in together. Although moving in together didn't mean they were pairing up as a couple.

"I don't know," Brian said, looking at Danny. He hadn't planned on it. "I suppose we can, but I wouldn't make any commitments until after we have completed our apprentice-ships."

"I wasn't thinking commitment," Danny said, but Brian wasn't so sure based on the sound of his voice. "If we were moving in together, then I would check the rest of the place out with you. If not, then this place is mine."

They ended up going through the place.

Brian turned every light on and then back off, so he would know which switch operated which light. Solar panels provided their electrical needs. The professor had told them toward the end of their training that there were enough pan-els to provide for twenty-five thousand men.

"Well, do you like it?" Danny asked.

"It's all right, but I would like to see some more places before we decide."

Half a day later...Brian found something he liked. It was on the perimeter, more private, and sat a little higher where Brian had a view of the fence and the woods beyond that.

"It's too far from the Research Center," Danny com-plained. "We could have had the first place cleaned and been moved in by now; besides, this place is the smallest we've been through so far."

"I like it, Danny," Brian said with a smile.

"It only has one shower; the other had two."

"It won't be as hard to keep clean."

They went back and forth.

"Okay, I'll tell you what," Danny said. "I'll help you clean this place; you help me clean the other. Your place will be mine and mine will be yours. If you ever want to sleep over or move in, you let me know."

Brian didn't want to disappoint Danny. Even though he hadn't thought about moving in together until Danny mentioned it, he didn't think it was a bad idea.

"Hey, that's a good way to put it. We now have two places for the both of us instead of one," Brian said, rewording what Danny said, changing the meaning to encompass the idea of sharing.

***

During the following week, Danny and Brian moved into their new homes, got them cleaned and settled in. They took a little more than two weeks off, wondering how long they could go before someone came looking for them. They visited Pete several times at his new place. He already had the kid. It was named Mark.

When it cried, it was loud and annoying.

Brian was fascinated by this and couldn't believe so much noise came from the little fellow. Pete even let him hold it, though it didn't do anything.

When they finally decided to report to the Research Center, Brian had a case of the nerves. It would have been worse alone. He was grateful Danny was with him.

The front entrance dumped into a decent sized foyer which leaned toward the larger rather than the smaller size.

They both recognized importance when they saw it. Adding to the atmosphere, Sandy's personal assistant sat behind a sliding glass window in the adjoining room.

Ken saw them immediately and slid the window open when they came through the door.

"Hi. You boys probably already know my name's Ken," he said and extended his arm through the window, hand bent at the wrist, "and you boys would be Danny and Brian?"

"Yes," Danny said, shaking Ken's hand. "I'm Danny."

"Pleased to meet you, Danny," Ken said. He then took Brian's hand, "Brian."

"A little obvious," Brian confirmed. Ken was wiry and stronger than he looked. "We're here to see Sandy."

Quite animated, Ken's hands were all over the place, turning circles, emphasizing every word.

"I'll let Sandy know you boys are here," Ken said, "have a seat."

"Thanks," Brian said.

When Danny didn't respond right away, Brian nudged him with a foot to the ankle, out of Ken's sight.

"Yeah, thanks."

They took their seats, and as Ken slid the glass door shut, Brian leaned into Danny. "I didn't know Ken manned the front door."

"Impressive, huh," Danny said. "This place is going to be decent to work at."

The longer they waited, the less apprehensive Brian became. His nerves began to subside, when suddenly, the door opened. They both jumped to their feet instantly. Brian's nerves kicked back into gear. But both sat back down when they saw it wasn't Sandy, just someone passing through the foyer.

An extended period elapsed.

"I wish Sandy would hurry up," Brian said. "I'm bored."

"Yeah, I wonder what's going on in there that it would take so long. You'd think they forgot us."

Brian leaned into him again. "Knucklehead, Ken's right there, ask him."

"No, he sees we're here."

"Then I doubt they've forgotten us."

Because there was no explanation as to why it was taking so long, it made the wait harder to endure.

Every time the door opened, they sprung to their feet.

"Man, there are a lot of people going through here," Danny said, complaining about the foot traffic.

After a while, they took turns pacing the foyer.

Most of the morning went by and they were still in the foyer. They had their heads resting on the back of their chairs, butts on the edge of their seats, eyes closed, half asleep. While in this position, having long since given up standing when someone came through the door, Sandy opened it, and backed into it to hold it in place.

"Hey," Sandy said, loud enough to make them jump.

Neither could help but stretch before proceeding through the door.

"Brian, Danny," Sandy said to each respectively, with piercing eye contact; intimidating, but, Brian thought, not meant to be. Sandy obviously was busy.

Sandy made no apologies or even mentioned the wait. Quickly they went.

From just inside the foyer, they hastily passed Ken's desk and right away found themselves in the think tank. It was a large room, with seven support columns running down its center. There, Sandy crisscrossed through a labyrinth of small cubicles. The whole place was a hubbub of activity with constant background chatter.

Sandy began to leave them behind. They had to hurry to catch up, then to keep up.

The narrow aisle between the cubicles was crowded in spots. It seemed as if every person at the Installation worked here.

Brian was apprehensive; he could feel his stomach churn as he took everything in. Courteous, he nodded to anyone acknowledging his presence. There were so many people, their passing distracted few. Most were enveloped in their work.

They traveled all the way across the room before Sandy stepped to one side and motioned for them to continue.

"These are yours," Sandy pointed. "I have two rules. Don't be late reporting to work and complete what you're assigned before its deadline. If you need help before you leave today, see Ken. I don't have time to baby sit; I am late for a meeting."

That quickly, they were directed, and left to themselves.

"I'm getting started," Brian said. "There is no way I'm letting Sandy get mad at me."

"Never," Danny agreed.

Over the next several minutes, they inspected their cubicles.

"It looks like they duped all this stuff this morning," Danny said over the cubical divide.

"I see that," Brian answered. "There's not even a speck of dust on my terminal or in the drawers to my desk. I wonder if that's why we had to wait."

"If you're right, that means they weren't expecting us. We should've taken another two weeks before reporting," Danny replied.

"A year would have been fun," Brian acknowledged.

"They never would have noticed, would they?"

They confirmed that their cubicles were identical. Each had a desk, a chair, a computer terminal, and not much more, and everything looked brand new.

"I can't access anything on my terminal," Danny told Brian.

After a moment, Brian said, "Me either."

With empty desks, non-responsive terminals, they didn't know how to proceed from there.

Nothing more passed over the divide, either.

Danny popped into Brian's cube, "Any ideas?" He kept it just above a whisper, so no one would hear.

"Yeah, sneak out and come back in a year."

"Wouldn't work now, we're already here. But it'd been nice?"

"Yeah, you're right, wouldn't get away with it now, so what'd think?"

"I'm clueless," Danny admitted.

"Well, I have an idea," Brian said. "You go find Sandy and ask."

"No way," Danny planted his rear firmly on Brian's desk, "you do it; I'm not budging."

"Sorry, my idea. That means you have to go."

Rather than sit and argue, Danny said, "A better idea. I'm hungry, it's after lunch, I say we go eat."

"That's the best idea I've heard yet," Brian concluded. He was conscientious. They were finally in a position to start, but after wasting the whole morning. "That'll beat sitting here wasting the afternoon. Let's go."

They left, via the back door. It was closer to the shuttle pick up.

"It feels like we're sneaking off," Brian said once they were outside.

"It does," Danny agreed, but they kept going.

They had a predicament to solve, but neither was sure the proper way to handle it. Everyone was so busy back at the Center. The idea of disturbing them—after all, it was their first day—was out of the question.

At the cafeteria, Brian picked a hearty gourmet soup which came with a steamy loaf of buttered bread. Freshly cut lengthwise, the butter was still melting into it. Brian broke the bread and dipped it into the soup. Danny picked steak and potatoes. Brian had that particular dish before and thought it overly spiced.

They took their time eating, enjoying lunch. Neither was in a hurry to return. After clearing and cleaning the table, they elected to do Danny's chores, giving them more time to avoid the situation at the Research Center.

Danny's section wasn't far from Brian's, which he had completed earlier this morning.

After they hauled the clippings to the Dupe, they spend a good portion of the afternoon over at Pete's house.

It wasn't until later that they decided they should go back and see Ken.

Ken slid open the window when he saw them come into the foyer, "Can I help you boys?" he asked.

"Sandy said to see you before we leave," Danny told him.

"You guys are done?" Arms and hands up in the air. "No, I don't think so, nope, surely not, no one's that fast.... You guys do any work? Couldn't have." Questioning, answering, and shaking his head back and forth. His whole body seemed to flail at the news.

"Sandy didn't give us anything to do," Danny explained.

"You haven't started! Oh my, that's not good. Sandy's terminal will be flashing your icons in the morning," he said, animated to the point of exaggeration, "and when that happens, I wouldn't want to be you boys. You were to see me for help when you needed it. You should have come sooner; you boys needed help."

Ken seemed comical apart from the news he was delivering.

He handed them each a booklet. "Here, I take it you haven't seen these yet," Ken said. "If I were you boys, I'd get started on them right away."

They went back to their cubes.

When Brian settled in, he opened the booklet. There was a short introductory; after that, a password to start his terminal. The rest of the pages were nothing but numbers.

Brian started his terminal and used the sign-in listed in the booklet. The numbers brought up training material and tests.

He breezed through the first page of numbers, going directly to the test, saving a ton of time. When he punched the number at the top of the following page, he hit something he wasn't familiar with. It took him over two hours to read the material, another forty-five minutes to complete the test. He had to backtrack through the text several times to ensure his answers were accurate.

Later, Brian noticed the think tank was quiet. He was concentrating so diligently he hadn't realized how quiet it had become. He listened, but heard nothing.

"Danny, are you still here?"

"What?"

"I think everyone's gone." Brian got up as he said this and shuffled through the aisle, checking several cubicles. He found each empty.

Danny heard him moving about. "Anyone here?"

"No."

When Brian sat, he leaned back in his chair, clasped his hands and placed them on his head. It was getting late. He was tired. He couldn't motivate himself to crank it back up. He stifled a yawn.

"I wonder how long we have to do this?" Brian said over the divide.

"I don't know. I haven't run across anything that said I'm done."

"You'd think they'd be more organized so we'd know what we're supposed to do." Brian yawned. "I say we take a break, get something to eat and then come back. We'll get more done when we're fresh."

When they returned, they found the building locked. Neither of them checked before leaving and assumed they locked themselves out. This didn't sit well with Danny. Brian, though, decided it was just as well; he was ready to call it a day, or more accurately, a night.

In the morning, Brian stopped at Danny's place. It was very early when he did so. Brian pretended to be shocked when he saw Danny on the front porch.

They did their chores by flashlight. While at the Dupe, they ate an extra large breakfast and duped sandwiches for later. They were prepared to stay and do whatever it took to catch up. When they arrived at the Research Center, they had to wait to be let in.

Ken found them in their cubes working away. He announced very loudly, so everyone nearby could hear, "I warned you boys yesterday, you needed to stay until you finished."

They explained how they got locked out.

It didn't matter.

Inside the office, they stood in front of Sandy's desk. They received a tongue-lashing that lasted the better part of ten minutes.

"...and I can't wait to tell the professor how poorly you guys did on your first day, and how inadequately he prepared both of you for the reality of work. That's what we do here, work!"

Sandy demoralized them.

When they left the office, Ken handed them both a set of keys.

"Take these, boys," Ken said. "We wouldn't want a repeat of that," as he lifted his chin in the direction of Sandy's office. "You'll be able to come and go as you please. Now, as you best know, you had better get back to work. I know that's what I would be doing if I were you boys, yes I would."

Once they were in the relative safety of their cubes, they buckled down for some serious catch-up.

Over the course of the first week, Brian figured they spent no less than eighty hours at their desks. A guess, he started to keep track. In the next seven days, they did ninety-eight hours. The pace they set was brutal. Breaks became practically nonexistent.

During the course of the next several months, the work Brian did changed. There was less of the standard testing, more essay-type work. Each assignment seemed modified, attacking the areas Brian showed the least amount of knowledge.

It was true, everyone worked long hours; Danny and Brian got into the habit of being the first there and the last to leave.

The essays that Brian did came back marked incomplete. He redid them. Each assignment took up huge chunks of time. That he always had several in the works at one time went without question.

He finally started to get the hang of it and a small percentage of his work came back marked complete.

They hardly did anything outside their cubes but sleep. Even when they took a whole day off, they slept most of it away. It allowed them to maintain the grueling pace.

Sandy seemed to be constantly over their shoulders. It was mostly figurative, but that first visit to the office wasn't their last.

Because of the punishing pace, in less than a year, most of Brian's first submissions came back marked complete. Eventually, everything he did was marked that way, the first time he submitted.

Chapter Five

It happened without warning. Brian signed into his email and opened the last one he had received. It was from Sandy and addressed to everyone at the Research Center. This was common and came as no surprise. What was a surprise was the subject of the email was Brian.

An announcement, it stated he had completed his apprenticeship and would receive his first project.

Brian wondered why Sandy hadn't given him a heads up. It would have been nice to find out in advance of everyone else.

"Danny," he called over the divide, "open your email."

"Give me a sec."

Nothing further came over the divide. Shortly though, Danny stormed into Brian's cube.

"What have you been doing, coming back here after we leave to work on this?"

Brian didn't know what to say. He was thrilled by the news, but it was obvious Danny was jealous. Brian looked at him and simply said, "No."

"Then how can you be done? I've been slaving away every minute you have."

"Aren't you going to congratulate me?" Although he wanted to kick him in the butt, and rib him for being so thoughtless, but valor won out. Brian just couldn't be hurtful.

"Sure, congratulations." With that said, Danny hurried out of the cube.

Brian shook his head and checked the next email. Another surprise; it was from the Professor.

"This is unusual, I wonder what Ed's up to," he muttered as he opened it.

The Professor congratulated him and wrote that he was delighted by his success and wasn't surprised at all when he heard Brian had done so well at the Research Center. Brian laughed, wondering whatever happened to 'poor fit'. The Professor further congratulated him on being in the top two percent of the graduates who had been through the program to date. This news sent goose bumps all through him, and he wondered why Sandy had made no mention of it. The professor went on to say he was impressed and honored to have had the opportunity having taught him.

Danny stuck his head into the cube. "I said *congratulations.*"

"Thanks," Brian said, turning to look up, smiling, but Danny never saw. He was already gone.

There was another email from Sandy addressed to him. Maybe he brought up that two percent thing in this one. But no, instead, there was a list; an extensive one, of things he could now get off the Dupe. He was restricted however to only getting two items. He breezed through the list, wishing he could Dupe more. Next, Sandy said to take a few days off before reporting to his office. At the end of the email, under the heading: Matter Transmission, was the project assigned to him.

"I was hoping we'd work together," Danny said, back in the entryway of Brian's cube. "Now we won't, because you're done. What I want to know is how you got done so quickly?"

Brian turned in his chair. "It doesn't…" But Danny had already left. Brian then heard Danny's chair protest as he dropped into it. This was upsetting him.

Brian got out of his chair and went into Danny's cube. He found Danny slouched in his chair, moving it from side to side, with one arm laid flat on one armrest, the other supported at the elbow on the opposite, with a finger to his lip.

"It doesn't mean we won't, later."

Danny swiveled around. "Fine, I'll see you later."

"Danny…"

"It's okay. Why don't you go see Sandy?"

"Danny, I'm going to take the rest of the day off," Brian informed him. "You should too, we could do something."

"No," he said stubbornly, "I have to get this done."

Danny then spun in his chair, turning his back to Brian, and scooted up to his terminal and started using the keypad.

Brian made a nasal, "Huh," then said, "Okay," and left.

***

Anxious, Brian couldn't wait to start his project.

But of more concern was Danny. If he turned resentful, Brian wouldn't be able to get anything done. This turned the two days off into a third. That Danny would display awful traits when he was upset was a spectacle Brian was avoiding. The third day turned into a fourth. He needed a solution and wanted to work out the details before he discussed this with Sandy. He spent time formulating a plan.

Late in the afternoon on the fifth day, Brian paced the foyer at the Research Center waiting for Sandy. Alone, his nerves were acting up something fierce with what now seemed a ludicrous idea concerning Danny. He decided he would come back later. He went to the sliding window and tapped on it. Ken slid it open.

"Ken, tell Sandy I need more time, I'll be back tomorrow."

"I can't do that," Ken said, with a hand going to his mouth. "He just told me you can go in."

Brian didn't know what to do. Debating, he sighed, which was followed by a deep breath. He then blew through pursed lips. Ken never closed the window. "Thanks," Brian said after too long of a delay.

He opened the door and went past Ken's desk dreading every step to Sandy's office. Although, once he reached the door, he knocked, and as he had seen Ken do in the past—didn't wait before going in.

Sandy stood and they shook hands across the desk. "Congratulations." There was no indication whatsoever that it was five days later instead of two.

"Thank you, sir."

"Sit down, Brian. We have a few things to go over."

For the next half hour, Sandy instructed him about what was expected. He defined the goals and went over how to set up a timeline. He involved Brian every step of the way and allowed him to participate.

When Sandy was through, he asked, "Any more questions?"

"No, not that I can think of right now, I'm sure I'll have plenty later," Brian said, thinking it was time to mention Danny. "I do have a problem though, sir."

"There are no problems, only opportunities," Sandy said. "So, what's the opportunity?" In saying that, Sandy made Brian feel like a colleague.

"It's Danny, sir. He's very jealous that I completed the apprenticeship before he did. We were hoping to work together."

"Problem solved; I'll have Danny moved to a different area."

"You don't understand; sir, you can't do that. Danny and I have talked about moving in together once we completed our apprenticeships. I don't want to jeopardize that."

"I see."

Brian knew Sandy understood, but the 'I see' spoke untold volumes of how petty he thought this was. Brian was no longer a colleague and Sandy wasn't going to waste any time dealing with something so trivial.

"Sorry, sir, I didn't mean to make my problem your problem."

This was turning out to be tougher than Brian had imagined.

***

Brian left the office and headed for Danny's cube. When he arrived, he peeked in. Danny was working at his terminal. He was in the exact position as he had been when Brian had left him five days earlier, typing away. Brian stepped in to surprise Danny with the news.

"Hey," he said, which made Danny jump.

"Geez, I didn't hear you come in!"

"Sorry."

"I thought you were taking the afternoon off," Danny said, "not five days. If I'd known that, I would've joined you."

Brian laughed; and this, before Danny even heard the good news.

"We're working together!"

Brian watched Danny's eyes light up.

Because Brian had brought a solution, Sandy hadn't had to spend time thinking of one.

***

The project brought a shift in Brian's mind set.

The apprenticeship had always seemed full of artificial pressure to perform, for the sake of performing. He now had something worthwhile, something where he could apply himself. It carried meaning and Brian wrapped his arms around it whole-heartedly. He sunk his teeth in—deep and hard.

Obviously, over the time it took Brian to complete his apprenticeship, he and Danny hadn't kept the same pace. Now though, with determination, Brian jumped in with both feet. He hit the bricks running, bringing Danny along with him.

His agreement with Sandy was to ensure Danny completed his apprenticeship within the next two months.

Ideas between Danny and Brian seemed to flow best late at night. Days flowed into one another. Any regular schedule went out the window. They both practically lived at the Center and didn't bother keeping track of how much time they spent there.

Brian attacked his project head on as was evident by the endurance they displayed. They worked well together and their strengths complemented one another. An excellent team, they made progress on Danny's apprenticeship, and simultaneously, raced to produce their first paper.

It was the thrill of a lifetime for Brian. He had never experienced anything like this before. He felt useful for the first time ever and loved it. It was such a confidence booster, and that he and Danny were doing it together was icing on the cake.

There was no standard flow on ideas; when one came along, they would dog it exhaustively. With the slightest hint of a new trail, they latched on and wouldn't let go.

In just under two months, with Brian's tutelage, Danny completed his apprenticeship. So engrossed was Brian in their work he never gave more than a passing thought to moving in with Danny. They already spent most of their time together, Brian reasoned; anything else would be a distraction.

After three months, the flow of ideas began to ebb. The hours they worked began to take on a semblance of normalcy. A month after that, they felt they'd exhausted every angle available. Eventually, it was hard to strive toward a goal with no apparent usable answers. At every turn, the bricks were no longer something they ran over; instead, they became a wall, with no way over or around.

After the sixth month came and went, Sandy called them into the office. They were accused of taking more days off than they worked, which wasn't true. Yes, they took time off, but not more days than they worked. This though, put a nail in the coffin. Brian decided it was time to move on. They would complete their paper and turn it in. It was a lengthy document, which took them more than two weeks to prepare for Sandy. They kept excellent records but had only kept it half organized. They used every bit of what they collected showing how extensively they had worked researching every avenue available.

They even included a section showing why Doctor Swanson had to create the Dupe. Atoms influence each other and that influence worked over a great distance, but the power needed to move atoms any great distance was tremendous.

Brian was discouraged with the final product. Overall, they hadn't provided anything in their paper that was doable. "This research paper sucks," Brian said, in a foul mood. Calling the project complete at this point felt like failure. "No one's going to be able to use any of this stuff."

"You know it's not the paper. It's the subject matter, no pun intended."

"Yeah," Brian said, feigning a laugh, "and Sandy's going to get a kick out of what we have here."

"Is there anything we should edit out to make it better?" Danny asked.

"Yep, using the sun as a power source."

"In theory that would work."

"I know. The sky's the limit; it's a research paper—and we're in the research phase—no dampers, but so what? We also need practical and we don't have any of that. Man will never be able to encapsulate the sun and harness its power. How could you ever make something that size accurate? And if you could, where would you get all the material, and if you did get material, by the time the matter reached the nearest planet, the diameter of its beam would be four times the size of its target. You'd lose seventy-five percent of the imposed information as it blew on by and the other twenty-five percent would cover half of the target planet."

"We can't turn it in without a power source."

"You know, the professor was right; I should have chosen child rearing," Brian said, thinking back and changing the subject. "Pete said he doesn't have it so bad. Mark is so cute once the little bugger is cleaned up and stuff. He doesn't even look like a pink larva anymore and he's adorable now that he's gone mobile. He stands so straight and tall, and comes right to you when you call his name."

"Where did that come from?"

Brian ignored the question.

"Mark is a known, not a theory," he continued, his mood shifting from foul to funk. "Pete doesn't have to figure anything out, just take care of a kid. You know, I haven't been over there in a while I'm going to go pay them a visit when we're through here."

This time Danny kept silent.

"It feels like we've wasted six months, Danny," Brian said, "and it isn't like we had a real choice to begin with by coming here."

"That seems like a lifetime ago, doesn't it?" Danny said, trying to lighten the mood. "The choices we had; what's it been—just over a year and a half?"

"At least," Brian answered.

"Well, if we're lucky, maybe our next project will be something easy," Danny said. "Maybe, let's see; maybe we'll have to figure out how to get water from a rock."

Brian chuckled. It didn't improve his mood, but broke his train of thought long enough that he turned in his chair and faced the terminal. Everything was ready. He and Danny were doing what they referred to as their salvage review, hoping they'd come up with something to save their paper. It didn't happen. Brian reached for the keypad. "Here goes nothing," he muttered, hitting send. The very act admitted defeat. But once done, Brian felt better. It was over.

"That's a wrap."

***

Every morning over breakfast and chores, Danny and Brian debated whether to go into the Center that day. They kept this up for two weeks and blamed Sandy for their poor behavior. He just didn't provide the proper supervision.

Late in the third week, "I don't know how much more of this I can take," Danny said, as he devoured his roasted turkey. It came with all the trimmings, and made an excellent breakfast. "I'm ready to go back. I'm bored."

"I could do another day," Brian said, enjoying a sampler platter. The dish was heaped to the edges with a variety of fresh and tender lamb. The layout of the food had a presentation about it that was flawless. There were five different types of specialty dips and each dip complemented every piece of lamb with a different taste. The dips, when mixed, offered an assortment of new flavors.

"Aren't you curious what the next project is?"

"Nope, don't care. I'm more curious how long it will be before someone comes and gets us."

"I can't believe we've gotten away with it this long," Danny said.

"That's my point."

"I get a feeling we'll be paying for this," Danny said with a chunk of turkey on his fork, pointing it in a stabbing fashion at Brian. "I bet when we get back we don't make it past Ken. He'll take us directly to the office, and when that happens, we're going to get our butts kicked."

"You bet, huh! Well, if it was so imperative, someone would already have dragged us back to our desks," Brian said, as he scooped out the last of the diced onions from a small ceramic cup onto what was left of the lamb, "and we'd be, how did you put it, slaving away."

"I want to go back before that happens."

"Fine. When we finish eating, we'll go," Brian said, rolling his eyes.

"At least we'll find out now if he's kept us together," Danny said. "He might split us after reading our paper."

"There's only one reason he would, and that would be if he thought we'd accomplish more apart."

This debate continued all the way to the Research Center.

"You said you wanted to bet," Brian challenged after they got off the shuttle. "What do you want to bet?"

"It was only an expression, like we can't dupe the same things," he said in a questioning tone.

"I was thinking time. If we're assigned different projects, then I help you on whatever you want," Brian explained. "If you lose, you're doing my chores."

"How long?"

"Fifty hours."

"Deal…"

"Another fifty says Ken doesn't take us directly to the office."

"Deal," Danny agreed again.

They walked into the foyer and then into Ken's area. Danny stopped in front of his desk.

"Good morning, Ken," Danny said, very deliberate, making a huge production out of greeting him. "Haven't seen you in a while. How's it going?" He didn't want Ken to miss the fact that they had arrived.

"Morning fellies," Ken greeted. "It's going." He seemed glad to receive Danny's unusual amount of attention. But Ken was always glad to see them. He was glad to see every-one.

"Morning Ken," Brian smiled. "Come on Danny, let's go." Reluctantly, Danny turned to catch up, as Brian had only stopped a moment. When Danny caught up, Brian whispered, "You didn't have to be such a bonehead. As you can see, I've won."

"Fellies," Ken stopped them.

"On-no you don't, I do. He's sending us to the office right now," Danny said with a quick little victory dance. "Told you so."

"I almost forgot. Sandy has your next project assigned. You'll find it on your terminals."

"Who?" Brian ribbed Danny, "did you say won?"

"Man, you got lucky, but I still have a chance to even it up. He didn't say we were working together."

"Oh yes he did. Ken said project, not projects," and then good naturedly, all the way to their cubes, he taunted Danny. "One hundred hours, I'll supervise every second so you don't waste any of it."

"Well, I hope we get that water from the rock thing," Danny said as they entered their cubes.

"If we do, you'll spend a hundred hours on it by yourself and I'll call in complete when you're done and turn it in," Brian said as he turned on his terminal.

"In that case, the theory will consist of you threatening the rock that you're going to take a crap on it, which makes it sweat a river," Danny shot back from over the divide.

"Before I turn it in, I'll change my name to yours, which makes that theory plausible. Then I'll take all the credit."

Danny retorted with something, but Brian had stopped listening. The next project glowed back at him from the screen.

"Danny, you got it up?" Brian asked as he leaned back in his chair.

"Yes."

"You already know I don't think this can be done and I can't deal with another dead end project right now." Danny didn't reply. "What do you think we should do?" Brian asked.

"Let's go see Sandy."

That made sense, but as Brian got up, he wasn't sure it was the right thing to do. How could they possibly change Sandy's mind. Danny was waiting for him outside the cube. They made their way back to Ken's desk.

"Ken, can you let Sandy know we need to see him?" Brian said. "We'll wait in the foyer." This was the second time they'd asked for an audience with Sandy; the only other time was their first day; every other trip had been at Sandy's behest.

With determination, Brian decided he wasn't about to be intimidated; he didn't want to work on this assignment, and he intended to stick to his guns on that.

They went into the foyer to wait and chose the same seats they used over a year and a half earlier. This time though, the seat of their pants barely touched chair and the door was still closing when Ken slid open the window.

"Sandy will see you now."

Brian caught the door before it latched shut.

"That was a whole lot quicker than the first time," Danny pointed out.

In the office, their demeanors changed as they presented themselves in front of his desk. Sandy was an imposing figure. Brian didn't cower, though; it was out of respect that he waited for Sandy to ask why they were there.

"What can I help you gentlemen with?" Sandy asked, once he finished what he was working on.

"We can't work on Duping memory," Brian spoke up.

"I'm the one who assigns..." Sandy said, establishing his authority.

"Sir, we'll just quit," Brian cut him off, standing straighter as he spoke.

Peripheral vision caught Danny's head snap toward him.

"Actually sir, we came to see if you could assign us a different project," Danny spoke up immediately, doing damage control. "We can tackle this one later, we're just asking for something easier this time around after working on the Matter Transmission Project."

For a second, Sandy contemplated this.

"You can't just quit; it doesn't work like that," he said, looking at Brian, but the nature of his tactics changed as well. "We have a lot of time invested in both of you. I want you to understand something here; it usually takes years before anyone is ready to tackle this project. I believe you guys are ready to do it now. Your first paper was excellent. Your ideas, original, and those ideas are displayed throughout your entire paper. I liked what you came up with for the power source."

"Can't you just assign us another project for now?" Danny pursued, knowing Brian wouldn't stand for it.

Brian thought it sweet of Danny to try to sway Sandy to change his mind on his behalf. And Sandy had even complimented their paper...this caught Brian off guard.

"Let me give you some advice," Sandy told them. "Change the method you approach this project. Keep a regular schedule. Take it nice and easy and don't go at it like maniacs. I'll even make it worth your while by moving you up one level of access on the Dupe. That'll give you a bunch of new things you can have."

"Really," Danny said. He liked that idea.

Brian heard practical.

"Yes, and I'll even throw in an assistant."

"An assistant! That'd be great, sir," Danny responded. The assistant sold him.

"I'll have Adam report to you in the morning."

This news made Danny eager; the idea of having an assistant was too much to debate. Although Brian felt slighted, he too got caught up in Danny's enthusiasm. He wasn't sure why. Sandy hadn't changed their assignment.

There was no putting a finger on it, but Brian couldn't help but feel nice and easy would ever pay them a visit.

***

Danny and Brian heeded Sandy's advice. They kept a reasonable schedule.

Working methodically, they collected everything they could get their hands on concerning the brain, and spent most of their time reading.

There was a ton of material, scads more than what they had found on matter transmission, but they left the Center each day after eight to nine hours and kept a sensible balance between the time they spent at work and away.

The only one who had endless days, was Adam. Danny and Brian kept him busy. They set up an inbox, which they filled throughout the day. The tray had to be empty by the next morning.

With so much information, and the experience with their previous paper, they put together a directory and kept it organized from the very start.

Each part of the brain received its own heading. Every heading was segmented: Composition, Electrical Activity and Chemical Activity. Within each of those three categories, they categorized theories on how each operated, what it controlled, and the influence it had on the rest, even if only subtle.

They made diagrams, with accompanying flow charts. They placed those onto clear overlays, to scale, which, once stacked, gave a complete and clear picture.

As time went by, their abuse of Adam took on new dimensions. He had to complete their chores and have breakfast waiting at their desk before they arrived at the Center every morning. It was fun having an assistant.

The brain was complicated, and the subject itself drew Brian in as he learned more about it. Engrossed by its study, he started taking material home that held the most interest each evening. With no brick walls in sight, and without realizing it, Brian stayed up later each night working on it. He developed a head of steam and bounced ideas around with Danny in the morning.

Every day, they stayed at the Center a little longer, until, more often than not; Adam was fetching dinner for them as well.

Eventually, just as before, they were camped in their chairs, talking over the divide for hours on end, discussing the theories of what made memory. Exactly how the brain stored and retrieved it. The days began to run into one another again. They woke Adam from his chair to send him for food, or let him know it was time to do chores.

This pace went on for better than three months, until late one evening: "I'm tired of living here," Adam screamed at Brian. "I'm going home, and tomorrow I'm telling Sandy how you guys have been treating me."

Instantly, Danny was with them in the cube.

"I was headed out too," Danny said. "I'll join you, Adam. We can walk together."

Later, Danny came back.

"I figured you'd still be here. I came back to let you know that I gave Adam a few days off," he explained. "He can't complain to Sandy if he's not here. He'll be okay in a couple of days. We're on our own, so we'll have to do chores in the morning, which means I'm going home to get some sleep."

"Guess, I will too," Brian said. He didn't want to stop, much less take time to do chores, but realized there was no choice. "What a setback."

"It'd be worse if Sandy found out how many hours we've been working."

When Adam returned a few days later, he apologized for his outburst.

Later that same morning, Danny excused Adam early and then left with him.

Danny had covered this with Brian, and they decided it was the best thing to do. Danny would take Adam out for a little one on one to ensure he was ready to embrace their grueling schedule.

It took three weeks before Brian realized that Danny and Adam were taking a liking to each other. This hurt. He didn't know what to say as they both began to work fewer hours and most times left together. He couldn't believe Danny was doing this to him. Brian believed it sparked that first night and he wondered why Danny allowed it to happen.

Brian piled more work onto Adam, giving him less time to complete it.

Danny took some of those things away. He told Brian he wanted to work on them himself. He extended due dates on what was left.

Brian saw a plane wreck coming. He told himself he wasn't jealous, but wished he had moved in with Danny after they completed their apprenticeships when he had the chance. He wasn't ready for it then, but would do it now.

Brian avoided conflict by letting them do as they pleased. He immersed himself into the project, making it his everything and it consumed him with a passion. He began to believe he could succeed with this one and convinced himself he wanted no part of the responsibility a partner required. Simply put, sharing his life would interfere with the project.

He began to leave when they did, wishing them well, which he meant, or at least tried.

At home, Brian spent countless hours reviewing everything to the point where it became second nature as he committed it to memory. Even though Brian didn't have a clue what was involved for memory duping, he found no reason why it hadn't worked for Stan. He became so absorbed it was all he thought about every waking hour.

Gradually, without forethought, it came about that he only worked at his desk when Danny and Adam were not there. It wasn't planned, but it was how he got things done. It wasn't blatant on his part, but he left work in the morning when Danny and Adam arrived.

Whether at home, or in the office, he was forever deep in thought, immersed in this puzzle. It was a puzzle in the abstract, on a microscopic level. Because he committed so much to memory, he was able to move the pieces around in his head. It was more than that, though, he became the puzzle's master. He developed the pieces and put them together any way he wished.

Even after six months, the bricks never became a wall.

One afternoon, after a fitful and long sleep, he woke and decided a long hot shower was in order. He wanted it hot, and the hotter he could stand it, the better. He had been in the shower awhile, when, eureka…it hit him like a ton of bricks! In the greatest revelation he had ever experienced, the pieces fell into place and he had the answer he had been seeking so diligently. He intuitively understood that this answer was only one of many.

Excited, he got out of the shower, dried and dressed. Danny wasn't going to believe it, but Brian would take him there. He set out for the Center. Impatiently, he waited for the shuttle. Danny was going to be thrilled.

He began to plan their next step. There was a lot of work ahead of them. He had to come up with a practical means to prove his theory so that everyone would understand and see, as he did, how it worked and could put it to use. Brian realized he would have to whittle this down into its simplest form. That would require time and patience.

When he got off the shuttle, bursting with energy, he ran to the Research Center. Soon, Danny would know!

This was going to excite every man and child living at Installation One-O-Seven. The news would travel fast. Every Installation would know, and they would speak his name. This sent chills through him, but Danny would find out first.

He hit the door so hard going into the Center; it nearly shattered glass. His shadow whipped through with him.

Ken jumped up from his desk as Brian ran through the door and headed for the think tank.

"Brian," Ken yelled, "Sandy wants to see you."

Brian turned, but continued going backward.

"Not now, Ken, I'll be right back," he shouted, "don't tell him I'm here yet."

When he turned forward, he ran smack dab into Sandy, stopping him dead in his tracks.

"You need to see me, sir?" He was astonished, then embarrassed.

"Yes, I do, but in the office."

In the office, the plane wreck happened.

"You're here early, today," Sandy observed.

"Yes, I came in to see Danny, sir. I have important information to go over with him concerning the project."

"Danny said you're not part of the team anymore," Sandy told him. "I happen to agree."

On the exterior, Brian chuckled, but inside, his mind screamed, <u>Danny</u>! He had a hard time understanding where this came from. He knew lately, he hadn't been here when they were but he had never considered himself 'not' part of the team. It hurt.

"Let me out. Assign me a new apprenticeship," Brian commanded.

"I can arrange that," Sandy said, showing his authority, but it wasn't what he planned to do. "Your work station has been moved. Take the rest of the day off and come back tomorrow ready to work on your next assignment. You never wanted this one anyway."

"How can you expect that of me? I can't stay here after this. Danny has hurt me, sir."

"Anything in particular you want?" Sandy was smart. He reasoned and decided quickly.

"Yes," he said, impulsively, "I'd like to fly the plane."

"I'll arrange it," Sandy told him. "Go home; get your head screwed back on straight. I'll send word when you can report to the Chief."

Brian stood silently in front of Sandy. He had the power to change it all, explain what he knew, get Danny and Adam removed from the project instead. Starting over was going to be hard, but the hardest thing now was letting Danny go. Danny was the only person he had grown to love. And now he had to let go.

"You said you had important information for Danny," Sandy inquired. "Anything I should relay?"

An opportunity, but just the mention would show where the real progress had come from and hurt Danny.

"No sir, it wasn't important." He decided this was best.

Done deal. The memories flooded back. They were strong. He had always felt bitter toward the professor for not giving them more choices. Now, when what he wanted originally was placed before him, it no longer seemed important. He had a lot of work ahead of him, a name-making discovery, and he couldn't even begin on it. Without the Research Center, it was for nothing. As he left the office, he was now confident he could put anyone aboard those ships with memory intact.

Brian didn't bother with his cube. It had nothing he couldn't replace with the Dupe. A chuckle accompanied an afterthought; he didn't even know where they had moved it. When he hit the exit, he reflected it had been a little over two years. This very door had seen him and Danny pass through day after day, together.

He was going to miss him dearly.

He vowed his shadow would never cross here again.

If only the hurt could be vowed away as easily.

Chapter Six

Brian sat under his favorite tree by the fence. He hadn't done this type of work lately and felt out of shape. That would change. Although it had been convenient, Adam would no longer be doing his chores.

He wiped sweat from his brow.

Mentally, Brian was a giant, matured beyond his years. But he felt out of place, like a kid wearing the clothes of a young man. This would be a turning point in his life and he knew it.

With his agenda cleared, he stayed put under the tree, contemplating the new path he would be taking in life. He had mixed sentiments from dearly wanting to tell Danny what he had accomplished to the anticipation of that first plane ride. Once, Brian had looked forward to nothing else. But that was two years ago, and a lot had changed. Apprenticing Henry's work would never replace the project. Just the thought of it made him antsy to work on it. But when he crawled out of bed he was the new apprentice to Chief Henry, no project. But to stop on it seemed a cruel joke. It wasn't going to be easy to stifle the urge that compelled him to proceed. He was so close to what everyone worked so hard to accomplish.

He wondered what Henry would expect. The thought made him uneasy. Wound up, he couldn't sit any longer. When he stood, he stretched and could tell he had gotten a workout; and still, the clippings had to go to the Dupe.

A creak sounded from the woods. Brian turned, taking in the panorama, trying to pinpoint where it had come from. Probably a branch, but something had broken it. Whatever it was had frozen. He knew it was there, had to be big and was watching him trying to locate it. The most numerous and dangerous predators were huge and sneaky. Even with their majestic fur coats, he seldom spotted them when he was the target of their hunt. Cunning animals, they managed to blend in. He decided to leave the area. Once, he had seen one almost clear the top of the fence.

Trotting toward the mower, he listened attentively. Sometimes, just turning your back and walking away made them charge after you. It was scary when they did; they were incredibly fast, but he heard nothing coming after him.

Cunning…reminded Brian of the foxes… He could never quite shake the feeling that he had discovered a new species. Depending on what Henry required of him, maybe he would find the time to look into it further, do some research, see what was available concerning new species.

With the mower in tow, he headed for the Dupe.

When he arrived home, he decided to clean the place and take a shower. Neither took long. Because he lived alone and wasn't there often, it stayed pretty tidy. Just a light dusting was all it needed. After that, he didn't know what to do with himself and began pacing the floor. This didn't last long and the house became confining. He headed for the door deciding to go for a walk; get outside again.

Out of habit, once outside, he found himself headed in the direction of the Research Center. Maybe he should see Sandy, explain everything. He did an about face. He had to burn off this excess energy. It was making him crazy. He needed to find something to do to occupy his mind. Walking wasn't doing the trick.

Brian wondered if anyone would care if he dropped in on Henry's office building. He would go there, familiarize himself with the place, find out where Henry's office was located and then leave. He wasn't reporting, just doing the prudent thing by checking things out ahead of time. That way, when it was time, he'd already know where to go. If, on the off chance he ran into Henry, maybe he would introduce himself formally.

Never having been there, feeling out of place, it played on him, even before he let himself in. Once in, he had to find a bathroom at once and began hurrying down the hall looking for one.

"Hey Brian, I heard you wanted to fly the plane," Henry hollered at him from an adjacent hall. He was loud. Brian heard his voice echo down the corridor behind him.

Purely coincidence, Brian backed up a step. "Sure, Chief Henry, eventually I hope to," he responded. By then, Henry was close enough that Brian extended his hand.

"Just call me Chief. Everyone else does," still loud. Brian knew from experience on the occasions he saw Henry at the cafeteria that he was just normally loud.

"Okay, Chief."

"I didn't expect to see you today," Henry spat out, sounding a little frustrated. "But I suppose you're ready to go fly that plane?"

"You don't mean right now?"

"Yes, right now! It's what Sandy said you wanted to do, fly, right? So, do you, or don't you?"

"Ah, sure," Brain said uncertainly.

"Let's go."

During the course of his apprenticeship, Brian had expected to go up in the plane, and eventually learn to fly, but not to be taken up within the first ten seconds of Henry laying eyes on him. He hadn't even been told to report.

Brian quickly scanned the hall looking for a bathroom. Henry was heading for the exit. Pressed with what was more important, Brian took off down the hall to catch up. Outside, he watched as Henry slid into his cart. A status symbol for the upper echelon; few people had them. Brian hesitated.

"Come on, get in," he snapped. "We haven't got all day."

He was barely situated when Henry slammed it into reverse and floored it. Brian caught the dash with both hands to keep from hitting it. Next, he slammed into the back of the seat as Henry took off. Brian was glad the seat was cushioned.

They drove to the cafeteria and parked practically inside the door. Henry's cart was much faster than the shuttle and he was a maniac behind the wheel. Henry was out and into the building in no time. Brian rushed, trying to keep up.

Inside, Henry worked the keypad, his fingers a blur, bringing up the sign-on screen. Getting food didn't require this step. The screen populated itself with more choices than Brian had ever seen. He wondered how many levels Henry was cleared to access. He must be at the top, or very close to it. He watched intently, realizing this guy could get anything he wanted. Brian began to stare at him in awe. All the while, Henry's fingers remained a blur over the keypad.

When the doors slid open on the Dupe, Henry grabbed a large flexible container off the platform. At the same time, he stuffed something in his pocket. Whatever it was sat behind the container which blocked Brian's view.

Henry sat the container on the floor and extended a handle from the top. There were wheels at the base. "Take this," he said, pointing the handle in Brian's direction. "Put it in the cart."

Brian was curious to what was inside. When Henry didn't offer, he wheeled it to the cart and threw it in back. Henry followed him out. Fearing the worst, Brian braced himself in his seat, ready for Henry to take off. He was glad he had done so.

Henry drove over the grounds, neglecting the roadways, taking the most direct route to the hangar. He was a madman with the thing. The grounds were hilly, mowed grass. It was hilly by design, providing more surface area for the grass. Henry ensured Brian's fears were not unwarranted, as Brian felt air under them several times and held on for dear life all the way to the hangar. Before they arrived at the hangar, Brian wished he had stayed home. The cart flew.

When they arrived, Henry hopped out yelling. "Catch the door, will you?" Brian, on Henry's heels, grabbed the door on his right. "No, the other one," Henry admonished. Brian expected Henry to call him some idiotic name. He and Danny had exchanged those all the time. "Slide it, like this." Henry demonstrated.

Brian moved to the other half, pushing. This brought the plane into view. It sat just inside the doors. Brian craned his neck to look up as he pushed. It was a behemoth. When the door hit a positive stop, Brian turned fully toward the plane.

"It never looks this big when you're flying it, Chief," Brian said, gaping.

Henry walked into the hangar, and proceeded under the plane. "You left something in the cart. Go get it," Henry ordered.

Rolling the container into the hangar, Brian promptly forgot the cart ride and anticipated getting on the plane. This was it. He had looked forward to this for a long time. He walked under the wing where Henry had disappeared.

Brian reached up and slid his hand along the underbelly of the plane.

"It's smooth, isn't it?" Brian called out.

"Smooth and ugly," Henry assured him.

Brian never thought it ugly, but by design it was nothing more than a wing. It looked like a piece of paper folded like a fan, although the bends were not quite as pronounced and at the top of each bend sat a propeller. There were eight propellers, making for a long wing.

"Come on. The entrance to the can is back here," Henry called.

Thankful, Brian had hoped the hangar would have a bathroom. He wondered how Henry knew, and hurried. Reminded, it was now imperative. ·

Henry was standing behind the plane, next to some crude looking steps, waiting.

"You ride in that?" Brian asked, following the steps to where they led. "Now that's ugly, Chief."

The can, Henry referred to, sat on top of the plane. "Come on, get in," Henry prodded. "And watch your tongue. It took the guy that built this a couple of months. It's one of the better ones around."

"I see he was creative," Brian commented.

"Don't get smart. That guy would be me."

Sorry he said anything, and against his better judgment, Brian placed a foot onto the first step. He hesitated because he really had to go.

"Come on, we don't have all day.

Reluctantly, he began to climb.

The can was located between the fourth and fifth propeller, nestled into the cradle of the choppy V configuration, right in the center of the wing. Brian struggled getting through the access door, not because the opening was too small but because the steps were out of kilter. Slightly slanted in the wrong direction, he couldn't maintain his center of gravity without grabbing the inside rim of the door to pull himself through.

It was just as crude inside the contraption. It was a strange environment; Brian had never seen anything like it. The floor was made of grated metal planks. The planks provided a flat surface between the V. They were not even and did not cover the area they should have across both sides. Bolted to the planks, were two seats toward the front. The flat wall in front of the seats contained a window that was long and narrow. There were also ten pull down seats, strapped in the up position. Five each were on opposite walls, facing each other.

It seemed small and didn't look safe. In no way did this help Brian's situation.

"Take this," Henry yelled up from the bottom of the steps.

Henry held the container above his head with the handle extended. Brian quickly got on his hands and knees to reach it. While there, he saw solar panels under him. He was sure the sun hadn't seen them in years.

Shortly, Henry was in the can with him, taking up more space. It felt cramped, but safer with Henry aboard. Brian wondered how ten more people would fit. Physically, there was room, but not mentally.

"Pick a seat and we'll be underway."

"Does it matter which one?"

"Nope, I already know my butt fits in both of them. If yours doesn't, we're in trouble."

Brian laughed, realizing for the first time that Henry was being cordial to him.

Henry closed the hatch and then secured the container to the floor with a bungee. Brian's eyes opened wide as Henry strapped the bungee in place. What was this going to be like? After the cart ride, Henry at the controls of the plane…strapping things to the floor…buckling in himself…. He hadn't waited on Brian to pick a seat. "Come on, I told you to take a seat," Henry repeated.

Brian took the remaining seat. His nerves were in high gear. He fiddled with his belt. He hurried to be strapped too. Once buckled, Henry reached over and pulled Brian's belt tight. One of Brian's legs began to move back and forth. The outside pressure caused a small release. His leg went faster, regaining control.

Henry sighed, closed his eyes and faced forward. Immediately, Brian grabbed the buckle and loosened it. It helped, tremendously. He checked, but it didn't look like anything showed through. With his leg still moving, Brian looked to Henry for what came next. Strange, Henry seemed to be meditating. Stranger still, Henry may be waiting for him to do something. Thankfully, there were no controls in front of him. And even stranger yet, it wouldn't have mattered which seat Henry sat in, there were no controls in front of him either. Weird.

The wait became intolerable; both legs were now in action....

"Chief, are we going to go?" Thinking the sooner they left, the sooner they'd be back.

"Quiet, Brian, I'm going through the preflight stuff." Then he chuckled, opening one eye to look at him. Brian's legs stopped. "Actually, I was wondering if I left any pressing matters back at headquarters."

Pressing matters, if Henry didn't hurry it along....

Henry undid his buckle and then leaned to one side in his chair. With one butt cheek up, Brian thought he was going to foul the air. There would be no escape inside the can. Danny would already be laughing. However, Henry reached into his pocket and pulled out a rectangular black case. It had to be what he had taken from the platform. Henry began unfolding it from the center. It wasn't a case. Each half went out to the side. The two sides, folded out again. Henry then flipped a handle down from the backside and locked it in place. It had finger style grooves. When done, the device had transformed, becoming much larger than when pulled from his pocket.

"I hope this thing works," Henry said, pushing a small green button embedded on the edge toward the top. "I can't find the other one. I have no idea where I sat it down the last time I flew this old thing." The whole face of the device came to life with a multitude of different displays. Henry touched an icon on the screen, and all eight propellers began to spin. A low hum filled the inside of the can. "Hey, it works," he said, alleviating Brian's concern. "I didn't know if I duped the right one. You ready?" The plane lurched forward. "You know, it scares the dickens out of me every time I have to take this old thing up," Henry yelled above the rising noise. "Maybe I'll have you build me a new one."

At that moment, it didn't sound like Henry was too keen on flying.

Maneuvering his thumb over one of the displays near the bottom by the handgrip the plane responded to the movement of his thumb. Brian set one leg back into motion slowly. Toward the top of the display, on the center screen, Brian leaned back to see the forward view on the monitor of where they were going as they taxied.

"How long are we going to be gone?" Brian asked when they reached the runway.

The plane surged forward. "We'll be in the air at least an hour, or more," Henry said, as he spun the edge of a dial in the handle turning the hum inside the can into a loud buzz.

Although Brian wanted off because it would be impossible to wait, he prepared for the long haul. The vibration inside the can became unbearably loud. Every piece of metal that touched, protested against each other with an ever-increasing whining pitch. The speed through the window kept coming at Brian faster until it no longer seemed real. It just was. The ride was bumpy and sloshed them both in unison from side to side. When they lifted, Brian felt it; the vibration inside stopped. An amazing contrast; it became quiet by comparison.

Brian tried to scoot forward. His belt stopped him. Reaching down, he undid it and got closer to the window. If it were important, Henry would have rebuckled his. With a better view, Brian saw how effortlessly the plane carried them up. He watched the fence pass beneath them. As it did so, an indescribable sensation washed over him. He tried to put a name to it. Thrilled, was all that came to mind, but it wasn't accurate, as least not totally.

Eventually, his forehead touched the window and his breath laid out a light fog over the glass, which vaporized immediately. Brian barely noticed; it didn't interfere with his line of sight, as the scenery below miniaturized. The smaller it became, the slower the details went out of view.

Very prominent, the forest extended from horizon to horizon. Brian looked at it all. He focused on one thing, then would jump to another with a continuous scan. The loss of pressure made him move his jaw from side to side. His ears popped. He wondered if that was normal.

There was water interspersed within the forest below; it came in all shapes and sizes. At the right angle, the color would turn white as the rays of the sun reflected up to where he sat in the plane.

It was all too new to Brian, keeping him glued to the window. The leading edge of the horizon continually brought something to study. After a while, Brian saw something ahead which stood out. A mass of shapes protruded above the forest. He began to study them intently. Closer, they became more defined. He saw that the edges straight-lined. They stood far above the trees.

Brian finally recognized them as buildings. They were taller than anything at the Installation as nothing there stood above the trees. Grouped together in one area, all rose to varying heights. Some of them reached up to a quarter of the distances they flew. A gush of wind from the back hatch stopped Brian from asking why they were there.

So engrossed, he never realized Henry had gotten up from his seat.

With the hatch open, Henry took a whiz out the back. Watching Henry as he relieved himself brought the need back to Brian with a vengeance.

The remote sat in Henry's vacated seat. "This is weird; now there's no one flying the plane," Brian said audibly, but barely. He couldn't wait for Henry to be done, and stood. Starting out pigeon-toed, slowly, balancing against the movement of the plane, muscles crying out against the flood, he kept control. As he made his way to the hatch, he prepared himself all the way. It didn't matter—he could hold it no longer as he grabbed and pinched it shut.

"Don't fall out," Henry said. Brian laughed; there was no way to do so, the hatch was too small. "And don't get any on the plane." The relief was so tremendous it almost hurt. There was no control over where it flew when it hit the wind. Brian's laughter turned to glee.

The view out of the hatch was better. From years of use, the front windshield was pitted to the point that it was slightly frosted. Through the hatch without the obstacle of the glass, it was clear.

He looked for the Installation; he thought it would be nearby, but didn't see it.

"Hey Chief, where's the Installation?"

"You see that ridge in the distance?" Henry pointed, bent over. Brian had to stoop, but shook his head yes. "The Installation is on top of it."

"How far away?"

"Hmm…can't be more than a hundred miles."

"A hundred miles!" Brian repeated. "You ever go far enough where you can't see the ridge?"

"All the time."

"How do you find your way back?"

"Sometimes landmarks, but the remote tells you."

Brian understood the landmarks. Even though he saw mostly the tops of trees, there were discernable differences all around that were readily distinguishable.

"How long have we been flying?"

"About an hour."

It seemed impossible. They had just left.

"You can get us back okay from here?" He knew Henry did this all the time, but this time he was aboard and wanted some assurance.

"That won't be a problem, Brian," Henry said. "Come on, close the hatch and get in your seat; we're going to buzz the airport."

When Brian got back to his seat, he noted that Henry had buckled in; and too, the buildings were much closer. Brian pulled the strap after buckling and began to ask about the buildings. His question turned out to be only, "Ah!" and then nothing came out. His stomach lurched to his throat and stayed there. His hands went to the chair. They were falling and he was leaving his seat.

"There, see it?" Henry yelled. Brian was looking out the window and saw nothing but the ground coming at them. It kept getting closer and did so quicker with each passing moment. With the plane in a nosedive, Brian thought Henry had lost control. His knuckles were white from gripping the chair. They were going to hit the ground. Every muscle tensed. Tight up against the belt, Brian was no longer in his seat. If he still had to go, it would have been over, which would have been the only relief he would experience through the stress of dying.

Brian took a breath ready to scream and turned away. He didn't want to watch when they hit. Henry was concentrating on the remote. Brian tried to see, but at the wrong angle, saw nothing.

Henry slid his thumb down on the sensor. As the thumb moved, so did Brian's stomach. It left his throat and slid all the way to the chair, gaining momentum before it got there. For a bit, he was glued to the seat.

Henry's thumb played over the controls again. Somehow he managed to make it go up, no, sideways, no, up and sideways.

"Good, nothing's there," Henry yelled. "Boy that was fun." Inside the can, things began to return to normal.

"Chief, what are you doing?" Brian asked, trying to figure out when fun had come into play.

"I told you, buzzing the airport. Hang on, we're going in. This may get bumpy," Henry warned.

Brian grabbed his belt and pulled it tighter, then latched onto his seat with both hands.

Henry flew the plane in a wide arc, while expertly descending to the top of the trees. Brian watched as a clearing came into view. They then went below the trees. When the wheels hit the ground, the speed and vibration returned. They were both jostled about, but nothing too bad.

When the plane stopped, Henry got up, opened the hatch and disappeared out the door. Brian stayed put. He was alive, and breathed a sigh of relief. He kept breathing sighs of relief before he got to his feet. Why would Henry land and go outside? There would be predators out there. He needed to find out what was going on but knew he could do nothing to help if a predator spotted Henry.

"Brian, we've got lots of work to do. Let's get started." That sounded as if Henry expected him to leave the can. He'd just survived what he thought was a crash; it would be less safe out there. "Come on, hop to it."

Brian looked out of the hatch. Henry had landed on some old concrete. There were straight lines leading to the plane where the wheels had flattened vegetation. He saw bare spots where the concrete showed under the weeds.

"Come on, we don't have all day."

With Henry watching him, Brian got out onto the top step. He waited there a long time before descending. When he touched the ground, it was the first time in his life that he had done so outside of the fence. This caused a stirring within his breast.

"Under the wing in the next bend, you'll find a compartment with tools. Get what you need and gather up what's on the runway." Henry pointed in the direction Brian would find the stuff. "Watch yourself; we're no longer inside the fence." Unaware, Brian's nostrils flared with the intake of each breath. He couldn't see past the trees. They had grown close together and thick on either side of where they had landed. He underwent a heightened sense of awareness. Someone had trimmed the branches off the trees, keeping them from overhanging the clearing.

"I said we don't have all day," Henry repeated. "Hop to it." It took Brian a while to figure out where the compartments were located. Everything on the plane looked so seamless. It took longer still to figure out how to unlatch and open the access door. He thought Henry would jump all over his case for taking so long.

Brian assessed the assortment of hand tools strapped inside the compartment. He grabbed a spade shovel and a rake.

He came around the bend in the wing to where Henry was at and saw that Henry had found a table and chair, which he set up under the shade of the wing. He was working with equipment he had placed on the table. The equipment had cords leading to the plane. Brian had no idea what he was doing.

When he finished he led Brian back around to the steps of the plane and showed him how to scrap the concrete clean with the shovel.

"Now that's how we do it. Start clearing."

Brian started his labor close to the steps. Their close proximity offered security.

It didn't take long to figure out how inaccurate Henry's statement was. 'We' had nothing to do with the manual labor Henry had assigned him.

After a while, Henry came around carrying a tarp. He saw Brian's progress and dropped the tarp on the area Brian had already cleaned.

"Lay this out over the grating in the can. That pathetic pile of stuff you've collected so far goes back with us. Put it on the tarp inside the can. Don't make any piles out here, put it in the can right away, now come on, hop to it. I don't want to be here all day."

Under the hot sun, Brian was already sweating.

By early afternoon, he had made some progress. He had gone back to the tool compartment and grabbed the flathead shovel. The flathead, when pushed across the top of the concrete, left a clean surface. Brian figured out he could roll up the accumulated dirt and roots with the weeds they supported. He put the rolls on his shoulder and carried them up the steps.

When Brian inquired about a bathroom break, Henry simply pointed to the trees; Brian never asked again. Every time he reached the edge of the concrete, it put him up close to the woods. It bothered him and kept him on constant vigil, searching, ensuring no predators were ready to pounce. He feared they were lurking just out of sight. He knew how they were; he wouldn't stand a chance unless he spotted them first, or was closer to the plane.

Later, Brian decided to get out of the sun for a bit and took an extended break under the wing. He wasn't as much tired as he was bored with the work. When Henry noticed this, he told Brian to fetch the container in the plane. When Brian returned, there was another chair set out for him by the table. He sat the container close to Henry and took the seat. It felt good to get off his feet. He hadn't felt so worn out until he sat. He was definitely getting some exercise.

Henry opened the container, and the aroma of food filled the air. Brian hadn't expected to eat until they returned. Before the smell of food, he was willing to hold out right along with Henry. A hot plate was set out in front of him, along with utensils. Brian was ready to dig in, but he waited until Henry was ready. Next, though, Henry set out refreshments. When Henry picked up his fork, Brian seized the drink.

It was unusually cold and satisfying.

"This is good and cold. Can I have another?" he asked, deciding he liked it this cold. "So what do you call the container, Chief?"

"It's a cooler," Henry answered, handing him another drink. Brian laughed; Henry could be funny. "Serious, it's a cooler."

"I've never seen it on the menu," Brian said, remembering Henry's tremendous amount of selections. "So why is it a cooler when the food is hot?"

"I couldn't tell you. All I know is on the directory it's listed under coolers and there's all different kinds of them."

"The drinks are cold, the food's hot. It should be called something else."

"Convince Ivan to change it. You could suggest five-dayers, seems how they don't perform well past five days." Ivan was the head administrator over Installation One-O-Seven. He was an old coot, and Brian would never approach him with anything so menial.

"How long are we staying, Chief?" Brian asked.

"That depends on you, Brian," Henry said in a challenging tone. "You don't have that much done yet."

Brian couldn't figure this guy out. One minute he's cordial, the next, intimidating. Henry's statement silenced Brian for the rest of their meal.

After eating, Brian pushed himself harder. He would show Henry what he was made of; he had accomplished much more than this, just not physically. It took him a while to figure out how to go about doing the work efficiently. With the flathead, he was now efficient. The only other thing that slowed him down was keeping an eye out for predators. He wouldn't bother with that anymore. Henry hadn't lifted a finger yet, he could watch Brian's backside.

Periodically, Brian had to go into the can to move the rolls forward and stack them, so he could bring in more. By early evening, the can was getting full.

"It's time to go," Henry told him.

"A little longer, Chief, I can get more done," Brian practically pleaded. With the trees providing shade, he was doing well.

"Who's the boss here?"

"You are."

"When I say it's time to go…" he began, waiting for Brian.

"It's time to go," Brian completed, intimidated into obedience.

"Stow your gear." Henry had already stowed his. Brian used the flathead to cut loose the roll he was working on. He hefted it up and loaded it into the can. He then put his things away.

As they took off, Brian felt the difference in the plane's surge when it hit the section he'd cleared. His pride swelled. He did that.

Henry did not offer Brian a chance to fly, and now that Brian had seen it done, he wanted to give it a shot. If given the chance; he'd take it, it didn't look so hard.

When Brian saw the Installation, he gripped his chair. He didn't know if Henry had to buzz the airport or not. He took a couple of deep breaths, getting ready. He knew what to expect and prepared for it. Henry didn't buzz the airport, though, and made a smooth landing.

The hangar doors were still open. Henry turned the plane around, reversed the propellers and backed it in. The viewer switched to the rear when the propeller did.

"Thanks, Chief," Brian said.

"Don't mention it." He was back to being cordial. "You can drive me to the office. I want to make sure you can operate the cart okay. Once you drop me off, use the cart to take this junk to the Dupe. The cooler goes too. Leave my cart at the office when you're done and I'll see you in the morning."

The cart was easy to operate. Brian was overjoyed and felt important. It was fun to be at the controls, having never experienced such power over anything. When he dropped Henry off at his office, Brian only heard, "Night," and Henry disappeared into the building.

Brian went back and forth to the Dupe, making several trips before deciding to eat. When he was done eating it was after dark, no one could see, so because of that, he couldn't resist taking the cart for a spin around the facility. He pushed it to the limit, putting it up on two wheels several times nearly flipping it. Immensely gratifying, he had a blast. Much later, he returned to his labor.

After a while, it began to remind him of the Research Center's long hours. He was tired and ready to go home. An unusual day, it had started with nothing on his agenda, and turned out to be packed with new experiences that both thrilled and stirred him. Thrown in for good measure, he had worked hard. If there was such a thing as having too much fun, this day had just approached it. He wanted to experience every bit of it again, except for maybe buzzing the airport.

Belatedly, Brian thought Henry had a reason for buzzing the airport. He did say, 'good, nothing's there' like he was expecting something.

Chapter Seven

The next morning Brian fought to get out of bed. Every muscle signaled the brain to quit moving and lay peacefully. He slowly sat up. Gradually, he turned, getting one foot to the floor, and then the other. He wanted to fall back, let the bed envelope him, rest. He resisted the urge and stood, but then, ended up right back on the edge of the bed.

Exhausted and sore from head to toe, he just sat there with his eyes closed. He promised himself no more late night spins with the cart. This proved how far out of shape he was.

He had chores yet to do. If he didn't get going, he would have to skip breakfast. It was important to arrive at the office before Henry. After all, he was Henry's new apprentice.

If he could get to the shower, it would make him feel better. He moaned getting back to his feet. Every muscle hurt. He took the first step; eyes almost closed, and groaned all the way to the bathroom.

***

"Well, look who's here," Henry said loudly, waking Brian.

"Good morning, Chief," Brian greeted him from the floor. He tried to make it cheerful.

He had beaten Henry to the office and sat on the floor to wait. The wall was too comfortable when he leaned against it...that was over an hour ago.

By the time he finished putting the clipping into the storage hopper, he had limbered up quite a bit. It didn't last though. Dozing against the wall brought all the soreness back, right to the bone. Brian put a hand on the floor to get up. Instead of pushing himself up to a squat using his hand for support, he turned all the way around onto his hands and knees. From there, he got up as quickly as he could.

Sleep-deprived and sore, he didn't know if he could take a repeat of yesterday. On the way to the office, he had resolved to work his butt off. The professor had told him Henry had other responsibilities. He couldn't help but hope those would be on today's agenda.

"Are you ready?" Henry asked.

"As ready as I'll ever be."

"Let's go."

Brian followed Henry outside and saw the cooler in the back of the cart. It only confirmed the reality for his day. He would be working his butt off.

His shoulders slumped as he got in the cart.

The thrill of the plane ride brought him back. It was all too new.

When Brian spotted the buildings on the horizon, he pulled his belt tight.

"Chief, are we going to buzz the airport again?"

"Yes we will."

Brian's stomach began to churn. He took in a couple of deep breaths. He clasped his hands and popped his knuckles. With his hands clasped, he put his arms over his head and bent his torso from side to side against the ache. There was no way to prepare for this.

Henry began to descend. They were still some distance off but Brian became concerned. If Henry were too close to the ground, he wouldn't have room to pull it off this time. They continued downward at a slow pace. Brian couldn't stand it; he wanted to warn Henry. Maybe he hadn't noticed what was going on. Somehow, Brian managed to remain quiet. He was only the apprentice; Henry knew what he was doing.

By the time they reached the runway, they were at tree top level and Henry hadn't slowed the plane. This was going to be dangerous. Every muscle tensed, despite telling himself Henry knew what he was doing.

Henry dipped below the trees and then simply flew low over the runway, pulling up to clear the trees at the other end. He then banked, making the same wide arch as the day before to line back up with the runway.

The next dip under tree level, Henry slowed the plane and they landed.

"I thought you said we were going to buzz the airport," Brian inquired as he got out of his seat.

"We just did," Henry said, already up and opening the hatch.

"That was it?" Brian found it hard to believe. "What about yesterday? We practically crashed falling out of the sky!"

Brian followed Henry down the ladder. It was going to be hot again.

"That was your initiation. Welcome to the world of flying."

"Oh!" He wondered if he should have caught on yesterday. "So why do you do it?"

"It's a tradition. I went through the same thing," he said headed for the shade of the wing where the table and equipment were located. Brian cut under the first bend to get the flathead.

"No, I meant buzz the airport. Yesterday you said 'nothings there' when you did it, like you were expecting something." He opened the compartment with the hand tools.

"Ah, lesson one, Brian," Henry began expounding. "There's a fence around the Installation it keeps the animals out. With no fence, you buzz before you land. Remember that, buzz before you land. It scares them off and you avoid hitting them and damaging the plane. They seem to like these clearings."

That made two things Brian thought he should have figured out on his own. He walked out into the sun to pick up where he had left off the day before. Brian didn't understand why Henry wasn't helping him. For that matter, why were they clearing a runway out in the middle of nowhere. By the way it looked, no one ever came here.

Shortly after Brian had begun working, Henry walked out from under the wing carrying the tarp and a hammer. He dropped the tarp by Brian's feet and kept walking with the hammer.

"You could have left it by the steps."

Henry didn't respond. He kept going down the runway and then stepped into the woods. He broke off a sapling at its base, and then bent the skinny end, breaking it on a slat. With the hammer tucked up under his arm, he separated the two pieces while walking back to the edge of the runway. Using it as a stake, he pounded it into the ground.

"If you want to continue your apprenticeship after today, Brian, you must clear the runway to here. If you don't, you're going back to the Research Center. We have to leave in time to get back before dark. I can't land if I can't see. Hop to it, you don't have all day."

Brian grabbed the tarp. Cordial had just gone on vacation. He wanted to ask what was going on. Nothing made any sense. This was supposed to be an apprenticeship. What was Henry trying to prove?

Brian began cutting the strips twice as long. He didn't stop rolling them until they were twice the diameter as before. He then bent them into a U shape and used the back of his neck and both shoulders to carry them to the plane and place them in the can.

It would be impossible to clear as much as Henry staked out.

If Henry had arrived sooner at the office, Brian believed he would have had a fighting chance. He picked up the pace a notch, it was the only thing he could think to do.

By mid-afternoon, the stake was still far away. Brian had marked where he started and was almost halfway. But more than half the day was gone. He wanted to convince Henry to move the plane closer, less time moving the rolls. But there was no point. Henry would have to stow equipment, move the plane and then set back up. It wasn't going to happen.

"Let's eat," Henry yelled out to him.

Brian had known this was coming and had a roll waiting to take to the plane. Inside the can, he took the time to throw everything forward, adding to the stack that went all the way up against the back of the seats and rose above them. It didn't look like there would be enough room for it all.

The food, once set out, was tantalizing.

"Chief, I'm starved," Brian said, seizing the drink practically out of Henry's hand before he could set it down. "But you don't expect me to waste time eating, do you?" He saw no choice but to trot back out and continue. It was too important. He had to succeed. Time was not on his side...

Early in the evening, the sun was behind the trees, providing shade. Several times, Henry stood in front of the plane with his hands on his hips, watching. Brian expected him to call out at any moment that it was time to go. With no room left in the can, Brian stacked everything along side the runway. Inside, there was only one aisle going to the front seats. If he continued to apprentice with Henry tomorrow, he would put this stuff on the plane then.

Brian had wished several times that Henry had shown up sooner at the office. Another hour's time would have made all the difference. Eventually though, Brian came to understand that Henry really had done him a favor. The placement of the stake was purely arbitrary. Henry didn't want him to succeed. With another hour, Henry would have placed the stake further away. Brian thought about moving it. It was tempting and would be just. If he could do it without Henry catching him at it, he would.

Brian didn't give up. In a desperate attempt, he cut and started the last strip, going all the way to the stake, easily making the last roll up to twenty-five feet long in spots. All he had to do was get it to the other side of the runway in one big roll. He stayed bent over and pushed the flathead under, lifted, moved over a step and repeated, back and forth, in a heated struggle against time.

"Okay, Brian, it's time to go," Henry yelled. However, Henry still had to put his stuff away.

Brian kept working, went at it harder, driving the flathead home, determined to have it done before Henry finished.

When he was done, he walked toward the plane, satisfied. Sweat was running down his arms, leaving dirty black streaks. Although he couldn't see, he knew his face and neck were the same. He put the flathead away and took the cooler from the top of the table. His only saving grace, there wasn't enough room in the can.

He took the cooler aboard and unstrapped one of the pull down seats, blocking the only aisle he had left. He sat on the seat sideways because there was no room for his knees. He opened the cooler and found several cold drinks inside. He took one, drank deeply, liquid escaping out both sides of his mouth.

Brian pulled his plate out of the hot section of the cooler as Henry came aboard. They stared at each other but never exchanged a word. Henry couldn't squeeze past. Brian leaned into the wall; Henry stepped over to get through.

The food smelled better than before!

As he wolfed it down, he felt the motors come to life. Starved, use to three squares a day it didn't take long for Brian to polish off his plate. When he was done, he unstrapped the next pull down. They were close enough that he lay across both. No sooner than he got comfortable...

"Brian, when you're done eating, come up here and sit with me."

"Sure, Chief," he said, but stayed where he was. Henry couldn't see him anyway with all the stuff stacked between them. He wondered what Henry wanted.

Brian wanted to rest, but sat up, knowing he was going to pay for it in the morning, and all the junk in the plane still had to be unloaded.

With his guard up, he went and sat next to Henry.

"Nice job out there today," Henry told him when he sat down. Brian noted cordial had returned from vacation.

"Thanks." He wasn't warming up to cordial.

"No, I mean it, here take this," Henry said, holding out the remote. "Now pay attention. It's on autopilot, so don't touch any of the controls. Just hold it," he warned. "Listen to me. I'm going to show you how this thing works."

Brian took it feeling self conscious because he was so dirty. Though the control felt very comfortable in his hand. He listened to Henry as he went through what turned out to be a haphazard lesson. Brian didn't ask any questions as Henry jumped from display to display explaining what they were for and then did the same for the controls. Henry went back over many things, repeating himself, but added new information all the time.

The remote was basic, but capable of a lot. Astonished, Brian realized he wasn't tired, as he soaked up everything Henry said.

By the time Brian surrendered the remote to Henry, so he could land at the Installation, he had an excellent grasp of how to use it.

After he dropped Henry off at the office, he unloaded the plane. He worked at it continually until done.

He parked the cart in front of the house. He would have it back before Henry showed up. Maybe someday he'd have one of his own. It did look nice parked out in front of his house.

Once inside, he wanted to shower but his bed was too inviting. A hard decision, he longed to feel clean, but he was so tired and based on the fact he needed new sheets anyway, the shower lost out.

***

In the morning, Brian waited in the cart in front of the office. The cart was so handy and such an immense help getting his stuff done he was very early.

He had aches, but nothing like the day before.

It was amazing what just a little more sleep could do.

As Brian waited, he recalled what Henry covered on the remote. He was glad for the lesson. He couldn't help but be leery of Henry, though. He kept sending mixed signals. So far, the only thing that compared to the apprenticeship at the Research Center was the lesson. He didn't know if there would be another today. Brian then wondered if there was a way with Henry to keep cordial from going on vacation. For all he knew, Henry would send him home because he hadn't gotten everything on the plane which wouldn't have fit regardless.

When Henry showed up, without ever saying a word, they drove to the Dupe and got a cooler. Brian then wondered what type of impossible challenge Henry had in store for the day.

After they were in the air, Henry began questioning Brian about the remote. Brian tried to recite verbatim what the displays and controls did, and could have done so, if not interrupted. Henry, not able to help himself, kept interrupting. He didn't seem interested in knowing if Brian remembered any of the stuff covered the previous day, but surprisingly, seemed to remember more himself which brought forth a much more in-depth explanation of how the remote worked.

At the old airport, Brian went to work loading what he had left on the edge of the runway. Henry parked close to where he was working. It took about a quarter of the morning to get it done. As Brian finished, Henry packed his equipment.

"We're leaving," Henry said. "There's been a change in plans."

Once in the air, Henry didn't head toward the Installation. This brought a new horizon for Brian to study and he wondered where they were going.

When they reached cruising altitude, Henry pulled another remote from his pocket.

"Here. I found the old one," Henry handed it to him. "Put it together. I'm going to teach you how to fly."

Brian folded the side panels out, and got the handle in place and turned it on.

"Now, all I want you to do is get a feel for the controls. They're touchy, so take it easy. I mean it; I'll send you back to the Research Center in a second if you don't listen." Of this, Brian had no doubt. "If you get into trouble, turn off your remote and I'll take over."

Brian became excited.

"Put your belt on," Henry said as he buckled himself.

Brian almost dropped the remote while fumbling with the buckle.

"Are you ready?"

"Unhuh."

"It's all yours," Henry said, touching his screen, leaving Brian in control.

The plane went to the right; Brian corrected this, but ended up too far to the left. He overdid it again going back to the right, and sent the plane downward a little too.

"We're not going anywhere particular; you don't need to stay in any one direction." Henry said this as the plane jerked back the other way. It also regained the altitude they had just lost, and then some, before dropping back down, giving Brian the willies.

"You're right, it's touchy."

"Don't worry. You'll get the hang of it. Just keep flying."

Brian banked the plane making a full circle, then tried to fly it straight again. He ended up making the same corrections.

"You'll find that once you're pointed in the direction you want to go, you can lift your thumb off the screen. It'll keep flying that way," Henry explained.

After an hour, still ecstatic, he was getting the hang of it.

"It's time to go home," Henry said.

Brian banked the plane and looked for a familiar landmark. He saw nothing he recognized. Even the ridge was nowhere in sight. He didn't know which way to go. But without asking, he punched in the coordinates for One-O-Seven, hit autopilot and allowed the plane to find its course.

"That's good," Henry said, impressed. "I had to be shown that a couple of times before I could set those on my own. You must have a better teacher."

Brian laughed; Henry was the worst teacher he'd ever had.

"You're doing great, Chief, thanks."

"Okay, take it down to fifteen hundred. Listen to me. All I want you to do is pretend you're landing at fifteen hundred. Got that, now make sure you don't go under."

Brian banked the plane and headed downward on a steep decline.

"I told you, nothing fancy. I'm serious. You're acting just like you can't wait to get shot back to the Research Center."

Brian slowed the decline.

"Sorry, Chief," he apologized, "thumb slipped."

"You're only getting one white lie." Cordial was on the verge of a vacation. "I'm not going to end up with my bones scattered all over the countryside because you think you know what you're doing."

"Sorry Chief, it won't happen again."

"It better not."

Brian tried to pin fifteen hundred without going under. He didn't quite manage it and was a little jerky after he went under.

"Not bad for your first try."

On the way back, at Henry's direction, Brian performed different rudimentary tasks with the plane.

Henry even allowed Brian to set the approach to the runway. Brian could tell Henry was amazed that he didn't have to repeat anything a second time.

"I'll land," Henry said. "But I want you to watch your monitor. You need to see everything on it at once. You'll get used to it."

***

From then on, every day, Brian flew with Henry. He looked forward to it and couldn't wait for Henry to hand over the remote once they were in the air.

During these days, for the most part, Henry remained cordial.

At the old airport, Brian made progress clearing the runway. When he reached the end, he found that it turned and kept going. Trees overhung where it led and the grass and weeds on top of the concrete were thicker. Henry explained that it led to an old terminal and they wouldn't be clearing any of that.

With the runway done, ready to go home, they sat in the can.

"Well, do you want to take a crack at it, Brian? We have a clean runway, thanks to you."

"You bet."

Henry laughed.

"You're not ready," he said, starting the motors. "You need to get a better feel for the controls before that's going to happen. Landing and taking off are the trickiest part of doing this."

Brian knew he could do it, but there was no way he would ever get Henry to buy into it. He was happy to just be flying and knew it wasn't a bad thing to settle for right now.

***

The following morning, Brian waited at the office. With the runway done, he anticipated what would be next on the agenda.

When Henry showed up, they went to the Dupe and got a cooler.

"Where are we going now, Chief?" Brian hoped there were no other runways that needed cleaning. He was tired of that.

"Same place."

"Why? We're done there."

"You think so," Henry said, with a smirk, but didn't bother explaining what they'd be doing.

***

After Henry parked the plane, Brian followed him down the steps, and waited to find out why they had returned.

"There's a ladder stored on the side of the runway, somewhere close to the center," Henry said. "Go find it."

"A ladder...oh, that's why we're here," Brian said, a palm to the forehead. "I should have figured that out when you said we were coming back. We have to trim trees. I mean I'm trimming trees," he corrected, putting a little slam on Henry.

"Yes, you are."

"Chief, in less than two weeks, I've lost my logic skills. They're shot and it's your fault," Brian accused him.

Henry chuckled. Brian was beginning to like him. If Henry could keep cordial under control...

Brian went to look for the ladder. He couldn't find it. He had cleaned up and down both sides of the runway and had never seen it.

When Henry was done setting up the equipment under the wing he came out and began kicking around where he thought it should be. He hit something solid on his fourth kick.

The Ladder was lying flat and overgrown with grass and weeds. Partially buried, it took both of them to work it free. Once free they each took an end and carried it along the runway. Henry led the way.

"It's a good thing these are made of stainless," Henry told Brian. "They can be stored out here indefinitely."

The ladder went against a tree and Brian followed Henry back to the plane.

On the tip of the wing, Henry opened a large compartment, revealing a self-winding disk, which held a retractable electric cord. Secured inside the compartment were motorized tools, which included an electric chainsaw. The plane was full of surprises. Brian wondered what else Henry had stored in it.

"You ever use one of these?" Henry said to Brian as he unclasped the chainsaw.

"No, but I've seen them used when maintenance cuts along the woods outside of the fence."

"That's a thankless job," Henry said. "Be glad you don't work in maintenance. I spray a growth retardant out there every so often or they'd be doing it continuously."

Henry carried the saw. Brian followed pulling the electric cord. The disc was large, the cord very long.

On the way back to the ladder, Henry went over safety issues concerning the saw, ensuring Brian was aware of how dangerous it was to operate it. He cautioned, "Be very careful with this." At the ladder, Henry repositioned it ensuring it was solid. He plugged in the saw and triggered it. Brian watched as the chain spun on the bar. "Please Brian, I can't stress enough to be responsible... Look, here's how you lock the chain so it doesn't move. Do that before you get on the ladder and before you climb back down." Henry then climbed the ladder. "Not only will this thing cut off your left nut if you're not careful, it'll take your left leg off with it."

Henry made two small under cuts at the bottom of a limb to demonstrate the proper cutting method to fell it. A little wedge dropped out. When the saw contacted the top of the limb, it made a funny buzzing noise that it hadn't during the undercuts. The sound didn't quite connect to the saw, but Brian continued to watch. It took Henry several minutes before the limb crashed to the ground.

"Oh, cool." Brian got a kick out of watching and was ready to try.

The buzzing noise didn't stop.

Immediately, Henry came down the ladder, throwing the saw, "Run, Brian, back to the plane!" Henry's arms and legs moved quickly coming down the ladder, as he yelled this at Brian. When Henry reached the third step, he turned and leaped.

Brian didn't know why Henry moved so fast. Alarmed, he took off after him. Henry had a lead, but Brian was faster and began to catch up.

A predator stepped out from under the wing. Massive muscles rippled under its colorful, orange, black and white fur. It was between them and the plane!

Its tail twitched at the sight of them.

Chapter Eight

Henry's feet slid over the fine sand left on top of the concrete from the cleaning. Easily staying in control, he became one fluid motion reaching into his pocket while coming to a stop.

Brian spotted the predator when he was almost upon Henry. Everything happened fast. At the last moment, trying to avoid Henry, Brian turned sideways, pushing his hands into the air, trying to redirect. Henry was already taking aim with what he pulled from his pocket.

The predator crouched; its ears went back flat against its head. Its tail still twitched.

Too close, but with a tremendous effort, Brian almost succeeded in missing. He clipped Henry's right shoulder and arm; caught mostly arm before sailing head first past Henry. Brian hit the concrete on his side and bounced.

Henry's right shoulder bent forward from the impact. With his feet firmly planted, Henry remained where he was, swiftly returning to an upright position.

Before hitting the concrete, Brian saw he had knocked a small canister from Henry's hand. He watched the canister as it landed and bounded away. The predator loomed beyond it. With no time to think, Brian got on his hands and knees immediately and scampered to retrieve it. It was no more than ten feet away.

Because they were in a state of disarray and halting, the predator launched itself toward them.

Brian watched it come. It sent shivers down his spine, almost making him stop, but Henry pulled the canister for a reason. Coming straight at him, the predator was going to reach Brian first. When Brian reached the canister, he scooped it up with a swiping grasp and rolled a half turn to his back. He tried to end up sitting, facing Henry.

Relief washed over Brian; Henry was still there. He hadn't come a step closer, but he hadn't turned to run.

Desperate and moving quickly, Brian threw the canister as he rolled all the way to his opposite side. For a moment, he watched it sail, and hoped he was accurate.

The predator was almost upon him. Purely reflex, now on his stomach, Brian pushed backward.

While he did this, he tilted his head toward Henry and saw him snatch the canister neatly out of the air. Henry's arm went up, aimed, and a steady stream of high-powered liquid pepper spray covered the thirty feet to the charging beast right over Brian's head.

The predator dropped to its front haunches, paws going up covering its face. It skidded on its stomach practically stopping on top of Brian.

Brian's eyes grew wide as the predator slid over the ground he had just vacated! Getting to his knees, he backed away faster. While on his knees, he'd seen that the bottom of the predator's chin, even lying on its stomach, would clear the top of his head.

It was big, and made an awful cry after being hit.

Brian scrambled to his feet and could smell the spray as he stood up into the path that it had traveled. He backed up, getting further away. His nose tingled. Adrenalin already pumped through his veins. His heart pounded in his chest. It pumped so hard he felt the throb in his temples.

The predator labored for breath, at the same time coughed and bit at the air trying to loosen the grip of whatever had hold of it.

Brian had never heard one make a sound like it. It reinforced the scare.

Facing the predator, Brian put both hands on his knees and sneezed, adding to the pressure in his head. He continued to take tiny steps backward, while bent over.

The funny buzzing noise still permeated the air. He sneezed again, and finally realized the buzzing noise came from the equipment under the plane.

A warning system—

Brian felt Henry's hand on his shoulder.

"You all right?"

"Yes." He sneezed again.

"That was close. We'd better get on the plane." Brian couldn't have agreed more. He straightened and wiped his nose. "They're pretty independent," Henry said. They kept ample space walking an arc toward the plane. "You usually won't see more than one at a time. But you never know. Even though they're solitary animals, it doesn't mean there won't be more around. They like to eat and will turn on each other over food when they travel together."

Brian wanted to run. However, out in the open, he wouldn't leave the security of Henry's side. He stuck close, keeping Henry between him and the predator. As they walked, Brian kept wiping his nose. He never wanted to go through anything like that again! He trembled.

When they got to the plane, they didn't go inside; instead, Henry went to his equipment and turned off the buzzer. Brian stayed at his side. Henry checked the display. Worried, Brian kept an eye on the predator. He felt a headache coming on.

"It doesn't show anything else. Go get the saw and put it away," Henry told him. Brian didn't move. Henry was out of his mind!

"What?"

Henry looked at him. "Hop to it. I said there isn't another one."

Horrified, Brian ran, unplugged the saw and ran back as fast as he could carry it. Henry said there wasn't another one, but there was one on the runway, recovering. Did Henry need more of a reason to get inside the can?

After securing the saw in the compartment, Brian pulled the cord to snap it. He didn't bother slowing it down. The cord wound onto the wheel at full speed. Quickly, Brian backed away, watching the cord dance while he wiped at his nose again. It didn't take long to wind into place. He closed the compartment and latched it.

Brian wasn't going to feel safe until he was in the can. He was going to get in before Henry gave him something else to do. Although compelled, he stopped and waited on Henry, and once he got acknowledgement, raced for the ladder and climbed in.

Inside, he closed the hatch, but didn't latch it. Henry was still outside. He then checked on the predator through the window. It was lying on its stomach, panting. Its eyes were closed, and tearing. Wet tracks ran down its face. Its nose dripped heavily, with mucus hanging. The panting was interrupted by a sporadic cough. It was nowhere near as menacing from inside the can.

Henry came aboard shortly after and they watched the predator together.

"Brian, didn't you hear the alarm?" Henry asked.

"Yes, I did. It went off when you started sawing. I thought it was the saw. If you'd have told me…"

Intently, Henry listened, "Sorry, I assumed you knew."

"If I had…we had plenty of time."

The predator jumped to its feet, startling Brian. It tried to run, but went sideways in a funny gait. It stopped closer to the plane, stuck a front leg out and began rubbing its face against it. Brian sat taller in his seat to watch. It then shook its head, and deliberately plunged one side of its face into the concrete scooting along. It ended up on its back, arching, rubbing its face fully into the concrete.

Brian noted it didn't show any evidence of being male. He thought about broaching the subject of the new species with Henry, but didn't know if he should. The headache was still balancing on the verge of becoming one.

"Chief, when he's out of the way, can we go home? I don't feel so hot," Brian said, cradling his temples in the palm of his hands.

***

"Brian, it's me, Chief."

It was dark.

"Brian…"

Brian got up, and slipped on his pants wondering what was going on.

Insistently, Henry beat on the door. "Brian!"

There was a light shining outside. Brian saw it through the window when he came out of the bedroom. Intolerant, Henry seemed intent on waking the closest neighbors. Brian moved across the floor swiftly, going to the door and turned on the outside light as he opened it.

"Chief."

Henry stepped in.

They had left the old airport before Brian had a chance to get any work done. Henry had flown them home because of Brian's headache. Now, Brian tried to recall if Henry said anything about leaving early to make up for the lost time. Thankfully, the headache was gone.

"Get a shirt on, I need your help."

"Now?"

"Look, I know how important this apprenticeship is to you, but I'm leaving. I don't have time to explain. It will either be with or without you. And if it's without you, don't bother showing up at the office anymore."

Cordial was on vacation. This was going to be fun.

Henry left the lights on in the cart. The beams lit up a patchy fog that floated in and out of the light. Henry had waited until the last moment to brake. There were skid marks, clearing moisture, showing the cart had turned sideways when Henry stopped. The cart was right up tight to the front porch.

"I'll get my shirt."

Brian went to the bedroom and got a shirt off the floor, and grabbed a pair of socks. He stuffed the socks into his pocket and buttoned the shirt on his way out. Henry waited impatiently holding Brian's shoes out to him as he approached.

"You can put these on while I drive."

Without stopping, Brian took the shoes and led the way.

Only inches away, Brian stepped off the front porch onto the edge of the cart, barefoot. It was wet. He threw his shoes onto the floorboard while taking the next step onto the seat. Before he sat, Brian made a couple of quick passes over the seat with his hands. Henry plopped into the driver's seat at the same time.

"I received a non-citizen report," Henry said, taking off hard. "We're responding. The report indicated several men are involved. We'll find out more when we arrive at Ninety-Two."

Brian had heard rumors of this happening.

When Henry stopped in front of the cafeteria, Brian put on his socks and shoes. The doors to the Dupe were opening when Brian caught up. The platform was loaded with bright orange containers, which Henry grabbed, set on the floor, and then connected together with their attached straps.

Without asking, Brian helped clear the platform and then grabbed the lead container when Henry finished. He pulled the convoy to the cart. The containers, connected together, were long, and Brian had to let go of the door before they were all clear. The door rubbed against the last ones.

It took Brian time to figure out how to undo the straps. His only light came through the glass on the door. He had half of them done when Henry popped the door with the next load.

"Chief, are these coolers?" Brian asked as the next convoy rolled toward the cart.

"Sort of, but they're special. Stack them. We're going to have a full load. Interweave them so they'll stay together," Henry instructed, as the coolers he had just shoved out came to rest against the cart. He didn't wait to see if Brian needed further clarification.

As Brian became familiar with how to take them apart, he made short work of loading them.

By the time Henry brought out the fourth load, Brian had quite a stack going.

With the way Henry drove, they weren't going to stay in place. When Henry went back again, Brian figured they were making two trips and stopped putting them on.

With the next load, Henry brought bungee cords. "Come on, why did you stop?" He dropped the cords by the rear of the cart and began helping load the coolers. "I want them all on."

Henry threw the bungee cords over the load when they finished.

"These won't stay on, will they Chief?" Brian said as he helped secure a bungee.

"Sure they will. I'll drive and show you how it's done."

Brian could have laughed, would have, if cordial was anywhere around. The load would have better luck with him at the wheel. He would take it easy, something Henry only seemed to do with the plane.

When Henry turned on the lights, he drove full throttle all the way to the hangar. The load bounced with the cart, but stayed on. The cords did the trick, which Brian would remember.

When they got to the hangar, Brian was out before the cart came to a stop and opened one side of the door. Henry sped in going around the plane. Brian ran the other door out to its positive stop, and then quickly went under the wing. Henry was undoing the last bungee.

"Get in the cart and hand them up," Henry said, now heading toward to the ladder.

Brian got right on top of the coolers, making the first couple of layers easy.

Three-fourths of the way through Henry was sweating. Until then, Brian had never seen that happen. It was more than a little. Henry didn't seem to notice. He was zoned. Completing this task was his only objective.

"We're almost done, Chief. Slow down. You're not planning to take off in the dark, are you?" Brian suspected maybe he was.

"Can't land, but I can take off."

"You won't be able to see."

"Enough to take off."

"That's dangerous, isn't it?"

"It can be, but once we're lined up with the runway, it'll practically be on autopilot. You don't have to risk it just stay here. I won't need you after this," Henry said, matter-of-factly. He reached down for the last container. Brian dodged sweat drops.

"You've done it before?"

"It's been awhile."

"Well I'm going. Now that I'm awake, I wouldn't miss this."

With the cart empty, Brian moved it away from the plane. By the time he parked, Henry had the motors running. The propellers generated an enormous amount of wind, which Brian fought against getting back to the plane. As he reached for the ladder, the plane moved. Brian missed it, ending up with a fist full of air. Henry wasn't kidding. Not only didn't he need Brian anymore, he wasn't waiting. With a couple of quick steps, Brian hoisted himself up. Henry hadn't even bothered to close the hatch. Brian wondered how long it would be before Henry realized he wasn't in the can.

Brian held on tight and climbed to the hatch. Careful, he tested every move. The plane picked up speed. He didn't want to fall.

The receding lights from the hangar showed into the can. Henry hadn't stacked everything. Coolers lay where they landed.

Brian made his way to the seat next to Henry. Henry's face took on the color of the display. Brian couldn't make out much through the window.

"The non-citizen report came out of eighty-five," Henry yelled when he noticed Brian taking his seat. "The report said there's at least two. It's a preliminary report so there could be more. We're going to Ninety-Two first to pick up Special Forces."

Henry was cruising right along still picking up speed. He was going faster than Brian had ever seen him taxi. It felt unsafe. He could barely see anything out of the window. Not only was it dark, but the window kept picking up moisture, making it harder.

When Henry reached the runway, under a rolling start, he powered up.

"I should let you take off, shouldn't I? You've been wanting to do this; here, take it." Henry held it out for him. Stunned, Brian shied away. Henry's face glowed green; he laughed. Moisture completely covered the window. Brian was sure Henry couldn't see a thing. It wasn't funny. But Henry still laughed. He had gone plumb nuts.

By the seat of his pants, Henry lifted from the runway. It became quiet and they climbed without incident.

Soon, they were above the fog. The window began to clear.

"Here. Take us to Ninety-Two." Henry tossed the remote to Brian while he unbuckled and left his seat.

"Sure, Chief. Nice take-off by the way."

"Thanks, I didn't think you noticed," Henry said, more at ease. Cordial was back.

Brian realized he was making his first trip to another Installation. It was so weird apprenticing with Henry. He never knew what to expect. Nothing was ever the same, predators attacking you one day, taking off in the dark to a different Installation the next.

Henry returned with a cooler.

"You want anything?"

"Sure," he said, putting the plane on autopilot.

"The sun will be up in less than a half hour," handing Brian a packet and a drink. "It's halfway clear, which is good. We'll have a nice view when it comes up. You've never seen that happen from up here, have you?"

"No, I haven't."

"I guarantee it's the best show around."

The stuff Henry was handing him was packaged differently then what the cooler had been. The drink wasn't cold. He studied the packet, turning it over, trying to figure out if it was food. It wasn't hot.

From the light of the remote, Brian watched Henry brace his packet on his lap. He wound a string attached to the packet around his index finger and pulled it free from the edge. "This will warm it up. Do you want me to do yours?"

"No, I think I can manage."

"Okay, leave it set for a second, so it warms up all the way." Henry then did the same for the drink.

Brian found the string on the drink. He unwound it, and when he did, it looked like a tail dangling off some animal. This reminded him he was going to cover his new species theory with Henry the day before, but hadn't, because of his headache.

"Chief, the professor told me we used to dupe animals." Throwing caution to the wind, Brian just threw it out there casually. He pulled the string to his packet next.

"I've heard before that we did. So I guess we used to, but I've always heard only the tigers were done," Henry said, taking a drink.

"That can't be true. I saw a fox and it was just like that tiger yesterday. I'm thinking I might have discovered a new species," Brian said as he opened the packet. He found a spoon attached to the side.

"Hold on …" Henry said interrupting him. The interruption didn't work, Brian kept on.

"Look, the tiger we saw yesterday didn't show any evidence that is was male. The fox I saw didn't either," Brian said. "Douglas duped more than just the tigers and he had them digitally remastered so none of them are male." It was getting lighter on the horizon as he began to eat. The drink was becoming cold between his knees.

"That's ridiculous," Henry said. "You don't know what you're talking about. Sure, Douglas was a sly one and that would be right up his alley, but the tiger program was done to keep the infestation away from the Installations. Douglas had them duped by the hundreds of thousands. Once they could make a go of it on their own, they were released."

The packet contained a hearty stew. Brian had slept from the time he had gotten home until Henry woke him. He hadn't realized how hungry he had gotten.

"I'll have another one of these, Chief," he said. "So you're saying no other animals were duped?"

"Maybe someone did one here or there, but that'd be it." Henry pulled the string and gave it to Brian.

"Then why are they different?"

"I don't know," Henry admitted. "But any change, had to be in us, not them."

"Why?"

Color was beginning to creep into the sky. Near the earth, it became a pastel blue.

"Call it a paradox," Henry said. "You have to remember, the Dupe's only been around for five hundred years or so. Where did we come from before that?"

Brian started on his second serving. He heard Henry's question, but didn't realize he was expected to answer.

"Well?"

"I don't know."

"You see, the animals, they die, just like us. But everywhere you look, there are still plenty around. It's more likely Douglas digitally remastered us and we're the ones who are different. That would be more his style."

Brian's spoon hesitated. This information made him shiver as he assessed, from the inside, whether he felt whole or not. He did, but knew he wasn't; and wondered why he had never thought of this before.

Daybreak had begun to take shape. Henry was right. It was a wonderful sight.

"Another stew, please," and then he asked. "Why would he do that?"

"Well, from what I gather, Douglas was bent on ensuring there wasn't another infestation," Henry pulled the string this time too. "Why do you think we're going out now? If the tigers aren't enough of a deterrent, then the Special Forces always step in."

From their vantage point, the sunrise was spectacular. The event went from ordinary to extraordinary, as multitudes of vivid color; both sharp and soft, magnificently displayed against pastel.

For a while, Brian ate and watched until the colors faded, turning the clouds to ordinary white and the sky from pastel to its usual blue. Feelings stirred within him. He wondered if he would ever have the opportunity to observe this again. The dawning of this day brought a paradox. He was alive, though different. The moment etched permanently in his mind. It would remain a part of him.

"I'm putting this stuff away do you want anymore?"

"Um, yeah. Why not? They're good."

"Why not! This will be your seventh one. I don't know where you put it." Henry said, shaking his head. "When you're done, tidy up. I want the coolers stacked and tied down before we pick up the Special Forces."

"You got it, Chief."

What had prevented him from thinking of this angle himself? It presented a challenge, one he was determined to research. Douglas had done something to him. He would simply find out what it was, and reverse it.

***

A little over five hours later they landed at Ninety-Two. Brian was hoping to get out and look around, but the Special Forces were waiting. Disappointed, he never had a chance to leave the plane.

The commander boarded first, letting himself in and made his way to the front.

"Chief, Sam," he said. They shook. "Prepare to take off as soon as I clear my men."

Henry nodded.

Dressed alike, the rest of his command filed in behind him. These guys looked tough. They carried a ton of equipment. The inside of the can came alive with activity. Seats were pulled down, gear arranged under them. Their weapons were kept close at hand. Brian had never seen a weapon before, other than in pictures. He was curious about them.

"How many planes have responded, Commander?" Henry asked.

"The last official word I received was five, there will be more. Not everyone had reported in."

When the hatch closed, Sam cleared his men with a quick head count and signaled Henry with a thumbs-up.

Everything was quick and efficient.

Brian was impressed. Henry didn't miss a beat. They were moving the instant Sam's thumb went up.

"Who's this?" Sam asked, nodding toward Brian.

"My apprentice, Brian."

"Hi, Brian." They shook too.

With no seats remaining, Sam had positioned himself almost between their seats. Brian wondered if he was supposed to offer his. He didn't, because he expected Henry to let him fly to Ninety-Two.

"Any confirmation on how many are involved?" he asked, as they lifted.

"There are two," Sam answered.

When Henry didn't offer the remote, Brian got up. "Sam, you can have my seat." Sam took it. Brian crawled on top of the coolers.

The manpower committed to this was enormous. Brian figured if there were five planes and each carried eleven Special Forces, then there would be fifty-five men on the hunt, which didn't include him or Henry, or the rest of the pilots. This was serious business. Sam had said more might come.

Mid afternoon, Henry descended, and they flew over Eighty-five.

Eight Special Forces got up from their seats. Four went to the hatch.

With binoculars, two went to their knees. The other two stood behind them. Three of them began searching down, the other, the sky above.

"The spotter is in place," the one looking up shouted.

"Keep an eye on him," Sam said. "Let me know when they signal."

Henry got up from his seat as well, keeping the remote and made his way to a vacated pull down. He began to circle the Installation.

While Henry made his way to the pull down, the other four Special Forces made their way to the window.

Tolerantly, within the confines of the can, everyone got resituated.

With every pass around the Installation, Henry flew out further.

Four hours later, "Commander, we're at least fifty miles out," Henry yelled. "I don't believe they made it this far. I'm going back to try again."

"You're clear to do so, Chief," Sam agreed. "Next pass, fly lower and keep a tighter pattern."

"Will do…"

Although bored, being on the plane twelve hours, with nothing to do over the last four, Brian was glad Henry took the time to get him out of bed. He wished they were landing instead of starting over so he could see the new installation. But so far, seeing the sunrise and learning of the paradox made this trip worthwhile.

When they were a third of the way back, things began to happen.

"There's the signal, Commander," one of the Special Forces called out from the front.

"Take it up, Chief. We'll get confirmation."

"Affirmative." The plane began to climb.

As they approached the spotter, another one of the Special Forces called out. "I count seven planes forming up."

"Chief, get in line. Acknowledge, now," the commander yelled. "Men, prepare to jump."

This command created havoc in the can as they hustled to get their gear and put it on in the close quarters. Meanwhile, Henry made the plane tip back and forth. Brian braced himself on the coolers.

"There's a latecomer, Commander."

"The spotter will hold for them," the Commander said.

Brian could see the other planes getting in line behind them through the hatch. He could also see planes in front of them. He had never seen so many. These guys knew what they were doing too, using the planes to communicate. He was amazed taking it all in. This close, he saw that all the planes were identical, except the cans on top which were different.

"Commander, the spotter is taking us in," Henry yelled.

"Boys, hook up."

Even though Henry was following the planes in front of him, he was not directly behind them. This held true from the lead plane on back.

Brian watched as the Special Forces snapped straps to a rod on the wall. Sam squeezed through, and began pulling the straps to ensure each was secure. He then hooked up himself.

"We're there, Commander," Henry yelled.

Unbelievably, through the window, Brian watched as people jumped out of the planes in front of them.

"Go, go, go," Sam yelled, startling Brian. Remarkably, when Sam yelled, his men jumped one at a time out of the hatch.

Sam was last; Brian got off the coolers and followed him right up to the hatch.

Parachutes were floating all over the place. Some were still opening as more Special Forces jumped from the planes behind them.

"Chief, you see that...that takes guts," Brian exclaimed. "Those guys are fearless."

"It's admirable."

"You ever do it?"

"No."

"You ever want to?"

"No."

Brian watched as the first of the Special Forces landed. He couldn't believe Henry said no. He watched as steer their parachutes avoiding the trees. He had been following Sam's chute and still had him in sight when he landed on the ground.

"We have to drop the coolers, Brian. Help me get them ready," Henry told him as he banked the plane and gave it a little lift. "You know, at one time, I used to think about doing that and maybe someday I'll think about it again, but not seriously enough to actually jump out of a perfectly good plane."

Brian was still watching all the action from the hatch. The formation behind them broke up. Each pilot chose a new path for his plane, as Henry had done.

"Come on, Chief," Brian pleaded. "If I did it, you would, wouldn't you?" Henry was Brian's only hope of ever getting a chance to jump like the Special Forces.

"No," Henry laughed. He began taking coolers to the hatch. "Here, I'll show you how to get these ready."

Henry unzipped a side pouch, and then pulled out a strap. It was rolled up. With both hands, he held it at the center. It spun as he reached for the bar to snap it in place.

They busied themselves with the work.

When they were better than half done, Henry said, "Turn us around and head back to the drop zone."

Henry left the remote on the pull down. Brian got it and performed the task. When done, he sat the remote down where he found it and then went back to hooking up coolers.

Working next to the hatch Brian caught a glimpse of a plane that had fallen in behind them. It was following and catching up.

"When we get there, I'll count down and say when to go. Then you can start throwing these out," Henry said after they finished.

Brian gave Henry the thumbs-up.

"Get ready. Less than a minute."

Brian got on his knees and stuck his head out of the hatch to look under the plane. He was looking for the drop zone.

As he did this, he noted the plane behind them kept getting closer.

"He's catching up to us," Brian said.

Henry checked.

"He'll be all right. He's getting ready to make his drop too."

As Brian searched, looking for Special Forces, he saw flashes concentrated in one area, off to the side of where they had landed. He wondered if it was their weapons.

Henry started the countdown. Brian pushed up to his knees. "Two, one, go…" And they began tossing coolers out of the hatch.

Henry used the top. Brian used the bottom. The straps pulled a little parachute out and then disconnected from the package.

The plane behind them dumped its load too. It had gained enough now that it bounced in their wake.

When the last cooler was out, Henry started gathering all of the straps up in his arms that were dangling out of the back of the plane preparing to pull them in.

At the same time, Brian stood and stretched. While he did this, a plane caught his eye through the front window. It was coming straight at them.

There was no time to tell Henry. Brian lunged for the remote. He stifled the reflex to pick it up; there wasn't time.

Desperate, though accurate, Brian touched the face of the remote as he got there, and pressed it against the seat with his thumb. He wanted to go down. Quickly, dive! Brian began to feel weightless. With one arm, Henry clutched tight to the straps. The other reached for the bar above him. By then Brian secured the remote from the seat. He continued to press down; it wasn't happening fast enough, although his feet felt like they were lifting from the grating.

Chapter Nine

Immediately, but for only an instant, the other plane filled the entire view through the hatch. It was close!

Brian left the floor, turned in the air, free falling. The hatch opening came toward him. Henry stayed in place embracing the straps and bar.

The plane behind them took no evasive action. Brian watched, unbelieving. Offset, two propellers from each became involved in a disintegrating match. The plane following them was lower. It ripped through the bottom of the V on the other plane. Taking the brunt of the impact, the V broke free. The stub, with a portion of the propeller remaining, passed over the lower plane's wing, tearing away huge chunks.

Their proximity sent a deafening shockwave through the can.

Brian's ears rang.

At the point of impact a profusion of fragments filled the sky. The lower plane, forced down, continued to follow. Brian moved his thumb.

The plane that broke, almost in cartwheel fashion, spun away.

Several small explosions occurred from within the damaged area of the plane which followed. Sparks spewed from the top, blowing pieces out into the developing contrail. Smoke began to engulf the top of the wing.

As they leveled, Brian met the grating with his back. He had his legs spread, ready to catch both sides of the wall to avoid going through. He didn't know which he was going to meet first and hit relatively hard. He was already banking the plane as he got to his feet. With his eyes on the remote, he made his way to the front.

"What was that?" Henry shouted. Brian could barely hear him.

"Another plane almost hit us. We barely made it out of the way. It caught the one in back of us."

Henry checked. "I don't see anything."

"Up front, Chief, we'll see it in a second," Brian yelled.

Henry pulled the straps and closed the hatch. Hastily, he made his way to the front.

Brian glanced across the horizon, for a moment, trying to spot the plane which went spinning away. He didn't see it. Easy to spot, a black contrail led to the diving plane that had been in back of them.

It had somewhat leveled.

The contrail showed an ever-increasing amount of smoke billowing from the wing and that it was still losing altitude. Small explosions continued to rip deeper into the wing. Brian dove to follow.

"The batteries are blowing," Henry said.

With two propellers gone, the next in line began to slow. It then sped, only to slow again.

"The motor's going on number five. If that stops and he can't keep it straight, he'll fly in circles. He won't be able to get to Eighty-Five," Henry said. "If the next one goes after that, he won't be able to keep it in the air."

The plane continued to descend.

"Come on, pull it up," Henry pleaded.

The number five motor continued to run, but kept cutting in and out.

The plane never gained altitude. After several minutes, it began to clip the top of the trees. The fifth motor cut out completely.

"He's not going to make it, Chief."

"Come on," Henry yelled. Brian could hear raw emotion in his voice.

They watched as the remaining propellers spun a path through the treetops.

The plane cleared a swathe of vegetation before it broke apart and disappeared under the forest canopy. The trees beyond moved and shook denoting its path.

"That could have been us." Brian circled the crash site. He went around a couple of times, but saw nothing they could do.

"Brian…." Henry looked at him with complete understanding. Brian didn't answer. "Thank you."

Solemnly, they flew to Eighty-Five and landed without saying a word.

From that day forward, cordial never went on vacation again.

***

Three days later, they were back at One-O-Seven.

In the cafeteria, Brian asked for, and anticipated getting his own can of pepper spray. Henry lifted it from the platform before Brian had a chance.

"Chief…"

It was so strange spending time at the other Installation. Nothing there was the same, except for the building which housed the Dupe. It was identical, different decor on the inside, but identical.

He didn't know anyone. Yet, there were faces that were familiar. Brian spent a lot of time observing while he was at Eight-five.

Henry had told everyone Brian was a hero. They wanted to know how he avoided the big crash. It was news they wanted to hear first hand, but it made Brian uncomfortable. He would much rather have received recognition for discovering Memory Duping. If they only knew…

"Here, I think this is yours," Henry teased.

"Finally." But when Brian reached for it, Henry pulled it away, and then held it out again, smiling. "Come on, Chief."

"Go ahead, take it. I promise I won't do it again."

Once it was in his hands, Brian turned it over looking for where the spray came out. Quickly, he went to one knee, extended his arm and aimed at the door. He could feel the power. No longer was he at the bottom of the food chain.

"Take it easy with that thing." Henry told him. "Don't fire it off in here, even by accident. Now put it away, and remember it's only good for two or three shots."

Brian wanted to slide across the floor and draw it out of his pocket, just like Henry.

But, as told, he put it away.

Brian picked up the cooler and headed for the cart.

Inside the plane, Henry prepared the remote.

"Brian, you know the more I think about it, the more I like the idea of having you build us a new plane. It would give the Installation a backup, and it could also be loaned out to any Installation losing theirs. Under that context, I should be able to get Ivan to buy into it. We can't do it without his approval."

"That'd be a big project."

"I know; we'd have to collect the materials, but it'd keep you out of my hair. Here," Henry handed Brian the remote. "Taxi us out and take off."

"You're sure…?"

"Sure, but don't think for a moment you're getting to land. One thing at a time."

When Brian reached the runway, he stopped. He had reviewed everything Henry had taught him as he taxied. He powered it up and performed a flawless takeoff.

After that, Henry took the remote and landed back at the Installation. When he reached the end of the runway, he turned around and handed the remote back to Brian.

"Do it again," he told him.

"Why, did I do something wrong?"

"Nothing that I saw. But no one's that good on their first try. I want to see you do it over."

Flawlessly, Brian took off a second time. When they lifted, Henry shook his head. With some things, it was easy to impress him. Brian felt like he had been doing it all his life. He noted, moving his jaw from side to side—that after the second takeoff, it was harder to hear.

***

They flew to the old airport and Brian buzzed it.

"Look, Chief!" Brian pointed.

"It's a whole herd."

Most of the herd was lying on the runway, sunning.

As Brian lowered the plane, he and Henry watched as they rose, almost in unison, and then, with their white tails in the air, headed for all they were worth into the woods. The majority went the same direction.

"There's so many of them," Brian said, delighted. "Have you ever seen that many deer?"

"I didn't count them last time and I didn't count them this time. So there's no way to know. But what I do know is you better buzz the runway again. Ensure they've all cleared."

Brian did so, and ended up doing it a third time.

After they landed, but before Henry shut the plane down, "Chief, can you do me a favor?"

"If I can."

"I want you to park next to where I'm working." Brian requested. "I know we've got a long cord, but we don't need to use it all. It would make my life much easier."

"We can do that," Henry agreed.

"Thanks."

The first few limbs, Brian had fun dropping.

Cutting them up and loading them into the can was another story. It took more muscle to do the work. It was tiring and became mundane. It didn't compare to the excitement over the last several days.

While he worked, Brian relived every moment since the predator and for some reason, went on to think of Danny. He couldn't help but think of the what-ifs. It made him sad and he longed to return. He could tell everyone about Memory Duping. He then worked at shutting it out and found success by organizing his ideas on how to launch the paradox project. That didn't last though; he didn't have enough information to go on, mostly questions. But it was a start.

With resiliency, he stuck to the work at hand.

The one thing he knew a lot about was Memory Duping. He needed to reduce it to its simplest form. And that, he could do from memory. While his body labored, he put his mind to work elsewhere.

Occasionally, he would look around and pat his pocket, drawing security from the small canister.

Only a couple of hours and he was ready for a change of pace.

***

During the following months, Brian made progress. He had one side of the runway completed and the other started. Henry made him weed-whack. Some of the saplings, which stood between where he had trimmed, and the runway, were too large for whacking. Those, he clipped off at the base with a pair of pruning sheers.

Daily Brian flew. Henry seemed content to watch, both from under the wing and in the can.

Brian became very proficient at flying, which now included landing. There were days Henry made him land and take off several times. When that happened, it always seemed to diminish Brian's hearing for a while.

One day, when they got back to the Installation, Henry said, "Brian, we're taking a couple of days off. You're going to fly solo after that."

"I'm ready now," Brian said, perking up.

"You may be ready, but I'm not."

"Chief—"

"Listen, you're taking me to the office and then you're going to unload the plane. I'm ready for two days myself, and that's all there is to it."

Brian didn't understand why Henry needed two days rest. He rarely lifted a finger.

***

The next morning, Brian didn't want to waste a day sitting around the house. He would find a terminal that he could use. There had to be others besides the ones at the Research Center. Using anything there, was out of the question. Brian was not about to break his vow. He would find one elsewhere.

The cafeteria had the main terminal, but everyone used it to Dupe food and other stuff. He couldn't tie it up. They had more upstairs, but Brian was sure those would be in use just like the ones at the Research Center.

Henry had one, but he kept the office locked.

He wondered about the Space Center. It was the largest building at One-O-Seven. Other than Ivan, he didn't know who worked there. There couldn't be that many; the Research Center had most everyone. The place was huge; surely they would have a terminal he could use. He decided to go check. If they didn't, he would see if he could find Henry and ask for the office key.

It wasn't until the professor told the class about the space program, that he even knew what the building was used for. The professor had said they were lucky, because only two other Installations had Space Centers.

Brian took the shuttle. It dropped him off in front of the building. He walked up the short flight of stairs and entered. Even though the place was big, there was no one like Ken staffing the front door. Brian's footsteps echoed down the halls as he searched for someone.

He stopped at one of the many glassed in offices. The door wasn't locked. Inside, he found what he was looking for; not one terminal, but three. The office hadn't been used for quite some time. Dust rested on every surface. The desks under the terminals were arranged for privacy. Brian was tempted to sit down and crank one up. Thinking he should avoid trouble, he shut the door and kept looking for someone.

Twenty minutes later, and countless office doors, he wandered into a large hall that curved out of sight. Thirty-five feet down the curve, large milky windows formed to the curve on his left. It brightened the hall. Though distorted, he could see movement through the glass. There were people beyond; no doors, but expecting one soon, he kept going.

The other side of the aisle had bricks to the ceiling. Evenly aligned, and made out of the same milky glass, the doors continued for as far as he could see. As he walked, more came into view. It seemed endless glass on the left, with bricks and doors on the right.

Curious, he opened one of these too. More office space, terminals, dust, like every other he looked into. He suspected the whole place was like this. The realization sunk in of the enormity of this place. At one time, there had to be thousands of people working here. He could spend the day and no one would ever know he was around.

There had to be an entrance into the glassed in area, and he was sure it couldn't be much further.

Ahead, the hall darkened.

The glass stopped and the bricks started back up. The milky doors continued on the right. Set in the wall just past where the bricks started back up again, there was a door.

Brian let himself in. It was quiet. Though he heard people muffled in the background, he didn't see them. The door squeaked, making Ivan look up from his work.

Ivan was the old geezer. At least in every conversation concerning Ivan with Danny and Pete, it was always how they referred to him.

Since he was the administrator and responsible for the Space Center, Brian thought it was a stroke of bad luck that he was the first person he'd seen. It made him nervous. This man had a lot of responsibility.

"Did the Chief send you down here to spy on me?"

"No, I came to see if you had a spare terminal I could use," Brian said, surprised Ivan even knew he was apprenticing with Henry.

Ivan looked back to his work. "There's one across the hall."

With these few words, Ivan excused him; and, at the same time, gave him permission, and told him where to go. The door squeaked when he left.

The office across the hall was loaded with junk. Unlike the others, it looked as if someone used it for storage. There were hard copies stacked against the walls, practically to the ceiling. In spots, they came out three or four deep.

There was only one desk. Brian thought about trying the office next door, but Ivan had said to use this one.

Facing the entrance, the desk was on the other side of the room. Brian made his way around it and brushed off the chair. There had been ample room before, between the desk and wall, but that was before the hard copies were stored on the floor. It didn't leave much room.

Brian picked up the keypad and blew. Not a good idea, dust went everywhere. Brian turned the keypad over and used his pants. It was better, but not much. Although it would do, he wanted to give it a thorough cleaning. He pushed the on button instead, and hoped it worked.

It lit up, and within an hour, the problem was solved. He'd only guessed, but guessed right.

Brian knew Henry was going to be surprised.

He then opened a file and started the next project. He titled the work, Project: Paradox and started listing questions he needed to answer. He had only been at it a little while when the door opened. Ivan came in and shut it behind him.

"I see you found it okay."

"Yeah, thanks for letting me use it," he said, clicking 'save'.

"You cleaned it, I trust."

"Not really, just wiped it off. It is dirty."

Ivan walked around the desk to look at the screen. "You got it to work, I see."

"Yes," Brian answered, wondering if there was a problem.

Ivan got too close. Brian pushed back in the chair, to regain his personal space. When he did this, he ran the chair against the stuff behind him. It stopped and caused Brian to lose his balance while getting up. Ivan caught him.

Ivan didn't let go. Instead, he gave Brian an embrace.

Brian froze.

Ivan was taller and kept a bear hug with one arm wrapped around him, while his hand found its way down the front of Brian's pants. At the same time, he gently kissed the top of Brian's head.

Brian tried to move. The old geezer was strong and pulled him tighter. Fearing Ivan, he wanted to scream but couldn't catch a breath.

"Stop," Ivan demanded. "I'm not going to hurt you." Brian continued to struggle, couldn't get free and then stopped. "That's better."

When Ivan realized that he had ended up on the wrong side of Brian's underwear, he removed his hand to try again.

He loosened his grip, a little, so he could see between them.

With all his might, Brian screamed and squirmed free. He jumped the desk, knocking the terminal to the floor, and ran from the room!

The crusty old fart nearly had him.

Brian went down the stairs outside, two, three at a time. He wasn't about to wait for the shuttle. He didn't stop running until he was well away from the Space Center.

He checked several times, but never saw anyone exit the building.

He wished he had remembered his pepper spray. He could have pulled it on the old geezer and made him stop.

Brian couldn't believe Ivan. He had been taught from the time he was Duped to save himself for a lifetime partner. Ivan didn't intend him for a partner.

It took several hours to walk home.

Once inside, he locked the doors, latched the windows, hoping Ivan wouldn't come. He had never locked the place before. That would change. He would carry the pepper spray on him at all times from now on.

On the way home, he couldn't get over his dumb luck at finding so many unused terminals. The Space Center was loaded with them. But he was too scared to think of returning.

He would get Henry's key and work from the office.

It would be another day before he saw Henry. He wondered how he would react to his discovery. It was for Henry's benefit that he wanted to find a terminal in the first place.

Henry probably already knew, but it wouldn't matter. Brian would print a hard copy and give it to him. He also had to figure out how to convince Henry to let him use the Dupe. It wouldn't be easy, but he would prepare Henry for that too.

Henry would be surprised.

Embarrassed, Brian decided not to tell anyone what Ivan had tried.

Chapter Ten

Footsteps echoed from the adjacent hall. Brian anticipated Henry would round the corner at any moment.

Somehow, he needed to convince Henry to sign in on the terminal at the Dupe, and then step aside so he could use it. A whole day had come and gone, and his best plan so far—ask Henry if he could be the one to dupe the extra key to the office. It was weak. He hadn't even asked if he could have a key to the office.

Henry rounded the corner.

Apprehensive, Brian was also about to find out what Henry had planned for his solo flight.

"Morning, Chief. What's on the agenda?"

"We won't be trimming trees."

"That's good; I was afraid you might send me out there alone."

"Don't worry, there's not a chance of that happening," Henry assured him, very possessive of his plane. "You will be making a supply run though."

"Okay," he said, with no idea what was involved.

"And, you're making an express run." This news heightened Brian's apprehension. He knew where the old runway was located and would rather trim trees by himself than do something totally unfamiliar. "We have to hook up pods and gather bags. And that means there won't be time for that solo flight today."

"Okay," this time with an understating there was a change in plans, "will we be getting supplies from the Dupe?" It sounded like they were on another mission. Even though he was prepared and prepped for the solo flight, hearing it was postponed didn't bother him, as long as he got to use the Dupe. It was important.

"Later, before we leave." The *we* confirmed Henry was coming.

"Let's get started then."

"Boy, that was easy." Henry put a hand toward Brian's forehead. "Are you feeling okay? I thought you'd be disappointed."

"I'm all right," he said, pulling away. "So, ah, can I make an extra key to your office?"

"And the reason…"

"So I can use your terminal. You know, in the evenings, or the next time we take a day off."

Henry hesitated. "I'll have to think about it. I don't know if I want you in there or not alone."

"Chief, please."

"Just hold it that thought; I haven't said no."

"Then you'll let me?"

"Brian, you're awfully needy. I haven't said yes, either. Just wait."

Henry was correct; needy was right; he needed a better plan. He knew this one was weak from the start and began to sulk wishing he could have come up with something better while Henry opened the office.

"Get the bag," Henry told him.

There was a large nylon bag in the corner. Brian went over and picked it up. There were only a few envelopes inside the bag.

As he carried it to the cart, he couldn't get over how badly he blew it with the key. Without the key, there would be no surprise for Henry.

Henry drove them to the hangar. They went to the back wall where Henry removed tarps exposing four cradles. Each had a pod nestled into it. The cradles, on wheels, were electric. Henry motored one into position under the plane. Once there, the cradle, capable of lifting, allowed him to place the pod up under the wing where he could secure it to the plane.

"You see how that's done?" Henry asked when he finished.

"Sure."

"There are three more…"

They hit the Space Center after completing the pods. Warily, Brian followed Henry inside. Leaning in the corner by the entrance there was one nylon bag.

"Load that and wait for me in the cart. I have to see Ivan. I won't be long."

This bag was over half full. At the cart, Brian took the contents from Henry's bag and added it to the Space Center's bag. After that, he waited. He wondered if Henry was asking for Ivan's approval to build the new plane.

Henry must have gotten bad news. When he returned, he was preoccupied and remained distracted as they drove away. Brian speculated Ivan had knocked his socks off.

Perplexingly, they stopped next in front of the Research Center. Brian's mind went racing a mile a minute.

"Ken has the bag," Henry told him. "Just ask, and he'll get it for you."

"I'm not going in there."

"Why?"

"A quick question…did Ivan tell you *no* on building a new plane?"

"As a matter of fact, I didn't ask. Now hop on in there and get it."

"I said I can't." Instantly, Brian's anxiety became intense. He half spoke under his breath, "I made a promise." Henry was already perturbed over something with Ivan. This wouldn't help. "Even if you told me I could no longer apprentice with you, Chief, I'm not going in there."

The wait was tense. Henry stared at him, unbelieving.

"Some promise. You're serious, aren't you?"

"Sorry, Chief."

Henry got out of the cart and went in. He returned with three bags that were practically overflowing. Throwing those in the back, he said, "You're going to have to tell me what happened."

"There's nothing to tell," Brian replied, as they drove off. He wished Henry would let it go.

"Something's eating at you. You've worked hard to avoid going back there. You're better off letting me know what it is, so I can help."

Brian couldn't bring himself to the point where he trusted Henry to understand.

"Chief, can we just drop it? There's nothing to tell."

They drove to several other buildings stopping to collect bags. Those, however, amounted to squat. Brian could carry what was inside of them in one hand. And he did so, stuffing what he carried out in hand into one of the bags already on the cart.

They went to the cafeteria last.

This was his chance.

Henry signed in with his usual speed, and made several selections.

"Don't forget, I want to dupe the key," Brian reminded him.

"Already done, and no, you're not getting it. Maybe if you open up and tell me what's going on," Henry said as he hit send. Disappointed, Brian gave up. He would wait another day, come up with a better plan. Henry would get his surprise. Brian would see to it. "I'm going upstairs to get the bag," Henry told him.

"Load the cart."

"No problem, Chief."

Henry left before the table descended. He hadn't bothered signing off.

Promptly, taking advantage of his good fortune, Brian jumped at the chance and began searching the directories. There wouldn't be much time. He stabbed at the keypad quickly. He would have to be done before Henry returned, or spoil the surprise. He needed two things and found the first item right away. He selected it and checked two of them. The second item was not in the same directory and should have been. It was more important that he have it then what he already selected. The clock was ticking. It took time to locate. When he finally did key it as a selection, he had to hurry to clear the platform. Henry had duped twenty or so items, which Brian threw to the floor, except for the key, which he pocketed as he ran back to the terminal pressing send for his stuff.

At the doors, he could hardly wait to get his hands on the stuff. Henry would be back at any moment. When the doors opened, Brian folded the hard copy lengthwise and crammed it into his back pocket making it bulge. The other items went into the same pocket as the key. Ecstatic, he rushed to get everything out to the cart.

Henry showed up while he was loading the last of it on.

"I thought you would have this done by now."

"I had to rearranged the cart. It was full."

At the hangar, Henry parked inside next to the ladder.

Fifteen minutes later, they were sitting in their chairs. Brian started the motors.

"Where to, Chief?"

"One-Thirteen."

As they taxied to the runway, Brian wondered what they would be doing. Henry had duped a bunch of stuff. It wasn't all coolers this time.

When Brian got to the runway, he stopped and reached into his pocket.

"Here," he said, handing Henry a pair of earplugs, taking the second set for himself. Henry opened the little plastic packet and pulled one out.

"Where did you get these?"

"I duped them while you were upstairs."

"That wasn't a good idea, Brian. I don't recall giving you permission."

"I wanted to surprise you with this. All you had to do was let me use the Dupe."

Henry became thoughtful and didn't say a word for a bit.

"That reminds me; the key please," he said, holding out his hand. "You didn't dupe another, did you?"

"No." He reluctantly reached into his pocket to hand it over. Henry was deviously smart; Brian wished he had thought to dupe an extra.

"Now, I suppose, because this was a surprise, you expect me to wear these?"

"It's up to you. But you don't hear well anymore. If you wear them while we're in the plane, you won't lose anymore of your hearing ability," Brian explained, while inserting the other earplug. He then leaned over and pulled the hard copy free. "Here, read this."

With the pods attached, Brian didn't notice much difference in the handling of the plane. It behaved about the same as when they had a load of wood in the can.

As soon as they flew over the fence, he set the coordinates for One-Thirteen.

The earplugs worked great. Stubbornly, Henry didn't use his and tucked the hard copy up under his leg, holding it between his leg and chair.

After setting the coordinates, Brian noted the display for distances read 984 miles.

"Chief, we're going nearly a thousand miles."

"984 to be exact."

Brian laughed, "You've made this trip before."

"Is it that obvious?"

They were in the air for the better part of hour when Henry opened the hard copy and began to read. He read it through from beginning to end. When he finished, he tucked it back up under his leg.

Brian could tell he understood what he read. He pulled the earplugs out of his pocket and wrestled with the idea of using them. With kind of a sigh, he opened the packet and put them in.

Satisfied, Brian made no acknowledgement of what took place.

***

They touched down ten hours and some odd minutes later at One-Thirteen. The closer they had gotten, the more enthusiastic Henry became. His mood was one of anticipation.

"Where do I park?"

"Anywhere by the hangar, just don't block their exit."

They got out, chocked the wheels and secured the plane with mooring ropes. The first time they did this was at Eighty-Five. There, Henry explained why they needed to do it. In the hangar, the plane was protected from the wind.

They went to the shuttle stop and waited.

"Chief, every one of these places is weird. Nothing is where it's supposed to be," Brian said. "So where are we headed?"

"To see Chris. He's head of security here."

The shuttle arrived and took them to the office building housing security. Chris and Henry acted like long lost pals.

It was a wonder Henry even took the time to introduce Brian. He did though, but after that, it was as if he didn't exist. Chris got drinks; they were alcoholic, and nothing was offered to Brian. He stood around like a bump on a log and became weary of their small talk while they yakked it up for what seemed like hours.

He became bored and wanted out of there.

"Chris," Brian tried. "Chief," he said more loudly, interrupting them.

"Yes, Brian," Henry acknowledged.

"I'm tired," he said. "I assume we're spending the night. If that's so, I'm ready to hit the sack."

It did the trick.

***

Brian woke alone in a strange place. The night before, even though Henry said he would return, Brian assumed he would not.

Hungry, he got up. Within fifteen minutes, he was showered, dressed, and out the door in search of the cafeteria. He figured it wouldn't be that hard to find and it wasn't. After boarding the shuttle he asked the person next to him if they were headed there. They told him yes.

The cafeteria was nearly identical to those at the other Installations; as before, only the décor was different.

To dupe his food, just like at One-O-Seven, no authorization was required.

He was clearing his table when Henry and Chris walked in.

"Hey Brian," Henry yelled across the room. "Get the express bags from the plane. We're taking the bags in the foyer at the office. Put the ones from the plane there. You can use the cart." He tossed Brian a set of keys.

Henry was loud. Everyone looked. Brian was glad for the opportunity to escape. He didn't know anyone, although, like before, some faces were familiar. He was embarrassed for Henry, who didn't even realize he drew so much attention to himself. If he would continue to use the earplugs, at least it wouldn't get worse.

When Brian was done with the bags, he parked the cart in front of the cafeteria. He checked to ensure Henry was still inside before departing for the shuttle. He was not going back in. He left Chris's keys in the cart. Who would take it? It belonged to the head of security.

He waited at the shuttle stop. When it arrived, he got on and stayed on until they reached the hangar. There, he began to prepare the plane.

He had just gotten started on the mooring ropes when Henry and Chris drove up. Brian stopped long enough to shake Chris's hand.

"It was nice meeting you, Brian," Chris said.

"Same here."

He went back to preparing the plane. When he finished, Henry and Chris were still saying their goodbyes. Brian went inside the can to wait. It took them forever.

Once inside and seated, Henry closed his eyes and relaxed into the chair.

"Home, Chief?" Brian prodded after a bit. With all the supplies, he knew that wasn't the case. But he needed to know what coordinates to set.

"No. Set a course for Twenty-Nine."

Brian punched coordinates and started the motors.

"That's over three thousand miles away."

"And not getting any closer sitting here." Henry never opened his eyes. The poor man was tired. Brian didn't bother reminding him to use his earplugs.

"Are we still on the express run?"

"No, most of the stuff we have is for us. Wake me when we reach the coast."

Henry said this as if he expected Brian to know what that was. He thought he knew, but wasn't totally sure. All the pictures he had seen were from far above the earth. He didn't know if it would look the same from the plane. With thirty hours of flying ahead of them, they'd be sleeping on the plane. Henry was getting an early start.

A couple of hours later, Brian spotted the coast. He waited until they were on top of it before he woke Henry. The amount of water amazed him. It went for as far as he could see.

Henry made a big show of waking. He stood, put his hands behind his neck, elbows in the air and arched his back. This was accompanied by a groan. He then used the hatch to relieve himself. All that, before he even said a word.

"Excellent. Now make a left and head south. Follow the coast."

"I thought we were going to Twenty-Nine."

"I never said we were. The coordinates were to get us here." Brian shook his head, realizing he still had stuff to learn. He banked and turned south. "Take us down and fly at five hundred."

At that level, details of the coast became clear. Where the green met blue, small strips of white were apparent in spots that separated the two.

Forty minutes later, Henry, very alert, pointed to a long and wide strip of white sand.

"I'll take it from here." Brian handed over the remote. "We're doing a flyover to make sure everything looks relatively smooth. Put your belt on, in case it gets bumpy. Let me know if you see anything. I'm especially concerned about washouts here." Henry descended and flew over the sand.

Brian couldn't take his eyes off the surf as they covered the length of the sandy area from one end to the other. Then Henry banked hard out over the water.

"You see anything?"

"No."

"Were you looking?"

"Sort of."

Henry banked hard once again, gained some height, resuming their southerly direction. He didn't go far before making a wide 180 degree turn landward, lining back up with the shore.

Once they cleared the trees, Henry descended, and ever so slowly, with a light touch, hit the sand. The plane bounced, went for a bit, and then touched again. Every time they touched, the plane lost speed. Henry stayed glued to the remote. He was in no hurry to set down.

When the plane stayed on the sand, Henry powered it up to keep moving. He turned toward the water and did not stop until they were within one hundred feet.

Henry did well and Brian knew it.

"This is where we'll park to avoid the tide. It gets rather windy here, so you'll have to tie it down." Henry took one of the zippered bags.

"Nice landing. When will I be ready to land here?" The bag had zippers all over the top and down both sides. Henry threw it out of the hatch.

"Thanks…and I believe you are ready. You just needed to see it done once."

Henry then scooted down the ladder. Brian followed, but paused. The wind whipped through his hair. He breathed in the smell of salt deeply through his nose. He heard the surf, a sound so unusual.

When Brian stepped onto the sand, he sank. This made him jump back onto the ladder. He then tested the sand with one foot, making a trench.

Once off the ladder, Brian stooped and picked up a handful of sand. Most of it escaped between his fingers. He tilted his hand and watched it pour. Some grains stuck. He brushed his hands together knocking them off. It was novel. He hadn't expected the sand to be so moveable. He repeated this several times before starting to look around.

This whole place was unusual and he grasped the phrase with a much better understanding, 'like a grain of sand.'

Henry had taken off and was nowhere in sight. But there were tracks showing where he had gone.

"Henry," Brian called. His voice became lost in the wind.

Brian followed the tracks. It felt strange to walk in the sand. It took more effort. This was unlike anything he had ever done.

Henry's tracks led to the water. "Henry," Brian yelled in that direction.

He kept looking at everything around him as he made his way to the water. He spotted the bag at the water's edge. Several pouches were unzipped, and Henry's clothes were in a pile on top of it. There was a blanket spread over the sand. Towels were on top of it.

Brian scanned the surface of the water and cupped his hands around his mouth. "Henry."

He caught sight of Henry waving his arm. He was way out in the water. It was nearly impossible to see him amongst the waves. Only his head showed. It wasn't until his arm went up and waved that Brian saw him.

Fascinated, he stood on shore and watched while Henry's head bobbed up and down over the waves and then disappear under it.

After a while, Henry swam back to where he could touch bottom. Then he walked. When he was most of the way back, he motioned for Brian.

"Come on," Henry yelled. "The water's great. It's not that windy right now we'll tie the plane down later."

Brian sat on the blanket and removed his shoes.

He wanted to do what Henry was doing, but wasn't sure if he could. But he was more than willing to try.

Once his socks and shoes were off, he took a moment to feel the sand beneath his feet. He shuffled them back and forth. It was so neat.

Henry had walked up far enough that Brian saw he had changed into shorts. He peered into the bag and found another pair. They were colorful. He undressed quickly and put them on.

It was scary at the water's edge; there was just so much of it!

Brian went closer and stopped where the surf brought warm water up around his feet. He went further, water engulf his ankles.

As he ventured out, the waves, only a couple of feet high rolled into him. Brian was overjoyed by the experience; he laughed and kept going.

When he got to where the waves crested, the water sprayed up over his head. He turned, laughing, and ran back toward shore. He didn't go far before turning to brave it again. Henry stood close by and watched.

"Try swimming, Brian."

For the next hour, Henry kept a close eye on Brian while he covered the basics of swimming with him. By then, Brian had mastered it well enough that Henry stopped keeping a constant vigil. Although later, when asked, Brian refused to go out over his head to swim with Henry.

He did handstands, body-surfed, dove into the waves and discovered stuff on the bottom. It was a blast!

"It's time to eat, Brian. Let's get out," Henry said. "You need sunscreen anyway before you turn into a cherry."

"No, Chief," he refused. "I'll eat later."

Henry swam over to him. Brian dove under to get away, only to be caught by his foot a few seconds later. Henry forcefully removed him from the water, dragging him onto shore.

Brian kicked and screamed all the way.

On shore, when Henry let go, Brian got up and tackled him. They both went down into the sand. They wrestled; being stronger, Henry pinned him down and began covering him with sand.

"You think you're a smart guy, huh. Are you smart enough to get back in the water?"

"Let me go, you big brute," Brian laughed. He kept laughing, until his side hurt. Then he got sand in his eye.

"Chief, stop, you got it in my eye," he said in a near panic.

Henry let go. "Sorry, I didn't mean to get so rough," he apologized.

"What do I do?"

"Stop rubbing them; get in the water and rinse."

The salt stung. Brian pulled at his cheeks close to his eyes, swishing his head back and forth to get it all out. The eye with the sand felt scratchy even after rinsing; it was hard to tell if all the sand was out.

Afterward, he went to the blanket and lay down. It took the steam out of him. Henry took one of the towels and covered him with it. He then went to the plane and got a cooler. Brian ate his lunch while resting his eyes.

When they finished eating, Henry put everything away and set a tent up by the plane.

"Go lie in the tent and get out of the sun for a while." Inside, Henry had pillows, and there were sleeping bags rolled out. It looked inviting. Brian crawled into the tent and got into one of the bags. He moved around, making the sand beneath him conform to his body. It was very comfortable. Soon, he fell asleep.

Chapter Eleven

Henry was snoring.

He was loud whether he was awake or asleep. It woke Brian.

Motivated, Brian got out of his sleeping bag and left the tent. He was still in shorts; the morning air touched him with a light breeze making him shiver. The sun wasn't quite up to provide its warmth.

On a mission, he kept going.

There were seagulls resting on the sand close to shore. They watched him approach as he made his way to the water. Some took flight; others scampered to the side getting out of his path.

The waves were nothing but small ripples. It was calm compared to the day before. The serenity reminded him of the early morning's hours at the Installation, yet it was completely different. Very peaceful.

There was a hose leading from the water to one of the pods under the wing. Henry had chocked the wheels and moored the plane. The warning system was set up.

Brian dug a hole and took care of business. Henry probably had brought something to use to clean with, but it was too late for that.

He could feel sand in his hair and his skin was sticky with yesterday's salt. He removed his shorts completely, which had sand in them. He dreaded the water, because of the chill, but had to go in.

Upon entering the water he found it was warmer than the air. Lacking shower facilities, he did the next best thing and took the plunge. The warmth soaked into him. He stayed and swam.

Henry had the towels placed over the tent poles. They were dry and after using one, Brian hung it back on the pole. He hung his shorts there too. They were now wet, but no longer sandy.

He found his clothes in the tent, all neatly folded.

He put on his underwear, then his pants. He searched his pocket for Henry's surprise. The pepper spray and earplugs were there. The surprise—gone! He checked through his other pockets, at the same time glanced around on the floor. This was the most important thing he had duped. Where could it have gone? He had to find it. He put his shirt on and went outside to where the blanket had been the day before.

After giving the area a thorough visual, he got on his hands and knees and began raking his fingers through the sand. "Where the heck could I have lost it?" He mumbled.

Brian was still on his hands and knees when Henry came out of the tent. Henry whizzed on one of the plane's tires while looking around. He spotted Brian, and then went to the pod that had the hose hooked to it. He moved the hose to the next pod before coming out to where Brian was searching.

"How's the eye?" Henry asked. He was in a good mood.

"It feels scratchy, but it'll be okay."

"Let me see." Henry stooped down. "It's still red. You shouldn't have rubbed it."

"It'll be okay, Chief. It feels better."

"So what are you doing?"

"Looking for something I duped."

"You duped more than the earplugs?"

"Yes, but it was for you. I had it yesterday."

"Could this be it?" Henry revealed a black case in his hand.

"You have it!"

"It fell out of your pants when I was picking everything up. I've had them in ever since," Henry said. He turned his head to show Brian. He was wearing the hearing aids.

"Do they work?"

"Yeah, they work. You know, I didn't think I had actually lost any hearing until I put them in. You're really something, Brian. You avoid that plane crash and save my skin, and now this. What can I say? Thank you." For the first time, Brian realized that Henry wasn't as loud. Victory! It was sweet. He had been prepared to wear Henry down with constant pleas to make him wear them. Feelings welled rampant at the thought of truly helping. "So what do you say you and I try some real fish for breakfast?" Henry asked.

Brian thought for a moment. "Is that a trick question?"

"How so?" He wrinkled his forehead.

"As far as I know, everything I eat is real."

"That wasn't the question." Henry chuckled. "We're gonna fish. So this meal won't be coming from the Dupe, which I'm sure you've never had anything but. Do you have your pepper spray?"

"Yes." He tilted his head to look over his shoulder at the word of caution.

"I'm sure you won't need it. I've never seen anything around here that would be a problem. We need some wood. You gather some and put it by the plane."

Pleased, Brian took off for some nearby trees. He was glad for Henry. The hearing aids made a difference.

Brian collected loose wood carrying it in his arms. He came across a large branch and worked it free. He threw the rest of what he collected on top of it and dragged the whole bunch to the plane.

He debated if he should cut it up with the saw, but instead, joined Henry by the water. He didn't know what Henry had in mind, but hoped there was enough wood.

Brian watched Henry cast, reel in, and then cast again. He had a serious look on his face while doing this. But at the same time, he was enjoying himself. There was a bucket at his feet with fish in it.

"You have to try this, Brian," he said, handing over the pole. Henry left the line in the water.

"Sure."

"Reel it in." Brian did so. "Not so fast." Brian slowed. "Not so slow."

"Chief…"

"Well, you have to do it just right," Henry said as he picked up another pole.

After casting several times, Brian didn't see the fun, or, understand the seriousness. He did get the line to go out farther with each cast. Then he caught a fish, and after that, *he* was hooked. He wanted to catch another. Together, they filled half of the bucket in no time.

"We'll clean these," Henry decided. "We can catch more later." He carried the bucket to the tent, and then went into the can and came back with an oversized flat case. Brian remembered wondering what was in that one because of its odd shape. Henry sat it on the sand and opened it. There was an array of knives and other utensils in both the top and bottom half. Henry opened a side compartment near the bottom of the case and pulled out a flat piece of glass. Its perimeter was almost as large as the case. He held onto that, picking out two large knives. He closed the case, and placed the glass into an inset on top.

Henry got a fish and then sent scales flying everywhere.

"What are you doing?" Brian asked.

"Cleaning."

"Doesn't that hurt?" Off went the head.

"Not anymore." Henry then opened the belly, and with his bare hand, scooped out the guts.

"That's gross."

When Henry was done, it looked like one of the fish plates from the Dupe. One that Brian happened to like.

"Here, you do one." Henry handed over a fish. He wasn't asking. Brian's first attempt was a hack job. His second try was better, but Henry did four to his one.

While Brian finished Henry dug a pit in the sand using the spade shovel. He smoothed out the edges, making it flat. He placed a circular grating over the pit. Henry had obviously done this before, the grating fit rather well. He removed the grating and set it aside.

"Get me some dried-out grass," he said as he began breaking up pieces of wood and throwing them into the pit.

Brian took off for some thick patches of grass closer to the woods. He retrieved a large handful. Wadding it all up, Henry stuffed it into the pile. He then broke up more wood, throwing it on top. Brian watched intently while Henry made these preparations.

When it was ready, Henry pulled a small object from his pocket. It was red and looked like it was made of plastic. He reached into the pit, and with a flick of his thumb, a little flame appeared. He touched it to the grass.

Brian backed away quickly; he had never seen a flame before.

"What if you catch the forest on fire?"

"Don't worry. That's not going to happen. It's in a pit."

"But it's against the Constitution, Chief."

"I enforce the Constitution. It's not going anywhere. Trust me on this one," Henry said, putting the grating in place.

Brian had come to considered Henry a friend, and trusted him. But he wasn't sure about this. The governing body, some five hundred years before had set down strict guidelines for the recovery of The Earth. This activity; inherently forbidden.

As the fire grew, Brian became mesmerized.

The smoke found him. It stung his eyes and made them water. It irritated the one he had gotten sand in the day before. He moved; the smoke followed. He went to the other side of the pit to get away. When the flames grew above the grating, Brian stepped up to the fire, overcoming his fear. He wanted to touch it. He passed his hand through the flame, and did so very quickly. It was warm. He did it again, slower, and then jerked back. It was hot and stung for a moment.

With the fire blazing, Brian flexed his hand from its touch. Henry tossed the fish onto the grating using a pair of tongs. Once all the fish were on, he began the tedious task of flipping, avoiding the smoke, and ensuring he flipped each in turn.

"You're going to like these," Henry promised. He was eager for the fish and explained the finer points of mastering the technique of flame and grating, the gist of which was turning the fish quickly and often to avoid burning them and to keep them from sticking.

With flames engulfing the fish, it didn't take long before they began to sizzle.

Brian stood in awe.

"Get the plates," Henry said. "They're in the tent. I cleaned the ones we used yesterday."

Henry had washed plates to reuse. It was unheard of. The Dupe provided plates with each meal and every plate was different. Some had exquisite designs. While growing up, Brian had selected the same meal several times in a row, just to study the plate.

When Brian returned, Henry announced that the fish were ready. He took a plate and loaded it with fish. They made the exchange and Henry cleared the grating.

Brian followed Henry to the table. He kept looking at his meal. Danny and Pete would never believe this. If Brian hadn't seen it with his own eyes… Henry made no attempt to place the fish onto the plates in any presentable, appetizing manner. He just tossed them on, letting them slide around, leaving black smudges. It didn't look very appealing and there was nothing else to go with it.

"It smells good, Chief," Brian said as he sat down.

"Tastes better," Henry said, indulging. Brian forked one and took a bit. "Watch it…"

Lengths of bone protruded from between his lips. The skin from the fish, stuck to the roof of his mouth; it was hot and tasted awful. He spit everything back onto the plate.

"You don't like it, after I went to all the trouble."

"Ah, it's all right, I wasn't expecting there to be bones. And it is a little hot." Brian explained, trying to recover. He didn't do very well.

"You're just used to the food from the Dupe. And why not…the menu is loaded with what the greatest chefs had to offer from around the world before everything went into the crapper. Come on, eat, but don't eat the skin and pick out the bones."

Obviously, the chefs knew what they were doing; Henry did not. Wisely, Brian chose not to point this out. With the way Henry was enjoying them, he would have gone to all the trouble even if he were alone. Brian was sure he had done so on many occasion.

"How often do you come out here?"

"Not often enough," still enjoying the fish.

Brian picked bones, and ate slowly. If he lifted the meat from the skin and scraped the slimy stuff off, it wasn't half bad. Maybe someday he'd acquire a taste, though with the Dupe's offerings, with all its variety—spiced to perfection, why bother?

"If you're not going to eat all those…?"

"I'm working on it. But, here, have a couple."

"I just hate to see them go to waste."

Afterward, Brian washed dishes and utensils. It was so novel; he had to give it a try.

"When we're finished, how would you like to go for a hike?" Henry asked.

"A hike in the forest!" Brian was thrilled by the idea. "It is safe?"

"Safe enough, like I said." He explained again he had never seen anything that would be a concern.

"That's a great idea! I've always wanted to see what was on the other side of the fence. This will be like that, won't it?"

"You're outside of the fence now, just not in the woods. And yes, it's very close; it's just a different place."

Henry went into the can, and slid two packages through the hatch. He let them drop to the sand.

The packages had a zipper which went three-fourths of the way around them. Brian unzipped one and found it was nothing more than a cover.

"They're backpacks," Henry told him. "These are light weight ones. They contain water and other essentials. Some of the selections for these weigh-in at over 150 pounds. Those have everything you can imagine to survive out here."

Henry helped him put his on. It fit well and was comfortable. Brian realized Henry had planned to do this all along, and not only cooked fish for himself, but hiked alone as well whenever he came here.

They made their way toward the woods. It was uphill, there were no paths, and soon the vegetation became thick. Wildlife was abundant, much more so than at the Installation. Squirrels seemed to follow from tree to tree. Other furry critters scampered about, as they weaved their way through the foliage.

Biting insects found them. Brian began to fall behind, slapping and swatting at them. It hindered his progress. It was a first. He had never encountered so many hungry insects that wanted to consume him.

"These darn things won't leave me alone."

"Turn around," Henry said. He unzipped one of the compartments in Brian's backpack.

"Here, use this." Henry had pulled a foil packet from his pack and opened it. A wet towelet was inside.

"Rub this over your exposed skin."

Henry opened one for himself. Brian started at his ankles and worked his way up.

"I spray for these things at the Installation. That's why we don't have them. But if you hopped the fence and went out a ways out, you'd find them."

They continued on. The insects were still a nuisance, buzzing around him insistently, but they no longer landed.

Incredibly, the foliage became thicker. They had to duck, turn sideways and force their way through.

Suddenly, they broke out onto some old asphalt. Brian could walk upright.

"I knew we were getting close," Henry said. "These things are all over the place."

The asphalt basically was clear, as opposed to what they had just gone through.

Like the runway at the turn, the vegetation would eventually take over. The road was canopied; and in spots, you could no longer see the asphalt and had to walk single file.

A breeze blew through the top of the trees, making them sway. The shadow from the trees moved about, causing circles of light to dance around them.

Wildlife continued to make itself known. For the most part, the animals scurried away to avoid them. That wasn't so for a skunk that crossed their path, unconcerned.

Henry slowed, giving it plenty of space and time to proceed about its business.

"Those things are fearless, Brian. Never approach one."

"It never crossed my mind, Chief. You don't have a problem with that, do you?"

"Although a story in itself, I'll never tell." Henry said, as if reminiscing. They both chuckled. Brian could imagine.

A cardinal flew overhead. Bright red, it flew the same direction, using the road, following the corridor on a higher level.

"I like following these things," Henry said. "There are thousands of miles of them, all connected together."

"Where do they go?" Brian asked.

"It used to be everywhere, nowhere anymore," he said, as they wound their way up the hill.

Toward the top of the hill they had been climbing, the trees thinned on the ocean side. It went from being steep on their right to a complete drop off.

Between the trees, Brian began to catch glimpses of the shore. Eventually, they had a full view. Facing fully into the wind, they stopped and gazed out over the ocean. The plane looked marooned out of time. The white caps on the water had returned. The breeze made the tent fluid.

Brian knew it wasn't the view, but he experienced an immense sense of freedom, and at the same time, tranquility and peace. The sensation lasted.

Life at the Installation had its difficulties, but life there was good. It just couldn't be compared to this. Although he couldn't put a finger on why he felt it, or what caused it to happen, Brian loved his apprenticeship with Henry; it had brought him here.

Henry removed his backpack and got a bottle of water. Brian did the same and they stayed for a while before continuing. The road was hilly, and curved along the ridge. They followed it for a long time before it twisted and turned back down the other side. The canopy returned above them. This stretch of road wasn't as overgrown.

It became warmer as the morning progressed. They both had worked up a sweat. They stayed on the road for a long time paralleling the shore.

When Henry chose to leave the road, they had to climb over a rusty rail. It was falling apart. They negotiated the embankment, going around large rocks that protruded above Brian's head. In spots, Brian slid, before getting his footing. He used trees to slow his pace. The embankment was steep.

The wildlife, still abundant, was easier to spot.

Where they reached the ocean, vegetation had grown right out into the water.

Henry stepped in with his shoes on. Brian followed him out into the water. Once out past the vegetation they followed the shore. It was hot under the sun. Brian kept cupping his hands to wet his face and arms.

They made their way to a narrow strip of sand. At the end of the strip, trees hung out over the water. They got back in, ducked under the bent trees and continued to wade until they reached more sand. This continued until they reached the shore where the plane was located. They had hiked for several hours. The walk and carrying the extra weight of the backpack tired Brian out.

"That was fun," Brian said. There had been no surprises, though Brian didn't know what he had expected. The experience, however, would stay with him forever. "Can we go swimming now?"

"Sure."

He couldn't wait to get into his shorts and dive in. The water was much more refreshing to play in then wade through.

Later, when Henry suggested they get out and eat, Brian was ready. He was starved. They enjoyed a meal from one of the coolers, with drinks that were ice cold.

While they ate, the pump shut off. When they finished eating, Henry showed Brian how to switch the hose to the next pod.

"When this is full, the pump will shut off automatically," Henry explained.

They spent the rest of the day lounging in and around the surf, and eating.

Later in the day, Brian checked the surrounding hills to locate the spot where they had looked down on the plane. He found it and asked if they could return. Henry told him it was already part of the plan.

In the morning, before they went hiking, Brian switched the hose to the last pod and turned on the pump.

"We'll be leaving tomorrow. That's the last one," Henry said.

"It'd be nice to stay another day, Chief." He wanted to extend their time. "This place is like paradise. I would really like to try your fish again."

"You're sure."

"Yeah." Using this as an ulterior motive to stay, Brian was sure he could convince Henry to do so.

"It's an excellent idea. We'll see."

That day was a repeat of the day before and when they turned in for the night, Brian couldn't believe how fast the time had gone. He was sure Henry would stay another day for the fish. He hoped he had him hooked.

In the morning, it was raining, and Henry decided to stay. Brian wasn't sure whether his ploy worked or if Henry stayed because of the weather.

The backpacks contained rain gear. Brian collected wood with his on, and they both fished in the rain.

By the time they finished making preparations, sand was stuck to everything.

To get the fire going, Henry had to coax it along. When he got it take hold, it blazed above the grating defiant of the rain.

They ate under the shelter of the wing. Even so, Brian left his raingear on. Henry enjoyed his fish. He ate it as if he hadn't had anything in ten years. Brian got a kick out of just watching.

Afterward, they hiked to the top of the hill. When they went down the far side, Henry turned onto a side road.

"We walked past this two times already and I never saw it," Brian said.

"They're easy to miss, just like the houses that are all around us."

"Houses?"

"Most of them have long rotted into the ground or were eaten away by insects, but if you know what to look for, you can find some decent remains."

"Can you show me?"

"I will…but before I do, we need to have a discussion about you and the research center…"

"Chief, that's not fair."

"But I can help," Henry said, as they left the corridor of the road.

"Help! As long as we're discussing help, how come you've never shown me anything at the office? I can help there." The vegetation was extremely wet and everything Brian touched imparted water. Sopped, his shoes squeaked with each step.

"That's rather complicated." He offered no further explanation.

"Complicated. It can't be that complicated. No one tells you what to do; you come and go as you please."

A very thoughtful, "Huh," from Henry, but still no explanation. Instead, he said, "You must realize by now, I've never needed an apprentice."

"Chief, you're not going to get rid of me now, are you?"

"I didn't say that, but I don't need you."

Brian almost broke down. "What am I going to do? Sandy's not going to take me back."

"Sandy's been waiting."

"I haven't finished the runway."

"That's not important."

"After all that work…?" They stopped by some mounded-up foliage.

"Brian, look." Henry pulled plant life away to reveal what was still standing of a brick wall.

"What about building a new plane?"

"It's a big project."

"I could do it."

"No doubt you could, but you're going to have to trust me before I would ever start you on something like that."

With that said, Brian opened up and began to tell Henry everything. He started with Danny first.

They left the remains of the old house for the road; the squeak in Brian's shoe continued and became louder.

When Brian explained Memory Duping, Henry surprised him. He asked some very pertinent questions. He had the basic knowledge, and understood what Brian covered. As a result, in a little over five hours, Brian took him there, as he had wanted to do with Danny.

When Henry made the mental leap through the theory to its logical conclusion, he became very excited.

Taking the detour made for a long hike. When Brian spotted the plane and tent, he was ready to get dry and eat.

"So I can stay with you and continue to apprentice?" Brian wanted to ensure his explanation was sufficient to keep him with Henry.

Henry was climbing the ladder to get a cooler and dry clothes.

"Brian, you worry me. I don't think you understand. You can have my job; I'll even see that you get it. No, you can have Sandy's job. Better yet, if you want, you can have Ivan's job. But you don't need to be tied down with any of that responsibility. You can have everyone working for you instead." Henry disappeared into the plane. After he got the stuff and came back down the ladder. Inside the tent, they stripped, toweled and put on dry clothes. "Do you know what this means?"

"Yes I do."

"I don't think you do. When we get back, we're going to set you up in the lab at the Space Center. You let me know what you need and I'll see to it that Sandy and Ivan provide what you want. Do you understand?"

"Yes." He hadn't said anything about Ivan's indiscretion and knew he needed too.

"The whole Research Center will be at your disposal. You tell Sandy what you need and when, he'll get it for you." Henry was so excited, Brian was sure they were up for the night. He had gotten over the excitement of his discovery long ago. And now there would be all sorts of expectations. For Henry, this was all new.

"Thanks, Chief."

"This is a breakthrough, Brian. I can't believe you've never said anything to anyone. I sure never expected this to come popping out of you. You're going to be famous. Here…" Henry gave Brian the key. "That key will open every door at the Installation. It's a master key and it's yours."

Very grateful, Brian thanked him.

Though rainy outside, it became darker as the sunset. Henry continued to make plans.

They both crawled into their sleeping bags. Henry positioned the cooler between them and opened it.

Brian filled his belly with a hot meal. It was cozy in the tent. It was dry and the sleeping bag provided warmth. The rain outside would get heavy at times, beating against the tent, only to lighten up for a while before it pelted hard again.

"You know, we're going to have to stop and see Chris on the way back. Ivan's not going to understand this, or take our word for it just because we tell him we've made a breakthrough. We'll have to cover this with the team there, so when we get back, Ivan will already be briefed and ready to go."

Henry was having a heyday and Brian could tell he held him in the highest regard.

"Chief, aren't we going to catch some sleep?"

"Sleep! I have half a mind to pack it all up and leave now."

Brian laughed. He wasn't ready to get wet again or have sand stuck all over him until the morning.

"Shush!"

"What?"

"Listen…"

Brian heard it then. The alarm was sounding. Henry's hearing aids were working well.

Henry got out of his sleeping bag, turned on the light and put on his shoes, then his rain gear.

"Stay here; I'll be back."

He fiddled with the zipper at the door before he got it to open.

Chapter Twelve

Henry, on his hands and knees held the door to the tent open with one hand and swept the light back and forth with the other shining it outside.

Brian caught glimpses of the rain as it dropped through the beam.

Henry proceeded on his hands and knees out into the rain. Suddenly, with a thud, he bounced back into the tent, landing on his rear.

Filling the tent; with its enormous size, a predator had latched onto Henry! It stood, tried backing away, but pulled up tent stakes instead.

"Brian!" Henry gasped; the tent moved. The predator shook to free itself, and backed away faster. Brian could feel the ground move under him. Then the tent collapsed.

Henry and the predator were gone.

Brian heard Henry scream in total panic.

He was slow to respond as he struggled to find the tent door. Once out of the tent, he saw the light. Incredibly, even though Henry was being dragged across the ground, he still held it.

Brian sprinted to get into range, pulling his pepper spray. He took aim and screamed,

"Chief!"

He hit the beast in the rear, which made it turn abruptly. Henry dangled from its mouth, looking like a rag doll, as he was jerked about.

In that instant, the predator let go and challenged Brian.

Snarling, it hunched menacingly.

Brian never hesitated. "Chief, run!"

Henry was already up. He dropped the light, reaching for his arm as he dashed away.

Brian sent a short burst of spray.

The predator, quick to respond, pursued Henry. It leapt and Brian missed completely

To recapture Henry, the predator made a quick paw against his legs. Henry tumbled to the ground. With a pounce and a head latch, it held Henry firmly in place.

With only another shot, maybe two, Brian needed to make the next one count. He screamed again as he continued to charge toward them. The predator tried to flee with its prize. Henry ended up between its legs, bouncing along the ground, dragged by his head. Then the predator stepped on Henry with a back leg. This pulled its head down and to the side. It didn't let go.

Brian never stopped and ended up along side of them—so close—he couldn't miss. He squeezed off another shot.

The predator made several barrel rolls, trying to escape the pepper spray. It ended up a short distance away.

Henry was face down.

"Chief!" Brian moved to his side going down to one knee.

The predator knew he was there. Breathing hard, eyes closed, it twisted and swiped at him several times attempting to connect. Brian was surprised by how quickly it had moved and how close it had came.

He turned Henry over, grabbed him by his shirt at the shoulders, and dragged him away.

When he stopped, he went back to one knee alongside of Henry.

Henry was gurgling.

"You're alive," Brian screeched. Relief rushed over him. "I'll get you to the plane."

When Brian went to pick him up, Henry's hand latched onto his forearm and gripped tight. This stopped Brian. Henry shook.

"What do you want me to do, Chief?"

Henry held Brian with a death grip, never saying a word.

The rain continued to fall. Brian leaned closer to protect Henry's face, hoping against hope that he would say he was ready to be taken to the plane. Instead, the shaking stopped and so did the gurgle. Henry let go and his arm fell away lifelessly.

A fit of rage overcame Brian. He got up and went to the predator stepping over a rock. Only inches away, timing the next intake of breath, he sprayed right into the predator's mouth. It leapt straight in the air, twisting and turning.

Brian went for the rock.

With raw emotion, and all of his energy, he delivered a head bashing—let go of the rock blow. The rock rolled away. Brian grabbed it before it came to a stop. He went back and bashed the predator's head again and again.

This went on, blow after blow, until he was on his knees straddling the predator. He didn't quit until he could no longer pick up the rock.

Brian felt no relief, as he fell back onto the sand, and screamed in anguish into the rain.

***

Wet and shivering, Brian slumped in the can on top of the grated steel. The warning system still sounded the alarm. When he sought the shelter of the can, he hadn't shut it off. Something he now regretted.

Water dripped from his clothes. He could hear it splatter against the solar panels beneath him.

At first, sleep didn't come, but when the shivering stopped, it did, though not for long. The rain pinged off the top of the can, waking him. After a while, he slept once more. Throughout the night, both rain and sleep came and went.

With the first hint of light, Brian opened the hatch.

The warning system was loud. He had lost his pepper spray. Not that there would be any left; he would get Henry's.

He left the safety of the can.

The rain had stopped, although everything still dripped water.

Along with his pepper spray, Henry too was gone. It weighed heavy on him. What would happen next? Brian's mind ran rampant with possibilities. None were good, especially for him.

He scurried across the top of the sand, keeping a constant vigil, looking to get to Henry. Alone, out in the open, he felt vulnerable and was scared shitless.

Henry was gray. There was blood in the sand all around his head, neck and arm. Brian wondered if it was Henry's blood on his pants.

Brian kept an eye out for any danger as he went through Henry's pockets looking for the pepper spray. It wasn't there. He ran back to the plane and reset the warning system. It showed there was nothing around. After that, he relaxed. It was the only satisfying thing he had been able to do in the last six hours.

He went to the tent and set it up so he could get inside. His socks were caked with sand. He removed them and put on a clean pair. The shoes were still wet. He put them on next and then began throwing everything out of the tent. As he did this, he came across Henry's pepper spray.

Mechanically, and without thought, he disconnected the hose from the pod and wound it around its holder in the storage compartment where it belonged.

Methodically Brian chose the next task and completed it. Over the last several days, they had used a lot of stuff. It took forever to put it all away. When everything was done, except for the warning system, he went for Henry.

He was drawn to the predator first. It was lying less than twenty feet away. He gave it a hard prod with his foot. Oddly, as he squatted, curiosity over came his fear. The thing was massive, but he was determined to find out what made it different. Although he was incredibly wary when he picked up its hind leg, he was surprised to find its fur so soft, and surprised again, when he saw that it was male.

"There goes my theory of duping the animals differently." He went to Henry. "I'm sorry I asked you to stay another day, sir, you'd be alive… I won't leave you here, though." Then he thought, "You know, you were right, Douglas Fairbanks remastered us."

He had to get Henry aboard the plane, go back to the Installation to let someone know what had happened.

Even though he had reset the warning system, he constantly took in his surroundings, ensuring he was not next.

This close to Henry almost made Brian cry. He had to suck it up. Being gentle, he cradled him into his arms and lifted. Henry's last breath of air expelled from him striking the side of Brian's face. Startled, he let go and dropped him back to the sand.

Realizing what happened; Brian cradled him again and picked him up. He tried to walk, but had to bend over backward just to stay balanced. After only a couple of steps, he put Henry down. He weighed too much.

Brian didn't remember Henry being that heavy when he dragged him away from the predator. With that thought, he picked Henry up by the shirt and dragged him toward the plane.

Brian made it halfway before he stopped to rest. Breathing hard when he reached the ladder, he laid Henry down at the bottom.

The steps presented a problem.

Still as gentle as he could, Brian hoisted Henry onto his shoulder.

With one hand, he gripped the edge of the steps and got both legs onto the first step. He was scrunched in a squatting position, but with great effort, straightened his legs. He did this for the next step too. On the third, he was shaking hard from the repeated effort. He couldn't make it up all the way, and lost his balance.

Henry was unwieldy, and Brian had to let go to catch himself. He slid against the ladder, and heard the sickly thump of Henry landing on the ground. Brian felt awful. He couldn't believe he had dropped him.

He got down and pulled his pants up to where he had torn them against the ladder to inspect his knee. Crude in their construction, the steps were made of grating and had sharp edges. The skin was lifted in spots on his upper shin and knee. It bled.

Brian was resolved to succeed at this. Five minutes later, he had one of the plane's mooring ropes tied around Henry's chest.

Once in the can, Brian raised Henry with the rope but discovered he couldn't hold him in place to get a new grip.

He tossed the rope back out and climbed down.

Every foot or so, Brian put a knot in the rope.

Back in the can, foot by foot, he pulled Henry closer to the hatch.

Brian used the lip at the hatch cut out. The knots held against the lip while he rested and got a new grip.

This worked and soon he had Henry up to the door. Henry, though, wasn't going to be easy to get through. Brian realized this and knew he had to lower Henry a little. Then he could get Henry's arms above his head and manipulate him through.

He lowered the rope to the previous knot. Brian got down and started pulling at Henry's arms to get them above his head. Unexpectedly, the knot slipped. The rope moved around Brian's arm and as the end of it whipped by his face it left what developed into a nasty welt.

Tiny droplets of blood welled up on his arm where the rope removed part of his skin. Both cheek and arm burned.

He found the first aid kit and took care of his arm and then his knee.

Henry was lying upside down, with one leg caught in the last step. The leg was bent at the wrong angle and Brian assumed it was bone protruding against his pants from the inside that made the defined point.

Brian favored his bandaged arm going down the ladder.

Sincerely, under his breath, he said, "Sorry, Chief," as he retrieved the rope, throwing it back into the can. "You would have been better off if I had just left you where you were."

While his arm ached, Brian stowed the warning system and went back into the can. With Henry, he had resorted to the only option he had left.

Brian took his customary seat and with the start of the motors, commenced his solo flight.

The plane felt sluggish as he taxied over the sand. It took extra power to move.

He went a third of the way to the other side and turned the plane around. This gave him twice the distance of the runway.

He turned the power dial, and slowly started to gain speed. He turned the dial up the rest of the way and felt it surge forward.

When more than half of the distance was gone, he wondered if he should power down and go all the way to the other end.

The plane hadn't gained any more speed. Brian pushed the power dial again; already maxed, it didn't move.

Ahead of him, there were rocks and trees all the way to the water's edge. If he was going to abort, now was the time to do so.

Just then, the plane lifted.

"Finally," Brian said aloud.

He was relieved, until he realized he hadn't achieved air speed. The wheels contacted the sand again. Appallingly, this put him past the point of no return.

He didn't know what to do. He needed to abort but couldn't. Henry said the results of that were always catastrophic. Brian had tied the rope off to his chair leg so Henry was off the ground. He was dangling out the back on the rope.

The pit of his stomach hardened. His forehead became hot.

If he didn't abort, it would be full speed into the trees. If he aborted, he would crash, but maybe survive.

Again, the plane lifted into the air. Brian waited. This close, he could see the plane wasn't going to clear the trees. He couldn't turn, without putting the tip of the wing into the ground.

He continued to wait for the plane to gain height. With clammy palms, Brian squeezed the remote intently. The remote held up under the pressure. Brian couldn't have applied more. As soon as he could bank, he did so, and did it hard toward the ocean.

Too late; he wasn't going to miss the trees!

With the tips of the wing pointing skyward and almost touching the ground, Brian grazed the side of a few trees. Eight large propellers generated a profusion of vegetation. It didn't slow the plane enough to be a problem as he headed out over the water.

Gracefully, Brian allowed the nose of the plane to dip toward the top of the water with a sweep back to level. This allowed the plane to pick up speed.

For the next several moments, mentally, Brian criticized himself for not going all the way to the other end of the sandy area. He then exhaled. "That was close."

He had totally misjudged the influence of the sand and the weight of the pods and the wet sand from the rain. It was his solo flight; Henry would not have been impressed.

Brian turned landward continuing to climb. He flew the plane until he reached cruising altitude and then set the co-ordinates for One-O-Seven. After that, he went to check on Henry. He left the remote on the chair, and headed for the hatch.

Secured to the other end, which was now stretched out behind the plane, Henry was there dancing in the wind.

"Sorry, Chief," he apologized as he unzipped. He knew he couldn't wait the twelve to fourteen hours until they got back.

Henry's clothes were tattered and torn, and the broken leg was now dangling precariously after having dragged him through the trees. His foot spun in one direction, stopped, and then spun in the other direction.

Unspeakably, while urinating, he watched Henry's leg detach. It seemed to float in the air, as if suspended for a short time. It then began to tumble and fall away as the plane left it behind. Brian watched until it went out of sight. He mentally marked the spot as he stood contemplating whether he should return and retrieve the leg and get Henry inside.

He couldn't decide what to do. After a bit, he went back to his seat, picked up the remote and sat down. He started tapping the remote against his lip. He nestled into the chair, continued to tap.

He tried to think; everything pressed in on him. Exhausted from the stress of the last nine hours, he set the remote in Henry's chair and tried to decide. Now comfortable in the chair, he fell asleep.

Twenty minutes later, stiff, the position awkward, he startled awake. He still hadn't decided what to do.

He got the sleeping bags and laid them out on top of the grating, one atop of the other. He climbed in, deciding he wasn't going back. Much more comfortable, he fell back to sleep.

A little over six hours later, he woke. He was starved. He didn't remember the last time he had eaten. Certainly, it wasn't yet today.

He went to check on Henry and pee. When he opened the hatch, Henry was gone.

At first, he felt disbelief, then instinct forced him back to his seat to pick up the remote. Though upset, out in the middle of nowhere, he saw the scope of how truly impossible it would be to go back and look for him. Even on the off chance he spotted Henry, going back over the last six hundred miles, he couldn't get to him without landing. There would be nowhere to do that. He concluded he had failed at the simple task of taking Henry home.

The only consolation, he wouldn't have to piss on Henry anymore.

He saw that the rope had sawed through on the lip of the hatch.

Numb, he picked up a cooler and sat in his chair. He opened it and got a hot plate. Without thinking, he ate.

He brooded over asking Henry to stay another day. He should have turned the plane around when he had the chance and gotten him inside.

Systematically, without thought, he devoured two servings from the cooler.

If he hadn't given up so easily.

After he finished eating, he fell asleep in the chair. Later, when he woke, he saw he wasn't going to make it back before dark.

When he was seventy-five miles out, he set the autopilot to circle around the Installation. He wasn't sure if they would be able to hear the plane during the night from that distance, but was hoping they couldn't. He didn't want to alarm anyone in advance.

When that was done, he got in the sleeping bag.

Sleep eluded him, though. He was no longer tired.

As he lay there, his most prominent thoughts were of Henry, how he had said he didn't want his bones scattered all over the countryside. Brian had accomplished that.

Brian didn't know what would happen now without Henry.

Henry was going to take care of everything.

Chapter Thirteen

Ivan's position dictated that Brian go see him with the news.

Hopping into Henry's cart, Brian drove to the Space Center.

When on the plane, he thought of Henry. It kept him up most of the night. Because of that, he slept late and landed later in the morning.

Brian parked the cart at the bottom of the steps. He slowly made his way up them and into the Space Center. As before, the halls were empty, and the door to the control room made its annoying squeak.

Fresh with Henry's death, Brian was numb. He had relived every moment during the night many times, and would do so again, this time with Ivan. Concern overcame Ivan when he looked up from his desk. With a welt on the side of his face, one arm bandaged, his pants torn and bloodstained, Brian was a mess.

"What happened to you?"

"The Chief is dead," Brian announced, immediately cutting to the chase. As word spread, a hubbub of activity surrounded Brian. He answered questions while he tried to explain everything that had happened.

Ivan sat at his desk in the open with his back to the wall. Unbelievably, from around the corner, Brian overheard someone say he thought Henry had decided to become a non-citizen and had convinced Brian to concoct this story about his death.

Eventually, Brian drove Ivan to the plane. He showed Ivan where Henry had been on the end of the rope. It was frayed and cut through just as he had said.

Brian pointed out the pieces of foliage stuck to the plane. He took Ivan inside and showed him the blood splattered solar panels, something he'd noticed when he got up. It was more than water that had dripped from his pants.

In a chronological manner, Brian relayed everything they did after they left One-Thirteen. He didn't mention the fire or that they had fished. Both would surely be rebuked.

Thankfully, Ivan didn't try to get personal. Brian was sure it was only because of the circumstances.

"Did you have anything to do with Henry's death?" Ivan finally got around to asking.

Astonished by the question, and feeling guilty, Brian explained that he had wanted to stay another day and they had done so.

It was well into the afternoon before Brian was free to go home. When he parked the cart in front of his house, it didn't feel right. The cart belonged to Henry. Once inside, he carefully removed the bandage from his arm. It was sensitive, and partially red. Some areas oozed, where the rope had removed more skin. He took a shower and redressed the wounds before going to the cafeteria. Though not in the mood, he knew he needed to eat. He chose a hot meal of steak and potatoes. The meat was tender, delicious and melted in his mouth.

When he returned home, he went to bed. It was still early, but it was the first chance he had in six days to tuck into his own bed. It felt good. It was a comfort just being securely inside the fence.

In the morning, Brian knew he needed to take care of the plane. It was full of their old supplies, which needed to go to the Dupe. He also had four pods filled with water from the ocean and he had no idea what to do with them.

He also had to deal with the matter of the Research Center. Henry said Sandy was waiting for his return. Brian didn't know if he was supposed to go there first or not. Showing up there would mark the end of his apprenticeship, even though he knew Henry's death had already done so. He wasn't ready to do that. Without Henry, he was leery of saying anything about memory duping. He decided it didn't matter what Sandy assigned him, he was going to commit his efforts to Memory Duping and Project Paradox.

Brian went to the cafeteria first and after eating he went upstairs to see Don, the supervisor in charge of the Dupe.

Don was not alone when Brian found him. He and Mike were discussing some issue concerning a maintenance procedure. Brian waited until he was acknowledged.

"Don, I've got four pods full of ocean water attached to the plane," Brian said. "I'm sure they're for you, but I don't know how to get them to you."

"I'll show him," Mike volunteered. "I've done it a couple of times for the Chief."

"Thanks Mike," Don said.

As Brian drove them to the hangar, Mike asked for the details of Henry's death. "It's too bad about the Chief. So what happened?"

Brian felt like the villain. His name would always be synonymous with Henry's death. In all truthfulness, it didn't seem fair. The experience was raw for him. For Mike, or anyone else, to go about casually asking.... Brian tried to be patient; Mike had volunteered to help with the pods. This was no different than explaining how he avoided the plane crash to everyone who wanted to know.

"The Chief was attacked by a tiger and it killed him." To the point and brief.

"I heard you had to kill it."

"I didn't have to kill it."

"That's what everybody's saying. You killed it trying to save the Chief."

"Is that so?"

"Yes, and I see it got your arm. You're lucky to be alive; those things will tear you up," Mike said shaking his head. "How did you do it?"

"A rock."

"A rock!"

"Yes, a rock."

Brian didn't clarify, hoping Mike was done with the questions.

Against the back wall of the hangar, Mike showed Brian which pipe would make the transfer.

"Use this pipe to pump the water to the storage tanks," he explained, as he went ahead and hooked it up. "The majority of what we dupe is food. Because of that we use a disproportionate amount of sodium and chloride molecules. This will supply those and more. A long time ago, one of the Dupes continued to run after they ran out of sodium, leaving just the chloride molecule in place. It made a lot of people sick, and some of them died. We have safeguards in place now."

Afterward, Mike flipped a toggle on the plane to reverse the motor.

"If you brought back a cubic mile of seawater, it would yield one-hundred-and-twenty-million tons of salt. As a bonus, twenty-three percent of the dissolved solids are something other than sodium and chloride. Most of the hydrogen and oxygen will be used to generate fresh water, which isn't as necessary because we can pump that from the ground."

When they were done, Brian drove Mike back to the Dupe and dropped him off.

"Thanks for the help," he said, appreciatively.

"It wasn't a problem, glad to be of help. You take care of yourself."

"I will."

Brian went back to the hangar and cleaned out the inside of the can. He started to clean the outside of the plane, but gave that up. It was a big project and would take all day. He wasn't in the mood.

While loading one of the supply hoppers with everything he had hauled to the Dupe, Brian wondered if he should go to the Research Center and get it over with, let Sandy know he was available. He continued to decide against that. He would rather clean the plane; and at that moment, it just simply wasn't going to happen.

Once the last of the supplies were in the hopper, he went to the cafeteria. He grabbed a snack selecting strawberry shortcake with a scoop of vanilla ice cream. He picked a table next to the wall trying to relax.

After the second bite, he lost interest in the shortcake. He couldn't stop thinking of Henry; and somehow it didn't seem fair to be enjoying anything after his death.

Ivan walked in and destroyed anything to do with relaxing. It hardly mattered; it wasn't working for him anyway. Ivan went to the terminal, keyed a selection and then picked a hot drink off the platform. Of all the places he could sit, Ivan came over and sat with Brian.

"I've been looking for you."

"More questions about the Chief."

"No, I received independent confirmation early this morning that there was a dead tiger at the collection point. They found Henry's leg too, right in the area you said it would be."

Amazed, Brian wondered how Ivan had gotten the information so fast, but he didn't ask.

"One more thing, as of now, you're no longer an apprentice for security." Ivan took a sip of his drink. Brian knew it was coming, but he had hoped not so soon on the heels of Henry's death. "I know this is unexpected," Ivan continued. "But I'm promoting you to the head of security of One-O-Seven. Congratulations."

The hairs on the nape of Brian's neck rose. Apprehensive, he gawked at Ivan. Something wasn't right. What was Ivan doing?

"I know Henry didn't have a chance to show you much of what he did around the Installation, but I'll be available to answer your questions."

Brian didn't know what to say. Perhaps a thank you would be suitable. But he just sat there too stunned; and being promoted to this level removed the responsibility of doing chores. There would be no more chores. All this crowed his mind and the appropriate time to express a thank you had passed.

"Surprised? You shouldn't be," Ivan said. "There is no one better qualified to take the Chief's position. When you're done here, I want you to come to the Space Center and see me."

Ivan got up and left.

Completely neglected, his ice cream had melted as they spoke. Had Ivan done this to make up for the improper advance? Brian was grasping at straws and knew it. He didn't have a clue how to handle Henry's position and yet Ivan had given it to him.

The snack went into the recycler.

***

Still apprehensive, Brian followed Ivan across the hall and into the office where Ivan had lost his discretion and accosted him.

Ivan sat down and turned on the terminal. A few minutes later, he had the clearance level setup.

"All right," he said as he got up, offering Brian the chair. "Just key a password and you're set to go."

Brian sat, keyed a password and hit enter. By default, after re-keying the password, he was now officially the head of security.

"Why are you doing this?"

"Because you know how to fly the plane…. Remember, I'll provide you with all the direction you need; just come see me."

***

Overwhelmed, Brian couldn't quit pacing the floor at home. He was excited because of his new clearance on the Dupe. Anything he wanted…. And yet, he felt terrible because it came at Henry's expense.

Everything swept through his mind.

The lure was too great; eventually it drew him to the Dupe. Using his new password, he began to view the directories. Amazed by everything available, he couldn't conceive what he should dupe first.

Brian signed off without getting a thing, and left. It was too overwhelming.

He needed time.

***

The next morning, Brian used the key to let himself into Henry's office. He sat at the desk and turned on the terminal. He worked in privacy until late in the evening of the following day. Starved, he hit the Dupe, ate, went home to shower and went to bed.

***

Several days later Brian was at the Dupe, a list in hand. He keyed several selections and loaded the cart.

Throughout the day, he made several trips back to the Dupe. Late that night, he had the most advanced terminal the Dupe offered. The desk and chair were new too. Beautifully designed, and very functional there was a host of other paraphernalia. He could now do his work without leaving the house.

Brian not only planned to work from home, he planned to camp as he and Danny had once done. The house, wired, gave him access to the mainframe located at the Space Center.

When Brian had everything connected, he turned on the terminal. In awe of his newfound power, he could do nothing but sit and stare.

When he began to work, the first thing he tackled was his Memory Dupping theory. In a step-by-step procedure, he outlined what must be done to make it work. Apprenticing with Henry gave him a lot of time to think this through, which allowed him to organize his thoughts and break it down into the simplest form to date.

Brian had just verbalized the whole process with Henry. That was the first he had done so with anyone and it was better than any refresher he could do on his own. Early in the morning, with two thirds of it completed, he encrypted the work and loaded it onto a storage device.

After two weeks, Brian had only left the house a handful of times. The third week was more of the same. With his new setup, he stayed very busy. He worked on more than Memory Duping, much more. By then he had the whole process recorded and anyone could follow what he laid out and use it. Primarily, what he added now gave clarification.

Hunkered down in the house day after day got old, he began to go to Henry's office more often. He went through the file drawers and found some of the things Henry did on a routine basis. An inspection of the fence was long overdue.

Over the next couple of months, Brian developed a routine, spending part of his time at the office, but most of it at home.

During this time, only three things came up that were related to his new position. He performed the fence inspection, bringing it up to date. He also took care of a spat between two men who were living together. It involved a third party and a fight had ensued.

He also used the plane to spray the growth retardant and bug repellent around the outside of the Installation.

One of the strangest things that Brian didn't understand was that Ivan never showed up to provide direction. Originally, he'd thought the old geezer would show up daily and try to make another pass at him. He was glad Ivan never came around, and Brian never had inclination to go see him.

***

Three months into the job, Brian received an email from Don asking for a replenishment run on the salt water. Brian knew this would be coming; he just hadn't known when.

Prepared, he went to the Dupe. He made five trips with the cart to the plane. He didn't need a list this time. When he loaded the cart with the last item, he went upstairs to confirm with Don that he would leave in the morning to make the run.

After speaking with Don, Brian collected all the bags for the express run, except for the one at the Research Center. That one could rot where it sat.

When the bags were all collected, he took them to the plane, loaded them in the can and connected the pods.

With everything ready, Brian went home and began downloading files to his latest addition from the Dupe, a neat little laptop. Recently, he had put a new terminal in Henry's office. While testing it, he had gone looking for the laptops. He knew one would come in handy on the plane, but hadn't had time to see what was available. He spent the rest of the day at home, and turned in early for an early start in the morning.

***

Before six in the morning, Brian had duped coolers and packed them away in the plane. Once underway, he turned on the new laptop. It was convenient. He was very pleased he wouldn't have to interrupt his work.

At One-Thirteen, Brian only stayed long enough to switch bags and pay Chris a quick visit to relay his condolences. Pressed for time, he wanted to ensure he landed at the collection point before dark.

When he reached the coast, he put the laptop down, glad for a break from the screen. While he sat there, he became nervous. Instead of grabbing the laptop again to occupy his mind, he went through the checklist ensuring everything was ready.

It was still light when Brian reached the collection point, but the sun wasn't going to be up much longer. On the horizon, the leading edges of the clouds took on a brilliant orange. He did a low flyover checking for washouts, saw nothing and banked out over the water putting the nose of the plane toward the sky. It began to climb.

Brian lined up with the collection point, still gaining altitude. He leveled the plane just before he got there and put it on autopilot. Mentally, he was prepared to do this.

He hooked up to the bar and walked to the hatch. He took a deep breath and opened it. He watched as the sandy area came into view beneath him. Hesitant, he waited too long to jump. When he had seen this done when he and Henry had responded to the non-citizen call, he was ready to do it in a heartbeat. Now when the moment arrived, he wasn't so sure. It was scarier than a dare to touch the fence. It was no wonder Henry had never done it.

As Brian turned the plane around, he was thankful he hadn't jumped. The remote sat on his seat, a habit picked up from Henry. A sense of humiliation stayed with him as he heard Ivan say,

"You what? You let the Installation's plane fly away while you jumped at the collection point?" He decided it was a bad habit; he would have to break himself of.

On the next pass, Brian jumped.

The chute opened immediately.

The exhilaration was phenomenal. He used the ropes to steer as he floated toward the sand. He thought there would be more control.

On the ground, Brian wondered what Henry would say as he removed the chute. He got the remote out of his pocket and folded it out and brought the plane around thinking eventually he could have convinced Henry to do this. It ended up being a blast.

When the plane came into view, everything was opposite of what it should be. It was disorienting. He stopped looking at the plane and used the screen to land. That kept everything in perspective.

Systematically slow, Brian was as cautious as Henry had been to land. Then he went to the place where he had fought valiantly to save Henry. There wasn't a trace of what had taken place. Indeed, someone had been there and removed all evidence.

Back at the plane, he took out the warning system and set it up. He then unwound the hose, hooked it to a pod and dragged the other end to the water and tossed it in. He retrieved the parachute. Once folded, he took it aboard the plane.

Brian latched the door behind him and then turned on a portable light. There was never a doubt in his mind that he would spend the night in the can.

Brian began rummaging through the things he brought, organizing them. He then laid out his bedding and switched off the light.

In the morning, the hose went to the next pod. It was cloudy and on the cool side. Brian had been looking forward to a swim and hoped the weather improved.

Back in the can, as he ate he reviewed the information for what he was going to do. It seemed straightforward enough.

When he finished eating, he tossed what he needed out of the hatch. He had chosen to do this to see how it worked. It should answer some questions.

He put on the backpack, got the spade shovel and rake and headed inland. He didn't want to go far but needed a spot that couldn't be readily seen from shore. When Ivan had called this a collection point, it was obvious that One-O-Seven wasn't the only Installation coming here.

Brian knew this spot wasn't ideal, but he had brought what he needed to correct that. When he found a spot that was useable, he dropped everything and went back to the plane for another load.

After the tenth trip, he was sweating and glad for the cloud cover. He hadn't carried a third of it yet. He wished he had the cart to make it easier. He thought he might get that swim in after all. When he had carried everything to the spot, he began to wonder if the results were going to be worth the effort, but he wanted to see firsthand what took place.

There was nothing directly associating this with what Douglas had done. But it would give Brian information, which so far had been sparse. Almost everything he read gave nothing but praise to Douglas for pulling man through the brink of extinction.

Brian began to dig. It was quite sandy; which made it easy, but it still took time to clear a large area and rake out all the debris.

With the shovel, Brian made several very shallow trenches. He opened the first bag and poured the contents into one of the trenches. In order to use all the bags, he had to dig another trench. By then, it was mid-afternoon and he took a break.

In the can, he ate, and afterward rested. It hadn't taken long to get out of shape. He could feel it and would have rather climbed into the sleeping bag. Instead, he got up and went back to it.

At the plot, with the tip of the shovel, he made a furrow in the dirt he had filled into the trench.

Brian removed a seed from the packet, and rolled it between his fingers inspecting it. With his thumbnail, he broke it in half. He wanted to see what was inside, find out what made it work. Even then, it gave him no clue as to its magical powers.

He had thoroughly read everything he could find on plants. One of the pieces of literature had caught his attention when it made a reference to not spraying the flowers with poison. The poison would kill or keep the insects away and the flowers wouldn't pollinate. If the flowers didn't pollinate, they could not reproduce. He was going to find out how this reproduced.

Brian had sprayed the Installation to keep the insects away. Did the act of doing that keep man from reproducing? He wondered if Douglas had designed the spray.

Henry's paradox was harder to figure out than duping memory. He was already three months working on it and knew he wasn't any closer. He saw no connection between himself and the insects, though he believed stranger things took place.

Following the instructions on the packet, Brian planted the seeds. He opened the backpack and used the water to drench each furrow where the seeds were located. When he discovered this on the mainframe, he remembered the professor telling them about farming and how man had grown things to eat. The pictures of the final product on the packets were familiar. It just came from the Dupe is all, not the ground.

When done, he used the empty bags to collect the debris and then carried everything back to the plane.

Once inside, he took a nap.

***

Later, after he woke, Brian tacked a target to the nearest tree. As he walked away, per the safety manual, he put in his earplugs. He had a nifty looking pair of safety specs that he put on. He then slid a clip into place and chambered a round. With the weapon on full automatic, he took aim and held his breath. He pulled the trigger. The recoil nearly landed him on his butt and the last round shot off straight up into the air.

Rubbing his shoulder, Brian could see he hadn't hit the target. There were leaves drifting to the ground from various heights out of the tree where the target hung and from the ones behind it. He laughed and put in another clip. This time, he kept better control.

From close up, Brian inspected the target. He was close but didn't hit it. The tree was scarred above and to the left of the target and there were no leaves this time floating from the tops of the trees.

A couple hours later, he was out of ammunition. He had meant to save a clip or two, but had too much fun and didn't stop until they were gone.

There were a bunch of targets left. The first ones he hung were pretty safe. The later ones he tore up right away. It was then he declared himself a Special Forces member, as he now had jumped from the plane and could use a weapon.

After switching the hose, Brian got a cooler and sat under the wing to eat. He went inside shortly after he finished and read from the laptop. Maybe tomorrow he would get to go for a swim.

In the morning, he opened the hatch and found that it had become very humid. He threw out a heavy backpack. He would eat from it later. He climbed out and attached the hose to the last pod. He would leave when this one was full, and sleep while flying back.

Brian had plans for when he returned. He hoped he could pull it off, and just thinking about it made his stomach crawl. It had to be done, though; if he was ever going to take the next step.

Even though it was still cloudy, with it so humid, maybe that swim wouldn't be out of the question.

Brian got the shovel next. There were empty shell casings and clips littering the top of the sand everywhere he had stood. Using the edge of the shovel, he scraped it along the top of the sand getting the casings and clips into several piles. Just working at this made him sweat. He then retrieved an empty topsoil bag, scooped up the shells, sand and all, and dumped it into the bag. By the time he finished, he filled four bags.

After putting on the backpack, he decided against going into the woods. Even though the backpack was manageable, it was heavy and he was already hot. He went toward the shore where the rocks and trees met the water. He was sweating profusely before he was halfway there. In the heat, he couldn't imagine trying to maneuver through the woods while wearing the pack.

He didn't go beyond the trees. He turned and followed the shore until he was even with the plane.

By then, Brian's clothes were getting drenched with sweat. Carrying the pack was tiring. He took it off and dropped it onto the sand and removed his shoes. He went into the water, clothes and all. He didn't stay in long and when he was back on shore, refreshed, he sat next to the backpack and opened it. As he removed items, he realized he needed the brochure so he would know how some of the survival gear was used. That was still on the plane.

There was a host of packets containing food. All were sealed in thick flexible bags. Some were clear, most were not. One interesting discovery, the bags had dates for how long they were safe to eat. There was nothing dated for less than a year; and most of it for much longer. The Dupe had some type of dating system it used to transfer the information to the packets based on when they were duped. Talk about advanced manipulation of the program! Brian decided he needed to find out how it was done.

He opened one of the packets and tasted its content. Different from anything he had ever had, it wasn't half bad. Even though there were many duplicate packets, there was a lot of variety too and after a while, he began just to taste each one so he could sample them all.

When Brian tried to repack everything, it wouldn't fit. He dumped it out and tried again. It was impossible; he gave up. The open containers of food were emptied into the ocean. He hoped the fish liked it. One trip later, minus several pounds of food and the water, he had everything back in the can.

Brian hauled the water to his garden and used it there.

***

Later in the evening, with his feet dangling out of the hatch, the laptop nearby and nervous about whether he could accomplish what he needed to do when he got back, Brian searched for Henry....

He knew it was pointless, but he sat there until it was too dark to see.

Chapter Fourteen

Early morning, there was just enough light to see.

Brian landed, and eased the plane over the tarmac to the hangar. After backing in, he stayed seated. He couldn't afford to waste time, but needed a moment to settle his nerves. Ironically, the first thing he was going to do was drive to the Space Center. It was precisely what he had done the last time, when he had returned from the collection point, but that was for an entirely different reason. He couldn't recall much of that drive.

Prepared, he felt he was ready. Wasting precious time, he stood uneasily, continuing to contemplate. He needed to be in and out of the Space Center before anyone arrived. If he didn't go now, he'd wait another three months before attempting again.

Brian carried two black cases off the plane. One was compact and disproportionately heavy for its size. The other, larger, was lightweight in comparison. What he carried, he had duped before leaving except for the reports he sorted from the express run.

The pods would wait until later.

Carefully, he arranged the cases in the cart. He tucked a blanket around them so they wouldn't bounce around and then drove off.

At the Space Center, he picked the cases up off the concrete after unlocking the front door. He glanced around to ensure no one was there. Technically, he wasn't breaking in. Henry had given him the key.

As he walked past the control center windows, he didn't see any distorted movement through the glass. Most of the lights were off, but a few were on in strategic locations. Edgily, he hurried past the entrance.

On the plane, he had studied an enhanced program he had uploaded to the laptop. It had a fancy 3-D display, which gave him a virtual tour of the Space Center. It had an overlay in the bottom corner showing him where everything was located. He was able to control where he went on the tour and had memorized his route through the sprawling complex.

Brian found the digitalizer without a problem. The room was large. He set his stuff on the equipment's table and immediately opened the larger case.

Quickly, he pulled a hard copy of the instructions to turn it on. He had it memorized, but wanted it close in case he ran into any problems.

The digitalizer began to cycle through its startup. As it did so, Brian pulled one of the memory units from the small black case and inserted it into the designated receptor. The memory units were heavy and compact.

Next, out of the lighter case, came the defibrillator, complete with timer. Brian had it rigged on a belt so he could just strap it on. He set the IV packet on the table.

While the equipment went through its startup, he went searching. He found a broom in one of the closets, which he leaned against the table.

He then attached the defibrillator to his chest, cleared the table and got onto it. As he was doing this, a green indicator light came on with a chime. The machine was ready.

Brian squeezed the IV bag, ensuring there was no air in the line. He inserted the needle anticipating it would hurt; he was hoping not quite so much. He couldn't tell if it was right. But in a hurry, he lay down on the table.

Before landing, he had eaten a large meal; and drank plenty of water. If ultimately successful, he would be full and hydrated.

Stan Swanson would be troubled to see someone else do this.

While lying on the table, Brian grabbed the broom and with the end of the handle pushed the start button located on the console. The table moved into the machine, taking Brian with it.

Vaporization was available and had to be initiated during the start up. He rechecked the console settings several times to ensure they were correct. It was the first time he had ever laid eyes on this thing, and he wanted it right. Any mistakes would cost him dearly....

A light encircled him, making one pass from head to toe. It moved briefly, stopped, then jumped back, only to run across him again going a little further each time.

It was painless.

Brian knew he couldn't lie there calmly knowing he was about to be vaporized. How had Stan done it? He didn't know. If it were his only choice, he would opt out. But then again, based on what he knew, he was actually quite sure he could go through with this. A contradiction with which he struggled.

Disturbed, he saw clearly why Stan had gone through with it.

The light which passed over him did nothing but note which portion of his body was encoding at the atomic level. When it was complete, the table ejected him. He stopped the timer on the defibrillator and took it off. It had nine seconds remaining. There was some guesswork setting it. He didn't want to cut it too close and get zapped now. Nine seconds was close enough when the time came to use it.

It felt good to remove the IV. He took a bandage from his pocket and put it on his arm. It was weird that the bandage would still be available when the time came to use it again. He pulled another memory unit from the case.

He plugged it into the next receptor and made a copy. He wondered, because of its size, how it worked. There was a lot of information he had put on both of them. They each contained his digitalization and were capable of reproducing him.

The memory units went back into the small storage case. He shut the equipment down and put the broom back in the closet.

He carried both cases out to the cart where he gently placed them in the rear. Before covering them with the blanket he pulled Ivan's mail from the larger case.

With more to do, Brian went back into the Space Center.

The control room was next.

He had been looking for, but hadn't located information on the spaceships.

Over the last couple of months, he'd found general information, but the details were missing. The information existed, or there wouldn't be a space program.

He had the same funny thought, as previously; what if there were no ships. It was ludicrous, and he dismissed it as he had done in the past. It was a way of life. Every day, day in and day out, their activity was designed to achieve one goal: When the ships arrived, have the ability to use them.

He wanted to know everything about the ships. Was there a list stating what was on board? How were they tracked? Why were so many lost? How much room was aboard each? And the most important: Where were they headed? He already had a directory set up to organize the information. He just needed something to organize.

Brian was beginning to feel pressed for time. He ran to the control room and squeaked the door going through.

He had no idea where to look, but suspected Ivan had access. He went straight to Ivan's desk and set the reports on the corner. Those had come from the express run and were addressed to Ivan. Unless caught, Brian would pick them up and take them with him before he left. He then sat at Ivan's terminal, turned it on and waited.

His password didn't work.

Frustrated, he tried again. Still nothing. Brian leaned back in the chair assessing whether to leave or try another terminal.

Not far from Ivan's desk, there were stairs leading up to a stage-like platform. Each step was a continuous run that conformed to the circular design that extended to the hallway. Brian could walk up at any point. When he reached the top, he stood looking down over the control center. Impressed by its sheer size, he took it all in. Workstations were distributed throughout the different levels. Every person would have a clear view of the four-story display.

Against both walls and down the center there were no workstations. It left access to travel up and down the different levels.

Brian proceeded down half way and cut across toward the center.

He chose a terminal and signed in. His password didn't work there either. He moved to the next; same result. He wondered why the one across the hall worked, but not these.

Suddenly, he heard his name, "Brian!" shouted from the top of the steps. He flinched. The rumbling voice brought an ill feeling which swept over him. He quickly got up blocking the view to the screen; and hit the off button at the same time. "What are you doing?"

It was Ivan.

He wanted to hide. He turned and looked up. Ivan glared down.

"Good morning," Brian said making it cheerful. His heart pounded as he walked into the aisle. He wondered how long Ivan had been there. "I just got back from the collection point and I thought I'd drop off your reports from the express run."

"How did you get in?" He was gruff. Brian knew Ivan had seen him turn off the screen.

"I used my key."

While ascending, Brian put his hands into his pockets, securing the pepper spray in his right. He turned the nozzle so it was ready. Ivan had better behave. "After I put the reports on your desk, I started looking around. I've never been given the tour. It's impressive."

Ivan had a determined look. He was holding the reports, already finding them.

"You're resourceful. Where did you get a key?"

"Henry gave it to me so I could use the terminal at the office."

Ivan seemed disappointed by this.

"I know I made you head of security, Brian. And you can use your access privilege everywhere except here." He then changed the subject. "So, we're getting special deliveries from now on, are we?" He managed a smile.

"Sure." Brian didn't want to do it, but knew there would now be no way to avoid it.

"Good. I'll email a list of everyone working here; you can bring their reports as well."

Brian thought, oh great…. "Not a problem, sir."

"Good. Now, listen to me. This is important. Make sure you deliver them when we're here. Is that understood?"

"Yes sir."

"I consider this a breach of trust that you used your key to get in. I assume I've made myself quite clear on that," Ivan admonished.

"Yes." Brian continued to grip the pepper spray. Right then, he wished Henry were alive. He would put Ivan in his place. Dropping off the reports didn't seem adequate; he wanted a viable reason to have shown up and felt compelled to justify further.

"I was hoping you'd be in. You saved me a trip later," he said, with more confidence than he felt. "I have a request."

"What is it?"

"I'd like to have an apprentice. I assume your approval is needed."

Brian saw this was unanticipated. It was what he wanted. He didn't need an apprentice in his way, and knew Ivan would never oblige.

Ivan began to smile. The smile turned into a laugh. It became a hearty laugh. Brian was embarrassed; he wanted to run away from this horrible man, but endured the wait until Ivan stopped. It took a while.

"What would you do with an apprentice?" Ivan quizzed, as if Brian had just made a mockery of the position. Still laughing, but every word was clear. "You couldn't show him what to do. You don't even know yourself. You haven't come here once to seek my guidance. And when you do show up, you break into the place and want to know if the position comes with an apprentice." Ivan's laugh became scornful.

Humiliated, Brian regretted saying anything. The ruse he had already used was sufficient.

"What if I died like Henry? You'd have no one to fly the plane," he retorted.

"You don't have to worry about that. I can teach anyone to fly or I can bring someone in from another Installation." Ivan continued, authoritatively. "I could fly it myself if I had to."

"You'd have time for that?"

"Brian, don't push me. If I have to, I'll replace you."

***

Not only did Ivan make Brian feel precarious in his new position, he had also escorted him right to the front door to ensure he left.

Brian didn't know what nerve he had hit to make Ivan threaten his position. He did know that he would have sprayed the old geezer had he followed him to the cart. He couldn't let Ivan discover why he was really there. He wished he hadn't pushed his luck to begin with, and had left before Ivan arrived. He should have never improvised at the last minute saying he wanted an apprentice.

All the way home, Brian kept repeating the terminal number for the last one he had used. When he got to the house, he ran inside and wrote it down. Back at the cart, he picked up the cases and brought them inside.

He had so much to do. He didn't know where to begin.

The last thing on his mind was pumping the salt water to the storage tanks and cleaning out the can.

He let it slide each day thinking he'd get to it later, until it was too late to bother going to the terminal. This went on as each day slipped into the next.

***

Brian checked the network trying to find the terminal number he had last used in the control room. It didn't exist. He wanted Ivan's terminal number too, and would have had it, if not interrupted.

The only thing that made any sense was the possibility that the Space Center was on a separate mainframe. No one would have access then, except the people working there. If it were as simple as another security level, he should be able to use the terminals.

Brian searched and found a decoding program. He downloaded it to the laptop. He needed to get into Ivan's terminal, using his password.

This meant another trip to the Space Center. It was a risk he didn't like. If caught, it would end his career. Wanting to make sure that didn't happen; Brian decided he would go in after dark when everyone was gone.

***

Brian was excited. If this worked, he could board any one of the ships. Entirely from memory, he performed every step, never referencing the database he had set up.

He barely slept; even so, it took better than five weeks to complete the remastered digitalization. The whole process didn't involve any one thing, but a combination of events that needed to take place. He had to locate specific files where the information was stored for his brain.

Step one involved providing an over abundance of neurons with axons that were extended beyond normal. The axon, a fiber-like extension of the neuron, carried signals within the brain telling other cells what to do. He made certain there was an overabundance by duplicating thousands of them.

It took time to disperse them throughout the digitalization of his brain.

Just having neurons with extended axons wasn't enough. In the next step, Brian added special proteins. The proteins would become the receptors that allowed the neurons the ability to connect to the nervous system.

Brian dubbed the work The Neurotrophic Factor, after one of the studies he read on the multitude of proteins that could be used. He made use of every known protein receptor available and provided those in abundance as well. This would guarantee the brain's electrical activity had a path to follow.

The brain, already capable of producing a host of different chemicals, needed to be induced into releasing them.

Brian worked out the sequence in which each had to be released to facilitate protein placement and axon connections to the proteins. This would speed the process for thought.

This was not as simple as providing juice to the heart to stimulate it into action, but basically it was the same principle. Stimulation was needed to kick everything into action and it had to be provided in a given sequence.

The chemicals, unlike the neurons and proteins, did not have to be provided in excess. He did have to go through the tedious task of locating each file for given parts of the brain and then program them when to release the chemicals they already produced.

Next, he heightened the brain's ability to produce electrical activity. He was unsure how much to change this. He didn't want to overdo it and scramble everything. But this was the key; he needed enough to jump any gaps to lock in the axons to the protein receptors. It needed to be done, because it wasn't happening on its own.

Brian pushed back in his chair to stretch his legs. Deep in thought, he was now ready to test it. He could do it as early as tonight, though he didn't want to take the risk without access to the ships.

He would spy on Ivan and crew. It was time to take another crack at Ivan's terminal.

***

He spent most the night spying on the Space Center. He stayed out of sight and had watched everyone leave for the day.

True to his word, Ivan had emailed a list of everyone working at the Space Center, expecting Brian to deliver their express runs.

Brian used the list to check off names as they left. The only name not checked was Ivan's. Brian sat waiting for him to leave.

But he never did. Disappointed, the boredom overpowering, Brian left before sunrise and went home.

***

The next day, Brian got to the office in the late evening. He spent little time there, printed a new list and went back to the Space Center. Later, the list looked the same. Everybody's name was checked off but Ivan.

This time though, a little after midnight, Brian decided Ivan was using a different exit. He left his cart under the cover of darkness, and used his key. Once inside, he locked the door behind him.

He had brought the laptop, which he carried it in a small backpack.

He sneaked around inside, staying flat against the walls, crawling on the floors or hiding behind desks when available. He took his time, stopping often to listen. He made little noise, and slow progress.

He couldn't help but feel Ivan was still in the building.

He bypassed the control room, opting instead to go directly to where the mainframe was located.

The room, only illuminated by the multi-colored digital displays, was long and narrow. An open balcony on the second level surrounded the entire room, and it too had equipment lining both sides of the upper walls.

A ton of conduit ran all over the place. After he took it all in, Brian didn't bother turning on the lights. He knew it would be a waste of his time. When he left, the room remained a mystery of equipment and conduit.

He went to the control room next, entering by the hall. This entrance was closer to the room housing the mainframe.

Brian plugged his laptop into Ivan's terminal, and clicked it on. He started the code-breaking program on the laptop. When the program came up, it asked for information. He didn't know what to type, other than Ivan. He doubted whether "old geezer" or "crusty old fart" would help, although it should.

He started the program.

As he waited, he slid to the floor behind Ivan's desk and listened for anything beyond where he hid.

It didn't take long. Ivan's password flashed onto the laptop. Iv@n1... Brian wondered if this meant, Ivan won...and chuckled to himself.

With the laptop still hooked to the terminal, he signed in as Ivan.

He found directories full of the information he was looking for on the ships. This was more like it! Quickly, he began downloading directories to the laptop. In no time, the memory was filled to capacity. Disappointed, he disconnected everything and turned off Ivan's terminal. He only had a small portion of what was available.

In a hurry, he forgot how loud the door squeaked.

Outside, he sprinted past the lights to where he left the cart. He checked behind him, but no one was rushing in hot pursuit. He threw the laptop in the back and sped off.

Brian parked right next to the cafeteria door, as Henry had always done and rushed in. This place was always open for business. He signed in and made his selection - quantity, six.

Impatiently, he waited by the doors. It seemed to take forever. He didn't have all night, and needed to get back. Brian grabbed all six laptops by their handles, taking three in each hand, and ran back to the cart.

At the Space Center, Brian parked away from the lights and made a beeline to the front door. He leaned three of the laptops from one hand against the wall, to free it, and unlocked door.

Hastily, he made his way back to the control room. He wanted to get this done. Carelessly, he walked quickly down the hall, the sound of his footsteps echoing ahead of him. He didn't notice there were more lights on in the control room until he was almost to the entrance. Stunned, he backed away until he was up against the brick wall, away from the glass. Then he heard someone coming from the other side of the control room door. Hurriedly, he ducked into the office across the aisle.

Brian had no more than shut the door when he heard the squeak. He flattened against the wall, opposite side, of the way the door opened.

"Where are you?" Ivan called out. "I know you're here."

In despair, Brian sunk to the floor.

"You might as well come out and save yourself some trouble," Ivan continued calling. "I can go to your house and confirm you're not there."

He closed his eyes and swallowed. What was he going to say?

"Okay, I'm going to your house…."

Brian let go of the laptops, stood, leaving them on the floor. He was reaching for the knob when he heard the squeak again. This stopped him.

He had expected Ivan to follow him right into the room. It was that close. He thought Ivan had seen him. But he hadn't. Ivan calling out was nothing but a clever ploy to see if anyone responded. The old geezer was crafty and Brian had fell for it.

He jarred the door in time to see the lights go out in the control room. He scurried down the hall to see where Ivan was headed. At the end of the hall, the building opened up into a large domed area. He spotted Ivan leaving through the door on this side of the control room. Surprisingly, Ivan was dressed in his pajamas and barefoot.

He could hear Ivan mumbling, and barely made out, "Impossible," then caught, "I don't know how?" then louder and clearer as he went out of sight down another hall, "…doors are locked."

Brian waited to see if Ivan would come back. He suspected he wouldn't. His manner didn't hold up to someone on a mission, more like someone for whom the mission was complete.

He went back and got the laptops. It was all he could do to return to the edge of the hall where he had watched Ivan leave, to confirm he hadn't returned. His nerves were shot, he was ready to bolt. Nothing but the rest of the information on Ivan's terminal would have kept him there. Jittery, but under the belief he could continue, he entered the control room through the same hall Ivan had just exited and proceeded to Ivan's terminal.

He hooked everything up and began downloading the next set of directories. While the download took place, Brian went back down the hall to ensure again Ivan wasn't returning. He knew how much time it took to fill the first one and returned after approximately that much time had elapsed. He started the third, staying there listening for any sound. He filled all six laptops and still hadn't gotten everything.

He quickly decided not to dupe more laptops. His nerves were too far gone to do more and return.

While shutting everything down and disconnecting wires, he made a correlation between the squeaky door and Ivan. Every time he squeaked that door, Ivan showed up.

Brian collected his stuff and decided to leave through the hall.

As he started to go, something moved further down the hall. Brian froze. It caught his eye a second time when it moved again. It was ahead of him, and had stopped. Clearly, Brian focused in on the perfect silhouette of a man.

In a desperate attempt to escape, Brian, witless with fear, burst through the door that squeaked. In the process, he dropped one of the laptops. It bounced off the floor, and then hit the wall dislodging chunks out of the corner of it. He kicked it trying to pick it up on the run. This sent it noisily down the aisle in front of him. He stopped, backtracked two steps, picked up the pieces, one of which was large with circuit panels imbedded, then ran, stopped again, and picked up the laptop. Then, for all he was worth, never looking back, he left the building.

He knew it wasn't Ivan; he never would have stayed in the shadows.

Once home, he prepared for Ivan. Whoever it was, would surely tell him.

He tried to find a place to hide all the stuff he duped. Every few seconds, he checked to see if Ivan was coming up to the front door. After he hid everything, he undressed, mussed his hair and climbed into bed.

Thirty minutes later, Ivan still wasn't there.

During that time, Brian kept getting up and changing hiding places for everything. Any of it, could be easily found. At one point, he got up, threw it all in the cart, drove several blocks away and put everything into one of the empty houses.

Two hours later, Ivan still hadn't shown up.

Long ago, the adrenaline had worn off and Brian was tired. He took a shower to stay awake. He wouldn't go to bed.

In another hour or so, he would leave and go to the office. He would see if anyone came by to mention anything about the Space Center.

Wondering what Ivan was up to, he stopped at the other house and took one of the laptops with him to the office. For whatever good it would do him, he began to go through the information, even though he expected this to be his last day on the job.

Chapter Fifteen

At the office, Brian spent his time skimming through the information on the laptop. He used the search function to speed the process. Even at that, it was going to take time to digest all seven laptops. The morning flew by.

Brian pondered the mystery of who had been in the hall at the Space Center. He didn't know what to make of it. As of yet, Ivan hadn't shown up to dismiss him. Either they hadn't reported him, and he couldn't imagine why not, or they hadn't recognized him, which was possible. Either way, Brian was thankful.

He was concerned that he might not have gotten what he needed on the laptops, which meant a return trip to the Space Center. He didn't want to do that. His luck wouldn't hold forever. He would end up facing Ivan, who, like a cunning predator, would devour him. He resolved, if need be, he would face a thousand Ivans. He would get the information he needed.

In the early afternoon, he went to the cafeteria. He checked the receptors to ensure one of them would accept his memory unit. There was one, so he didn't foresee a problem.

Sitting at one of the tables, Brian tried to remember the last time he had eaten a meal without performing another task at the same time. It had been a while.

He enjoyed his dish of succulent broiled shrimp, which were glazed with an exquisite garlic sauce and thought of Ivan. Something had alerted him last night and he came without taking the time to dress. Brian wondered if it really was the squeaky door.

Still hungry, he got up and selected another dish of shrimp. When he was finished, he went home. He had been starved, but wished he hadn't eaten the second plate. He felt sluggish, overfull and sleep-deprived. He needed to be sharp when he tested his digitalization. He laid down for a short nap.

***

Brian woke the next morning. Realizing he had slept through the night, he rolled over onto his stomach and went back to sleep. Later, when he crawled out of bed, he decided he'd been burning the candle on both ends for too long and it had caught up with him.

Now, fully rested, he was ready to test, but he would have to wait until tonight when there would be total privacy. He took a leisurely shower, and went to the Dupe. He knew if he hadn't slept through the night, he would already know if it worked. This excited him, and he wished he hadn't let the opportunity slip through his fingers.

Antsy, he decided to kick the routine. He had been working too hard.

After he ate, he searched the directories for a new headboard. He wanted a place where he could hide his stuff.

He found one that he liked and duped two of them.

At home, he took the old headboard off. While assembling the new, he used the encasement pieces from the second headboard to create an area between the base and drawers. It gave him a large, well-hidden space.

He then went to the other house and grabbed his stuff. He kept two of the laptops out, and hid the rest in the dead space. He loaded the cart with the old headboard and leftover pieces and took them to the Dupe.

Later, he headed for the plane. The pods, though empty, were still attached. He disconnected them wishing that job was already complete. He cleaned the inside of the can thoroughly by getting under the grating and washing the solar panels. This was something he was sure hadn't been done since the can was installed.

Doing the manual labor left his mind free. He tried to think of any last minute preparation he needed to make.

He took everything he removed from the can to the Dupe. While there, he finalized plans to leave the Installation and duped some things to take with him.

He stopped at the office long enough to confirm there wasn't any scuttlebutt on the Space Center and checked emails. Nothing….

A little over an hour later, Brian buzzed the old runway. The place looked the same, except the grass and weeds had grown tall where he had weed-whacked. A job never completed, one side of the runway still needed the limbs trimmed. "Some day," he said, under his breath. But it wasn't why he had come.

Standing behind the plane, he strapped on a holster. He removed a pistol from the case it came in, loaded it and chambered a round. It fit neatly into the holster and slid in and out smoothly. He put on a backpack and loaded a clip into the automatic weapon. Extra clips went into a belt made to carry them.

The weapons would provide long-range protection, and Brian wondered why Henry had never carried them on the plane. Although for close encounters, the pepper spray would work best.

The warning system stayed in its compartment. Brian left the plane and walked to the end of the runway where it curved. Henry had said it led to a terminal. He stepped into the foliage and the plane disappeared from sight. Easy to follow, the runway was wider than the road at the collection point so the trees hadn't canopied the whole thing.

Brian exercised extreme caution, ready for anything. He knew there were predators in the area and this effectively took his mind away from work.

He ran across another path where planes had once traveled, but kept following the one he was on.

He hadn't gone far when he spotted what looked like an expansive building. He couldn't see it clearly; but caught bits and pieces through the thick foliage. Cautiously, he approached. At an entrance, after checking through the glass of the second set of doors, he looked behind him and ducked under what remained of the glass in the first set.

Still intact, the second set of doors wouldn't open. With one foot up against the other door for leverage, Brian applied a tremendous amount of force. He got it to move, but barely. It groaned in protest the whole time he pulled. A whiff of air made him turn his head and stop. The door stayed where he had pulled it to.

After another hard pull, Brian stepped inside. Birds took flight overhead. He crouched while they flew back and forth before roosting again. He had disturbed their peaceful existence. He was sure it was a first for them.

While crouching, Brian took measure. The place was dilapidated. Large chunks of stuff lay all around and everything was covered in bird dung. It smelled strongly. He stood and headed down a wide corridor. This created another commotion above him. He walked over the bird droppings; something he couldn't avoid. The stuff covered everything and was even in piles in some areas. It crunched under his feet. The recent stuff stuck to the bottom of his shoes and oozed up around the edges. The older crunchy stuff stuck to that.

Farther down the corridor, a large tree had taken up residence inside. When he got closer, he could see that long ago the roots had pulled up out of the ground from one side. It had crashed through the side of the building, taking out the glass and part of the metal framework that held the glass in place.

The tree, still alive, had turned back on itself toward the sun. The vast majority had successfully reached back outside where it now grew. As Brian approached, glass added itself to the mix on the bottom of his shoes.

He noted that the limbs had grown thick and now encapsulated part of the framework where glass had been. A good portion still grew inside and filled the aisle all the way to the ceiling. Brian made his way through it.

On the other side, as far as the corridor led, there were bird droppings. He had seen enough and decided to exit where the tree had come through.

Once outside, Brian scraped the bottom of his shoes off against the trunk and then on the ground, twisted in place.

Staying close to the building, he scuffed his feet as he went, turning them from side to side and dragging the tips of his toes to finish the job. He stopped at different windows to see if the floor was still fouled. He wasn't going back in unless he found an area to which the birds didn't have access.

In spots the vegetation was thick and he couldn't stay next to the building. Massive trees had grown up under the overhang in spots and had broken it. He knew that trees grew from the top so he attributed this to the diameter growth where the tops had bent and curled. While gaining purchase, wind provided the energy to do the job.

When he rounded another corner, he found a set of double doors. Surprised, when he looked through he didn't see any bird droppings. He tried to get in, but neither door would budge. Even using his foot didn't work.

Brian took off the backpack and searched through it. He found a tool, which he used to shimmy between the doors. When he got it stuck, he kicked it to the side and the door snapped free. Even though it was ajar, it still wouldn't move. He found a hefty branch and used it to persuade the door open enough so that he could squeeze through.

Albeit very stiffly, the second set of doors opened just fine for him.

This section of the building had fared better over the years.

He investigated all the nooks and crannies, opening doors as he went. Surprisingly, most of the doors worked and behind them he found mostly office space or storage rooms.

Later, he stopped in one of the offices on an outside wall with windows. He took a seat in a plastic chair and snacked out of the backpack. He enjoyed the candy and refreshment.

By mid-afternoon he had gone all the way around the building. Realizing his stamina wasn't what it should be, he vowed to start exercising on a regular basis. It felt wonderful to be out in the fresh air; it cleared his head. He was on verge of making history and this was a much needed break from that work.

Back at the plane, Brian set up the warning system, and brought out the cooler and both laptops. He sat under the plane and ate while he refined the search to glean the information he was looking for. Still afraid of missing something, he spent much of his time going over each directory.

He worked with both laptops until early evening. He enjoyed having his office outside for a change. It was no wonder Henry had done it all the time. It was very relaxing.

Long before daylight ended, Brian packed everything and flew back to the Installation. He continued working on the laptops while flying until it was time to set his approach.

After landing, he still had several hours to kill. He wouldn't go to the Dupe until there was no chance of anyone showing up. He loaded his cart, drove to the Dupe, threw the empty cooler into a storage hopper, and went home. There, he hid everything within the new headboard.

He thought about catching a nap, but went out for a walk, going to the fence. Napping was out of the question. He was too wound up. Walking would burn off his nervous energy. He knew he would soon know whether his digitalization worked. Once at the fence, he stayed alongside it. In the calm of the evening, Brian focused on what he would be doing. He didn't return home until well after dark.

With the lights off, Brian drove to the Dupe. After he parked, he went inside without the memory unit. He went upstairs and made use of Ivan's trick, calling out to see if anyone answered. There was no one there. Back at the cart, he retrieved the memory unit.

He signed onto the terminal and inserted it into the slot. He clicked the proper drive and then selected his file.

The decisive moment had arrived.... He was a simple click away from knowing whether it would work. It seemed too easy.

A chill ran down his spine.

Brian hit cancel, pulled the memory unit, signed off, and went home.

***

Over an hour and a half later, Brian was back at the Dupe.

While his hands shook, he got everything ready, and prepared to try again.

With his digitalization in the slot, he selected it and took a deep breath.

When Brian was just one click away, he hesitated, but only for a moment. He hit the button and waited by the terminal. He wanted to go closer to the platform when he heard the elevator start its descent, but couldn't bring himself to move. He took another deep breath, which he was still expelling when the elevator stopped. As the doors opened, an odd sensation ran over him. There he was, on the platform wearing the clothes he had on the night of the digitalization.

He watched as his chest moved, eyes blinked.

A moan came from the table.... This scared the living crap out of him. He backed away. Then the left arm lifted and went to the chest. He turned his head and saw Brian. "No, you removed the defibrillator. Why?" One leg pulled up, pointing a knee into the air. It swayed back and forth. "Brian, don't let me die! Please, don't do this to me." The words were a struggle, but they cut powerfully through every part of his being.

Brian hit himself hard in the chest while lying on the platform. The other leg came up at the same time. He began to moan…. While on his back, he turned on the platform, and swung his legs out over the edge. He sat up, but bent too far forward. The IV bag, which was lying on his stomach, fell to the floor. Brian fell too. Then, in a desperate struggle, he got to his feet, surprisingly quick.

"Brian, it's me! It worked. Get the defibrillator." The words streamed together, franticly. He tried to walk, stumbled, kept his balance, stopped and swayed.

"I'll get it." Brian ran down the hall in a flash, looking back at the pain and despair on his own face as he exited the cafeteria.

"Hurry!" At what was almost a whisper. "Please, Brian, hurry!" pursued him down the hall, almost a scream.

Quickly, Brian pulled open the door of the box housing the defibrillator. He rushed back opening the package.

He never imagined this. Near panic, he went as fast as he could. In a moment of doubt, after he canceled the first try, he had gone home and deactivated the defibrillator on the digitalization. If it hadn't worked….

When Brian entered the cafeteria, he found himself lying on the floor where he had been standing moments before.

He initiated the charge on the defibrillator. When it was ready, he placed the pads onto the now bared chest and released the charge.

Both Brians jumped….

The charge made one body jerk; the other, compelled to respond.

He put his head to his chest and listened. Only moments before, he breathed, begged for life. It didn't work.

He tried again. Same result.

Even though he knew it was coming, he jumped every time he released the charge.

When the defibrillator crackled and the smell of burnt flesh assaulted his nostrils, Brian went to get up. He fell back to the floor, shaken. He began to cry out in sobs. It wasn't out of anguish or despair, but frustration for not knowing what to do. The sound he made became a howl. He could no longer tell if this was victory, or sacrifice. He wished he had used the vaporizer, like the good doctor.

A part of Brian was ready to give up. He just wanted to leave and go home. He didn't want to deal with this. The other part, detached, dragged the body to the recycler. He threw it in and started the equipment so it would pull his body out of sight and into the enclosed conveyor.

He didn't understand how he could have been so blind. He knew he had tried to avoid the pressure Stan brought upon himself to succeed by letting everyone know. There were no expectations; Brian hadn't let anyone know but Henry. Henry's help would have made a difference. Stan saw a transporter. Brian saw a memory dupe. Brian now understood that he and Stan were both blind beyond those goals.

He needed to get out of there.

Feeling like a monster, he retrieved the memory unit.

He went home and began pacing the floor. For a long time he could do nothing else. It was him that woke up on the platform. He couldn't imagine. The stress was tremendous.

He had killed himself. He felt trapped. He had to get away.

Before daybreak, Brian sat in the plane, waiting at the end of the runway.

With the first hint of light, he took off. He left without a plan, or food, or water.

When he was seventy-five miles away, he put the plane in the same holding pattern he had used before, flying around the Installation.

He had all seven laptops with him. Why he had brought them, he didn't know.

After the first day, he came to the realization that it wasn't quite the same situation as Stan. Stan jumped the gun to show everyone that it did work. Brian jumped the gun to prove to himself that it worked.

Brian would avoid mistakes of this nature in the future. He would update his digitalization so it would include what he had just gone through. Explaining what happened would never take the place of the experience. This made it necessary to return to the Space Center. It also made him wonder if Henry kept an updated digitalization. If he did, Brian could dupe him. He would have to find out.

The broken laptop never did work. He removed the hard drive putting it into a different laptop. It was the only one that he hadn't seen any of its content. During the third day, he made a discovery on this hard-drive, and immediately returned to the Installation.

***

It was late morning.

Brian realized someone was knocking at his door. He leapt off the bed, coming fully awake. He had fallen asleep among laptops that were still on. He ran to the door and opened it with an annoyed pull. Alarmed, he saw Ivan. What now? He had stopped expecting him weeks ago. Several laptops sat out in plain view. They contained evidence that he had been to the Space Center.

The moment became awkward.

"You don't have to stand there in your underwear with the door wide open," Ivan told him. "Invite me in." It was the last thing Brian wanted to do and it was why Ivan was still standing outside.

"Sure," Brian said, stepping aside. Feeling vulnerable, he wished he had put on his clothes. He needed his pepper spray too. "I'll get dressed."

Upon entering, Ivan immediately began to survey inside.

Brian didn't want Ivan to follow him into the bedroom; there were more laptops on his bed. Luckily, both memory units with his digitalization were in the headboard.

"Wait there," Brian held up a hand as if he could keep Ivan by the door. "I'll be right back." Brian didn't want Ivan to think he had an opportunity to take liberties. He was sure Ivan would feel free to do so. He didn't bother dressing in the bedroom, instead, he rapidly chose clothes from a pile on the floor, and ran back in front of Ivan put his pants on with the pepper spray in the pocket.

"What's with all the laptops?" Ivan asked.

"My luck, you know," Brian improvised. He kept his distance while he dressed. He was very uncomfortable doing so in front of Ivan. "I keep breaking them."

"That's unusual; I've found them to be quite reliable. I believe I still have the first one I ever duped."

Brian found and picked up the broken laptop to show Ivan. "That's not the problem," he explained, wondering why Ivan was here. "They keep falling out of the cart. I haven't come up with a good means of securing them."

"Are all of these broken?"

"Sort of. I've been taking them apart and replacing pieces."

"That's wasteful. It would be a better use of your time if you recycled them and duped another."

"I've been trying to save the information I have on them."

"No backup; that's a shame. You still need to recycle them."

"I plan to."

"Good. Now the reason I'm here; I wanted to let you know I have an apprentice lined up for you."

"Really?" This was the last thing Brian expected.

"Ed told me he has a candidate. His name is Gary. He'll be available in a couple of weeks."

"That's excellent, it's what we need." Brian's mind raced trying to figure out what this meant. Did Ivan expect him to train his replacement?

"Yes, well, as head of security, I thought you'd expect nothing less, especially after requesting it."

"And here I thought you'd forgotten." Ivan was toying with him.

Neither of them said anything for a bit...Ivan was still surveying the room.

"One thing before I go." Brian thought, oh great, here it comes...Ivan was going to ask why he was at the Space Center. "I want you to understand this is nothing against Henry, but he didn't set a very good example. His strong point wasn't having an apprentice. He didn't know how to deal with it. I want you to put together an apprenticeship program for Gary."

"No problem, sir."

"Good," he said, smiling, as he opened the door to leave. "I want to review it when you're finished."

"Sure."

"Have a good day then."

"You too." Brian stood in the door and watched Ivan walk away.

If Gary was going to be his replacement, then Brian wasn't going to take time to show him anything. Ivan would have to find somebody else to do it.

He added one more thing to his list of to dos. The next time he was at the Space Center, he would use Ivan's terminal and give himself a new sign on and password. He could accomplish memory dupping; he couldn't be put out of business.

The apprenticeship program would have to wait. Of more concern, what could he come up with to keep Gary busy? He would have to hurry on the transmission. He also had to get to the collection point to see how his garden was doing.

There was no time for this.

Chapter Sixteen

"Good morning, Brian. What brings you to the second floor?" Don was in his office, feet up on the desk.

"Morning, Don. I came to see you because I'm building a new plane."

"Is that so? You know, if that old thing is broken, we can dupe parts. There's no need to replace it."

"It's not broken." Brian shrugged. "I've never had a problem with it."

"They are reliable, aren't they, but a second plane? That'll have to be cleared through Ivan."

"I've already seen Ivan. I'm getting an apprentice in a week or so. You wouldn't know this, but the Chief was going to have me do it. He never had the chance. After those planes crashed, he thought there should be a loaner available. I'm including it as part of Gary's apprenticeship."

"Well, that sounds just like him, always thinking of everyone else. But you'll still have to have Ivan's approval. That might be tough to get. Though if you do, you'll need to collect materials."

"That's why I'm here; where do I start?"

Don took his feet off the desk, and pressed his keypad into action. He had hard copies printing shortly afterward. It took several minutes for everything to print. He handed the stack of papers to Brian.

"Here, take these. The first page is a list of materials for the original design. You'll need extra steel for the can and other materials, depending on what you add. Even though steel isn't an element, it's listed here because the iron and carbon are available together where you're going to collect it from."

Brian took the pile of hard copies. He had no idea it would be so easy for Don to whip them out.

"Ivan's expecting a hard copy of Gary's apprenticeship program so he can review it. When I turn it in, I'll include copies of this before Gary starts work on it. So there'll be no need for both of us to cover it with him."

"You sound confident."

"I think the Chief had the right idea. How can Ivan refuse having a loaner available? It'll convince him."

"It might."

"I'm planning on it."

"If you'd like, I can print another copy for Ivan," Don offered.

"Just the materials list," Brian decided. "I can't imagine why he'd need more than that. How will I know when I have collected enough?"

"You'll find that information in the pile of papers I just gave you. But basically you weigh what you bring back. If you always collect more than you need, it won't be a problem."

"Okay, another question. If I made an early run for saltwater, do you have room to store it?"

"Oh yeah, we have plenty of tanks we can use. You could probably make twenty trips and not fill them all."

"Thanks."

Brian stopped downstairs to grab a bite while he was there. He had a leisurely meal and went through the stack of papers from Don.

The first page listed the elements needed in sequential order by weight. Brian went down the whole page. This was going to keep Gary busy for months.

If they made a trip for each entry, some locations would require more... He needed the plane's capacity to figure out which ones needed more than one trip. The one thing he didn't know was how long it would take at each location.

The following section contained blueprints, a parts list, and the assembly instructions for the plane. After that, an unexpected bonus, maps showing the best locations to go pilfering, with coordinates. On the maps were handwritten notes explaining how to resolve problems others had run into.

When Brian finished eating, he went to the office to continue his assessment.

At his terminal, he couldn't find the load capacity for the plane. With an educated guess, based on the number of gallons the tanks held, he keyed numbers to calculate how many trips he would have to make to each location. He calculated his airtimes.

Brian broke the days into whole numbers for any decimals by location.

He set up a percentage table that added another five, ten and fifteen percent to give him a range. He then added his extras. This method wasn't scientific, but he had a time range that would be close.

Brian's extras included a mainframe for the house. He needed some heavy-duty computing power. He would have Gary build a new cart too, to test his ability to assemble the plane. The plane was going to be a perfect guise to lump everything together. He would push it all through the dupe together so the material for the mainframe would go unnoticed.

Ivan would be a problem.

***

Very late, Brian unlocked the door to the Space Center.

He carried a black case of newly duped memory units.

Around his neck, he wore a strap. Attached to the strap was a digital recorder. Tense, he took it slow and easy.

Wary from the moment he approached the building, he hoped there wouldn't be any problems. He made his way to the computer room, closed the door behind him and turned on the lights. He started the recorder.

He never felt as if anyone were watching over his shoulder, but that in itself was eerie. If there was someone, something should tip him. He didn't believe he had missed anything. But he always wondered, which kept him on his toes.

After making a complete sweep with the recorder of everything in the room, including the second level, he shut the lights off and cracked the door. It was clear. He didn't expect to see anyone, but after the last time, he was extra careful. From the computer room, he proceeded to the digitalization equipment. He brought no defibrillator or IV this time. He would copy and paste those files to the new digitalization. It meant less time inside. No instruction manual either. He found the broom where he had left it, and in no time was shutting the equipment down and putting the broom back.

Next, he made his way to Ivan's terminal. Keeping an eye over his shoulder, he was anxious to get the additional sign in and password. He would have it before he left. He worked the keypad for almost a half hour and couldn't find where Ivan had set it up.

He wondered if he had to go across the hall where Ivan had done it originally. He was getting antsy; but took the long way around to avoid the squeaky door. He was getting nervous about the amount of time this was taking. He had hoped to be in and out without a glitch. Across the hall, he signed on under Ivan's name and found it right away.

He realized at once, he could have done this from home.

When he left, he locked the door, wishing his previous visit had been as smooth and uneventful.

***

Once home, Brian didn't go to bed. Instead, he worked on the new digitization. The copy and paste function was making quick work of it, still though it would take time. The following morning, still working, his terminal chimed with an email. "Who the heck…?"

Brian checked the time. He'd been at the terminal for over ten hours.

He wanted this done so he could make the transmission before Gary started apprenticing.

He opened the email. It brought a halt to his progress. From Ivan, it said he was to report at once to the Space Center. There had been a serious breach, which required his immediate attention.

"No, how could he have caught me?" A sickening feeling overcame him. "There'd be no way?"

There was maybe another two hours of work and he'd have this finished. He was going to view the recording next. He was now certain with the way Ivan's sign in worked across the hall that there was a second mainframe.

No longer frustrated by the interruption, he tried to come up with a reason for having gone back into the Space Center without Ivan being there. He had expressly told him not to do so.

"He's going to have my head. What do I tell him?"

The sickening feeling wouldn't go away.

***

The door squeaked.

"Oh, good, you're here," Ivan said, getting up immediately from his desk. Ivan was glad to see him. When he reached Brian, he walked by, whispering, "Come with me." Ivan then opened the door taking them back into the hall and in a friendly gesture, held it for him. This was totally out of character. Brian became concerned. Ivan acted awful friendly. Not expecting this, he questioned what Ivan was up to.

"You emailed."

"Not here," he said in a confiding tone, ensuring only Brian could hear. The old geezer was too friendly. Once they were both in the hall and the door closed, Ivan checked in both directions to make sure they were alone. Brian's hands dove into his pockets; clutching the pepper spray. What was he up to? "I have something you need to see."

He thought, 'I'll bet you do,' but said, "What?" as they proceeded down the hall.

"Somebody broke in last night."

Immediately, Brian felt himself flush. He had been caught, but Ivan didn't seem to know who it was.

"Really; anything missing?"

"How should I know, it's a big place."

"But you're sure someone broke in?"

"Oh, yes, after I locked up."

"If you're not missing anything, how do you know?" he pressed.

"I'll show you in a minute." This scared Brian. What could Ivan possibly show him? Did he suspect him after all?

Ivan stopped at the front entrance where Brian had entered the night before. "I thought someone broke in once before. You see this." He pointed to a piece of string taped to the top of the jamb.

"The string?"

"Yes." Ivan pulled it from between the jamb. "I left it like this when I locked up." he opened the door and let it shut. "This is how I found it this morning."

Unreal. They stood in the Space Center, with an active space program that would take them to distant planets, which only Brian knew how to use, and he was being undone by a low-tech piece of string Ivan taped to the top of the jamb. He would have laughed, except it had worked.

"Any idea who…?"

"No, but you're going to find out for me."

"How am I supposed to do that?"

"Look Brian," Ivan snapped. "We've never had a problem with this before. Put the place under surveillance. This is happening on your watch. Take care of it. I don't want to regret putting you in charge."

Brian didn't know what to say. "Okay."

"Good. I want you to keep this entrance under surveillance. You should catch who ever it is in short order."

"Sure, I'll sit just inside the door here."

"No—no one comes in here after hours. That includes you. I thought I made that perfectly clear before. When you catch whoever it is, report him to me."

"It'd be easier from inside."

"Absolutely not. And don't let anyone know what you're up to; we don't want to tip them off."

***

Brian worked a finely made flexible piece of plastic through the doorjamb and pushed the string back into place.

The second mainframe now had a Y connector hooked to a feed that supplied every building at the Installation. Unless someone from the Space Center went looking for the hidden directory on an outside terminal, no one should pick up on what he had done.

The broken laptop said there was a Dupe on the Space Station. He had just used the transmitter at the digitalizer to board there.

If Ivan suspected Brian of breaking in, and if he thought simply by letting him know he suspected—that this would stop him, then Ivan had another thing coming. Brian thought about leaving the string between the jamb. It would eliminate him from the suspect pool. Too bold—Ivan would replace him for not doing his job and catching the culprit.

He hurried home.

***

Brian stirred.

It felt like someone kicked him in the chest.

He felt funny too, almost dizzy; he didn't understand why. The pain in his chest subsided. Pieces began to fall into place. He reached for his chest. The defibrillator was there. Grateful to be alive, he extended his lower jaw wetting his upper lip.

The dizziness wouldn't go away. It was an odd sensation. He associated it with floating. He wanted water.

He blinked, opening his eyes. There was no one around; everything was unfamiliar. He tried to move, which only heightened the sense of dizziness.

"Oh, great." He realized he was the one who had went. "Why did it have to be me? All that work yet to do."

He calmed himself. It wouldn't be up to him any longer. It was so strange, everything, gone in an instant, just like that, totally out of reach.

Brian sat up on the edge of the platform and almost floated off. He wondered where and when he was. Some place without gravity. But where? He held the edge of the platform so he would stay in place which kept him from floating off. He carefully removed the defibrillator, let it go, and watched it float away with a slight rotation. "Strange." The IV in his arm still hurt. He pulled the needle. It barely bled. He reached into his pocket; the bandage was there. This made him smile. He wondered how he missed the fact the needle wasn't in the vein and put it off to being in a hurry; hadn't noticed, or he would have corrected it.

He was dehydrated; the Dupe wasn't perfect. He reinserted the IV, this time getting the vein. He wanted water and wished he had brought some with him.

He began to feel nauseated. It was all so disorienting. He lay back on the platform; he needed time to adjust.

Though it seemed no more than an instant, it could be months, years. Actually, it could be a couple of centuries into the future; his old self long dead? The strangeness of it all wouldn't go away. "Wow." He needed to find out. He couldn't rid himself of the feeling about all the work he had yet to do. He heard the defibrillator when it made contact with the opposing wall instead of the floor. "This is so weird."

***

When Brian got to the office, Gary was waiting. Not since Adam was his and Danny's assistant had anyone tried to impress him; he would provide Gary with many more opportunities to be impressive.

"Good morning, Gary. How are you doing?"

"Fine, Chief."

"Don't call me that. You didn't know the Chief, so don't even go there."

"That won't be a problem," Gary answered a little smug.

Brian shook his head and led the way into the building. He unlocked his office and went in with Gary in tow. Gary stopped and stood at the front of the desk where he waited while Brian seated himself starting his terminal.

Four new emails displayed. The first three were from Ivan.

The fourth, encrypted, came from the Space Station. He was there! Excited, Brian opened it. It felt strange reading something from himself that he had not written. It was short, and made Brian wonder if everything was okay. It read: "Knock, knock, this is so weird, are you there? If you are, what date is it?"

"Hmm, I hope everything is okay."

"What?"

"Nothing." Absorbed with the communication, Brian had forgotten Gary. Having him around was going to put a crimp in his style.

Brian emailed the date and wanted to know why he needed it. He asked what it was like being duped, and if there were any problems. He asked that he keep him updated with any concern.

He then hurried through the emails from Ivan. Starting at the top, Ivan wanted to know why he had not received anything on Gary's apprenticeship. "Ivan must have known you were starting today." The second email asked if he had caught the culprit breaking into the Space Center. "He's an idiot," he said under his breath so Gary wouldn't understand.

"What?"

"Nothing!"

The third was a complaint that Ivan forwarded from the Research Center. Ken had sent it wanting to know when Brian was picking up their mail.

"It took them long enough to figure that out."

"What?" Gary wanted to know.

"Nothing." He decided Gary was going to be a royal pain in the butt.

Brian used Ivan's first email and replied that he was still working on Gary's apprenticeship program and hadn't completed it as of yet because he was spending his nights keeping the Space Center under surveillance; and no, no one had showed up. He didn't like covering for himself in this manner, it led to trouble. In reality though, he had been back once at night to splice the Space Center's mainframe to an outside line and make the transmission to the Space Station. Thankfully, he hadn't seen anyone.

Adding a PS, he told Ivan to consider the Research Center's mail taken care of. After sending, Brian opened the sent copy and forwarded it to the Space Station. He pleaded for help with the apprenticeship program and let Brian know he would be gone for a couple of days on a saltwater run. He ensured it went out encrypted.

"Are you ready to fly the plane?"

Gary lost the smug look, but recovered quickly. "Sure, why not?" He sounded a little cocky. Brian wondered if he had been as transparent to Henry.

This was going to be too easy.

"Use the bathroom before we go." Brian told him.

"We're leaving now?"

"You bet. Grab the bag in the corner, we have work to do."

They left for the Dupe.

Once the platform was down, Brian pocketed several things from the table.

Unlike Henry, Brian couldn't stand waiting for Gary to do everything and helped him load the cart.

They made the run through the Installation gathering mail. They stopped at the Research Center last.

"Go get their mail. Ken will have it. He keeps the stuff behind his desk. Tell him I said hi."

When Gary came out, he carried two full bags and had to return for a third.

"Why is there so much from this place?"

"It's because there are a lot of people in there and they have nothing better to do all day other than generating junk mail," Brian told him.

Once at the plane, Brian had Gary load everything from the cart while he wheeled one of the pods under the wing. Now that he was preparing to go, he was anxious to see how the garden was doing. When Gary finished loading the plane, he immediately began helping Brian with the pods.

When done and seated in their chairs, pods attached, Brian reached into his pocket.

"These are earplugs," he said, handing a set to Gary. "You need to use them whenever we fly."

"Sure."

They taxied to the runway and took off.

It didn't take long before Gary was glued right up tight to the window. Brian set the autopilot and opened his laptop satisfied Gary was going to get a long time to enjoy the view.

Brian then settled in for a marathon session on Douglas Fairbanks.

Thirteen hours later, Brian knew more about Douglas than any other historical figure. Nothing though, explained or hinted at any changes Douglas had made to them. There was more to read but he didn't hold out much hope of finding that information. It seemed like he was fishing in empty waters.

At One-Thirteen, Chris set them up in one of the houses. It was small, but had a couple of beds in one room.

After Chris left, Brian sent Gary to make the exchange on the bags; then he went to bed.

***

Brian came awake with a start. At first, he didn't realize what had aroused him.

"Gary, please, I was sleeping."

Gary froze; there was a long pause.

"Brian," he whispered close to his ear, "you don't seem to be hooked up with anybody and I thought…"

Brian cut him off and tried to let him down easy. "I'm not," he confirmed. "Let's just say I'm saving myself for whoever that will be."

"I can respect that." But Gary didn't move. He stayed there. "So you're sure?"

Trying to be nice hadn't worked. He put the refusal on a firmer level. "Gary, get in your own bed. And from now on, you better call me Chief." He was very stern, deciding Gary didn't want to be let off the hook easily.

Slowly, Gary crawled from under the covers and went to his own bed. He didn't take the rejection well.

A short time later, Brian could hear him weeping silently. He wanted to console him, but thought better of it. Gary might get the wrong idea and think it was okay to hop back in his bed. Brian rolled over and faced away; he tried to go back to sleep, but couldn't. Thoughts of Danny surfaced to trouble him.

***

In the morning, Brian stepped outside and soaked up the rays from the sun. There wasn't a cloud in the sky. It was already hot. It would get sticky before long. Just a few hours away from the sea, he knew a swim had his name written all over it.

Brian worried about Gary. He was gone by the time Brian got up. Maybe the upcoming experiences waiting by the sea would lighten Gary's spirits.

Brian made his way to the cafeteria. Gary wasn't there. He ate and went to the plane. He found Gary seated, earplugs in and ready to go. He was still sulking. Brian didn't bother to say good morning.

He started the plane and they took off for the coast. Brian turned on his laptop and began working. They flew silently, with each wrapped in his own thoughts.

Several hours later, Brian banked the plane and followed the coast south. Neither had said a word.

When they got close to the collection point, he prepared for a jump.

Glued to the window, Gary paid no attention to what Brian was doing.

When they arrived, Brian did the flyover and then banked out over the water. Because they had cruised over the treetops, Gary's attention was now both outside and inside on Brian. He didn't want to miss a thing.

Brian lined back up with the shore, taking the plane higher. He waited until they were almost there.

"Gary, go open the hatch for me," he ordered.

While Gary did so, Brian removed a battery wire from the remote. Still by the hatch, he got up and handed the remote to Gary. Never hesitating, Brian jumped. He did a half turn in the air and watched as Gary gaped, stunned.

His eyes became wild!

Brian thought he saw Gary tremble.

Chapter Seventeen

Brian wondered if he had gone too far. Gary would be going nuts.

Initially, Brian thought he had come up with something better than Henry had. But his eyes…Gary was scared. Brian was going to put the plane through its paces, take Gary for a joy ride, but was having second thoughts.

Free falling, he pulled the ripcord and floated the rest of the way to the ground where he promptly removed his chute and began assembling the other remote. He put the plane in a tight holding pattern over the forest, keeping it out of view. At the same time, he trotted up the hill toward the garden. He was anxious to see what had happened, and he needed to do this while he had Gary out of the way.

Troubled, he saw that the plot was barren. Had he done it wrong? Or did Douglas do something to the seeds too?

As he got closer though, something was there. When he reached the edge, he bent over and pulled up a stub by the roots. "It worked. They ate it." He looked at the animal tracks. "All that work…at this rate, I'll be dead before I figure out what Douglas did. I'd be further ahead making matter transmission work."

Discouraged, he made his way back toward shore and brought the plane around. All that water on the plane too…though now, he wouldn't have to sneak it to the garden.

It was only a setback. He began planning what he needed to do to start over. "I'll have to protect it, build a fence."

Brian stopped walking when the plane came into view and concentrated on landing it.

When the plane quit bouncing off the sand, he powered it up and taxied it toward the water. While he did this, Gary came barreling down the steps. He jumped; taking a tumble in the sand, but was up at once. His arms swung in an exaggerated arc while his legs stayed almost straight at the knees. His whole body pumped quickly, heading straight toward Brian. He was upset…and he hadn't even gotten the joy ride.

"Did you do that because I climbed into your bed last night?" Gary screamed.

Brian wanted to say, 'when will you catch on, before or after I take my foot out of your keister?' He refrained. "No," he said, realizing he had brought down an ego. Maybe he had gone too far.

"Then why?"

"Gary, it's an initiation. I followed a tradition. I went through it and now so have you."

Gary's jaw moved. He wanted to say more, thought about it, and didn't.

"I hope you're not as dumb as a box of rocks," Brian scolded. "Last night, I told you to call me Chief. You had better start doing so, or I'll see to it that what you just went though becomes a daily part of your life. Every day, it'll be something. You'll know it's coming, but you won't know what or when. Understand?"

Gary shook his head.

"And another thing, if you're going to apprentice with me, you're not going to get yourself killed. I don't want to see you jump from the plane before it comes to a complete stop. If I ever see that happen again, I'll find a new apprentice."

***

Three days later, Brian set a course for One-O-Seven and they left the ocean behind. It was almost dark. He couldn't wait to get back so he could check his communications from the Space Station. He hoped the apprenticeship program was in his email. He would simply forward it to Ivan. That would be sweet and simple and save a ton of time.

Almost magically, the trip's sour start contrasted dramatically with how it ended. Brian had brought Gary to a far away place and enjoyed watching him experience everything for the first time. The awe of seeing Gary outside the fence, the hikes, swimming, and yes, a fire, with which Brian, against his better judgment, had cooked fish.

Gary took a liking to the fish, which reminded Brian of Henry. Hesitant to do the fire and fish, he didn't want Gary saying anything to anyone. Ivan would hear about it at some point and Brian was hoping he could trust Gary.

Gary's attitude improved dramatically after that. Taking him into his confidence had worked wonders.

Even though Brian's time away from his daily tasks left him rejuvenated, he could tell he had overdone it with the hikes and too much time in the water. He really needed to get in shape. But exercising on a regular basis hadn't worked for him. With everything that vied for his attention, there just wasn't time to maintain a regime. He had started several times, even hitting two or three days in a row before something came along and knocked it off his schedule. He vowed then, once back to the Installation, nothing would interfere. He committed himself to starting when they got back. Mornings would work best.

As soon as they were in the air, Brian had Gary spread their sleeping bags out over the grating. Brian set the autopilot and climbed into one. Gary did the same.

Brian fell asleep soon thereafter.

***

Mid-morning they arrived at One-O-Seven.

After landing, Brian parked outside.

"Gary, tie it down out here. Then run the hose to the transfer pipe. Hook it to a pod and start the pump. When you're done with that, clean out the inside of the can. Stack everything on the tarmac. You can take it to the Dupe later. Set yourself up a place to work inside. If I'm not back by the time you're done, then sweep. I'll be back with a load of parts so you can start on the cart."

"Say again, Chief."

Three minutes and forty-seven seconds later, Brian left. He only had to show Gary where the transfer pipe was located. Eager to find out how it was going at the Space Station, he went straight to the office. Brian would Dupe parts when he finished there, and then start exercising. He planned to start slowly, and work his way into a rigorous program. His one and only email from the Space Station had caused concern, and he couldn't help but worry since they'd left for the collection point. He didn't know what to expect and wished there had been a few more days before Gary had started his apprenticeship.

When Brian signed in, he found a host of messages. With a smile, Brian paged down looking for the apprenticeship and counted how many he received. Toward the bottom, there was one tagged important. "What have you been up to? I don't see anything on the apprenticeship." He clicked the tagged message, making a mental note of how many came from the Space Station.

What he read caught his full attention immediately. It started: 'You need to take care of this right away before anyone discovers what I did.'

He read the rest, in total disbelief. His head spun, digesting the information. After a pause, he reread it. He hoped it was true. "But how at the Space Station?" Without opening another email, he shut the terminal down and ran from the office to his cart.

***

Brian raced home. Inside, he quickly hit the on button to his terminal. Then, just as quickly, he ran to the bedroom. From behind the headboard, he pulled the original non-remastered memory unit. The most expendable, he figured he wouldn't need it again. He double-checked, ensuring he had grabbed the right one.

Back at the terminal, he signed in as Iv@n1 and put the memory unit into place. Impatiently, he waited while the terminal readied itself. Excited, he couldn't wait to view what was sent from the Space Station.

At his command, his terminal whined into action. He erased his digitalization, then as instructed by Brian at the Space Station, quickly located the directory on the Space Center's mainframe and went to the file he needed to copy.

The sooner he deleted this file from the Space Center's mainframe, the less likely anyone would discover it.

A pop up displayed. The time to perform the task populated a field. Uneasy, he watched as the counter continued to increase. When it hit twelve hours, he left. A mainframe at the house would solve problems of that nature.

Brian ran to his cart, jumped in and headed for the Dupe. He would get another memory unit and copy the file at the Dupe.

He walked into the cafeteria and saw that the place was too busy for him to stay on the terminal long. After procuring the memory unit, he went back to his cart and headed full speed toward the Space Center. On the way, he tried to come up with an excuse for showing up in the middle of the morning. Everyone would be in, including Ivan. He didn't want to chance running into someone without a ready excuse. Preoccupied with the message in the email, he didn't dredge anything up for why he was showing up there, but kept going.

He wondered if the other Brian was correct. He said he had located files which solved Henry's paradox. If his terminal at home had more oomph behind it, he would already be reading what Douglas had done to them. When he found out, he would simply reverse it.

Neither Brian could afford to have someone discover the file. It could be traced back to its source. He needed to hurry, retrieve it and delete it.

At the Space Center, he parked off to the side so the cart couldn't be seen from the front of the building. He walked in as casually and calmly as he could. No one was around. He went downstairs; figuring he wouldn't be as likely to run into anyone. Fast and efficient, he would use the terminal on the digitization equipment. But first, he had to find the stairs close by that led back up.

Having never been on the lower level, Brian hoped he could find his way. When he reached the stairs he thought he should use, he went up. Recognizing where he was, he made his way quickly to the room. He was relieved when he checked inside and saw it was empty. He turned on the terminal. Once up, he inserted the memory unit and located the file. He started the download, only to get another pop up. It told him the file was in use.

He had left his terminal running at home.

With his luck, Ivan would pop up next. Brian could just hear him. "Why are you here?" Frustrated, he shut it off, pulled the memory unit and hid it inside the room. Cautiously, he went back into the hall and made his way to the mainframe. He ducked in and turned on the lights. He hurried to where he had installed the splice and removed it. That would sever his communication with the Space Station too. With no choice, he hoped it didn't present a problem while everyone was using the system.

He turned out the lights and cracked the door. Hopping out, he got halfway down the hall when he heard footsteps coming. On tiptoes, not to make a sound, he quickly ran back to the room with the mainframe and ducked in.

There was no place to hide. He leaned into the door, turning to listen. The footsteps got louder; adrenalin filled his veins. When they passed, he sighed, remembering Henry said it was complicated being the head of security. Brian hadn't found anything complicated about it. Though unrelated, doing this was very stressful.

"You set me up Brian. You made it so I'd have to do this right now, didn't you? While everyone's here." He wanted to leave, and if he didn't know how critical it was, he would be gone.

This warranted an email with a piece of his mind attached. The other Brian, far away, had too much time on his hands. He wanted to tell him right then, "Learn to be cautious. Plan ahead; keep everything simple, low key. No risk!" Those were just a few things that came to mind.

With the sound of the footsteps fading, Brian creaked the door once more. He stayed calm and headed back to the digitization equipment. Mercifully, the room was still empty and no one had seen him. He still hadn't come up with a reason to be there.

Within a matter of minutes, he had the equipment up and running and was copying the file; once done, he deleted the original and then shut everything down. Taking the memory unit, he went back to the mainframe and reconnected the splice. Done with that, he headed for the stairs.

As he approached the stairs, he heard footsteps again, and assumed it was the same person on the return trip. He bolted, made the turn at the head of the stairs and flew down them as fast as he could go. He didn't stop running until he was by the stairs at the main entrance. He walked up those trying hard to breathe normally. Satisfied, he walked out of the building with the answer to Henry's paradox in hand.

At home, his terminal displayed a different icon: Continue or Cancel. Brian hit cancel. It didn't respond. With the ultimate power at his disposal, he pushed the off button and held it. Few things were more satisfying than having the power to fix these blasted things with that button.

He turned it back on, only to have the screen freeze again. He gave it time, but nothing happened. He applied the ultimate power again. After an hour, with only a bright blue screen to show for his efforts, he gave up. It no longer worked. He had tried everything he knew, which was only enough to be dangerous. He wondered if he had screwed up all the terminals connected to the mainframe. He hoped not. His was the only one he had disconnected. But if there was a problem detected, they would test the whole system and discover his splice.

He didn't have the proper receptor for the memory unit at the office and Henry's paradox sat right in front of him waiting.

Stuffing the memory unit back in its case, he couldn't bear to wait any longer; he had to know what was there. The other Brian already knew; and soon, he would too.

Brian got up and left for the Dupe. He would use the terminal there.

When he entered the cafeteria, there were people sitting at the tables eating but the crowd had thinned. Either those left were having a late breakfast; or early lunch, he had hoped the place would be empty. Brian duped himself a plate. He would wait it out. He sat the memory unit on the floor between his feet and began to observe gauging the time each table should clear.

He ate slowly.

One person finished shortly after Brian sat down making him antsy for the rest to go. They took forever; it was all he could do to wait for the others to go. Eventually, another got up and cleared their table, while they were still doing so, another got up. When the last person started clearing their table Brian set his fork down and headed for the terminal with the memory. He was signed on before they were out of the door. He would now find out what Douglas had done.

He clicked the proper directory as they headed for the door. As he did so, someone else walked in. Brian promptly signed off and stepped aside to let them to use the terminal. He didn't pull the memory unit and drifted back to his table where he resumed eating.

He hoped the man needed something other than food. If that were the case, they would be in and out in no time. But he lingered over the terminal, pushing Brian's patience. When he heard the distinctive whine of the elevator as it descended, he looked at the doors waiting for them to open. When they did, he saw food. Disappointed, Brian took a deep breath, and prepared to endure another wait. He thought maybe he should dupe a new terminal, take it home, get back in business, but then, the man picked up his plate and headed for the door.

Back at the terminal, determined to get this done before any one else came in, his fingers became a blur over the keypad. When the menu displayed, there was only one option. Enter to continue. He knew then the program material was old, or maybe someone had thrown it together. "Enter to continue," he repeated, with his finger hovering over the enter button. "Hmm, what's next…?"

Chapter Eighteen

In a hurry, bent on finishing before another interruption, Brian tapped the enter key and watched the screen intently. Instead of displaying more options, the screen went blank and initiated the Dupe. "What?" Brian continued looking at the screen, waiting, but it didn't display anything further.

By the time the elevator reached the bottom, Brian was at the doors. His hopes began to fade, wondering if Brian at the Space Station was playing some sort of joke.

"After all I went through, this had better explain everything."

When the doors opened, his eyes went wide.

Something had gone terrible wrong.

"What the heck?"

Focused on nothing else, and bewildered, the whole building could have fallen in all around him, and he wouldn't have noticed. This was no explanation.

Did he copy the incorrect file?

It wasn't possible, and he knew it.

He just stood there unbelieving and mystified.

Audibly, the defibrillator thumped. The face scrunched, turning red. A cry rang throughout the cafeteria.

The pink larva on the platform screamed. It didn't seem humanly possible for something that small to be so loud.

He had to stop it. Everyone upstairs would be down to see what was going on. He couldn't explain this.

Immediately, Brian grabbed it up by the first thing he could get a hold of, lifting it from the platform by an ankle.

Shocked, he almost dropped it.

It was the new species.

How? It looked just like Mark when he was little.

A failed experiment; Douglas had done this.

The cry dissipated as it ran out of breath, hanging upside down, mouth wide-open, lungs still trying to expel. A moment of silence; no time to think, Brian cradled it, "Shh! Shh!" he said, putting a hand over its mouth. It inhaled. Though muffled, Brian was sure, even then, the cry traveled upstairs.

Unsure of what to do, he headed for the door unbuttoning his shirt, knowing, at the very least; he had to get out of the cafeteria before anyone came in. As fast as he could, he got his shirt off. The kid was trying hard to improve upon its previous wails. Bareback, Brian hit the exit wrapping his shirt around the thing to hide it.

With every wrap of his shirt, covering it from head to toe, it got quieter.

He cradled it tightly in one arm while climbing into the cart. The pedal went to the metal and didn't come up until he was home.

Once inside, he went straight to his room. It had gotten quiet as he drove. He laid it on the bed; and began unwrapping. He hoped he hadn't hurt it. With the shirt off the thing, he stared at it in disbelief. What did it mean? Space Station Brian said this answered the paradox. He removed the defibrillator. Other than being small, it looked fine. The sight of it both excited and distressed him. He couldn't connect the dots, and stopped trying.

"No one will believe this. You're not one of Douglas's experiments. You're the new species."

It explained nothing.

"What am I supposed to do with you?" At the cafeteria, he had left in a hurry and realized while driving home that he hadn't signed off, or pulled the memory unit. It was getting close to lunch; he needed to return. "I have to go back, but you can't come."

Brian looked around his room, wishing he could go to the office and retrieve the emails from the Space Station. He went to his dresser and emptied one of the drawers onto the floor. He took his pillow, placed it in the bottom and then gently took the kid and put it inside. He covered it with his shirt, leaving its head exposed.

"You can't crawl out of there, can you? Probably not…." Brian pushed the drawer shut to make sure. His fingers lingered. Hesitant to leave, he slowly pulled it open, and looked at it again.

"Unbelievable, a new species."

He then closed the drawer more gently, and raced for the cart.

***

Brian parked practically inside of the door to the cafeteria. He half expected to see several new species lying all over the floor because some idiot kept trying to get food. He burst in so suddenly, everyone turned to see. The place was getting busy. They looked at him as if they suspected he was harboring something at home. Then he realized that he hadn't put a shirt on.

Undaunted, Brian walked to the terminal, which was in use and checked the slot. The memory unit was gone.

He panicked, quickly surveying the room; someone had it!

Unexpectedly, he spotted Gary at one of the tables. Brian went over and slid into the chair opposite him.

"Hey Chief, new look?" Gary smiled.

"Don't ask." He wished everyone would quit gawking. "How long have you been here?"

"I waited, Chief, but you never came back. I got everything done."

"That's not what I wanted to know. How long have you been here?"

"I saw you leave wrapping up your shirt. Did you spill something hot?"

"That's none of your business. You didn't happen to sign me off to get your food, did you?"

"No, Don was at the terminal when I came in." It had to be Don…. "He asked if I was making all the noise."

"What did you say?"

"My exact words, 'you saw me walk in.'"

"What else?"

"Nothing."

"You didn't mention you saw me?"

"No."

It probably didn't matter; Don had signed him off…. Brian didn't like the sound of that.

"Listen, Gary, I have an urgent assignment for you." Gary perked up. "I need you to go upstairs and get everyone out of the building."

"What's up?"

"You're on a need to know."

"Okay, so I just go up and ask them to leave?"

"No, be more creative. Go up acting like a raving lunatic and tell them you saw something fall out of the sky."

"Saw something fall out of the sky?"

"Yeah, and it crashed in the woods. They'll come down to see that."

"That's creative," Gary agreed, "but it doesn't have to be that, does it?"

"Look, this is your first assignment. Don't blow it. Just get everyone out."

"I'll try."

Brian stood; Gary sat, motionless, debating.

"Come on, you need to do it now. After you're done, you can have the rest of the day off."

Reluctantly, Gary got up from his half-eaten plate of food and slowly, headed for the stairs. He turned. "Any other ideas?"

"Not that I can think of. Just use it."

Brian left wishing he had his shirt and drove the cart to the corner of the building where he waited until he saw people coming out. From a distance, it looked like they were all joking and having fun. He sped to the next entrance wondering what Gary had told them. Inside, he flew up the stairs.

He went to Don's office and looked around. He didn't see the memory unit. He walked around the desk to check the drawers and spotted it sitting underneath the desk.

He took it and split, automatically scanning around him to ensure no one saw. He hoped Don never missed it.

In the cart, back by the corner, he saw Gary still had everyone outside. When Gary spotted him, he waved. Brian gave the thumbs up, and they all proceeded to go back inside.

When the last person went in, Brian drove up, parked, and went in himself. Of all things, he had to stop and get baby supplies and a shirt.

***

It was quiet when he walked into the house. Concerned, because he didn't know if he had roughed it up too much, he went into the bedroom and carefully opened the drawer. He didn't want to wake it.

Relieved, he watched it breathe.

In awe, Brian whispered, "Breathing isn't all you've been up to." He gently removed the wet shirt and replaced it with a blanket. "Don't know where you expelled that from, but it works." The whole time he made the exchange, he couldn't keep his eyes off it. "You're a little snot, you know that. I don't recall giving you permission to pee on my pillow." Because it was lying quiet, and he knew how much noise it could make, he didn't disturb it further.

He closed the drawer just as gently as he had opened it and picked a shirt up from the floor that had once been in it and went to his terminal. To no avail, it still wouldn't work. He left with a laptop and headed for the office.

***

Brian downloaded emails, resisting the urge to read them, knowing if he opened even one he wouldn't get back to the house until he knew what was going on. Without a clue as to what the kid needed, he didn't want to leave it to long by itself. He wondered how long it could be left alone.

Since he'd gotten back from the collection point, the morning was a blur. It was confusing. He couldn't stop thinking of it sleeping in his drawer. There was no connection as to why it answered Henry's paradox.

When the downloads were complete, he hurried back.

As he came to a stop in front of the house he heard cries. They were faint. But it was no longer sleeping. The emails would have to wait. Opening the door, the cry escaped. Worried, Brian pulled back a step. Although his house was somewhat secluded, he checked up and down the street to ensure no one was nearby.

When he lifted it out of the drawer, it seemed to calm a little, but started right back in once he sat it on the bed. If it kept this up, someone would come knocking.

Carefully, Brian cleaned it from head to toe before diapering it. It seemed awkward, but he dressed it too. He didn't know what size to get, so he had a variety of clothes to choose from. The close inspection left him amazed. He didn't know what to make of it. The only thing he knew for sure was that it was different, and very fussy.

"I don't know, but am I suppose to feed you now or something?"

He carried it from the bedroom with its head in the palm of his hand, legs draped over each side of his arm at the elbow. He prepared a bottle. Even with the tip securely in its mouth, it wouldn't suckle, but it could and did cry. He came to the realization he wouldn't likely be able to hide the fact that he had it in the house and prepped it for travel. Twenty minutes later, he had it strapped in the carrier and loaded into the cart with all its supplies.

When Brian pulled up to the plane, he saw the pods. He wished he had told Gary to remove them. Too late for that now, he would have to do it himself.

He grabbed the carrier. "Look, it's a plane. You're a lucky one; I didn't get to fly on my first day."

Once inside, he put it in on the grating and left it there. Inside the hangar, he grabbed a pod holder and ran it up under the wing. In less than two hours, he was done, and would have been sooner, but he had to keep responding to the cries from within the can.

No matter how many times he offered, the thing wouldn't take the bottle and seemed to insist on being held. His experience with Mark said it should take the bottle.

While donning his earplugs, he stared into the carrier, which was now bungeed to the grating next to him.

"Oops, forgot about you. We can't do that now, can we? You need something too. But what?"

It was too important, so Brian took the time to go to the Dupe. When he returned, the kid was all red in the face. "You look like you've been doing that the whole time I was gone. You can give it up anytime." He felt sorry for it though, and tried the bottle again, which he was still unsuccessful at. Brian put little muffs on its head and stretched a headband around that to keep them snugly in place.

"There, you're set. You just let me know if it doesn't work." He went back out to the cart. Three trips later, he had the rest of the supplies onboard.

While the kid cried, he put in his own earplugs thinking he would have to wear them from then on. He wished he knew what else to do for it. He zipped the carrier closed, and started the motors, which drowned out its cries completely.

***

As the plane climbed, Brian turned on the laptop. With anticipation, he opened the first email and then set the auto-pilot. A response, it stated: "Glad you're still with me," and then went on to explain the date request. The mainframe at the Space Station was not running on the same time as that of earth. There was a fifty-year difference. Brian at the Space Station admitted he didn't know which was correct, if either, but would research.

The next email was a rather lengthy dissertation about being the one who ended up on the Space Station. He wasn't pleased. Brian read this with great interest; and compassion; related totally, and saw how unprepared he was to take that step. He had thought this over beforehand and hadn't fore-seen it as a problem. It was him that went. He composed an email at once, offering support. He would send it when he returned. Being his only contact, he began to wonder if he had done the right thing.

The next two emails were more of the same; a broken disc, of how strange it was being the one. Every conceivable aspect was gone over with the last email saying, "Oh by the way, digitalize water and take it with you next time."

In the fifth, he read: "I've discovered a treasure trove of information, stuff I've never seen before." When Brian reached the end of the email, he was disappointed there wasn't more detail.

Several emails later, with still no details, he opened one with a single word: 'Girl….'

"Girl," it sounded foreign on his tongue.

In the next, Douglas, referred to as a visionary, was in total control. The email went on to explain Douglas's vision for the recovery of the earth. He would rid it of the infesta-tion, and prevent another one. That decision generated a tremendous amount of internal controversy at all the Instal-lations. Only males would be duped, no females. Another new word, prefix on male. He looked down at the carrier, and then turned off the laptop.

It didn't seem an hour, but they had overflown the runway.

He banked the plane, set his approach and began descending. He buzzed the place on the return trip, watching several small furry critters scamper into the woods. They looked just as confused as he was.

Brian landed and pulled his earplugs as the motors were stopping. There wasn't a sound from the carrier.

He made preparations, emptying two backpacks exchanging their content for baby supplies. Eventually, what he was taking ended up organized at the bottom of the ladder.

He wished he had brought more than just the pepper spray for protection.

"When I get back I'm duping a weapon to keep on the plane," he said in the general direction of the carrier, now sitting at the top of the steps.

He placed one backpack on top of the cooler and bungeed it to the handle. The other he put on.

Loaded to the hilt, he set out, pepper spray clenched between his teeth, the cooler in tow behind him, and the baby carrier in the other hand. When he made it to the terminal, everything went onto the ground, including him. It wasn't an easy stroll through all the foliage.

The kid began to fuss once the carrier was released. Brian was tempted to check, but couldn't afford to be caught out in the open with his attention on it. He didn't know if its cries would attract attention. Right away, he got up and proceeded around the building. The motion seemed to soothe and it quieted.

Although now exhausted, Brian didn't stop until he made it to the double doors. The first set were still a problem, but worked. Then everything went onto the floor and he pulled on the second set of doors to ensure they were securely in place. Brian sat on the floor to catch his breath. As he did so, the new species fussed.

"Not again. You know, you and your stuff are heavy. Give me a break, we just got here." He said while catching his breath. "There's a room here that'll be perfect for you."

The fussing turned to a cry. It forced Brian to get up and collect everything. "It's not much further. So what are you doing in there anyway? Will you eat something now?" He was using the most soothing tone he could manage. The room he had in mind was on an outside wall with windows.

He traveled more comfortably without the foliage obstacle course, though now in a hurry, because the kid was becoming annoying. It wanted something.

When he reached the room, he offloaded. "We're here. I'll have you out in a moment," Brian said, unzipping the carrier. The first whiff made him gag. "No wonder you're so fussy. Did something crawl in there with you and die?" He turned up his nose, gently lifting the new species out of the carrier, not wanting to find out what this was all about.

He used his free hand to unzip one of the backpacks, found a blanket and spread it on the floor. He laid the baby on it and got a bottle. It never stopped crying. He knew Pete had been through all of this and wondered how he had done it with Mark.

"If Pete can do it, so can I. You just watch me," he muttered, bracing for the task. "You know when I'm done with this, I'm going. I can't stay, but I'll be back." He offered solace with his voice, if not his words.

He finished and offered the bottle, but decided after so many times it just didn't want it.

On his way out, Brian tossed the diaper onto the ground, then thought better of it and picked it back up. Who knew what it would draw?

Back inside, he went to the section where the birds had access, opened the door and threw it in, adding to the foul odor.

When he was half way to the plane, feeling guilty, he turned around to go back and check on it one last time. As he approached the room, it was still crying. He didn't want to go in; he had already done everything he knew to do.

"Hey new species, I told you I'd be right back," he said, as he opened the door.

Brian picked it up and walked with it around the room cradling it in his arms. He could feel its warmth penetrate his chest. He tried a pacifier, but it didn't take that either. After a while, as he walked, its eyes closed. After a while longer, it was sleeping comfortably in his arms. He put it on the blanket. It woke. He grabbed another blanket from the backpack and lay down next to it covering them both.

He placed a hand on its chest and gently patted. It went back to sleep.

***

Three hours later, disoriented at first, Brian woke to a cry, and everything came back in a rush.

"I've got to go," he addressed the new species.

Brian checked, but it didn't need a change.

"You should eat sometime." He offered the bottle, but it continued to cry. "What else do you want?" He picked it up, walked around again, which had worked before. "I can't do this all day, obviously you can. You don't seem to be able to do anything besides want to be held and cry."

Compelled to leave, he sat the kid back on the blanket. He needed to get back to the Installation. He would read emails on the way. Gary couldn't be left standing around in the morning with nothing to do.

He left it on the blanket, walked out, escaping the cries. It was hard walking away, harder still to start the motors of the plane. He didn't want to leave. With resolve, he took off. When he hit cruising altitude, he set the autopilot and put the remote down. He reached for the laptop anxious to read emails. Torn, he ended up with the remote back in his hands. The urge to return was very strong.

Chapter Nineteen

Brian yawned; at the same time, he concentrated on landing at the Installation.

Unlike working through the night, which he had done on many occasions, the night before was nerve-racking. He had turned the plane around as soon as he had taken off and returned to the new species. It felt like the responsible thing to do. But between the female, who was simply impossible, and reading emails, sleep was never an option.

He debated whether to bring it back with him and leave it on Pete's front porch. That would be news. 'Mysterious kid left on porch. Where did it come from?' The first time it needed a change.... Brian smiled.... It wouldn't just be news; it would be the news of the century while everyone tried to figure out what it was. Someone though, would eventually find out who had left it; and that couldn't happen.

Gary was waiting at the hangar when Brian taxied up. Unprepared to deal with him, Brian went down the steps heading for his cart. He had things to do, none of which included time with his apprentice.

"Hey, Chief, where have you been?"

"Business," Brian spat, picking up his pace. Gary matched him as he headed toward the cart.

"Anything I can help with?"

"No."

"I'm just asking Chief. So, in the morning, am I supposed to wait for you here or at the office?"

"Here is fine." Brian climbed into the cart and then asked, "Yesterday, how did you get everyone to leave the building?"

"I told them you were having a fire drill."

"That was smart."

"Thanks, Chief. It worked, too, didn't it?"

"Yes it did. You know, you're going to do all right. Look, for that, take the morning off. I'll have parts in the hangar before this afternoon. When you come back, get started."

"Okay. Do you want me to tie the plane down?"

"No, I'm leaving again."

"Can you give me a lift home?"

"No, catch the shuttle."

Brian pulled away, taking off for the office. During the night, he had learned many things. The biggest surprise, because he had anticipated finding out what Douglas had done to him, was that Douglas hadn't done anything to him.

Brian turned on his terminal before he sat in the office chair. Once up and running, he sent composed emails to the Space Station. He downloaded what he received, another host of them. He checked the email directory for Pete's name, and didn't see it. He then generated a parts list for the cart and left.

He raced across the Installation heading for Pete's.

As he drove, he thought of the daunting task Douglas had set out to do. Every record, within every mainframe, changed, removing or replacing all reference to anything feminine.

An incredible find. In total wonder, Brian came to understand why the animals were still around without the Dupe.

He parked in front of Pete's house feeling uncomfortable because he hadn't been in a while, and now only came for information. He knocked tentatively and waited. He became anxious. He couldn't stay, and if Pete wasn't home, he didn't know what he was going to do. He had to find out what he came here for.

Brian heard footsteps approach the door.

"Hey, look who's here, nice to see you. Come on in," Pete said when he opened the door.

"Can't, no time. Sorry, but this has to be a quick visit. I have a question for you."

"Brian!" Mark yelled, running across the room and out onto the porch. He ran into Brian's legs, hugging them.

"How are you, rug rat?" He bent over and picked him up.

"I'm not a rug rat. I'm a big boy."

"You are, huh. Who told you that?"

"My dad."

"Well, he's right." Brian wanted to know how Pete got Mark to eat when he first brought him home. "Pete, has anyone asked you to update your digitization?" He asked instead, not knowing how to go about asking the other because there was no reason for him to ask.

"Do you want me to do that now?"

"No, nothing like that."

"Has someone asked you to do yours?"

"No."

"Can I go for a ride in the cart?" Mark interrupted.

"Not today buddy," he said, putting a finger into his belly making him squirm and laugh.

"Pete, do you have email?"

"I don't have a terminal. But I'll earn one when I'm ready to raise another child."

"When will that be?"

"Within a couple of years."

"That long!" Brian set Mark down. "I've got to go buddy, give me five."

Brian said goodbye, telling Pete he would be back. He drove to the Dupe and did cart parts, after which he went to the hangar and unloaded everything inside. Since it was quicker than programming a new system, he went to the office, gave Pete an email account, and deleted all his files. He disconnected the terminal and loaded it into the cart.

On his way back to Pete's, he couldn't stop thinking of what he read in one email where he learned Douglas was a happy man. At least that was what he had thought when he read that Douglas was gay. The term gay received a lengthy explanation, with all the innuendo from four centuries earlier, and explained that leaving the female out of the equation was the logical choice for Douglas. It fit his lifestyle.

That decision didn't go without a tremendous amount of internal struggle. Not everyone agreed. But with absolute control over what he set out to do, Douglas triumphed.

At Pete's, Brian took the terminal and set it on the porch. He knocked for the second time.

"Hey," Pete said, "I didn't expect to see you again today."

"I told you I would be back. This is for you and Mark." He pointed to the terminal sitting on the porch.

"For us?"

"Yes, but don't tell anyone where you got it."

"Will you get into trouble?"

With a genuine laugh, he said, "Only if you tell." Although, for Brian, this hardly mattered.

"That won't happen."

"You now have email."

"Great."

"Out of curiosity," Brian said, taking a step back. "How did you get Mark started on the bottle when you first brought him home?"

"It wasn't easy, because they don't know anything when they're first duped. I just kept pressing his jaw against the bottle. It took time, but he caught on."

"Pete, I appreciate that," he said, backing away further. He started to go.

"You seem stressed," Pete noted. "Is the new job getting to you?"

The question gave Brian pause while he climbed into the cart. "Actually no, but you know how it is."

"Are you thinking of taking up child rearing?"

"No," Brian said. "Maybe," he added, reconsidering, knowing that would cover for the question he'd just asked. Mark came out and stood next to Pete. "I'll be back to give you that ride, Buddy."

"You should; I know you were thinking about it once before. You look like you could use a change of pace. Thanks for the terminal," Pete said.

"Bye, Brian," Mark yelled. He waved as Brian pulled away.

Brian waved without looking back speeding toward the Dupe. He smiled thinking the last day had been more of a change of pace than he would ever have planned. He hoped he hadn't raised any suspicions with Pete.

In another email, Space Station Brian said he had discovered the mummified remains of someone in one of the crew quarters. In those same quarters, he found the digitalization for the new species, along with the information on Douglas.

"It's no wonder you didn't get Gary's apprenticeship done. You've been very busy."

At the Dupe, Brian stocked up on baby supplies and did more cart parts. He did several coolers for himself and duped a pistol with a shoulder holster. He selected a vest to conceal the weapon.

With everything in the cart, he went to the hangar.

***

Apprehensive, and in a hurry to start feeding, Brian went through both sets of double doors and into the terminal. There wasn't a sound from inside the room as he approached, raising his worst fears. When he walked in, the new species was lying quiet on the blanket, still covered, sound asleep.

He resisted the urge to pick it up by preparing ahead of time. He set out a change of clothes, a diaper and a bottle. He then lay down next to the baby, turning on the laptop to continue reading emails. Later, when the kid woke, he changed everything on it from head to toe. He nestled it into his arms and tried feeding.

While it cried, he depressed its jaw as Pete had told him. It coughed and choked a few times, but after a while, he could see progress on the bottle. Encouraged, he kept at it.

With the bottle almost gone, Brian caught himself nodding. He gently laid the kid on the blanket and covered them both.

He woke ten minutes later to the sound of the new species crying. For some reason he recalled he was supposed to start exercising the day before. He promised himself nothing would interfere.

"What was I thinking?" he spoke gently to the little girl next to him. He picked her up. She belched loudly in his ear. "Where did that come from?" he laughed.

When he cradled her in his arms, she went back to sleep. Brian lay down, this time leaving her across his chest.

***

The next morning Brian returned to the Installation and walked into the hangar. It was a mess. Gary had parts all over the place. Some were in different groupings. The groupings were in various stages of assembly.

"Gary, are we making progress?"

"I am, Chief."

"We're doing the plane next. That'll need to be organized better than this." He ignored Gary's emphasis with frustration because he expected the cart to be further along. As he walked out, he added, "I'm getting the rest of the parts."

Busy with the little girl most of the night and all morning, he now took time to eat a quick meal; it was the first he'd actually sat and relaxed since returning from the collection point two days earlier. Afterward, he worked on the list.

The Dupe spat out mostly large parts. Brian stacked them in the cart. He filled it quickly, with the largest pieces overhanging the edges. He wanted to finish the list in one trip; duping and programming a terminal was high on the agenda. He needed to retrieve and send emails.

With the cart stacked full and more yet to do, he saw that one trip wasn't going to do it.

He hurried to the hangar, drove in, off loaded onto the floor, making another pile, and then went back to the Dupe. Again, more large parts came out, but this time he was able to finish the list and get it all onto the cart.

He had room for the terminal too, which he did and headed home with it.

Brian disconnected the old terminal and set it on the floor. Once he had the new one hooked up, he turned it on and loaded the operating system.

While the terminal performed its task, Brian thumbed through the small memory units looking for the email download. He thumbed through them a second time. He rifled through the desk drawers wondering where he'd put it. He was still looking when the terminal beeped it was ready.

Fifteen minutes later, feeling pressed for time, he left. He hadn't planned to be gone long. Programming the terminal would wait. Without it, though, he had no communication link to the Space Station. Going to the Space Center and using the terminal across the hall from Ivan was not an option. He wasn't prepared to face Ivan.

Brian knew he couldn't put this off very long. Someone would email something that would bite him in the butt. If he had left his stuff on Pete's terminal and password protected….

At the hangar, he parked next to the pile he had unloaded earlier. "Gary, here's the rest. I'll be back in the morning to pick you up. You need to have this done. There are other things to do."

***

"What a couple of days this has turned out to be." Brian spoke softly to the baby, setting her on the blanket. "I sure didn't expect you when I landed two days ago."

With the kid fed, he proceeded to change her. It still amazed him every time he had to do so. She was very different than Mark. Then he laid out maps and went to work on where he and Gary would begin pilfering materials for the plane.

While he did this, pent-up demands crept in keeping him from concentrating. He had to complete Gary's apprenticeship program. Ivan already questioned why it wasn't done. He wondered how Brian at the Space Station was doing. Worst, he had to get Ivan's approval to build the plane and he needed that before he could start.

When he screwed up his terminal disconnecting and re-connecting the Space Centers mainframe, he wondered if it had caused problems for anyone else. Then there was the incident at the Dupe where he had to recover the memory unit out of Don's office. He wondered if Don remembered; or reported it to Ivan. Above all, he needed to get his email up and running.

"Because of you I'm not getting anything done. Pete's porch is an appealing option. If I left you there, I'd be back on track in no time."

In the morning, Brian left with little choice. He knew he would be gone longer than any time previous. He didn't like it. He wanted to stay, protect, and provide for this little life. But he had work to do.

It was hard to leave, and proved more difficult every time he had to do so.

***

When Brian landed at One-O-Seven, a quick inspection showed Gary hadn't made much progress on the new cart. Gary was nowhere around. Brian's cart was gone too. Irritated, he walked to the shuttle pick-up carrying a laptop. After waiting twenty minutes that he didn't have, he boarded the shuttle.

He stayed on when it stopped at the office. The cart wasn't there.

Brian departed at the Dupe. There was no one inside. He had hoped to find Gary. He began duping supplies for the trip, wondering why he bothered. Deep down, he knew the answer. He had to do this for Henry. This would be his legacy; a loaner plane stationed at One-O-Seven.

A margin note said to bring dynamite. He selected it, and the instructions. Brian lined everything against a wall where it would be out of the way. There were coolers, a half dozen pepper sprays, and dynamite. A new memory unit for email downloads went into his pocket as he exited the building.

He made his way back to the shuttle to head home. He didn't like leaving the stuff unattended, didn't like waiting for the shuttle. "Gary, where are you?" The Installation was large; and could prove more than a day's search.

The largest volume of material they needed to collect for the plane was aluminum. Surprisingly, glass was right up toward the top of the list. Brian figured it was for the solar panels and wondered why plastic wasn't used instead.

The coordinates on one map placed one collection point for steel in the city by the airport he had just left. It made the decision easy. They would go there first. He would be close to her.

He caught the shuttle for home. Frustrated, he wanted a shower. But since Gary had made himself scarce, that wouldn't happen.

He got off at the closest stop and began walking. It was further than he remembered. He wasn't accustomed to this and had forgotten how long it took. At home, he installed the email program and reestablished the connection to the Space Center's mainframe. Everything worked. He sent and downloaded emails. There was one from Pete. "Decent, his worked."

When done, Brian walked back to the shuttle pick-up and waited. He knew how impossible it would be to find Gary. If he didn't have supplies already waiting at the Dupe, he would simply leave and go back to her.

Brian rode back to the Dupe and picked up what he could carry from inside. He then rode to the hangar. There, finally, he found the cart, parked by the door, with Gary sitting in the driver's seat, eating.

"Good morning, Chief," Gary said. "Are you staying or leaving?"

Brian restrained himself. "Slide over; we have a busy day ahead of us." He set off for the Dupe. He would have continued to use the shuttle until he had gotten everything aboard the plane. Not getting a shower aggravated him. It was all he could do to keep from strangling Gary for being so inefficient and taking off with the cart.

"Chief, I broke one of the parts for the cart. You'll need to replace it."

***

When they reached the outskirts of the city, Brian flew in low looking for a place to land.

He found a spot, less than ideal, but doable. He used it.

From the time they had taken off, Brian let Gary know what he expected. A captive audience, Gary couldn't help but listen to him, though Brian realized Gary had given up hearing what he had to say long ago.

After they landed, Brian opened the hatch, Gary got out and Brian threw packages down to him.

When they were both standing at the bottom of the steps, Brian reached into his pocket for a pepper spray. He gave it to Gary.

"There are predators around here; keep an eye out," Brian told him. "These things are good for three or four shots. Go for the eyes." He demonstrated, pulling another from his pocket.

"Think you can handle that?"

"Sure, looks easy enough."

Brian thought it would be an entirely different story if something came after him, and gave him an additional pepper spray.

"Try it."

Gary did, hitting the same target.

The spray fouled the air. Brian rubbed at his nose.

"You have a cooler, your gloves…" and then Brian pointed to a spot along side of the plane.

"Stack what you collect right there."

"Will do, Chief."

"I'm sure you've never used dynamite."

"Nope."

"Me either. Be careful." Brian pulled papers from his back pocket. "Follow the instructions. I'll be back when I can."

"You're leaving?"

"Yep."

"You're pissed because I didn't finish the cart. You don't have to turn this into an object lesson."

"This has nothing to do with the cart."

"Chief, I worked on it most of the night."

"It doesn't matter. You'll finish it later."

"Come on, Chief. You can't leave me out here alone."

"Look, there's nothing to argue. As long as you keep your wits about you, you'll be fine. I have something that's pressing, or I would stay."

Brian reached into his pocket and gave Gary another pepper spray. Gary looked so apprehensive, Brian didn't want to leave. But it couldn't be helped. His priority had to be with the kid. He climbed the ladder into the can telling Gary again to be careful.

The airport, not even a three-minute flight, took longer because Brian had to make a wide arc to line up a decent approach. He did the usual fly over and watched several small fury critters scurry away.

After landing, he took a few moments to empty a backpack and the cold side of a cooler. He repackaged baby supplies into them. He had wanted to do this during the flight out, save time, but couldn't very well with Gary on the plane.

Brian carried the cooler to the ground while he continued to worry about Gary. He didn't have any useful experience outside of the fence. "And naturally, I leave him out here alone. I can't believe I did it."

Brian hoped nothing happened. If he returned to the Installation alone a second time, Ivan would simply replace him. There wouldn't even be a second chance, much less a new apprentice.

His worries shifted to the baby. Being this close and gone so long, he trotted, with the cooler bouncing in tow.

Following his usual route, Brian made his way around the building.

At the back, when he rounded the corner, he immediately spotted a predator! It was up against the building, standing on hind haunches, stretched, front paws clutching a windowsill. Brian watched it pull itself up. Intently, it looked through the glass. Its back paws continued to scrape against the wall and foliage to maintain position.

It didn't see him.

The entrance was close to the corner Brian had just rounded. He could walk in before the predator got there.

Weary, anger began to motivate him. It was her window. Could it break the glass? It licked its chops; staring. Cautiously, Brian drew his pistol. He transferred it to his left hand to get the pepper spray. The predator turned toward him sniffing the air. Brian froze. It didn't pick him out and looked the other way, still sniffing.

It turned back to the window, repositioned itself, getting higher, improving its view. Slowly, Brian began to draw the pepper spray.

A hard repercussion rocked the air. The explosion was close.

Brian jumped, losing the pistol.
He bobbled the pepper spray.

Chapter Twenty

The explosion triggered the predator to jerk and twist off the wall. Unexpectedly quick to recover, it came like the wind; and before Brian could regain control over the pepper spray, it flew past him in a blur and was gone.

Shocked by its speed, Brian stooped to pick up his pistol, the pepper spray now ready. He hadn't thought it would get to him before he ducked into the building. He reassessed its ability.

Was Gary hurt? Did he just kill himself? Worried, Brian knew Gary just set off the dynamite, his concern though didn't keep him from backing hastily through the double doors which he pulled tight ensuring they were secure.

Safe inside, the world outside vanished. He heard her cry where he stood. He turned with a hastened step, running after a bit. She became his only concern.

"It's all right, I'm here," Brian cooed, entering the room. The cry changed to a nasal hesitation mimicking a laugh. She had heard him, responded, glad he was back.

Brian placed her in one arm and prepared a bottle. Her face was tear tracked; lips, pouty. She had been crying hard and for some time. It pulled his heartstrings.

"I'm sorry, I'm here now," he murmured, but he knew he would leave again, and soon.

He pushed on her little chin, teaching her to suckle. It was so easy to do; he wished he had figured this out on his own without involving Pete.

He interrupted her feeding to change her, eliminating the smell before it became nauseating.

"Your little butt is so red." He gently wiped her clean. "Does it hurt?" He wiped her face as well.

Brian went from his knees to sitting on the floor while he picked her up. He finished feeding her and she fell asleep, contented, cradled in his arms. She had looked terrible when he first picked her up. Now, she seemed none the worse for wear.

"I'm going to find you a suitable room," he whispered in her ear while setting her down.

"Something upstairs where that mean old predator can't get to you."

Brian began moving her supplies. On the last trip, he wrapped her in the blanket. When he laid her down in the new room, he was amazed she had slept through the whole ordeal. Because she did, he left the blanket wrapped around her.

"You don't even know you've been moved."

Afterward, Brian left for the plane. He was extra cautious as he made the trip. Inside the can he shuffled through the contents on the grating, which he had dumped earlier from the backpack. He found the first aid kit, tore it open and removed the antibiotic ointment.

"This should do the trick." Since he had started getting formula into her, she had supplied an infinite number of surprises. "I'll have this on your little bottom in no time."

He grabbed his laptop and brought it with him. Close to her, he stretched out on the floor; and worked while she slept.

There was an email from Ivan. Uneasy by what it might contain, he had ignored it on the trip out. The email said that fire drills were something they hadn't performed in a long time. There was nothing concerning the memory unit. There were numerous people involved in the fire drill. Anyone of them could have said something. Only Don removed the memory unit. Brian composed several responses using the same document. None of them viable; he reread Ivan's email, and tried to answer it again. Later, when he came back to the document, he deleted it. He decided Ivan's email was more of a directive than a question.

He continued trying to work while sleep entreated upon him. Almost gone, he remembered Gary. There hadn't been another explosion. Was he really dead? This concern formed too late, and Brian drifted off.

***

The windows vibrated from the second explosion. Brian jumped, and looked at the laptop's clock; a little over an hour had passed.

"That answers that," he said, relieved.

She slept through it. A little surprised, he thought the first explosion had scared her, made her cry so hard. Apparently that wasn't the case. Once assured she would continue to sleep he rejoined her in slumber.

Two hours later, the baby fed, wearing a fresh diaper and a layer of ointment protecting her little bottom, Brian left to check on Gary. Wide-awake, she lay there so cute; he wanted to stay.

Although he wouldn't admit it to anyone else, he had become more fascinated with her with every passing moment. He wouldn't admit either to his sense of accomplishment by providing for her or his growing fondness.

On his way out, he dropped the dirty diaper into the birds section. The collection was starting to mound.

***

When Brian landed, he was pleased to see a pile of material sitting where he had instructed Gary to put it.

When he got out, he was disappointed to see the size of the pile. It had looked bigger from inside the plane; at this rate, it would take days to fill the can. This threw his whole time line out of whack. Having her didn't help. He would have to recalculate.

He loaded the small pile, wondering where Gary was. When he finished, he walked down the road. There were tall buildings on either side; all were in various stages of decay. At the crossroad, he called out Gary's name; and waited, but got no answer. He did the same at the next.

"Hey Chief."

Brian jumped.

"Up here. I thought I heard you."

"What are you doing up there?"

"Working." His eyes rolled.

"You found steel up there?"

"The test kit you provided says so."

"How did you get up there?" The building was wide open, with no windows on any level.

"I'll come down and show you." Gary disappeared. When he reappeared, Brian walked in under the building to meet him.

"I'd have more done, Chief, if I didn't have to carry this stuff up the road." Gary said this as if he knew it would be Brian's only concern.

"Show me what you mean."

With Gary leading the way, they walked up an incline that kept turning to the left at each end of the building.

On the third level, there were heaps of old junk metal on wheels with rotted rubber. They too were in various states of decay, with a few now in shreds.

"I've been throwing this stuff over," Gary said as he picked up a piece of metal and tossed it out past the edge to demonstrate. "If that's all I had to do…"

"Come on, Gary, it's obvious I can get the plane down here. The only reason I chose the spot I did, it's where we parked. Think for yourself."

"Well, that's settled. Are you sticking around? You can watch the next blast. It's a riot."

"How long will it take?"

"It's almost ready."

"Finish it."

Brian gathered pieces and threw them over while Gary prepared the dynamite. His hands turned a reddish black from the rust and dirt. There were pieces that would require both of them to lift. If they could man-handle them through the hatch, they would fill a fourth or more of the plane.

He drew blood on the sharp edge of one piece trying to pick it up. His gloves were on the plane. He went and got them.

When Gary was ready, he called Brian to the opposite end of the ramp where they huddled behind a large pillar. Gary held a wireless remote and began to push buttons.

"This thing has a ton of safety features. I have to sequence through them all to get it to work. Put your earplugs in; I'm still recovering from that first blast. This will blow in a few."

Brian put his earplugs in seeing that Gary had already done so. Maybe he had never taken them out after the first blast which could be the reason he hadn't heard the plane.

In dramatic fashion, Gary held five fingers high above his head, and then put his hand to the floor, bending at the torso. When he came back up, four fingers showed.

Brian, reminded of Ken's comical posturing at the Research Center, thought 'oh brother.'

When Gary reached one, he held the count for an extended period, then spread his legs, bent his knees, bracing, and brought his hand down pushing the button. The repercussion was hard. The whole building shook. It felt as if it was on the verge of collapse.

"Isn't that awesome?" Gary said, grinning from ear to ear. "You can feel it through your whole body."

It was a rush, but scary, as dust surrounded them and blew out over the edge. Ozone filled the air.

The only thing Brian considered awesome was there wouldn't be a predator within fifty miles. "Have you stayed in here every time?"

"Yes, it's neat, isn't it?" Gary had found his calling.

"Not if it kills you. Next time, get out," Brian told him this as they entered the thinning cloud of dust. He didn't know which was worse, the predators, or the danger Gary posed to himself. Brian knew he had been right to worry when he had left him alone.

"Sure, Chief." Gary put his gloves on. 'Whatever you say,' wasn't said and Brian stopped the safety lecture. He recognized the active, inactive listening. He had done it himself to Henry. It made him feel old; somehow, he had turned into the Chief.

Pieces of concrete had fallen from the ceiling and pieces of embedded metal pockmarked the ceiling as well.

Working together, using a crude assessment, they sorted the larger pieces. They put what wouldn't fit through the hatch onto the next heap of steel to be blown. The rest went over the edge.

At first, neither could avoid watching the stuff they threw over as it crashed onto the concrete below. But that wasted time; Brian pushed to get everything over.

"I'll get the plane. You can handle the rest of the stuff."

"Okay."

Brian parked as close as he could and called Gary. Together, they struggled to get the large pieces aboard.

In all, Brian was there more than three and a half hours.

"I'm leaving."

"Again? Okay, bye." Gary walked away, disappearing up the ramp.

Brian left.

The plane was almost half-full and a few things shifted, settling to the grating when Brian made the wide arc to land.

He was pleased with their progress. There would be time to take care of the kid, fill the rest of the plane and return Gary to the Installation. While Gary unloaded everything, Brian would get that shower, and be back long before dark. There should even be time to dupe the first plane parts.

The feeling didn't last. Ten to twelve trips from this location and the steel requirement would be filled.

Brian anticipated collecting aluminum next. The problem; the closest location was six hours away from her, five from the Installation. There wasn't time to make the trip, collect material, and make it back to her in one day.

In less than two weeks, they would go.

Because aluminum was the largest volume of what they needed, they were going to be there a while. She might have to spend a night or two alone.

If Gary knew how to fly, Brian would send him. But Gary hadn't touched the remote; at least with batteries in it. Then Brian realized it wouldn't work. He needed the plane to take care of her. Solving logistics, providing for her, he felt guilty. She had to be his first priority. Everything else had to be planned around her. The feeling was strong. She wouldn't get the short end of the stick.

There would be no nights alone for her. He would come up with something.

The afternoon was peaceful, expecting an occasional explosion. Brian relaxed, worked, and didn't allow his worries to play another significant role.

On the flight back to the Installation, Gary received his first flying lesson. Brian had learned more about the remote since Henry passed than Henry had ever told him. Henry probably knew it all, but either considered it unimportant or had forgotten it by the time he trained Brian.

It was all available on the mainframe.

**

Brian set the autopilot, anxious to return to the old airport. He set his laptop on its namesake and opened the first email from the Space Station. Brian at the Space Station was like a machine; he cranked out emails like there was no tomorrow.

Thankfully, as a reprieve, there was nothing from Ivan, although Brian felt his silence would be short-lived.

While Brian was at the Dupe, he had done shelving units to organize parts for the plane. He told Gary to assemble those before continuing with the cart. It felt funny duping parts for the plane. He still needed to ask Ivan. Not ask, but convince him the loaner was necessary. If Ivan found out now, he would put the kibosh to it.

He had to get something into Ivan's hands, and soon; but Ivan would want to know why Brian worked on this instead of Gary's apprenticeship.

That made Brian sweat a little; and the minor detail inched forward that as head of security, he hoped Don would report the missing memory unit to him instead of Ivan. He hadn't done so, and Brian wondered if Ivan knew.

To top it off, he hadn't emailed the Space Station Brian about the little girl. How was he going to explain it? "Hey, how is this for news? We started a new infestation."

Brian tried to concentrate on the first email: "I don't want to cause undue concern, but I don't know how long I can stay on the Space Station. Even though it's set up for long-term use, there isn't much organic material aboard. By no means have I searched everywhere, but I doubt I'll find more."

In another he wrote, "I'm having problems adjusting to weightlessness. Not in and of itself, but I found a manual that said I'd have to exercise four hours a day just to combat the long-term effects of it on my body. Even then, it won't provide the same benefit as gravity."

This reminded Brian; he had to start his own exercise regime.

The next email had an attached file, information that went as a greeting on all spaceships. It was available in case any ship ran into intelligent life. It gave man's location in the cosmos, saying he was a peaceful species.

Brian opened the attachment. It contained drawings of two people.

Both drawings were of identical poses. Full frontal views, both showed the range of motion of the arms and legs; neither had clothes.

Immediately, Brian recognized the male and glanced past it. He focused on the female.

She was depicted with long hair drawn below her shoulders. It cascaded to her breasts. Overly enlarged, compared to the male, they gave her a shapely look. Very distinctive, her body was very unlike his. She looked quite exotic.

Although the baby looked nothing like this, Brian recognized the connection between the drawing and her. She would grow to look like this.

There was an email from Pete. He opened it next: "Since you were here, Mark has asked twenty to a hundred times a day when you'll be back. He's waiting for that ride on the cart. The day you told him later, he went off sulking. That was the reason you didn't see him right away when you came back."

"Mark, I promise, you'll get that ride."

He started to compose an email to let Pete know he'd be there to give Mark that ride, but stopped and reopened the attachment to the previous email and studied the picture again.

The drawing was informative; Brian kept returning to it.

***

"For someone so small, you can belt out the volume, can't you," Brian said, climbing out of his sleeping bag. He had duped the bag on his last trip. In its box, the air mattress was still aboard the plane. He had gotten back too late to retrieve it before dark, and wasn't able to carry everything in one trip.

The room was getting cozy.

Several days before, Brian had brought paint. After completing that, he cleaned and disinfected the floor three times.

He had toys neatly arranged along one wall, which were decoration for now. She would play with them later.

He still needed a crib, highchair, and all those things he saw at Pete's for babies.

He held her comfortably sitting in the rocking chair while she fed on her own.

"It didn't take you long, no it didn't. You're smart. Pete said it took Mark awhile, but not you."

As if solving the paradox wasn't enough, the last email he'd read from the Space Station said he discovered the reason for the communication problem with the spaceships.

That email explained there were seven satellites which worked in conjunction with the Space Station. All were similar and provided the communication network for the spaceships. At some point, the onboard computer system had shut down and rebooted. When that happened, it came back fifty-five years out of date.

This put the satellite network out of alignment. They had to be precise to send and pick up signals. Over time, the further away the spaceships were, the more important this alignment became. Eventually, the earth would lose contact with all the ships unless the system was rebooted with the correct date.

Brian at the Space Station was going over manuals to see how to proceed. He would send an assessment of how difficult it would be to shut it down and restart with the correct date. The onboard computers controlled everything, including his life support, and until he was assured he understood how to do it, he wasn't taking any chances. He would be signing his own death warrant if it didn't work.

When the baby finished her bottle, Brian changed her and set her on the floor. Her rash was worse. It had gotten better at first, but the ointment was no longer working. It didn't make sense.

"I'm going to go get Gary. I'll be back in a couple of hours." She lay there; eyes wide open, just looking around. On the way out, he stopped at the door. "I hope you don't mind that I talk to you."

***

"I started on the plane, Chief."

"You've finished the cart?"

"Yes."

"Does it work?" he asked. Gary laughed. "Sorry," Brian said climbing in. "I'm going for a shower." He started, and then stopped. "Hey, why'd it stop?"

"It worked for me." Gary looked puzzled.

Brian pushed on the pedal again. The cart moved. "Kidding. Now we'll see how you do on the plane."

At home, he emailed Pete. He'd spent the entire flight back to the Installation trying to compose something to ask what worked for rashes. He ended up telling him he had one and wondered if any of the baby products Pete used on Mark ever worked. He hated to depend on Pete for help, but hoped he responded while he was in the shower.

***

Over the next week, Gary kept getting further behind assembling the plane.

Every day, he would collect materials from the city, at the Installation he would toss it all out onto the tarmac, and then take everything to the Dupe, weigh it, and return to the hangar loaded with parts for the plane. The earlier they got back, the more parts Brian duped, putting Gary further behind. When the shelves were full, and Gary started using the floor, Brian duped more shelving, and pressed Gary to accomplish more.

Gary would work late into the night, and Brian would pick him up earlier each morning. Gary complained he needed more than four hours of sleep and wanted to know when they were taking a day off.

Brian told him he would be able to sleep on the plane ride to and from the aluminum collection point when they started there; until then, he needed to accomplish more, sleep less. There would be no days off.

On the thirteenth day, the last load of steel hit the tarmac. "That's it," Brian said. "I won't be back in the morning. Tomorrow, you'll have the day to catch up. I expect to see a good portion of those parts on the shelf gone. You can even sleep in an extra fifteen minutes."

"That's mighty generous of you, Chief, but don't you think that's pushing it? An extra fifteen minutes could mean the difference between using them all and not using them all."

"Okay, a half hour."

"Now you're really going overboard with the generosity thing. You're killing me with it."

"Enjoy it while you can."

***

In the morning, Brian loaded the plane on the runway. When he was done, he had her and all her things on the plane.

"You come with a lot of baggage, don't you?" Brian said, pushing the last of it through the hatch. It took several trips to get it all to the plane. "You're going far away; but with any luck, we'll find a nicer place than this one."

He saw nothing else to do, other than move her.

He got everything situated and started the motors.

"You're a lucky one, being the wee little thing you are, and already flying on the big plane a second time."

Brian took off, and once the autopilot was set, grabbed his laptop to read emails. On the rest of the flight, he had prepared for the trip; and once with her, had no opportunity.

It seemed as if he had composed the email forever; but reluctantly, and feeling like an idiot, he let Space Station Brian know he had duped the kid.

The reply should be in this batch. He had tried hard to capture accurately, without placing blame, what had taken place.

No surprise, it was there. "Haven't you learned anything?" Brian laughed out-loud. It was precisely what he thought when he had to delete the file at the Space Center during the middle of the day. The email was nonjudgmental in its nature; and Brian was relieved he had broken the news.

In the next email, the Space Station announced he would shut down and reboot the system. When he did, it would cause a complete loss of communication with the remaining spaceships. This would be cause for great concern at the Space Center, and likely raise a stir. He was sure to hear about it. They wouldn't know what was going on. "And if it doesn't come back up, you'll know I couldn't get it to work. If that happens, this will be my last transmission."

He said he planned to proceed at once.

Brian breathed in deep and read on. Space Station Brian was messing with four centuries of work, the hope of man. 'Unless there are underlying problems this should work. When I bring it back online, the Space Center will have communication with all the spaceships.'

He hadn't given any specific time; but it was possible he had already pulled the plug. Ivan was responsible for the space program; he would be pulling his hair out.

The baby began to fuss. Brian used his foot and gently rocked her holder on the grating. He continued to read while he rocked her. It didn't help and she began to cry. Bending over, he pulled her from the holder. She quieted.

"I just fed you before we left." After a quick finger check between her and the diaper, "You're dry. You know what, you're becoming a pest."

Brian nestled her into his lap.

"Look, now there's no room for the laptop. You're so blasted cute, but don't think for a moment I won't leave you on Pete's porch."

The rash was going away. Pete had told him to use a powder instead of ointment; and that it might be necessary to alternate between the two.

There was barely room for the laptop, but he wanted to continue reading. Balancing it, he rearranged her. She flexed, as if falling, and hit him on the side of the head with her hand.

"I can tell already this is going to be an adventure."

Chapter Twenty-One

At their destination Brian double-checked the coordinates on the remote to confirm they had arrived. There was nothing below them but trees.

He began to circle, getting out his binoculars.

Haphazardly he checked the area not quite certain how to identify what he was looking for. The trees were tall, the canopy thick. After ten minutes, he began a more systematic search, and then expanded the area covered.

A half hour later, in the distance among the trees, he caught reflections of something shiny. Unsurprisingly, it was back at where he'd started. He took the plane lower and returned. As he did this, he caught more reflections dispersed among the trees. The angle the sun had reached showed him where the stuff was at.

"That's got to be it. Hopefully, that's our aluminum, kiddo, but I haven't seen a place to land."

She was sound asleep; had been for quite some time.

Brian continued to look through the binoculars, but when the sun was no longer at the right angle, he saw nothing but trees once again.

"What kind of place is this? It's so overgrown. If I can't find a place to land, what good is it? We might as well head back."

Discouraged by the prospect, he began to hodgepodge it again, already knowing there was nothing available. He had seen enough to know only one spot could have worked, except for one very large tree. "Remove the tree and clean it up and that spot would be ideal," he said, surveying it again.

Twenty minutes later he gave up, "What a waste," and set coordinates for the old airport. He would take her back. As the plane climbed he continued to search.

Six and a half minutes away, a road caught his attention when they were perpendicular to it. He seized the remote. It wasn't close to where he wanted to be, but it was the first thing to present a possibility.

Brian lined up at one end, and checked his air speed. He timed the length; it was more than enough. The foliage however, was tight; and with no intention of landing, he made a second pass slightly below treetop level concentrating on the open space against the wing span.

Even after the second pass, he still wasn't sure if he should land, and pulled up going around making a third pass.

On the third pass, he went lower than before. Halfway through, shuddering, the plane pulled to the left, shaved a few trees, and made a terrible racket.

The noise changed as Brian pulled it back straight. "That's got to be a bearing, I don't think I hit the trees first," he told her, pulling up. The plane responded. His adrenalin pumped. The noise changed to a beating sound, and then changed again to a rattle.

Once they were above the trees, the noise stopped, and the plane became sluggish.

Brian keyed the mode button on the remote; changing to diagnostics. The display blinked a red square over the number three motor. It had quit.

"The plane's broke, kiddo."

He decided to land. He knew he'd catch foliage with the tips of the wing, but he hadn't seen anything major that would damage the plane.

"We don't have time for breakdowns." If he flew back to the Installation for repairs, it meant a prolonged absence from her.

"You're missing out on all the excitement," he said, gazing down at her for a moment, letting her know what they were doing; though through it all, she continued to sleep. "Must be nice not to have a care in the world."

Taut at the controls, Brian circled and descended down to the road. As they touched down, and until they stopped, he caught foliage.

"Gary would wet his pants." He shut the motors off. Astonishingly, once he shut it down, the kid stirred.

She began to cry.

"Glad you could join us. But you'll have to stay put and guard the plane for me." Brian said, trying to soothe her. He figured it didn't matter what he said to her. Although, just as if she understood, it didn't help. He found the pacifier and stuck it in her mouth. "Bad timing; I have to go see what happened." He let go of the pacifier. She hadn't latched on and it fell between her and her holder. "Great, you'll just have to cry this one off."

Brian went to the hatch. Climbing down, he became weary. He couldn't see into the foliage; and stopped. It would hide a lurking predator giving him no time to react.

For the first time, he realized if he died out here, she would too. He had to be careful. He wouldn't be able to protect himself under such close quarters.

He pulled the pepper spray, deciding to set the warning system first. He saw in his haste, he forgot to close the hatch. He climbed up, peeked in. "You can stop anytime," he told her, pulling the hatch shut and securing it.

When he made it to the ground, instead of setting up the warning system, he walked under the number three motor. He was sure he had scared off anything close by during the landing. He saw the problem right away; there was a length of wire dangling from the propeller. It had wound itself around and pulled up under the base of the cone.

He knew he caught the wire on the second pass. There was damage to the skin on both the number two and number four motor housings. If he brought it back for repairs like this, it would leave him open to questions about what he had been doing. Gary might say something to Ivan.

Brian grabbed the dangling end and pulled. Securely in place, it didn't budge.

Though now muffled, he could hear her continue to throw a fit. She wasn't happy and was letting him know.

Brian gripped the pepper spray with his mouth, wrapped the wire around his left hand, got a good grip with his right and pulled. He lifted himself from the ground.

Just then, he heard a rustle in the bush. Quickly, he let go, landing on his feet with the pepper spray aimed. He heard it again; this time he saw the leaves move. It was just the wind…he needed to set the warning system. She still cried.

Brian went around to the other half of the wing and went under to the compartment with the warning system. He got it out and set it up.

When done, the pepper spray went into his pocket.

Still crying, she had long since passed annoying.

Frustrated, he climbed the ladder.

"Give it a rest, will you." Brian yelled while opening the hatch. "I can only do one thing at a time." At hearing his voice, she cried harder.

Upset, he crossed over the grating quickly.

"Okay, okay, I'm right here. When I'm busy with something else, you're going to have to figure out it's time to be quiet."

He picked her up, and his anger dissipated at once.

"You little snot, you can tell I'm not happy with you, can't you?" He couldn't help but sooth her. "I'm sorry; I didn't mean to make you wait. You just need a little care, and you know I'm supposed to provide it."

Accepting this fate, he started to change her.

"…I wasn't mad at you, anyway. I'm mad because I broke our plane. I don't have time to spend on it. We have to find you a place to stay. Then there's all your stuff, and I need to go get Gary in the morning and bring him here so he can collect aluminum and you see how far away we parked from the aluminum."

He knew he was carrying her understanding a bit too far as he prepared her formula. But she enjoyed the attention whether she understood everything or not.

"Do you think I can get that done today? If you stay in your carrier, I might." Brian put her back in the holder and stuffed a blanket in on one side of her head. He manipulated the blanket to hold the bottle. "There, now I have work to do, you leave me alone."

Brian went out, got a pair of nippers and the stepladder. Because the wire had wound many times and so tight around the shaft, it had bunched and pulled into practically one smooth piece. He couldn't get the nippers around any of it to cut it free.

Brian tried to remove the cone. It too wouldn't budge. The wire had jammed up under it.

The longer he worked, the more tools he had lying around.

Much later he completed the repair. He went into the can at dusk knowing Gary just got an extra day to clear the shelves of plane parts.

***

In the morning, Brian proceeded north to locate the reflections he had seen from the air.

He debated whether to bring her, saving time; but there was no telling what he'd run into, and being unfamiliar with the lay of the land, he left her safely on the plane.

In his backpack, he carried most of her supplies. It would be fewer things to carry later if he found what he was looking for.

He brought a compass to ensure he stayed on track.

The forest canopy was high above him. It was thick and left the ground he traversed mostly free of any thick undergrowth.

Three hours later, he didn't know if he was hopelessly lost or still on track to locate the reflections.

Based on the time he'd flown before seeing the road the aluminum should be five to seven miles away.

Everything he encountered looked the same; the hills, the trees, although everything was different with its configuration, shape, and placement. Brian looked back often, picking out landmarks.

In less than three hours he ran into some thick undergrowth, which slowed him considerably.

He broke out into a small clearing. There was one very large tree standing in the center. He was sure it was the same place he had seen from the air. It looked small and needed much more work than his assessment from the air.

With the amount of time it took to walk, he already knew he would spend another night. If Gary finished the parts on the shelves...he'd get that day off he was looking for.

Brian crossed the clearing, knowing he was close to the reflections. It wouldn't be long and he would find out what they were.

He hit thick underbrush on the opposite side, mentally assigning time to the tasks that needed to be done to clear a swath for the plane to land. Without the plane and the chainsaw it held, he had to come up with a means to take down the tree. He knew no matter what he came up with, it would be faster than hauling the aluminum back to where the plane sat now.

He spotted the first reflection when he cleared the underbrush, and then another as he got closer. There were yet more beyond them.

He stopped and studied the first one. A weird design, it had no propellers, but a large, elongated body leading back to smaller wings that supported a fin. It looked nothing like what he flew.

"Strange looking things...and they sure are ugly. All those reflections, there must be hundreds of them." He got out his testing kit.

Impossible to land with all the trees, he decided there couldn't have been any trees when they were landed and parked.

He hadn't seen a building yet and this concerned him. She needed a place to stay, something secure. After confirming it was aluminum, he kept going.

The old planes were interspersed among the trees all over the place.

He walked for hours and never found a building she could stay in.

***

Brian bent over. He kissed her on the forehead.

"It's time for me to go, kiddo. I'll see you later. Don't worry, okay." Brian clicked off the lantern.

Slowly, so as not to wake her, he opened the door. It was still dark.

He ended up using one of the old planes for her shelter, where he had just spent part of the night with her. He never located any suitable structures for her, and had given-up searching. It was a three-hour walk back to get her and another three bringing her here. It only made sense to make do with what was available.

It would be no less then sixteen to seventeen hours before he returned.

Brian tied several bottles to her holder. A couple more, he had suspended above her.

They were close enough she could get her mouth around any of them. That might only happen by accident, but in twelve hours, she could accidentally do it several times.

This would be the longest stretch yet she would be by herself. He didn't like it. She required constant care.

He was concerned too, because in the very early hours, he'd heard something sniffing around outside. He had looked out the many windows, but they were too dirty to see anything, and with no moon, he couldn't spot what it was. He hadn't heard it since and wished he knew what had been out there.

For his own safety, he didn't want to make the walk in the dark. But he had kept her up until late, hoping she'd sleep a good portion of the time he was gone. He would get his sleep on the ride back.

The pepper spray was out and ready. He assured himself this was a safe place for her to stay as he closed the door behind him.

***

Because Brian had an early start, he landed at One-O-Seven late morning.

Gary came running out of the hangar as he taxied up. Brian was relieved to see him. One less worry; he didn't have to waste time finding him and decided then he could dupe a load of plane parts.

While Brian was still shutting the plane down, Gary opened the hatch.

"Chief, did you hear the news?"

"What news?"

"About the spaceships."

"What about them?" It had been rolling around in the back of his mind, but had never risen to a conscious level once he'd left.

"We've lost communication with all them, Chief," Gary said, concerned. "Ivan's doing everything he can to reestablish contact. But everyone's worried. It's all they talk about."

"Really!" He wanted to stay above suspicion. "When did this happen?"

"Early yesterday."

"Nothing more today?"

"Not that I've heard, but they said they were going to work on it through the night at the Space Center."

Space Station Brian didn't say how long he anticipated it would take to complete that whole process. But turning off and restarting a terminal didn't take all day. He should have it back up and running by now.

"All those years of work and Ivan lost it on his watch," Brian said. It felt good to get that dig in on Ivan. But at the same time, he hoped Brian at the Space Station knew what he was doing; he needed to check his emails, see what he said.

"Yeah, and there's even talk of replacing Ivan."

"Is that right?"

"Yes. If we never get it back, all that work will be lost…it'll all be for nothing. Ivan's head will roll."

Brian was glad no one knew he was at the bottom of it. Ivan would just be getting what he deserved.

"We need to get supplies," he said, changing the subject, "and more plane parts." Brian got out of his seat. "We're leaving for a few days."

"We're leaving? Now? What about the ships?"

Even though he wasn't totally sure, and if he didn't need to stay above suspicion, Brian would have assured Gary it would only be a matter of time and they were going to have communication with all the ships.

"I'm sure Ivan and his staff have it under control." He went down the ladder leading the way.

"I'm glad you think so. No one else does."

Brian couldn't assure him further, and headed for the carts. They were parked side by side in front of the hangar.

"Follow me in the other cart," Brian told him.

"Aren't you going to check on what I've done?"

"Are you out of parts?"

"No."

"It's been two and a half days, Gary. You should be."

"But Chief, the spaceships."

"That news should not interfere with your work." Brian climbed into the new cart, and backed up. Gary backed the other almost in unison. Brian jammed it forward without coming to a stop and floored it. "I'll see it when we're back."

They raced to the Dupe.

Brian held his laptop under a butt cheek to keep it from bouncing out.

At the Dupe, he filled the platform with supplies telling Gary to put the stuff in his cart. On the heels of that, he then did a load of plane parts.

When done, he walked out to the carts, which Gary was in the process of loading his.

"Look, Gary, I need a shower in the worst way. Don't leave anything in the cafeteria. Put the supplies on the plane. Plane parts go on the shelves. You do have room, don't you?"

"Chief, what do you think?"

"I'm just checking. Now make sure you're waiting for me when I get back to the hangar." Brian wanted to ensure there were no delays. He was in a hurry to return.

At home, Brian's routine was down pat. Hooking his laptop to the terminal, he started them both. He hurried to the bathroom and started the shower.

He ran back to the terminal and initiated the macro to perform email downloads. It would send his composed emails as well.

Feeling pressed for time, he undressed on the way back to the shower, dropping a line of clothes leading there. He quickly jumped in, soaped down, rinsed and jumped back out drying as he did so.

He put the same clothes on, which were in the order he needed them, taking him back to the terminal. They were fresh; he'd put them on this morning during the flight back taking them fresh from the packages the Dupe supplied.

Displayed at the top, he saw an email from Pete.

"No time today, buddy, but you'll get your ride."

Next, and happy to see them, a couple from the Space Station; he hoped they would supply more insight into Brian's progress with the reboot. There was one from Ivan and another from Don.

"I wonder what Ivan's problem is?"

He shut everything down, folded the laptop and ran to the cart wishing he were back with her. She was probably crying, but he eased his concern picturing her peacefully asleep.

He flew to the hangar. Gary was inside unloading the cart.

"Did you get everything?"

"That's the last of it on the cart."

"Gary, this is looking good. It's better organized," Brian complimented him after a cursory look. With Gary replenishing the shelves before he saw them, he wouldn't be able to tell how empty they were. "You can finish putting that stuff away when we get back. Let's go; you're flying today."

"Chief, aren't you worried about the communication problem with the Space Station?"

"Yes, as a matter of fact I am," Brian said, "but hanging around here waiting to see what happens won't change the outcome; let's go."

Gary could never imagine Brian's worries. They were on a completely different level. Even a very long explanation would be unbelievable. Even though Brian wanted to stay and get the latest as it happened, he needed more to return to her.

Once on the plane they took off.

***

Brian ensured Gary understood he had to take it easy with the plane before handing over the remote. Henry had done the same with him, and now he understood why.

After a couple of hours of instruction with Gary at the controls, Brian made him set the autopilot.

Eager to read his emails he had patiently waited giving Gary his lesson.

"If you want any sleep, now's the time to get it," Brian said.

"After that, you expect me to sleep?" Gary scoffed.

"When we get there, I'm putting you to work," Brian said. "Just roll your sleeping bag out next to the dynamite and get comfortable. Even if you don't sleep, you'll still rest. It's up to you, but I don't want to hear any complaining you're tired when the work starts."

"I'll lay down," Gary said, "but I won't sleep."

While Gary prepared a spot, Brian opened his laptop and turned it on. He dreaded having to open Ivan's email, and opened the first one from Brian at the Space Station instead.

A strange feeling overcame him when he read it. What he received amazed him. Unfamiliar with the equipment on the Space Station, he couldn't follow along as he read through it.

It listed a procedure for what he was attempting to do to correct the date problem with the operating system. It was quite elaborate and it impressed him that he was able to figure this all out.

What amazed him the most and made him feel so strange, was that it was his brain doing the work here and he didn't have a clue what was being referred to.

Brian knew if given the chance, he would; but right then, it was just strange.

The email stated the procedure would take approximately three hours. He wondered what had gone wrong.

After that, Brian at the Space Station said if his attempt didn't succeed, then Brian needed to come back to the Space Station wearing a spacesuit.

The email went on and gave two other methods to reboot the system.

Trying to figure it out drained him. He needed to come back to it later, become very familiar with it, in case he had failed.

Curious as to what Don had sent him, he opened his next.

"Stop making parts," he said under his breath as he read it. "It's a little late for that; I just did a load."

"What?" Gary unexpectedly asked.

"Nothing, I was reading out loud."

"Oh."

Don explained that they were running low on copper and until Brian could bring some in, he needed to hold off.

Brian thought the maps were at the house. He knew he didn't have them on the plane. He decided then to make an additional copy, and carry a set with him. If he had them now, he could plan ahead and avoid any interruption in the flow of parts.

He knew there was a place to procure copper close to where she was. Without the maps, he wouldn't know how to get there. That alone meant a delay.

He opened the email from Pete next. He was looking to tie Brian down to a date and time he could give Mark a ride. Besieged, he wanted something to satisfy the little bugger for a while. Brian didn't know how to respond. He would have to wait.

The other Space Station email had been sent just before pulling the plug; it was stranger than the first. It asked that Brian communicate more often with him when the system was back on line. Space Station Brian threatened to spill the beans to Ivan about everything if he didn't do so. "I'm sure Ivan will be more than appreciative of the information on how to board the spaceships with his memory intact. He might even come see you about the female."

Brian stopped reading and contemplated this for a long time. This was his brain at work as well. He'd have to do more than offer support.

He had deferred Ivan's email until last.

A general issue going to everyone, it stated there had been a breakdown in communications with the Space Station resulting in a loss of contact with the spaceships. He would keep everyone posted with additional news as it became available.

Brian sighed; glad that's all it was as he listened to Gary snoring behind him.

Chapter Twenty-Two

"Gary, we're almost there. Get up," Brian called over his shoulder.

He had to call a second time before Gary took his seat. "I told you I wouldn't be able to sleep," Gary said.

"Um hum." Preoccupied, he was antsy this close to her. "I was up here yesterday scouting around. You brought your pepper spray?"

"Sure thing." Gary got it out to show him.

"There's a little hike ahead of us. I couldn't find anywhere to land close to the aluminum. But there's a spot we're going to clear so we can land there. It'll be tough, there's a bit of work, but that will put us where we need to be. You'll see what I mean." By then, he was descending into the trees.

"You're not landing here?"

"Why not?" Brian smiled, completing the flyover. The poor man just woke up.

"You'll hit the trees; that's why."

"I know; I did that yesterday too." Brian turned, lined up, and went straight down to the road. "But we can land," he said, easing the plane in.

White-knuckled, Gary held his seat.

The hike was still ahead of them, and Brian had yet to cover with him what to do when they got there. Once on the ground, with no time to waste Brian pulled the last strap tight on his backpack and handed Gary one of the shovels. He began at a brisk pace.

It didn't take long for the shower he took to seem like it never happened. Working up a sweat, Gary began to complain. Brian thought he should get his earplugs out, make a big show of putting them in, but the hint would be wasted.

There were a few creeks to cross. At one, no wider than a large step, Gary misjudged, ending up with one foot in the shallow water. As they continued, his shoe began to squeak. It became just as annoying as Gary.

"What did you put in these backpacks?" Gary asked, an hour into the trip. "They're heavy."

"Food for me; you did bring something for yourself, didn't you? Because yours is full of dynamite."

"That's funny, Chief. I suppose now you're going to tell me we're hopelessly lost."

"Hopelessly? I don't recall saying that out loud. Besides, I don't think you're hopeless all the time."

Off and on, these exchanges continued until they arrived. Gary undid his backpack; it fell to the ground. He sat on it. Brian undid his, and untied the pruning shears from the side of it. He showed Gary where to start.

"…and haul everything to the edge. I'm going to scout around."

"I thought you did that yesterday."

"I didn't finish."

"See you when you get back." Gary seemed unconcerned. It made Brian feel as though he needed to stay and supervise. Until now, Gary had done all right when left alone. The hike had worn him out. He looked tired.

"I won't be long; get something done." Brian handed him an additional pepper spray. "And keep an eye out for yourself."

Once he was through the thick undergrowth, He took off running. When he was closer, he returned to a walk and caught his breath. He had chosen a plane located away from where they would be working; but it was closer than he wanted her to be but his was one of the better planes he'd seen.

Brian climbed into the plane and found her as he'd imagined, peacefully asleep. He was sure that hadn't always been the case.

The bottles suspended above her were empty. Her face was dirty where formula had dripped. The bottles tied to the side of the carrier were mostly full.

Brian gently removed her from the carrier. The back of her neck and clothes were crusted with dried formula. She made a funny face as he moved her and began to suckle, as if hungry.

"I'll have something for you in a moment." Brian carried her the short distance to the supplies.

He washed her head; she began to cry. "Look at this; I'm waking you instead of the other way around. Are you hungry?" He removed her clothes and cleaned her neck. "You need a bath."

When the formula was ready, Brian laid her on the floor and held the bottle using his free hand to change her.

"Poor thing…." The diaper was full, and overly soaked. The rash had returned. "You haven't had one of those in a while." Brian worried. She had endured too long without care. Over the next several weeks, it would be nothing but more of the same. He would have to figure out a way to change that. The only foreseeable decrease in time was getting the plane close to the aluminum.

He held her close. She hadn't opened her eyes as of yet, but continued to suckle. "You didn't get anything, did you? It all dripped out."

When the bottle was gone, Brian held her. "You're being so good. Sorry I left you so long." She gave her customary burp. He gave her a little squeeze, letting her know he cared deeply.

"You know I'm glad to see you." He set her down and she began to whimper. "Sorry, but I have to go help Gary, or you'll run out of supplies. We can't let that happen now, can we?" He gave her the pacifier.

He opened the door and half expected to see Gary waiting for him. Gary could easily have followed. Brian hadn't considered this until that moment. In the future, he would keep Gary's whereabouts on a conscious level when he left him to come to her.

There was no image in his mind ever explaining this to Gary; it made him wonder how Gary would react if *'female'* should ever escape his lips.

Brian himself was still coming to terms with this incredible find. Found at the Space Station, no less. He could have spent an entire lifetime on Henry's paradox and never had a clue.

When he returned to the clearing, Gary was busy clipping away. When Brian saw how he was going about it, he became frustrated. Everything lay where he had cut it.

"Give me those." Brian took the shears and punched the tip into the ground at the base of the growth. He pulled them together, cutting it off just below the ground. "That's how it needs to be done."

"You'll wreck the cutting edge doing it that way."

"You can't leave six-inch spikes sticking out of the ground. They'll blow the tires on the plane."

"I was going to dig them out."

"That'll take ten times longer."

"You won't get far once you've wrecked the shears."

"I'll dupe more."

"I thought you wanted to get it done."

"Go cut the tree down. I'll do this."

Brian relieved his frustration clipping away. Twenty minutes into it, the shears were getting dull. Gary was sitting under the tree doing nothing. With brute force, Brian made another cut on the largest root he had attempted yet. They were getting nowhere; not even a dent. Brian went to join Gary.

"Chief, this sucker is big. It'll take me a year to cut it up and move it."

"Maybe for you; I could have it done in the time you'd waste sitting there."

"I needed to rest."

"I do too, so let's eat. That way we won't be wasting time."

***

Two hours went by.

"That's enough, Gary. You can't use it all."

"We've got more on the plane."

"You're going back to get it."

"Not tonight, it'll be dark soon."

"So hurry up."

Gary had the dynamite packed into a notch they had cut out of the tree. Both of them had taken turns with the axe cutting the notch. It was a fourth of the way into the tree. Gary was wiring the last stick into place.

"Okay, it's set." They ran away, Gary giggling. "I can't wait to see what this does."

Once through the thick underbrush, they kept going.

"How far will that transmitter work?" Brian asked.

"How should I know? I only read enough to use it," Gary admitted. "Is that the aluminum?" He was pointing to one of the old planes.

"Yes."

"Is it a plane?"

"It looks like an old one to me. So yes, I'd say so."

"That doesn't look like it would fly." They came to a tree, every bit as big as the one they were blowing. "This'll do, Chief."

"Don't forget your earplugs." They positioned themselves behind it.

When ready, Gary began the countdown. Five, four.... Brian bent his knees; cupped his hands over his ears. Gary had said it was ten times what he had used on the steel.

An intense flash. The ground shook.

Huge chunks of wood flew by, snapping what they hit.

Gary was in awe of the power he'd unleashed.

Then it happened. Pieces began to rain from the sky. Brian could hear chunks pinging off the old planes. The baby...! A large piece came through the branches and landed next to them. Brian aligned himself under a very large branch and hugged the tree.

"I told you, you didn't need that much."

Three minutes later, they still heard pieces traveling through the leaves dropping to the ground. Brian longed to run to her.

"Let's go see, Chief," Gary said.

"It's not safe yet," Brian told him. "We'll wait."

"How much longer?"

"Until it's safe."

They waited until they hadn't heard anything for quite some time before making their way to the clearing.

"Look at that, Chief. There are paths clean through the underbrush."

Brian could see into the open space through them. He moved his head, changing his line of sight, trying to locate the tree, but it was getting dark, and maybe because it was getting dark he couldn't see it. When they reached the clearing, the tree was completely gone.

"Impressive," Brian said, satisfied. "You just saved yourself a year's worth of work."

They walked out and found a hole where the tree had once stood.

"I think I overdid it," Gary observed with a chuckle.

"You finally figured that out. Guess what's next?"

"Fill in the hole?"

"You're on a roll. Although that'll be tomorrow," Brian said.

"That's fine by me."

"Pick a plane, Gary, any plane; and it's yours for the night. You will be sleeping alone."

"You're not sleeping out here, are you?"

"And you were doing so well."

***

Brian went to her, passing torn foliage along the way. He hurried, and as he approached, he inspected the plane. There was one large dent. Up close, it was the only one. There was a jagged chunk of wood lying on the ground. Thankful that the damage was minor, he went inside. He found it darker. She was fussing. He had expected much worse after what they had done.

"Hey, I wasn't gone very long."

He kept the lantern off and took care of her needs in the waning light. Gary might spot a light and come like a moth. By the time he was done with her, it was completely dark. He removed his shoes and lay on the floor. He kept her with him.

"We'll give you a bath in the morning, okay?"

Restless, he tried to sleep. He kept thinking of how much there was yet to do before they could get the plane. He tried to clear his mind and rest. It didn't help that she kept kicking her legs, moving her arms.

"Do you want to burp?" Brian sat up, picking her up in the process. It always calmed her when she did so.

He patted her on the back and got more than a burp; it wasn't just a little.

In the dark, he gave her a bath, and after he cleaned and replaced everything on her with new, they lay together on the floor again. It had taken nearly two hours to do everything in the dark. Later, when she slept, he opened the door and left.

Brian's eyes, which had adjusted to the pitch black inside of the plane, found it a little lighter and easier to see outside. He made his way to the tree they had used for cover and picked up the pruning shears. An owl was hooting nearby.

He walked out into the clearing, where it became much lighter. It was a clear night and the stars seemed close enough to touch. A light breeze blew the tall grass in the clearing.

As he made his way to where he had been working, he stumbled over a piece of wood hidden in the grass. He was sure the clearing was full of them. It added yet another chore. The open area would have to be 'weed-whacked' in order to locate and remove them. When he got to where he had left off earlier, he bent over and began cutting. When he had no more than an armful, he gathered it up and carried it to the edge.

He returned intending to continue cutting, but spent time looking at what he had done. Compared to what they needed to do, it was simply pitiful. The spot Gary had attempted was a mess. They'd still be a year doing what needed to be done.

He collected dried grass, placing the base of the stalks together. Once he had a hand full, he reached into his pocket for the lighter. A shooting star caught his attention as it shot across the sky. Holding the stalks at a forty-five degree angle, he lit the ends.

Fire quickly consumed the stalks.

He touched his homemade torch to the grass around him. It caught quickly. Brian walked with his dwindling torch to the ground starting the grass as he went. It spread, grew tall, and became hot. Brian dropped what remained of his torch and fled the heat.

He turned to watch. The fire threw off a surprising amount of light; it continued to get brighter as it spread.

In wonder, he saw that the breeze moved the fire in the direction it blew.

Once the fire reached the thick growth along the edge leading back to the old planes, it towered into the air. Unbelievably quick, it spewed sparks into the forest canopy above, catching it on fire.

In panic, not knowing it would be so fierce, he ducked into the thick underbrush behind him and began to circle the fire back to her. He needed to get there before it did. Gary! He needed to get him too; but after waking him, he wouldn't be able to get rid of him to save her. At that point, Brian decided it didn't matter.

The light from the fire cast an eerie shadow around him as he made his way through the underbrush; able to see, he broke free, and ran through the forest.

As Brian made the turn skirting the open area, he knew Gary was closer than she was. He would get him first.

After he made the turn, he could see the fire wasn't advancing into the forest much past the edge of where the underbrush stopped.

He stood and watched. Although there were pieces of burning embers dropping to the ground from the canopy above, the fire below no longer raged. As it died down, the flames above extinguished to glowing embers. The embers threw off smoke and began to fade.

Brian walked the edge and was amazed by how quickly and completely the underbrush had burned away. He kept checking above him to ensure the fire wasn't advancing anywhere into the forest along the way.

When he reached the opposite end of the clearing from where he had started the fire, it had encroached into the forest. The flames raged well into the canopy. Embers showered to the ground. The wind pushed it, keeping it alive.

Brian wanted to put his arms above his head and run through the dropping embers to check the other side. He knew how hot it burned; headed away from the planes, he turned and rechecked their side of the forest again to ensure he didn't need to evacuate them.

He understood now why the Installations maintained the clearing around the fence; it would stop a fire. He needed to check his timetable, spraying the growth retardant was probably past due.

As the sun rose, Brian shoveled ash and dirt into the hole. Dispersed columns of smoke continued to rise all around him. He smelled like smoke; soot and ash covered his shoes and the bottom of his pants. Dead tired, he continued to push. Only the hole remained. He had made progress on it, but it was big. Using the shovel, he skimmed it across the top of the earth to collect a shaving of dirt, which he then carried to the hole. A thick column of smoke filled the sky off in the distances to the east where the fire still raged.

He spotted Gary standing at the edge watching. When he looked again, Gary was gone. The next time he saw him, Gary was walking out carrying the other shovel.

"Chief, it's taking shape," Gary said, in total wonder. "Smart. That was the way to clear it."

"Only the hole is left and if you hadn't...."

"Take a break, Chief, I'll get it. I can't believe you stayed out here last night. I would have been scared to death," Gary said, in total admiration.

Brian took him up on the offer; he needed to check the baby and catch a nap and he was dying of thirst. He walked away knowing it would take them longer to fill the hole than anything else they had done; and it wasn't even on the agenda to begin with.

He checked making sure Gary didn't follow.

***

Four hours later Brian returned. There was still smoke in the distance.

Gary was using the head of the axe, stomping the head of it on the ground, compacting the dirt in the hole. It was almost ready.

"It's soft, Chief. The plane will sink when it hits this."

"Keep packing." Brian got his shovel. As he gripped the handle, his palms ached where they touched it. His fingers were stiff and sore from handling it most of the night...

"Hey, Chief, go get the plane. I'll finish this. It'll be ready before you're back."

"I was thinking you should go set the first charge and I'll finish this. We need to get the can loaded today, even if we have to work on it through the night."

"Chief, I can have this done, one plane blown and the aluminum sitting out here before you're back with the plane."

"Okay, this I'll have to see." Brian reached into his pocket and took out the remote. He unfolded it and started the plane. "You better hurry. You've got less than ten minutes."

"The remote reaches that far?"

"You bet."

* * *

"Gary, when we land, just throw this load out onto the tarmac and then go get a shower. We're going back as soon as we can."

"I'm going to find out what happened to the Space Station first."

"No, I'll find that out and let you know."

"It'll only take a second."

"Precisely, and that's why I'll let you know. You won't have a second to spare."

"Why the rush?"

Caught off guard, Brian didn't know how to answer. He finished setting the approach and then turned to Gary looking him square in the eyes.

"I'm running the show here, Gary. You're the apprentice. Remember that." Gary looked away. "You got it?"

"Sure, Chief."

"I'll find out, get a shower myself and more supplies. You'll need to be quick to get everything done before I'm back. I expect you to be waiting on the plane. It doesn't matter if you wait all day on me. Just don't make me wait a second for you. Understand?"

"Yes."

"And don't forget, not a word to anyone about the fire."

* * *

As Brian walked to the cart, Gary was inside the can fuming. Demonstrating forcefully, he banged stuff around; aluminum flew out onto the tarmac, accompanied by an ongoing tirade from inside. Brian decided it was no skin off his nose; Gary would get it done, and quickly.

He left, headed for the office. He had to have the maps. He wished, though, he hadn't resorted to intimidation. Gary hadn't been obstinate; he was concerned. It was the question Brian wasn't prepared to answer that started it.

Although moving away from her, the fire only served to increase his sense of urgency.

At the office, he searched for the maps; they weren't there.

He took off for home. Maybe they were sitting on the desk after all; he hadn't really looked. When he got there, a quick glance of the desk proved they weren't there.

"Where did I use those last?"

Brian started the routine; he would find them before he left.

After the shower, he toweled dry in front of the terminal, checking it for emails from the Space Station. There was nothing, save one from Don. A three-hour task for the space station was now into its fifth day.

"I'll have to get a spacesuit and start over. What went wrong, buddy?"

His composed emails had already gone. In one, he congratulated the Space Station for resetting the time and rebooting successfully. It didn't matter whether he sent them or not. If he wasn't successful, he would never see them.

Brian searched for the maps, trying to remember the last time he'd had them in his hands. Nothing else came to mind but his desk. They have been there.

Nevertheless, he looked in the bedroom. It was the only other room besides the bathroom, which he had been in over the last five days. They weren't there either. Back at the terminal, he pulled up the directory Don had used and initiated another copy. Instead of just waiting while they printed, he made use of the time by opening and reading Don's email. He dressed at the same time.

Very seriously, Don reiterated he had to stop on the plane, and bring copper; he let Brian know if he couldn't do this on his own, he would involve Ivan.

Brian began to sweat. He needed to go see Don right away. This was a breach of trust for which Ivan would dismiss him as head of security. He didn't have time for this. Being able to land near the aluminum knocked well over six hours off the time they'd be gone, it was still to long for her, and these guys' were trying to chew up more time than he just saved.

While Brian disconnected the laptop, he realized the maps were the second thing that had come up missing. He wondered if someone had been in the place and went back into the bedroom. He checked behind the headboard. The memory units were there.

He couldn't imagine, but if someone had been in the place, and returned to do a thorough job of searching, the memory units would yield the secret behind the memory duping process. Although Ivan would resort to this sort of thing, he was too busy. Could it have been the man in the shadows at the Space Center? Had Ivan sent him?

Brian pulled the memory units out of the headboard and placed them into the cart. He went back in and taped a piece of his hair above the door. It would take too long to return with string.

On his way to the Dupe, he became concerned about Gary. It might not take much of a nudge for him to run tell Ivan everything they had been up to. Brian regretted treating him so poorly.

As he headed for the Dupe to see Don, he tried to come up with another place to store the memory units. As he parked, his mind raced. He ran upstairs; Don was sitting at his desk eating; didn't he ever work?

"Brian, I've been trying to reach you."

"I know, sir. Sorry I did more parts, but I didn't see your email right away."

"I figured it had to be something like that. In any case, you have the copper?"

"No, in a few days, though."

"We're at a critical level, Brian. I informed Ivan of how serious it is. I didn't want to burden him; he has enough to deal with. The Space Station has kept him up for the past five days. To keep him abreast of the situation I told him you were taking care of it already."

"I'll see what I can do to get it sooner."

"Is that what you want me to relay to Ivan?"

"I'll have it tomorrow."

"You don't understand, Brian. To conserve, we've already blocked copper content from being duped."

"Yes, I do understand. You need it today."

"Ivan said you would cooperate fully."

"You'll have it today."

"Brian, that's what I needed to hear."

Chapter Twenty-three

In a hurry, Brian stopped downstairs for supplies. When the doors opened, many of his selections were missing. Don had blocked even trace amounts of copper. Wrought with the pressure to procure copper, there wasn't time to see what he did or didn't get; except for her new holder. She *needed* it, and it wasn't there.

Next, he brought up the search function and keyed in spacesuits. As they displayed, a hand squeezed his shoulder with a knowing grip.

Brian pulled away and was surprised at who he saw.

"Danny! I didn't see you come in."

"I'm at the table over there with Adam. I saw you come down from upstairs. It's Chief now, is it?"

"I suppose."

"So how's it going?"

"It goes." A myriad of feelings surfaced.

"I can call you Chief, right?"

"Sure."

"Chief sounds so official."

"I know. It does, doesn't it?"

"You're lucky. But you always were. I won't get a promotion. There are too many people ahead of me for Sandy's position. And he's such a grisly old cog; he'll outlive everyone down there."

"That's too bad." It was all Brian could do to keep his composure. There were so many things he wanted to say. It would be so easy to pick up where he had left off, *running* to tell Danny everything....

"I've seen you buzzing around in that cart when I'm riding the shuttle. That has to be a riot. You always blow right on past. You'll have to let me take it for a spin sometime."

"Sure."

"Hey, why don't you come join us?"

"Yes—No! I mean, I can't. I would, but I can't."

"Keeping you busy are they, or are you still jealous of Adam?"

"*Danny!*" All along, at the forefront, he stayed focused on the problem at hand; resolve the copper issue, return to her.

"It's okay, Brian, I understand."

"You can't understand, Danny. You could have, you should have."

"What's that supposed to mean?"

"Nothing." Brian's hands went up, both palms facing Danny. "Look, I have to go, but it was nice seeing you."

He signed off, went to the platform and pulled a cooler to the floor. He extended the handle and began to stack the rest of the stuff on top of it. Danny stood at the terminal and watched. He never offered a hand. It was so like him.

Brian stopped when he finished; he longed to stay. He looked at Danny, hurting inside, he didn't understand *why*.

"I'll see you around," Brian said.

"Yeah, we'll catch up with each other later."

There was a slight hesitation before Danny turned to go. Brian watched him walk back to his table; then he nodded to Adam.

He left with the supplies and raced to the hangar. She couldn't wait until tomorrow. But he was committed to getting the copper. He would have to see to it that Don got it. Why did it have to be today? And one concern continued to nag at him since he had left her. What *if* the wind changed?

***

Gary was sitting in the opening of the hatch, feet on the first step. Elbows rested on his knees. Sweat dripped from him.

"Well, did Ivan get it?" Gary asked. Brian shook his head *no*; Brian at the Space Station had failed. "By the way you look, I didn't think so."

"No shower?" Brian inquired.

"I just finished, Chief. You didn't leave me time. Besides, I was waiting to hear."

Brian tossed up what supplies he had.

"You still have time. Something came up that I have to deal with."

"Need any help?"

"No, I can handle it. It'll get rank in the can if you don't shower. I'd hate to have to string you out on a rope to let you air out on the way back. The cart's empty, take it."

"You're a thrill a minute, Chief."

As Gary left, Brian took the memory units under the wing and placed them inside the storage compartment with the warning system. He walked into the hangar next. The old cart sat where Gary had parked it, still loaded with the last group of plane parts he had duped. Brian drove it to the Dupe. He had worried about losing a day because the maps weren't on the plane. He dumped everything into the storage bins; this was much worse than any delay the maps caused. He went upstairs to let Don know he had loaded the hoppers.

Brian watched while Don ran the equipment, bringing what he had loaded to the Dupe. After a half hour, Don smiled.

"That did the trick, Brian. We're back in business. We're still low, but no longer critical."

"You'll have more in a few days."

Brian stopped downstairs and used the Dupe for the second time. Not knowing what was missing, he reselected everything he had tried earlier, and then added one item that he hadn't before.

***

Gary was waiting at the hangar when Brian drove up.

"What? No parts."

"Let's get on the plane. You don't have time for more; we should have left hours ago." Brian drove the short distance to the plane.

"What did you do with the parts that were on the cart? I was going to put them away."

"I took them back to the Dupe. They were low on copper."

They made quick work of the supplies, and when Brian handed up the new laptop, he said,

"Gary, this is for you."

Gary's eyes went wide. "Chief!" Brian knew how longingly he had looked at his, and had decided to do something special for him. Even though he intended this to keep Gary's mouth sealed, he didn't say it.

"You're doing a fine job, Gary. Keep me impressed."

On the flight back, with Danny still fresh on his mind, Brian opened the email containing the procedures for rebooting the system. He tried to concentrate. He needed to become very familiar with it; understand it completely. He would go again to the Space Station when they got back.

He was worried because he could only transmit from the Space Center. Because of her, it meant going there while Ivan and crew were in the building. He wouldn't leave her alone at night. He hoped they were too busy there to take notice.

***

Brian opened the door and went inside. He could only stay long enough to clean and get something into her. Without yet taking off or landing, Gary couldn't solo. If he could, Brian would have sent him on his way. The copper was less than an hour's flight.

Barring problems, he could procure it and return before dark. He would instruct Gary, preparing him to load the aluminum when he returned. They would leave early, and get more copper to Don in one day instead of two.

"Hey, look at you." One of the bottles tied to the side of the carrier was almost empty. "You got one. Good for you." He hadn't tied any above her.

He got her out and inspected her bottom. She wasn't clean, but not as bad as before. The rash had cleared some. Before leaving, Brian cut a hole in the bottom of her carrier. It wasn't perfect, but it wasn't half bad.

When she was cleaned and diapered, Brian placed her in the new carrier. He had transferred it into a backpack while Gary slept, along with her supplies.

He propped a new bottle in place with a blanket. Her little hand came up and grasped at it.

"It won't be long and you'll have that on your own."

He picked up the carrier with the hole and folded the diapers he had placed under it. They had caught the mess. He held his breath opening the cockpit door and threw it in. He was glad it had a door. If the plane sat out under the sun, he was sure he would no longer be able to open the door to toss more in. He cleaned around the hole on the old carrier so it was ready for reuse.

Before leaving, he bent over and kissed her. As he pulled away, he thought her eyes tracked his movement. He did it again, pulling away further. Sure enough, she followed him.

Spontaneously, he hovered over her and swayed from side to side making a funny noise. She watched. He then got on his knees, bent over backward, trying to disappear from sight. Loosing the bottle, she turned her head to see.

He wanted to stay, but couldn't afford the time. He needed to get the copper; then return to the Space Center so he could transmit himself to the Space Station.

But because this had turned into a magical moment, he played with her a little longer. Later, he decided Ivan could sweat it out another day waiting for him to reconnect the Space Station. The copper would wait until morning too.

Only if he could turn Gary loose.

***

Brian's thumb traversed over the face of the remote, lifting the plane from their makeshift runway into the rising sun.

His newly printed maps sat on Gary's seat where he could easily reference them. When he reached cruising altitude, he punched coordinates from the page for the copper and set the autopilot.

In less than an hour, he flew over the old city.

Reaching the outskirts, he descended. The plane bounced in the wind. It was the worst Brian had ever encountered; he didn't know how much the plane could take, and pulled his seat strap tighter.

Large portions of the terrain below were barren. Trees were few and far between; the wind tossed their branches about mercilessly. Lower still, he recognized some of the barren areas as concrete.

The city was larger than the one by the old airport, where most of her stuff awaited her return. Brian wondered what it would have been like to live in such a place. A margin note on the map said he could land in an Industrial Park where the copper was located. As he approached the area, going lower still, the plane continued to handle roughly. He concentrated on the remote.

Less protected from the elements, the buildings hadn't fared well; many high-rises no longer stood.

When he reached his destination, he turned with the wind, and then turned again, putting the nose of the plane into it.

Never having seen so much open concrete, Brian could set down almost anywhere. A good thing, since the plane bounced around.

Once on the ground, watching the display, he taxied up to a building with a large faded sign hanging from its side. The indicator on the display told him this was it.

The sign was too faded to read; he taxied past. Traveling along the length of the single-story building, he didn't stop until he reached a door. The margin note said this place once refined metal. It told him he only required an empty backpack to collect copper. It sounded too easy, and more than just copper was available.

Brian shut the plane off. Even after the propellers stopped, the can moved about with the plane. He needed to tie it down.

Brian opened the hatch. Catching his hair, the wind blew in around him. Out on the first step, a chill engulfed his bones. His clothes pressed against him and flapped in the wind. Pushed along by the wind, an endless supply of rubbish blew by. The chill wasn't from the wind. Out in the open, this was the first he could ever recall not seeing a tree in sight. This was a strange place.

He walked to the door, squinting against the wind. The door looked out of place, set into an imposingly long wall.

Brian tried the knob. It didn't turn. Tentatively, he kicked the door. It was in surprisingly good shape.

He went back to the plane and held the panel against the wind getting tools and the marooning ropes. He spent time pounding stakes into the cracks of the concrete.

Back at the door, he tapped the knob with a hammer trying to loosen it. He ended up giving it a couple of good whacks, knocking it off. He bent the latch out of the jam. Corroded, the door didn't budge.

With a chisel, he worked his way around the door, trying to free it from the frame. He busted the outside portion of the hinges completely off. Forty-five minutes later, with a wrecking bar, he made it under the top corner and used a chunk of brick against the jam to leverage it free.

The door fell to the ground with force, landing flat on the concrete. The wind howled through the opening.

Brian stood in the doorway. The wind blew around him as he took it all in. Part of the ceiling on the west of the building had collapsed and pushed a large portion of the wall away. All he had to do was simply walk around the corner and he could have come in over the rubble. If he had circled in the plane, he would have seen that from the air.

There was a lot of stuff inside to identify. Brian walked in, pulling his test kit. The copper was here; he just had to put it in his backpack.

With no idea what they had been used for he tested several large contraptions. They weren't made of copper.

As he continued, something nagged at him. When he was half way through the room, he realized what it was. There were no birds roosting in the rafters; not even a mouse had scurried about getting out of his way. A total absence of life.

Before entering the next section, Brian turned and surveyed what he had been through; from this angle, he planned his exit for what he would check on the way out.

Only a breeze followed as he passed through the door going into the next section.

A huge area, dark and dank, it contained endless shelves separated by skinny aisles. There was a track set into the floor that shot back and forth across the main aisle. He walked, looking into the rows.

Ransacked, no shelf was left organized. Brian could see he was but only one of many visitors over the years.

Part of the way down, small drums littered the floor. When he reached them, he wiped at one of the grime-layered labels and made out the word *copper*. A stroke of luck, except the drum was empty. He scanned over the shelves. At the very top, he spotted more drums. It was a long way up to where they sat.

Excited, he pushed drums aside with his feet as he passed. All were empty. To get into the aisle, he picked up more empties and threw them out into the main aisle. They rang hollow as they bounced away.

He began to climb. Everything he touched imparted dirt. Staying close to the crossbars, he rubbed against them. He couldn't avoid the grime. A wire mesh served as the shelf. The mesh, only laid in place, felt rickety once he laid on it at the top. Too scared to stand, he crawled on his hands and knees to the drums.

From the higher vantage point, he could see yet another main aisle with more shelving beyond it.

Down several rows, he could see more drums; and, across the main aisle there were more yet.

He was disappointed when he could read the label; it said gold. It wasn't what he wanted. They needed it, but gold wasn't critical.

He used his feet and pushed one of the gold drums off the shelf. He would come back and get it later. It crashed into the stack of empties below. It both crushed and pushed them into the feet of the stanchion he was on. The whole unit moved. Brian almost screamed as the top swayed back and forth.

Shaken, he climbed down. Luckily, the stanchion was attached at both ends to the other units. He didn't want to think of what would have happened if they weren't. He was extra careful coming down.

The drum had split open. Granulites of gold poured out onto the floor.

After three hours of climbing around reading labels, his clothes were ready for the recycler. His hands were black. With no rhyme or reason where stuff had been stored, he had gone through everything. Other metals he found; but no copper.

Fearing he had arrived a century or two too late, he was ready to go. There were fresh clothes and water on the plane. He wanted to dive into those and remove the grime. Wandering further into the building, he wasn't ready to fly two hours to the next location for copper.

He came to an abrupt stop in an older section of the building. The floor, made of wood instead of concrete, had fallen into the lower level. Whatever it landed on left peaks and valleys through out; shelving and drums lay in twisted heaps where they had slid into the low areas. This whole section was much larger than what he had just gone through. There were thousands of drums.

He searched for an easy way down. He saw some stairs, but with no floor, there was no access to those.

Brian returned to the plane. The wind hadn't let up. He got the ladder, knowing it wasn't tall enough, and undid one of the anchoring ropes from the plane.

Returning to the building, he went back to the edge which had stopped him before. He tied the rope to the top of the ladder and lowered it. With nothing level below, the ladder came to rest at an unsecured angle. He tied off the rope and went down.

When he set foot on the floor, it creaked and groaned under him. He made his way across the floor. It was difficult to negotiate the inclines. At all angles, some were steep. Cresting a splinter-filled peak, he slid down the other side slowly. He covered the short distance catching his foot on a twisted stanchion. He pulled upright using it, and swung along the side of it ducking into the carnage.

The first drum, already open, was only partially full. He tested one of the black balls from inside. Getting a positive result, he removed his backpack and filled it. It was heavy, but he put it on and climbed the incline with his hands on the floor. He took the backpack off at the top and let it slide down the other side on its own. He followed it down picking it up and putting it back on when he reached the bottom.

At the ladder, Brian dumped half of the balls and grabbed some broken pieces of wood. He used the wood to reset the ladder, getting it close to level. He stepped onto it, testing it, and climbed up grasping the rope. He shimmied up. Strenuously, he pulled up onto the concrete laying his upper body onto the floor before he could swing one leg over the edge. On top, he dumped the contents of the backpack, then threw it over the edge and went back down himself. He loaded it with the other half.

After a while, the work became drudgery. He counted each step as he took it, knowing every one, was one less. The hardest thing he had to do was climb the rope with a load. It didn't take long before he was throwing each ball up one at a time

Incredibly, all the drums where he worked were copper. He couldn't imagine why anyone needed so much of it.

Over four hundred pounds later, Brian sat in the can preparing to take off. He hadn't collected any other metals. Too long away already, and too tired, he would come back another day.

When he took off, he was glad he had not attempted doing this the night before.

***

Trees swayed in the wind as Brian checked the time flying over their makeshift airstrip. Wind-fed, the fire now covered a tremendous area; it blackened the horizon.

He flew to the fire, and once there, checked the time again and guessed it was roughly thirty-five miles away. He set the map on the remote to see if there were any Installations in its path. There were, though it was a little to the north, and better than three hundred miles away. He wondered if he should report it to them. Based on how far it had traveled, it wouldn't take but a couple of weeks to get there.

He turned around and went back.

After landing, he pulled up next to the pile of aluminum and stopped. Gary was waiting.

"What took so long?"

"It wasn't as easy as the map said it would be."

"Dirty job?"

"Worse than what I look, I've already cleaned and changed."

"Glad I didn't go."

"Me too, load the plane and get more aluminum brought out here."

"You're not going to help?"

"No."

"I was hoping we'd leave later."

"We're waiting until morning; I'm tired," Brian told him as he continued to walk away.

"We should really go see what's happening with the Space Station."

"Isn't there something else you'd like from the Dupe?"

"Of course!"

"Load the plane, get more aluminum out here, and get some sleep yourself."

"Not a problem, Chief."

"I didn't think so."

Brian went into the forest wishing he didn't' have to go to the Space Station a second time. Leaves, falling from the canopy above danced in the wind on the way to the ground. After Gary was out of view, Brian circled back and watched him. There was no reason to worry about Gary following; he was working away; whistling.

"Everything should be that easy," Brian mumbled. When he turned to go, he spotted a deer. Because the wind moved everything, it never spotted him in return as it walked by.

At the door, he could hear her cry faintly.

She stopped at once when she heard him come in. It was neat to watch her focus in on the sound of his voice and find him. "What kind of cry was that? Stop as soon as I come in." He removed her from the carrier and gave her a hug. He wet a towel and wiped her face. "Did you miss me, huh? I missed you, yes I did."

He provided for her needs and then lay on the floor with her close. He could feel her warmth. He rubbed the nipple of the bottle against her lips. She opened her mouth; both hands came up and gripped the bottle. Brian busied himself with the laptop and barely noticed. He needed to review the procedures once again, be totally prepared.

He started to read; too tired though, he drifted off while she took control of the bottle on her own.

***

"We should have left yesterday, Chief. It's so foggy, you can't see a thing."

"Do you want to try?"

"Hardly."

"Even on a clear day, hardly is the correct answer. Although it's nothing more air time won't solve."

A dramatic change from the evening before, the wind had died, leaving a fog.

Brian throttled the motors and released the brake. Besides the fog, it was dark, making it impossible to see. He hoped visibility returned before he did. It would be nerve-racking circling close by her without being able to land.

Gary held his breath. Beads of water formed on the glass and streaked away.

"Shouldn't we have lifted off by now?" Gary screamed above the whine.

Chapter Twenty-Four

Brian remembered when Henry's face glowed green from the remote. As they lifted off, he bet his face looked the same. With complete understanding, he knew how accomplished Henry had been at flying. He was there; he had to take Gary there. Depending on the cloud cover, Gary might miss out on this flight, and not get time.

Keeping the plane on a steep climb, Brian tried to break clear of the clouds so Gary could have the controls. When it started to get cold in the can, he leveled off. Higher than he ever had been, with no break in sight, he descended back down to cruising altitude.

Brian set the autopilot and opened his laptop. Likewise, Gary opened his.

Three hours into the flight, they broke free of the clouds. Brian had begun to worry they might not be able to land. Any delay would postpone returning to the Space Station. Any delays at all, and he would cancel the space station trip in lieu of returning to her.

Brian picked up the remote, set it to manual and handed it to Gary.

"Fly for a while."

Gary looked up from his laptop, took the remote, reset the autopilot and handed it back to Brian.

"I can fly. You need to let me take off."

Brian took it back. "I thought you wanted something from the Dupe."

Gary put his hand out. "Okay Chief, give it here. I've changed my mind; I can use the practice."

"Ah, there is yet hope, words of wisdom from the apprentice."

Gary laughed, putting the laptop away.

Later, as Brian set the approach, he instructed Gary to offload the copper first and get it to the Dupe; he also made sure Gary understood to let Don know it was there after he got it into one of the hoppers.

On the ground, with Gary in the can, Brian grabbed his remastered memory unit and headed home. There was so much to prepare before he could transmit himself to the Space Station.

Once home, he climbed in through the back window, which he had unlocked before leaving. At the front door, he checked his strand of hair. Someone had been in the place. Ivan…. He had to be responsible for this. Though now that he knew for sure someone was breaking in, there wasn't much he could do to prevent it. Who would he tell? Ivan?

Feeling better that he had put everything of value on the plane; he set the email download. He had only one outgoing message for Pete.

He jumped into the shower, quickly soaped, and rinsed. Since he'd only been able to use a washcloth on the plane, the first water to hit the drain was dark. Wanting to linger in the spray, he delayed a little, turning the dial hotter. He moved around, letting it massage over him before giving it up to other pressing matters and shutting it off. He hopped out, grabbed a towel and used it on the way to the terminal.

Astonished by what he saw, the towel fell to the floor. He then plunked down into the chair.

"It can't be." The display was full of emails from Space Station Brian. The top one titled:

"Open please—urgent!" kept repeating itself, filling the entire screen. The last one had come just moments before.

He opened it.

"Please respond at once."

Just then, the terminal chimed. The same message appeared again.

Brian's hands went to the keypad. "I'm here," he typed, relived. "I thought you died."

The reply came back quickly. "Finally, you answer. I've been trying to reach you all morning. I'm alive? But of course. What's meant by that?"

His adrenalin flowed. He had just emailed someone he thought was dead, and that someone happened to be himself. He sat, frozen. It was so strange. Brian at the Space Station had it back up and running. He wouldn't have to go to the Space Center after all. No risk of getting caught there. Plus, it saved a ton of time; he could do plane parts instead and get back on schedule. While grasping all of this, his computer chimed again.

"Are you there? Or did you know or something?"

"Yes, I'm here." He emailed at once.

"It's nice to finally get a hold of you."

"This is awkward," he emailed again at once.

"I know, get used to it. I knew if I keep at it, I'd catch you sooner or later. You have to take care of something."

Brian didn't know how to respond. The last time the Space Station had something for him to take care of he ended up with her.

"So how are you doing?" He asked, ignoring the request.

"There's no time for that. There's a problem."

Now it was a problem.

"Look, two days ago I thought you were dead. I was coming to the Space Station this morning to reset the computer."

"Look, two days ago you sent a message congratulating me. Why would you come?"

"Five days—two days ago—that's why! What took so long?"

"I explained that in an earlier email, no time to explain again. Besides, it was fun making Ivan sweat it out."

"Brave of you. Ivan wasn't the only one waiting."

"Sorry, there were tests to run. Those tests weren't designed for one person to perform. It took time. Look, back to the reason I needed to contact you; we have a problem."

"What problem?"

"You have to go to the Space Center and remove the splice. Ivan is about to discover it."

"How do you know that?" A moment before the good news was finding out he was alive and he didn't have to go to the Space Station. That quickly changed to he had to go again.

"I told you I've explained everything in earlier emails. You're still building the plane?"

"Yes, but it's not very far along."

"Build it to spec, I'll email everything you need to know. The little girl, she's doing okay?"

"She looked thin to me this morning, but otherwise fine."

"Send me a picture."

"I don't have one, but I'll get one. Did resetting the time work?"

"It's in an earlier email. You don't have much time. Ivan has already begun to check and test everything."

"Fine, I'll go, bye."

"Not yet. I want to let you know you're in trouble. Ivan has emailed you like mad. He's been trying to contact you too. Now go, bye."

"Wait, why?"

"It would take too long. You need to go. You can read why later. It's in his emails, bye."

Quickly, Brian typed, "Give me the short version," and hit send.

"You took too long."

"What?"

Brian waited, but Brian at the Space Station didn't respond. 'You took too long,' was too short to understand what was meant.

Brian stood ready to leave. Realizing he wasn't dressed he stopped for a moment adjusting to the adrenalin running through his veins. This was so bizarre emailing back and forth to himself like that. He debated whether to read his emails, or go.

Important, Space Station Brian had said to read them later.

He dressed and left.

***

In the cart, Brian skirted the Space Center driving to the back.

Entering the building from the rear put him closer to the mainframe. He would only be inside briefly. No longer required to transmit himself to the Space Station, with all it involved, he would finish here and use the extra time to dupe parts for the plane.

He had no problem finding the room, even though he was coming at it from a different direction. He walked the whole distance without hearing or seeing anyone. Quickly, he ducked into the room and went to the splice. He didn't want to remove it. Doing so severed his only connection to the Space Station permanently. He wound the wire and stuffed it into his pocket as he headed out of the room.

When he was close to the exit, he heard someone running in one of the halls close by. He couldn't tell if the sound was headed in his direction or not, but picked up his pace. He wanted to run, get out, but by the time he could tell it was coming his way, it was too late. They were too close and coming too fast for him to make the exit without being seen.

"Brian, hold up." It was Ivan. His voice was commanding, and gruff. Brian stopped; hands automatically went into his pockets. Of all people…how did he find time to run around the halls? Did he find out Brian was building a plane? "What are you doing on this end of the building? I've been trying to reach you all morning," he said.

"I was making the rounds and stopped to use the bathroom," Brian lied. Caught, he wondered what trouble Space Station Brian referred too.

"You weren't coming to see me?" Dangerous ground, he didn't know how to respond.

"You said you were looking for me?"

"Yes…making the rounds. You're not still watching the place are you?"

"Most nights. Why?" Brian squirmed inside. It felt like he was cutting his throat.

"I never see you out there," Ivan said as if he knew.

"I wouldn't be very good at it if you did."

"You wouldn't be, would you, but you can stop. I had cameras installed on all the doors. There hasn't been a break-in since that was done." Ivan enjoyed expounding this piece of information. Smug as ever, he acted as though he had gotten rid of a nuisance permanently.

Brian was grateful he hadn't come in carrying a space-suit; Ivan would have tied him to a chair in the control center with the video playing over and over on the big screen of him with it until he confessed to everything.

"You could have told me, sir. I didn't need to keep spending nights out there watching the place." Brian didn't like to continue to lie, but jumped at the chance to admonish Ivan. He couldn't resist.

"I thought I did. Anyway, someone spotted you on the camera just now. Do you have answers to my emails?"

"Not yet, sir."

"The itinerary is important. At least confirm now that you and Gary can take care of it?"

"Gary and I will take care of whatever it is, sir."

"You haven't read the emails?"

"Not yet." He hadn't expected to run into Ivan, and now wished he had taken the time to read the dam things.

"You need to do so. I want this handled promptly. If you need help, let me know. I'll see that it's provided. Speaking of Gary, how's he doing?"

"He's doing fine. The professor chose a good candidate."

"I never got his apprenticeship."

"You didn't?" Brian hesitated. "I emailed that a long time ago." Another out and out lie, but it was too late to take back. "I'll send it again."

"Good, I'll review it later when it settles here."

"So I hear congratulations are in order," Brian said, speculating. He didn't know what happened with the spaceships yet.

"Thanks. It's hard to believe we got them all back but two."

Brian was surprised by the degree of success, and noted Ivan didn't seem to mind taking all the credit.

"It's keeping me busy," Ivan continued. "Speaking of which, I have to get back to the control center. You need to go to the office and respond to my emails at once. I'll expect to see everything by this afternoon."

After Ivan left, Brian walked out. He didn't know what to do about Gary's apprenticeship. At this point, he couldn't tell Ivan Gary was building a plane. Convincing Ivan had been the drawback from the beginning. If Ivan was approachable, he could have resolved this earlier. If Brian at the Space Station had worked on the apprenticeship program all of this would have been resolved before now.

If he had to tack on time to complete the apprenticeship, with everything else that needed to be done, he wouldn't get back to her for days.

And an itinerary? What was that all about? Nothing was ever easy when it involved Ivan.

Something had to give.

***

Brian postponed reading Ivan's emails and went to see Don. He had to have time to think. Don was at his desk. As usual, he didn't seem busy.

"Don, I want to apologize again for the copper shortage," Brian said.

"It was critical."

"Did Gary come see you?"

"Yes, he did. We're all set."

"We can continue on the plane?"

"I don't see why not."

"So I don't screw up again, is there anything else we're low on?"

"How much of the list have you done?"

"Not enough to worry about."

"Okay, let me check." Don brought up a spreadsheet and began to scroll down the list. He stopped at an item and his finger traced across the screen. "Based on what I see here there won't be enough silica. What else do we need for glass? There, calcium, but there's plenty of that."

Don went through the rest of the list, finding nothing more.

"Thanks, Don."

"Just because you're good to go, you still need to replace everything."

"That won't be a problem, we will."

Brian went downstairs and started on the parts list. It would take time to replace everything he had brought back to eliminate the copper shortage.

He was still busy at the terminal when Gary walked in. Brian had parts stacked along the wall. The floor was getting full.

"You heard about the spaceships?" Brian asked.

"Yes, great news. You were right, Chief. Ivan had it under control. Not only did he get it back, but fixed whatever underlying problem prevented communication with the rest of them. He knew what he was doing."

"Of course he did. Do you know what you want off here?" Brian asked. He stepped aside, palm out to the keypad.

"Yes." Gary took his place.

"Make it quick."

"Don't worry," Gary said, finding what he wanted. "Can I have this?" It was some sort of software program.

"Sure." Brian selected it. "Is the plane unloaded?"

"Almost."

"Load your cart, make me some room on the floor."

When Gary finished loading the cart, he said, "My cart's full, Chief. Do you want me to load yours?"

"No, get going. Finish unloading the plane. Come back when you're done."

All the while, Brian felt he should stop to work on Gary's apprenticeship so he could send it to Ivan. Encouraged by the progress on the list, and since some of the parts coming off the Dupe now were large; he stayed and cranked more out.

As he worked his way through the list, he tried to come up with a means to complete the apprenticeship in one fell swoop. Dupping parts kept his mind free to think..

Brian refilled the area Gary had cleared, leaning the large stuff against the wall.

There were several times the Dupe only took one entry; those parts were not only big, but heavy. Brian had to slide them off the table and push them across the floor. There was no way for one person to pick them up. Gary would be on his own getting them to the hanger. Something he'd have to figure out on his own.

When Gary returned an hour later, he was surprised by the small mountain of parts against the wall.

"I take it we're spending the night here." Gary stated.

"You are. I'm not."

"I get a day off?"

"Gary, please. You now have a ton of work. It's the only reason you're staying."

"One of these days, Chief!"

Brian thought, one of these days when I can start exercising on a daily basis.

***

Brian duped supplies and then left for the house.

He still wasn't sure what to do for Gary's apprenticeship other than spend time on it and see what he came up with. Once home, he felt pressed. This was something that was a waste of time. Wishing he had come home first to let the quiet of the house help him whip through it, he turned on his terminal to start working.

There was another email from the Space Station. Brian there couldn't have had much time to compose it. Pete had responded too. Brian set the download and scrolled through the list of emails looking for Ivan's itinerary.

He opened it and got the gist immediately. He had to pick up two people at Twenty-One in three days and bring them to One-O-Seven.

Brian replied, "Gary and I will take care of this."

He left that open and composed a separate email. This came down to doing the apprenticeship or going back to her. He knew what he had to do.

"Ivan, I've tried to locate Gary's apprenticeship. I believe it was stored on one of the broken laptops. You told me to recycle those and I did. Sorry for the delay, but it'll have to be redone."

Both emails were on their way before the download sequence completed.

***

Brian took off alone rising above the runway.

In the air, autopilot on, he quickly opened the email from Pete. It concerned her. He had asked Pete how he knew Mark got enough to eat when he was little.

Instead of an answer to that, Pete had written, "I wish you hadn't told Mark '*later*' for that ride. He spends part of some days waiting for you out on the front porch to come. I thought you'd at least give me a date so I could let him know."

Brian felt guilty. He needed to get over there and wondered if he could fit it in somehow when he returned.

But more importantly, he did get his answer; there were attachments to the email. He opened the first of two. It was a picture of a scale. The second was a spreadsheet. It contained the average weight based on weeks since duped. Brian didn't know it was important to remember the day she was duped. He wasn't sure when that had happened. Everything was a blur since then.

He began deleting the 'please respond at once' emails from Space Station Brian, as he tried to calculate back to the day she was spit out of the Dupe. There were hundreds of emails to delete.

When he finished he opened Ivan's itinerary. He had scanned it earlier, but now read it closely.

Ivan wanted to ensure Brian understood he ran a respectable organization. It was set in stone for the day after tomorrow. Brian was expected to show up at precisely the appointed time.

Brian grabbed the remote. He had to find out where this place was; and saw it was over seven hours from One-O-Seven.

In an instant, solving the logistics, Brian decided at once to bring her back to the old airport. She would be close. It wouldn't take long to fly to her when he finished.

Ivan mentioned there would be others. Itineraries for those would be forthcoming once arrangements were finalized.

In the next email, Ivan asked him to respond confirming he was available to perform the pick-up. Because Brian hadn't responded right away, the next asked about the apprenticeship and when it would be sent. There were several more, and each got progressively sterner. Ivan had gotten tired of waiting for Brian to respond. He took too long, which Space Station Brian had told him. The last email only said, "Please report to me at once."

"I didn't know how much trouble I was in," Brian said. He wished he had read these before running into Ivan. Because of the cameras, he could never go back. He felt vulnerable, precarious, all Ivan had to do was remove him as head of security and it would put him back to being a bottom feeder.

The rest of the emails from Ivan were general issue concerning the success with the spaceships. Brian read those expecting to see gloating; although none was apparent, the crusty old fart had to be doing so.

Finally he opened the email from Space Station Brian which had come after he had left to pull the splice. It had attachments.

He was surprised to read that the plane he used wasn't a plane at all, but a drone.

Planes built for people to travel could exceed two thousand miles an hour. The drones were slow in comparison, one hundred miles per hour tops, and they weren't designed to take a person anywhere. In fact, they weren't designed to go anywhere.

Part of a communication system, they replaced towers once built on the earth and flew in circles, in a predetermined, permanent position, twenty miles above the surface of the earth. Originally, they were only brought down once every two years for maintenance, but maintenance intervals increased as materials used to build them improved.

Because it was designed to fly for long periods, and didn't require fossil fuel, it was a good fit for the Installations and every Installation made use of them.

That's why the cans are added, just a place for you to sit your butt, Space Station Brian explained.

"Interesting. I wonder if I can make this thing go faster."

He opened one of the attachments. It contained a parts list. The first column had + and – marked against various parts. A legend indicated the pluses were parts not on the original list that needed to be duped, and the minuses weren't needed. Everything not marked had to be duped.

Brian needed to check this against what he already had done.

New assembly instructions were in the next attachment. He needed to get those into Gary's hands or he'd end up having to redo a bunch of it.

A further surprise, all the Installations had drones above them. "Ivan uses his to communicate with the heads of other Installations."

That's how Ivan got confirmation on Henry so fast, Brian realized. He had expected this email to be short. Because of its length, he knew Brian at the Space Station had been working on it for quite some time, and hadn't sent it until he confirmed the plane/drone was being built.

Without the splice, there was no way to let Space Station Brian know the drone was in jeopardy. If Ivan found out, he would put an end to it.

The next email was an explanation saying the ships sent a continuous beacon and communications with them reestablished instantaneously once the satellites realigned. The next portion Brian at the space station had already told him. It said there hadn't been a need to reset the time; and he shouldn't have bothered.

"Why? You just pulled off something no one else has been able to do."

In another, Space Station Brian gave him three months to get into the best physical shape of his life, after which he was to re-digitalize himself. It would improve their chances of survival.

There was no explanation as to what they had to survive.

In another, he told Brian he didn't need the IV, but to bring water. He explained the digitalization for the IV currently was wrong. "Do not use it on the new program."

"I wondered about that when I did it."

If Brian wasn't already concerned enough, the last email read, 'the spaceships are obsolete, I think I'll take them all off line. That'll put Ivan back in his place and give him heartburn.'

Brian racked his brain, but could think of nothing that would send Brian down this rabbit hole.

"Obsolete? We just reestablished contact with most of them which is the greatest news of the century and you did it buddy. Are you going insane up there, or what?"

Without the splice, there was no longer a way to know what was going on.

Chapter Twenty-five

On the return flight to her, he ran back into the clouds. He hoped it was clear at their new airstrip, but he wouldn't find that out until he arrived.

When he did, it was cloudy. He flew in under them. It was raining. Visibility was poor. "I'm sure you can hear me and I know you're hungry, so I can't just waste time circling."

Motivated, he did a flyover of the runway. He could barely see, but made out enough to know the dark areas to either side of him were trees. He turned the nose upward and reduced his airspeed as he cleared the trees at the end of the runway. He turned the drone, slowed some more, going as slow as he dared as he flew over again. He decided to land.

Concentrating on the final approach, knowing Henry would scold him for using poor judgment, he touched down, and felt the pull of the water on the wheels; it forced the drone to slow abruptly pressing him against the belt. The uneven ground jostled him about. He feared worse and was thankful it wasn't as bad as he had anticipated. He pulled up next to the pile of aluminum and parked.

Because the cloud cover was so extensive, he couldn't see if the fire still burned. Possibly, the rain had extinguished it, which would be one less worry.

Outside, Brian avoided the puddles. Pushed by the propellers, most of the ash had collected at the edge of the airstrip. Taking the first step onto it, he slipped and landed on his butt. Automatically, he checked to see if anyone had seen him. Out in the middle of nowhere, he laughed at himself for doing so. Staying on two feet was a chore; he slid just getting up. Managing the rest, he shuffled through without his feet leaving the ground, after which he ran to the abandoned plane.

Inside, he picked her up and gave her a hug. With a hand under each arm, he then extended his arms holding her out. He bounced her, testing her weight. He couldn't begin to guess, but because of the chart, he knew approximately the range she should be in. She began to pout when he had bounced her. He grabbed a bottle filling it half full and let her have it. She nursed while he carried her around.

He cleaned her first; then tidied the place, leaving a wet trail everywhere he went. Anything that could spoil went into the cockpit.

"I've got something for you on the drone. It's guaranteed to stimulate your palate and put weight on you," he told her. Now nursing, she just stared at him. He had cereal on the drone and couldn't wait to get some into her.

He planned to bring her back in several days so he left most of the supplies. Putting a diaper on her, he put her into the carrier and covered it with a blanket. He picked everything up and took her outside into the rain.

When he reached the ash, keeping his knees bent, he shuffled through.

Once inside the can, anxious to try the cereal, he sat the carrier on the grating and removed the blanket. She was so aware. He kept glancing over at her while he prepared the cereal. She watched him intently. He continually talked, sharing his hectic day.

One rather large mess later, still sharing his day, he couldn't tell how much cereal he had gotten into her.

"We should have started you on this before now, huh. If I knew what I was doing, you wouldn't be so skinny. When we get that scale, we're going to find out how bad at this I've been doing, yes, we will."

He cleaned her, and prepared more formula. After giving it to her, he took it away. She didn't like it one bit and protested, kicking her little legs and carrying on with a loud cry that continued in volume.

The cereal was nothing but mush. Brian unscrewed the top of the bottle and scooped some into it. After putting it back together, he pinched the tip closed and shook it vigorously.

"Mean old Brian, took your bottle away. Here, you can have it back."

She latched on with one tear escaping down the side of her cheek.

He picked up the carrier. "You have to move you loud thing, I'm bringing the aluminum aboard and you can't be in the way." He placed her in front of the seats.

Working in the rain, he hurried to get as much done as he could before they had to go.

His butt was already wet from falling in the ash. The rest of him, partially wet, and it didn't take long for the drizzle to soak the rest of the way through. His clothes stuck to him, constricting his movement.

Getting almost half the pile of aluminum, he worked past the time he needed to leave.

***

Cutting it close, he and she landed at the windy city just before dark.

In brand new clothes he had changed into getting out of the wet ones he worked in the old factory by the light of the lantern collecting titanium, magnesium, gold and silver, all metals he needed. It was after three in the morning when he finished. His new clothes were in total ruin.

They took off in the dark and once coordinates were set for the old airport, using the lantern, he undressed and cleaned up. He changed into newly duped clothes as he had done earlier. She was still awake and watched.

"You're going to spend the night on the plane," he cooed. "It scared me the first time I had to do that. You won't be scared, will you?"

Glad for her company, he made another bottle with cereal. He was surprised she took it. Since picking her up, he had kept a steady supply available, which mostly he dumped, keeping what she had fresh.

She really didn't want it. Most of it seeped out of the corner of her mouth.

"Can't fit another drop in there, can you," Brian said proudly.

In the only clear spot in the can, he spread out sleeping bags and got in. Exhausted from the long day, he felt immediately comfortable.

Tired, he tried to calculate when they would arrive.

***

Brian woke and turned off the lantern; he hadn't managed to do it the night before.

Sleeping soundly to the hum of the drone, he wondered how long she had been crying. He picked up the remote, checked the time, their position. He had overslept and over flown the old airport. He had to turn around to go back.

"You like your cereal? Is that why you're crying? You want more."

By the time they landed, she was set. He carried her down the steps into the bright morning sun. Birds were flying about, chirping. He made his way along the familiar route to the terminal. Everything that moved or made a sound caught his attention.

Squirrels, performing their acrobats, curiously, seemed to come watch their passing. A flickertail scooted across in front of them.

The forest was alive with life.

Although the stroll was enjoyable, he knew there were predators. He stayed watchful, as she depended on him for her safety. He moved cautiously, the pepper spray out and pointing at everything that moved.

In the terminal, he took her upstairs to her room.

"You remember this place don't you?" Brian said, laying out a fresh blanket.

He retrieved a fuzzy toy from against the wall and gave it to her. She grasped it with both hands. It went into her mouth.

"Yuck. Silly, that's not food."

He got another toy that had gadgets all over it for her to pull, move and press. Every control set something into motion. Brian showed her what each did. The one that caught her eye was a button that set a spinner going like mad whistling noisily as it spun.

She reached out, trying to grasp it.

"You're not quite ready for this one, are you?"

Knowing he had to go, he prepared a couple of bottles.

"I won't be long," he told her, tying them into place on her holder. "I'll get a scale, do a few parts, and be back before you know it."

He didn't want to leave. There was no telling what he'd run into at the Installation. Every time, it seemed to be something different. Of all the irons in the fire, time with her was the most precious. He preferred it over everything else, but he had to go pick up passengers, and before that could be done, the can had to be emptied and cleaned. He needed to print the new assembly instructions, and get them into Gary's hands before he got too far along. And he wanted badly to make time for Mark.

And Ivan...ever present and lurking in the shadows.

Before he left, he gave her back the fuzzy toy.

***

When he landed at the Installation, taxing to the hangar, he saw Gary come out to wait for him.

"I wish you wouldn't do that," Brian said under his breath. After he parked, he opened the hatch, yelling down at Gary. "I was on my way in to see you. You didn't have to stop working."

"Sorry, chief. I just wanted to make sure you heard about Ivan?"

"No." He wondered if the old geezer had a heart attack and croaked, then realized Brian at the Space Station probably pulled the plug.

"Yesterday, the counsel promoted him to chair their meetings."

"They did!"

"Isn't that great?"

A long pause. "Yeah, it is." It wasn't the enthusiastic response Gary expected.

"It was the least they could do, considering what he accomplished."

The counsel was the governing body for the Installations. One representative per, they didn't meet often, but when they did, they had the authority to initiate change. Ivan was now its chair, a coveted position which carried an enormous amount of prestige. Although the news shouldn't upset him, Brian knew Ivan wasn't deserving of such a grand honor.

"Gary, get everything off the plane. When you get that done, I want you to wipe down all the seats, the walls, and then pull up a section of grating and clean under it. I don't have time. I have to leave shortly to take care of some business for Ivan. I'd hate to be you if he found out you delayed me."

Brian drove off wishing his counterpart at the Space Station would pull the plug.

Taking the irony of it all out on Gary wasn't fair, though he doubted Gary would ever work as hard or as fast again. Not even for something from the Dupe.

At home, he started the routine. Though there would be nothing from the Space Station, Ivan was another story. He expected finalized itineraries and some sort of directive on the apprenticeship.

Out of the shower, he printed the new assembly instructions for the drone. There were no emails; Ivan was silent. Brian would have preferred something from him, anything to indicate what he was thinking.

He dressed, and drove back to the hangar. He climbed the steps of the drone. Gary was under the grating cleaning. He had already emptied the can.

"Chief, I'll be done in fifteen minutes."

"Great. I'm headed for the Dupe. When you finish, I'll have more parts." Brian held up the new assembly instructions. "You'll need to throw away the assembly instructions you have. Ivan replaced them with these." He put them on the pulldown which Gary had yet to put back in place.

Brian left and went to the Dupe. It took Gary longer than fifteen minutes to show up. But when he did, he went straight to work clearing the wall.

Before he could get out with the first load, Brian told him, "Gary, put that in my cart."

"I thought you had to go?"

"I do, so let me know when it's almost full."

When Gary finished with the cart he informed Brian. At that point, Brian completed his entries, which included a scale and supplies for the trip.

"I'll be back late tomorrow. When I return, there will be a couple of men with me. You'll need to make yourself available at the hangar to take them to the Space Center. I won't have time."

"Is that what you're doing for Ivan?"

"Yes."

"Can I come?"

"No."

"You know I haven't flown in a couple of days, Chief."

"It'll be a couple more."

Because Gary expected him to go, Brian had to postpone Mark's ride. He almost told Gary to do it, but decided against it. It was something he needed to take care of himself.

***

Brian drove to the hanger, loaded the can and took off. An hour later, he landed at the old airport and made his way to the terminal.

Inside, he ran up the steps carrying the scale.

Once he was in the room, anxious to get her on it, he removed his backpack, tossing it next to the wall.

He knelt on the floor, putting the package in front of him and began opening it. She knew he was there; and because he hadn't picked her up yet, she began to fuss.

"Just give me a minute. I'll pick you up and have you on here."

He pulled the scale out of the box. Setting it on the floor, he reached for her, pulling her to him across the floor by a foot. He then undressed her, picked her up and put her on the scale. Once he had her, she didn't want to be set back down. She kicked and screamed when he let go.

"Hold still."

Unable to catch her weight, Brian put a hand on her stomach to steady the scale and prevent it from falling over.

It was impossible, so he took her off and prepared a bottle. When it was ready, he weighed the bottle, gave it to her and put them both on the scale.

"I should know better, huh. You'll only be happy if I feed you first." He was relieved by what he saw. Even though she was at the low end, she was within her weight range. "Not bad. After you suck that down, we're going to try the cereal again."

Later, they spent part of the day outside enjoying the sun. After that, they went exploring through the terminal.

By the end of the day, Brian began to believe that maybe the professor's profile of him was right. He had a knack for child rearing.

***

The next morning, sitting in the rocking chair, Brian rhythmically rocked her.

He was ready to go, but waited. It didn't make sense to arrive at Twenty-One before the appointed time. If he arrived early, he'd just have to wait there, while she waited here.

She had stayed up late the night before. He had kept her going until she could no longer keep her eyes open. Diaperless and fed, she peacefully slept in his arms.

When it came time, he slowly got up and placed her gently into the carrier. She stirred, but slept. He would get her another new holder, as this one now had a hole punched through the bottom of it too.

He left for Twenty-One.

As he flew, he spent part of his time working on Gary's apprenticeship. What he put together though, couldn't be given to Ivan. He had laid it out as if Ivan had already approved the new drone.

Butting a head wind, Brian arrived late. He expected them to be waiting on the tarmac as the Special Forces had done. Instead, the two yahoos were nowhere in sight. The delay bothered him, as it added to the time she would be alone. He didn't like it and fought the temptation to leave and return to her.

It was a lesson in timeliness, because if he took off, they were sure to be ready when Ivan made him come back. Already at the bottom of Ivan's popularity list, Brian climbed out to go find them. Even though leaving without them was rational to him, he knew from Ivan's point of view, it wasn't.

From the air, the Installation had looked as large as One-O-Seven. He knew how impossible it was to find someone there, and knew here, he would need help. The whole situation reinforced with certainty that if Ivan wasn't involved, he would already be gone.

After a ten minute walk, Brian waited at the shuttle stop. He would ask the driver for help. Every second that passed gnawed at him. Aggravated, he didn't wait five minutes, and headed back to the drone. He would buzz the entire Installation announcing his presence. It would get their attention. They would come.

He kept checking over his shoulder on the way back, trying to convince himself, buzzing the place would be the best thing to do. When he was almost to the drone, he saw the shuttle passing the stop. He ran to catch it, waving his arms to ensure the driver could see him. The driver turned, heading toward the airstrip. Brian changed direction again, heading back to the drone. There were two passengers riding in the next car. It had to be them.

The shuttle pulled to a stop at the same time Brian made it back. Both passengers disembarked, unloading luggage. He wondered why the luggage, since they could dupe everything they needed at One-O-Seven.

Stepping up, he offered a hand. "Hi, I'm Brian."

"Rod," Rod said taking Brian's hand.

"Stewart," said the other, as the shuttle pulled away.

"I'm ready when you guys are," Brian said, heading for the drone.

Inside the can, he started the motors, while closing the hatch. They had both taken seats next to each other on the pulldowns. He ensured they buckled up properly and handed each a set of earplugs.

As Brian turned the drone, he opened a cooler and offered a hot plate to Rod. While taxiing, he offered the next to Stewart, and as the drone sped down the runway, he gave them each a cold drink. For the comfort of his passengers, he kept the drone on a slight but steady incline.

"Do you guys know why Ivan is having you come to One-O-Seven?" Brian asked.

"We're putting a timeline together to test equipment at the Space Center," Stewart said.

"Someone there has made an adjustment of some sort to bring all the ships on line, we're going to find out what they did."

"We'll be assigning names to perform those tests based on the people best qualified," Rod added.

"Good luck," Brian said. He went to his seat. Having to fetch them was a waste of time, and Ivan had plans for more. They would come, but never figure out what happened. If Brian at the Space Station pulled the plug, it would only serve to confuse them for the rest of their days. If Gary could solo, he would be here instead and Brian would be with her.

Gary needed more fly time under his belt. Brian had to see that he got it. He was tired of being stuck doing this stuff.

***

Brian climbed down the steps of the drone with a piece of luggage. This was the longest he'd been away from her to date. He hurried to get them and their stuff off the drone. Gary came out of the hangar.

Stewart had followed Brian down the steps. Rod was next and while Brian waited at the bottom of the steps, he said, "Gary, this is Rod and Stewart."

Once Rod cleared, Brian raced back up the steps going back into the can calling Gary. He handed down the rest of their stuff.

"Gary, I'll be back in the morning."

"Okay, see you then."

"How's the plane coming?"

"You should go look."

"I will, later."

Brian stood to go, but then bent over and stuck his head out of the hatch.

"Guys, it was nice meeting you. Gary's taking you to the Space Center. Ivan is expecting you."

He wanted to check his emails. He didn't need to upset Ivan; the old geezer could have sent something else he considered important, which would require Brian's immediate attention. But the urge to return to her compelled him.

He closed the hatch.

***

At the bottom of the steps, Brian heard the little female screaming at the top of her lungs. Riddled with guilt, he sprinted up the stairs.

He quickly lifted her out of the carrier, and then tenderly put her to his shoulder. Slowly, he swayed in place, patting her on the back.

"There, there, I'm here now."

He had never seen her so distraught.

In that instant, it became clearer to him than it ever would. She was very aware of him; knew when she called out crying he was the only one who came. She depended on him completely to provide. No one else cared for her.

"I'm sorry; I came back as soon as I could."

He wet a cloth and began to clean her while she suckled the bottle.

"Aw, you're so hungry."

He decided if he wasn't able to keep his time away short, he would give her to Pete.

The idea of that no longer appealed to him. He couldn't explain it. Somehow she had managed to get a hold over him. Even though small, she had managed to fill a huge spot in his heart.

But he could no longer keep doing this to her; she needed him all of the time.

If he left her on a porch at a different Installation, it wasn't likely anyone would trace her back to him.

He knew he didn't want to do that, either. Not only would her gender be the news of the century, but he cared too much for her to put her through it.

"How can I give you up? You kind of grew on me, kiddo." Struggling with all of this, he tried to put himself above his personal feelings. He had to see that she got what was best for her. "I vow, some way or another, I'll solve this. I promise."

Brian had never made a vow he didn't keep.

He knew that as he committed this one to her.

Chapter Twenty-Six

Brian's commitment to her was strong.

He didn't know what else to do, and had to stop at One-O-Seven to find out what the latest was from Ivan. Parking further away than usual, he watched Gary, who, like clock-work, strolled out of the hangar. Once the drone stopped, she fussed. If not for Ivan, he would have gone straight to their make-shift airstrip to collect aluminum.

He had to avert Gary. Prepared, he practically jumped to the tarmac and ran to him. He couldn't let him anywhere near the drone.

"Hey, Chief, want me to help with the supplies before we go?"

"You're not going anywhere."

"Aw, come on, I can use a break. All I've done is work on the plane."

"Well, you're right. You need a break."

"Yeah, and you know I need the practice."

"True enough. However, I stopped to let you know I've changed my mind. I'm giving you the day off. How's that for a break?" The news was so unexpected Gary at first seemed confused.

"Go on—get out of here before I change my mind."

"Can I take the cart?"

"Yes."

While Brian walked to his cart, Gary ran to the other. Hopping in, he drove off erratically, head back, hooting in the air. One fist pumped above his head. Brian just shook his. From far away he heard Gary yell, "Thanks, Chief," which made him smile.

Excited, Gary bolted so quickly he hadn't bothered clos-ing the hangar door. Brian changed direction to shut it, but when he got there, he went in.

Some of the parts he had duped were support stan-chions. With them in place, the outline of the drone began to take shape.

"Man, oh, man, if Ivan walked in and saw this…." Brian couldn't imagine. Gary's progress was impressive. Brian wished he hadn't given him the day off.

After shutting the hangar door, he went back to the drone. He knew Gary wouldn't be back and because no one else used the hangar but them, he got his laptop, and left her there.

Once at the house, he took a shower. Afterward, he checked emails. Still nothing from Ivan. He anticipated Ivan would have at least sent the next itinerary. He wished he could email Brian at the Space Station; find out what was going on.

He drove to the Dupe and duped a new carrier along with some supplies. He brought the parts list, but only did what could fit in his cart.

Back at the hangar, after loading their supplies into the drone, he parked inside. Still impressed, he admired again what Gary had accomplished.

"If she ever comes here again, you'll only get the morning next time."

He went back to the drone, and together, they took off.

***

At the make-shift airstrip, she sat in her carrier under the wing. Brian had placed her on the table beside of the warning system. A breeze fluttered her hair.

She watched while he loaded aluminum.

Eventually, he connected what she was doing with his memories of Henry, and laughed at her.

"Are you supervising? Well, you're doing a fine job. I'm still working. But you know what, you're so blasted cute, anyone would work for you."

The day before, he had taken half of the pile. There wasn't enough left to fill the can. After he loaded what was there, he went and got her.

"We're going to make a big bang; yes we are. Just like Gary." He carried her inside. "When I come back, I'll get you something to eat."

Brian worked at placing a charge inside the tail section of a different plane. When finished, he went back to the drone and closed the hatch. He made her a bottle, got a cooler, and sat on the grating next to her. He put her into the muffs she used while flying; then sequenced through the safety functions on the remote.

"I'm ready; are you?" he asked, while taking her little hand. He separated her index finger and pressed it against the button. They both jumped. "Look at what you did." She pouted. He laughed. "Oh, it's okay. Gary couldn't have done it any better." He gave her the bottle and removed the muffs.

After he ate, Brian gathered pieces. They were all over the place. As he walked about finding them, he realized how much work it had been for Gary to generate the pile he had made. It took the majority of the day to load the can. By the end of the day, he had only a small pile left on the ground of extra pieces.

It made him wonder if the amount of work Gary had done recently was the result of having gotten the laptop. It seemed Gary had stepped it up a notch since receiving it. If Brian had known from the beginning that was going to be the case, he would have duped it sooner. Not only sooner, he would have done a hundred of them. He wondered what else Gary wanted. What ever it was, Brian would see he got it.

Quitting before dusk, they took off heading back for the old airport. He would have to leave her there for a short time in the morning, because he couldn't keep giving Gary days off.

Managing his time, he restricted what he did at the Installation to duping parts, checking emails, and of course, the ever necessary shower. He never gave in to the urge to give Mark a ride, though he felt he could make time for that.

Over the course of the next five days, he varied little from this routine.

All along, his email remained unnaturally silent.

She went with him on every trip; and Gary never got an opportunity to fly.

***

On the sixth day, Brian landed early at One-O-Seven.

After shutting everything down, he got out of his seat, stretched, and watched Gary come out of the hangar.

Brian went out the hatch. Becoming old hat, they greeted each other in passing.

"Good morning," Gary said as Brian came down.

"Morning, Gary. How's the plane coming?" he asked, heading for his cart.

"It's another day along, Chief. You're going to have to crank out more parts than you've been doing; the shelves are getting bare." Gary reached the steps and began to climb.

"Wonderful. Is there anything you want from the Dupe?"

"Yeah, I'll pick it out when I get there."

"See you in a few."

Brian drove home to catch a shower. Afterward, even though he'd anticipated it, he dreaded finally seeing the email from Ivan. He wondered why it had taken so long. Stewart had said they were assigning names. Maybe Ivan had to wait to get that information. Brian sat down to open the message.

Surprisingly, he was headed back to Twenty-One. Ivan explained that both Rod and Stewart had been ferried via plane to Twenty-One, and a team of ten men from around the globe would be available for a pickup there in four days.

The pickup time was slated for late evening. Brian emailed Ivan letting him know he would make the trip, but asked for a change in the time to the following morning. He would take her, and find a place somewhere around the halfway mark where she could stay. He would make some excuse to land there while returning. He didn't like the idea of having a team of ten men waiting for him in the can while he took care of her, but there was little choice. He wasn't going to leave her as long as he had last time.

It would make two back-to-back seven and a half hour stretches for her, longer than he wished, but better than leaving her alone throughout the entire trip.

Brian decided then it didn't matter whether Ivan approved the time change or not. He would arrive the following morning regardless. He had to do what was best for her.

There was an email from Don; Brian decided to read it later. He needed to Dupe parts. He shut off the laptop and folded it.

Brian drove to the Dupe and spent longer than usual doing parts. He needed to stay ahead of Gary.

***

Over the next three days, Brian continued to collect aluminum. He never left her alone. On the fourth day, he prepared her to come along while he took care of Ivan's itinerary.

"Hey kiddo, you're not going to like this, but you're staying by yourself for a while. I know I promised, but I don't have a choice right this second." She cooed, playing with the fuzzy toy as he carried her out of the terminal.

Brian hated to do this to her; over the last three days he'd come to grips with the situation by making a very tough decision.

What he came up with scared him, but every channel of thought funneled him to the same conclusion; end the chaos from the Installation, and devote all his time to her.

It meant leaving, becoming a non-citizen. Doing so meant he had to outsmart and avoid the Special Forces at all cost. They would come for him. And, as if avoiding that threat wasn't enough, he had to survive the wild; and contend with predators.

He would take the new drone, which, though not ready, was moving right along. While Gary worked on it, he would plan, which he had to do very carefully. One mistake and it would cost them their lives.

"Did you know you've always been a non-citizen? You haven't spent a day at the Installation since you were duped. I guess I won't be spending anymore time there either."

It was the only way to provide the proper care for her.

The email he had received from Don told him it was time for a saltwater run. He would dupe supplies, take them with him on that trip and drop them within fifty miles of the ocean. He would take her there, and build a shelter. The closest Installation was over five hundred miles away.

"They'll never look for us there. And don't you dare tell anyone where we're going. Even though it'll be a big change for us, it's our little secret."

Although they wouldn't know where to search, they would search. Brian wondered if there was any way they wouldn't bother. Nothing came to mind that would stop them.

"You know what, there's something else we've been putting off. You're going to grow up thinking your name is kiddo. It's time you got a name. So what should it be?"

Brian was fond of Danny, but he didn't want her to remind him of Danny. Along the same vein, Henry might not be bad.

He had considered the professor's name, but somehow Ed just didn't work for her. Neither did Sandy. She wasn't an Ed or a Sandy. None of the names seemed right for her.

"Do you like Henry? It's a fine name. How does it sound? Henry." She continued to play with the toy as he carried her along the path, which now bore signs of continued use. "You're not paying attention. Just for that, I'm picking a name that doesn't remind me of anyone. Jack…. That's it, Jack. I hope you like it."

She continued to play with her toy.

At the drone, he carried her on board and they took off.

Two and a half hours into the flight, he turned south and began searching. He kept an eye on the horizon looking for telltale signs of high-rises. An old city would have ample space to set the drone down. Plus, it should prove an ideal location to find a safe haven for her.

After three quarters of an hour, he turned again, went fifty miles paralleling his route and then turned north.

Passing through his original travel route, he continued north an additional three quarters of an hour before turning again toward his destination. He kept crisscrossing in this manner until he spotted an old city.

As he approached the outskirts of the place, he continued to descend; keeping a straight line until he flew within the tall structures themselves looking for a long stretch without rubble. When he found a spot that was doable, he used it.

After landing, he prepared formula. Her fuzzy toy lay on the grating next to the carrier.

"You dropped this, Jack." Calling her by name seemed odd. He had gone so long calling her kiddo, he wondered how long it would take to get used to it. "You know, I think I like kiddo better. Maybe we should stick with that." She reached for the toy when he handed it to her.

"You don't care one way or the other, do you?"

He opened the hatch.

"It's either I get used to calling you Jack, or change it," he told her over his shoulder while looking around outside. "Does Bob or Robert sound better?" He got out onto the first step, pepper spray clenched between his teeth. "You let me know when I get back."

Brian closed the hatch and made his way to one of the high-rises. He found his way in and located the stairs. Going up several levels, he left footprints everywhere he searched in the layer of filth on the floor.

With much of the glass missing from their frames, he looked for a room that wasn't on an outside wall. He found several, but either they were without doors, or the ones still in place were broken, or wouldn't open. If he had to wrench any of them apart, he wouldn't be able to latch them in place securely. He had to have one that worked, or he couldn't leave her. He ended up back by the stairs and went up another flight.

Eight floors later, on the eleventh level, he found what he wanted and went to get her.

Back on the eleventh floor, with her in the carrier, breathing hard, he said, "If I did that three or four times a day, I'd get in shape, wouldn't I? We should have eaten before coming up here, kiddo. Now I have to go back and carry our food up. Sorry, I mean Jack."

He set her on the floor outside of the room, removing his backpack. He had filled it with blankets. Unzipping it, he took one into the room, spread it out over the floor in one corner and went back for another. When all the blankets were in place, he had nearly covered the entire room.

Impulsively, he started calling her Robert to see if he could get used to that.

"Robert, you're sleeping on the floor tonight. You shouldn't feel bad about it; it's all I've done since you showed up. I haven't spent a single night in my own bed."

Toward evening, he put two chairs side by side facing west on the edge of the eleventh floor. She, secure within her carrier, sat on top of one. He sat in the other, with a steaming plate from the cooler.

Without windows, a breeze blew in around them.

"Nice view, huh, Robert?"

He looked around, but preoccupied, really wasn't taking it in. He ate slowly, contemplating. Leaving the Installation would be a tremendous change; but he would do it for her.

When he finished eating he couldn't help but take his plate and fling it like a saucer. Spinning away, it went far before losing power. Then, flip flopping, it traveled to the ground. He watched it hit and shatter.

Moments later, a spectacular sunset went unnoticed by Brian.

The peaceful scene played out its array of colors while his fingers raced over the keys of his laptop, listing the things that he needed to do before he became a non-citizen.

A lone hawk screeched its presence.

She gazed out tracking the hawk until it flew out of sight.

Long after dark, she asleep, he picked up the carrier and took her into the room.

"Robert, because of you I didn't pick those guys up tonight. I hope I don't get into too much trouble over it," he said as he secured the door behind him for the night.

He had tried Robert now several times. He didn't know if it fit her any better than Jack, but he needed to settle on something. One thing he knew, he had to decide, and not change it, or she would never catch on.

In the morning, Brian left her there and flew off for Twenty-One.

Ivan had not approved his request for the time change.

***

Arriving a half day behind Ivan's schedule, Brian landed at Twenty-One. Surprised, there was a shuttle waiting on the tarmac with a driver. After parking, Brian got out of the can, the shuttle driver got out of the cart.

The team was not in the shuttle. He didn't expect they would be around, and had flown in low over the Installation announcing his presence.

They met halfway between the drone and shuttle and offered hands. "Brian."

"Jim," he said. "Where have you been?"

"Mechanical issues."

"I'll let the guys know. Some of them weren't happy you didn't show up last night. They complained long and loud about traveling so far to be held up here waiting for you." Ivan probably already heard. There would be an email asking for an explanation. Especially since he had requested the delay in advance. "The complainers got the whole lot of them going. I had to sit here and listen to them the whole time."

"Where are they now?"

"I put them up last night and took them to breakfast this morning. After a night's rest, they were a cordial bunch..."

Brian laughed. "Well, I'm here to take them off your hands."

"Give me a half hour, and they're yours."

Brian waited in the drone working on the list, adding, refining and prioritizing the things he needed to do before leaving the Installation. Collecting sand for the solar panels sat in the number one slot. It was the only thing the Dupe needed in order for him to complete the parts list for the drone.

In under a half hour the driver returned with the team. He had kept an eye out for them and descended the ladder when he saw them coming to offer help with their luggage.

Because he was the only one by the drone, the whole team had watched him descend to the tarmac. They continued to stare while he put his hands behind his back waiting at the bottom of the ladder for the shuttle to come to a stop.

Brian noted that nobody was conversing. Not one of them had a smile. They just stared. "This is great," he said under his breath.

Once the shuttle stopped, Brian put on his best smile and stepped forward.

"Sorry for the delay, it couldn't be helped."

"I already told them," Jim said. He had gotten out and was pulling their luggage off the shuttle and handing each piece to its respective owner as they came forward to claim what was theirs.

The team formed a line at the ladder waiting their turn to board. No one said a word to Brian. They didn't need his help either, as no one had more than one piece. He wondered what information they had fed to Ivan. It was hard waiting patiently at the bottom while they boarded. He was in trouble because of them and contemplated how much damage control he would have to do. The old geezer wouldn't put up with much more of this before replacing him.

After ensuring the men were settled, Brian took his seat.

In the air, he worried about her and was anxious to get back. Picking these guys up only confirmed the need to end the chaos.

Three hours later, he set the approach and began to descend. He told them he needed a bathroom break and accommodatingly, would make a courtesy landing so they could enjoy the rest of their flight.

He parked the drone so the building she was in was out of view. They couldn't see where he went as he raced to her, even running up the stairs two at a time all the way to where she was on the eleventh level.

Entering the room, he found she had rolled up next to the wall.

"Hey Robert, are you going mobile on me?" Her whole body twisted to catch a clear view of him. She let him have a big grin. He picked her up. "I'm glad to see you too." Quickly, he prepared formula and laid her back in the center of the room. He had left a couple of full bottles by her side when he had left. Both lay on the floor sideways, and were empty.

After changing her, he cleaned out both of the old bottles and refilled them.

Shutting the door to leave, it tore his heart to listen to her cry when he said goodbye.

***

It took over nine hours before he laid a hand on that doorknob again.

She lay sleeping, and was across the room against the adjacent wall from where she was last time he came in.

"Robert, it's time to go, sweetie." He brought her up to his shoulder, giving her a big hug.

"I'm taking you to the ocean. I can't wait until we get there. You're going for a swim. That'll be so much fun?"

With all new supplies on the drone, Brian left everything where it lay. When he picked her up, she woke, saw him and then went back to sleep while he put her into the carrier.

"You wore yourself out wandering all over the place."

The following morning, within fifty miles of the ocean, he began to circle, dumping their supplies for the future. On parachutes, he watched as most of it caught in the tops of the trees. He grabbed the remote, punched their coordinates, saving them so the drone could return on its own.

As the drone circled, he carried her to the hatch.

"Look, Robert, this is going to be our new home. Do you like it?"

Within two hours, he had the hose in the water, pump running….

She splashed in the surf giggling. Brian had never heard her laugh. He had her by the chest and kept bouncing her along on top of the water. He enjoyed watching her while she deliberately slapped the water with her hands.

There were no emails from Ivan when he had returned with the team. Now that they were working at the Space Center, Brian was sure his inbox was filling up.

He didn't look forward to returning in three days, and decided then, staying a fourth might not be a bad idea.

Chapter Twenty-Seven

On the third day, they left the ocean. Brian wanted to stay a fourth, but was concerned Gary would run out of parts. Their time together was wonderful; she really enjoyed herself; but all the preparations he still needed to make; and those emails after delivering the team late to One-O-Seven, they were surely piling up. It all breached in on his rest and relaxation. He needed to get back, start damage control.

He knew if he never saw another email, it would be too soon. That was one thing he would never miss. The one thing he would miss—something fierce—and he didn't see how he could do without, was a shower. Other than that, he could walk away from all of the comforts of home and devote his time to her. Though she was more than worth giving up the shower, he knew he could jury-rig something which gave him some semblance of one.

He'd finished loading the last of their things and prepared to take off. He started the motors when she began to cry.

"Not now, Robert, you're just a little late eating. Wait until we're in the air."

Once the propellers reached velocity, he taxied to the end of the sand where he turned and powered to full throttle. It was loud, drowning her cries as they rolled along over the sand. Maxed to capacity, the drone strained to reach air speed.

Using the entire length of the shore, Brian lifted up over the trees, and turned toward the old airport.

After setting the autopilot he took her out of the carrier, and slipped a finger between her skin and the diaper. She needed a change.

"Honestly Robert, I'll have to stop feeding you all of the time. I know you didn't do that because I fly poorly."

Once changed, he got a jar of mashed peaches, one of her favorites. He was getting good at spoon-feeding her. He no longer made a big mess of it. When the jar was empty, he mixed cereal into her formula. He took her with him, and sat in his chair while she fed.

"You're going on the scale when we get back. I'll bet you've gained five pounds. Just look at those rolls jiggling on you." He had a hold of the inside of her thigh, shaking it back and forth. She clamped down onto the nipple to retain it, and smiled at him. "Isn't that precious? You had fun, didn't you? You sure liked playing in the water. I know that. I'm going to have to find something that'll hold water so you can play in it all the time."

Later, while she slept, he put her into the carrier, and opened his laptop and began working.

When they arrived at the old airport, Brian buzzed the runway. Soaking up the evening sun, three predators got to their feet and watched him approach. Fearless, they didn't budge until the drone was almost on top of them. Then they disappeared into the trees. Brian circled and flew just over the forest canopy headed in the same direction they had fled to drive them further away.

After landing, he grabbed his rifle and got out. Carefully, he searched along the edge where they had disappeared into the forest. Next, he scoured the whole area to ensure they weren't around.

Once on the path, her with him, he stayed in tune with what was going on around him.

Relieved when they were safely inside the terminal, he took her to the room and removed her clothing.

He placed her on the scale. "Oh my goodness, look at you, Robert, almost four pounds. You're now at the top of your range. Looks like I'll have to ask Pete how I'm supposed to keep you from going over."

Brian took the dirty diaper to the bird section. He had gone in once and moved the heaped up pile so he could continue to throw more in. He wasn't looking forward to doing that again.

He wondered how long she would need diapers. He needed to drop a stockpile of them where they were going; it made him wonder how many trips in the drone it would take to keep her in full supply. Looking over his shoulder, he sized up the pile and made a mental note to collect a little data and perform some calculations. It wasn't going to be a small number.

Once settled in her room, they didn't venture out for the rest of the day.

***

When he arrived at the Installation the following morning, Gary was backing the cart away from the hangar.

"Where do you think you're going?" Brian asked.

"I'm caught up with you," Gary announced proudly. "I'm leaving for the day."

"I see I made it just in time. You're not going anywhere."

"Yeah, but, Chief, I was just taking off…."

"Not a chance."

"Chief!"

"Listen, remove the pods and take them inside. I'll get an auxiliary pump so you can transfer the water. After that, prepare to restock the shelves for the rest of the day."

Gary got out of the cart hem-hawing, obviously frustrated, he adjusted to the fact he had just lost out. One foot scraped across the tarmac before kicking up into the air, and then he said, "I'll need solar panels soon."

"You read my mind. The next trip I make will be to the collection point to get sand, but you won't have to wait, I'll dupe a bunch of panels today."

"Can I go with you this time?" Gary asked.

"No, but when the plane's finished, we'll get you back in the air. I hope you haven't forgotten everything. I'd hate to start over."

"You can't expect me to remember everything."

"And why not?"

"Just kidding, Chief. And you can bet I won't hassle you anymore about the practice. Anything's better than working on the plane every day."

At the Dupe Brian stayed until it became busy with lunch patrons. Mostly harnesses of battery wire came off the platform. He had piled them on the floor on top of each other.

When done at the Dupe, he went home for a shower. Once there, he checked his terminal for emails, and mentally prepared to do damage control. There was one email from Ivan, but he unexpectedly thanked him for the timely pick-up despite the mechanical problem with the plane. Further, as a heads up, Ivan said there would be another team coming to One-O-Seven. He would let Brian know when, but anticipated it was still a couple of weeks away.

The new drone wouldn't be ready before then. She would have to endure another long absence without him. Though he'd never asked, Brian believed now that Pete had never left Mark alone. The sooner he could be there for her, the better.

He wanted to email Ivan asking if Twenty-One would be his destination again, because he wanted to make a suggestion about scheduling the pick up in the morning, but didn't push his luck.

At the Dupe, the last things he keyed into the terminal were the largest backpacks available containing the preserved food items. He did diapers too.

Needing something to carry the sand, he duped empty backpacks as well.

He hadn't completed the aluminum requirement yet. He was close; two or three more trips would finish it. With things the way they were now, it somehow no longer seemed important to replenish the raw materials, just get what was needed to finish the drone.

The same went for Gary, though it would be a shame not to finish his apprenticeship, because he had already spent a considerable amount of time getting Gary to where he was, it really wasn't important either.

Gone longer than he anticipated, he hurried to return to her.

***

Mid-morning of the following day, Brian landed on the shore by the ocean. He got out, and carried her under the wing to the access panel containing the warning system.

"Look, Robert, hear the water. It's got your name written all over it. I'll bet you're ready; I know I am. And as soon as I get this set up…."

She watched, blinking against the wind which blew hard. Brian felt grains of sand biting against his legs. He had turned her carrier so the back of it took the brunt. Once the table was out, he put her on it while he finished with the equipment.

Excited by the size of the waves, he was ready to try his hand at body surfing. They were higher than on any previous visit. He would catch a ride and outdo Henry's best.

While flying out, he had dropped the supplies. Now, there were parachutes covering previous parachutes, all stuck in the trees.

Before he reached the wet sand, Brian sat the carrier down getting her undressed.

Once in the water, the force of the waves knocked him over. Going under, she cried when he stood back up. Brian took her back to shore.

"You're going to have to wait until it calms down, Robert," he told her, wrapping and rubbing her with a towel. Getting her redressed, he put the towel over the carrier to shield her from the sun and wind. Brian went back into the rough water and played in it until he wore himself out.

After eating, he held her while she worked on the remainder of the bottle. Her eyelids, streaked red, were heavy. She would slowly close them when she stopped nursing, and then reopen wide when she continued. As she repeated this cycle, Brian yawned.

"You're as cute as a whip when you do that, but you're making me tired."

Brian laid out his sleeping bag and joined her for a nap.

Later, he shoveled sand into the backpacks. He carried those up the steps one at a time as he filled them and then stacked them inside. He only filled them to the point where they remained easy to handle. After he had been at it several hours, she fussed for attention.

"I'd take you swimming, but the water's still too rough. Shall we eat? I could use something."

When they settled in for the evening, Brian had filled more than half of the bags. He never took her into the water. If anything, the waves had gotten larger and the sun had completely disappeared behind the clouds.

During the night it rained. The wind howled. Brian got up and went outside to stow the warning system. The table had blown over; the equipment was now wet and had sand stuck all over it. He hoped it still worked.

By morning, the ferocity of the storm increased. Many times, Brian couldn't see the ocean through the window because of the driving rain. When he could, the waves were white-capped for as far out as he could see. He turned on the lantern to lighten the place. Dreary, they held up in the can most of the day waiting it out.

Late evening, shoveling wet sand into a backpack, Brian decided to stay another day. After spending most of it lying around, he couldn't motivate himself to work very long, or very hard. He quit before dark.

The next morning when he came out of the can, he took a deep breath. Everything was fresh. The rain had cleansed, and renewed, making the vegetation greener. They both spent the morning enjoying the surf. The waves were still up, but nothing like before.

After a leisurely day enjoying the water off and on, and a slow pace filling backpacks, they left late in the evening and flew overnight to the old airport.

***

Once set up in her room at the terminal, Brian left for One-O-Seven with the sand.

When he arrived, the routine down, Gary began unloading the can before Brian made it to his cart.

"Come see me as soon as you get the first load weighed."

"Sure. So you know; I came across something neat I'd like to get off the Dupe."

"That won't be a problem."

"Thanks, Chief, I appreciate you letting me get what I want."

"You're welcome."

At the Dupe, Brian pulled solar panels and more battery wire from the platform. On the downhill run, there were less than four pages to go on the parts list.

When Gary showed up, he gave Brian the weight, and selected what he wanted, and then complained about Brian stacking the harnesses. "They get all tangled when you throw them on top of each other." Afterward, Brian sent him to collect the mail run.

He had stopped at the house first, and read a forwarded email from Ivan. Originally from the Research Center, they asked about their mail run. Ivan added: 'Brian, this is nonsense. This is the second time I've acted as a liaison for something you should take care of on your own. In the future, this needs to be done in a timely manner.' He then asked Brian where he was at on his other duties; all of which were behind; eventually, the email cumulated with Gary's apprenticeship.

To save time, Brian decided not to build a can on top of the new drone. He would have Gary make something simple. Something that wouldn't require a lot of time, yet provide enough comfort for travel. He had a couple of ideas in mind; which he had drawn up on one of the laptops.

One iron that never made it to the fire was duping a mainframe for the house. He had postponed that idea after discovering someone had been in the place. Now, he would never need it.

After that email from Ivan, the first thing Brian did when he boarded the drone was turn on his laptop and delete the work he had performed to date on the apprenticeship. It had been a thorn in his side from day one. Deleting it, removed the thorn. It felt good doing so.

Calculating the weight of the sand Gary had given him, Brian figured he could get the rest in one trip. It would be a heavy load, but nothing the drone couldn't handle.

Then he would help Gary finish the drone and he and she would leave permanently.

Brian at the Space Station was going to be surprised, and Brian wondered how he would handle the news when he found out.

***

At Ninety-Two, there was no one at the hangar, usually wasn't, and Brian had more mailbags than he could carry. A lot of bags had accumulated at the Research Center since the last time they had taken them. He turned the drone, positioning it so it was ready to go. He would finish this delivery and leave. He threw the bags out onto the tarmac wishing he'd told Gary to leave them in the hangar at One-O-Seven. It would have saved the delay caused by stopping at Ninety-Two.

"Robert, I'll be right back," he told her, after the bags were all out.

Dragging them over the tarmac, Brian made a couple of trips getting them next to the hangar. He went to the shuttle stop and waited. It was a hot day. When the driver showed up, Brian asked if he would make a side trip to the hangar for the mailbags.

The driver agreed to help and Brian climbed aboard.

While loading the bags into the rear car, ever so faintly, he heard her as she began to cry.

"Do you hear that?" one of the passengers asked the man next to him.

"I'm almost ready to go," Brian called out.

"Hear what?" the other man asked.

Brian hurried, tossing in the last bag.

"It sounded like a baby."

"I'm ready," Brian called out again, louder than before to the driver.

"I don't hear anything."

"No wait, listen, there it is again…."

"Driver, I've got everything loaded," Brian yelled this time. He could get a lot louder if need be.

"It's crying. You hear it now?"

"Let's go, I don't have all day." The shuttle pulled forward making a wide turn. The driver passed close to the drone. "Thanks, Driver." Brian knew she wouldn't stay quiet. "I see it's going to be a wonderful day for the trip home," he said, now obviously very loud, distracting their attention to him.

"Do you have a baby on the plane?" the one who had heard her turned and asked.

"Sorry, I'm with your friend there, I didn't hear any baby," Brian said as they pulled away. "Besides, who would ever stick me with one of those to carry around on a plane?"

The man beside him stifled a laugh.

"I could have sworn I heard a baby cry," the man said, "and you didn't hear it?"

"No, I didn't," the other replied, still chuckling.

At the security office, Brian got the bags inside. He said hi on his first trip inside and goodbye after his last trip. There was a bag going back with them. He hurried carrying it to the shuttle stop.

When he walked up to the drone, she still cried.

"Sorry," he said, getting in. "I heard you the first time, and so did everyone else." She was sweating from the workout. Brian picked her up and gave her a bottle. "That was a close call, Robert. You don't know how close. What would I do if they found you? I would miss you if they took you away."

***

Returning with the next load of sand, Brian buzzed the old airport. Nothing scurried off the runway. On occasion, there would be nothing, but that was the exception, not the rule.

The drone, loaded with backpacks of sand, handled differently than when it had full pods of water under the wing. Brian made a wide and graceful turn taking his time.

Once on the ground, he shut it down and used the aisle he had left on one side of the can.

She watched him approach giving him a big grin. "Yeah, I'm coming to get you, and you know it." She was strapped in one of the pull downs in her carrier. Without much room left, Brian had put her there so he could use the seat next to him for his stuff. He removed her muffs, and unstrapped her from the carrier to see if she needed a change. "You're just wet. I suppose that can wait until we're in your room."

He picked up the carrier taking her with him. Unlatching the hatch, he looked outside. As of yet, the morning sun hadn't broken over the trees. Streams of light came through and glistened off the dew present along the side of the runway. It was a quiet morning.

While he carried her down the steps, something began to nag at him, like he'd forgot something. He didn't know what it would be and transferred the carrier to his other hand when he reached the bottom, he kept thinking he had left something inside that they needed. He looked around and then set her on the concrete and climbed back up the ladder. Looking in, his view was blocked; he could only see the backpacks of sand.

He couldn't imagine what it could be that he'd forgotten. Looking back down at her, he was torn about leaving her unattended to go inside. He was already at the top, and though it troubled him, he stepped inside and followed the aisle around. He would only be a moment. He spotted her fuzzy toy, but knew that wasn't what nagged at him. He picked it up and went back out closing the hatch. At the bottom of the ladder, he gave her the toy.

"You lost this again, Robert." He picked up the carrier and walked across the runway heading for the path. He continued talking to her as he tried to figure out what bothered him. "You've been getting around lately, haven't you? So tell me, what do you like better, where we dumped the supplies, or the ocean?" The nagging felling had started when he came down the ladder.

On the path, it was very quiet. Whatever was nagging at him wouldn't stop.

As he walked, the vegetation imparted water onto his clothes wherever he touched it in passing. Further down the path he took note on a conscious level that, as of yet, he hadn't seen a rabbit bouncing around in front of them. This deep into the forest, there were usually several he would have seen by now.

No flickertails either.

"I've been thinking, wouldn't it be nice to live by the ocean? We could play in the water whenever we wanted. You would enjoy that too, I'm sure. I'd have to start over with the supplies, but it'd be worth it." Looking up, he searched the trees looking for a squirrel, but saw none. "I can't put a finger on it, Robert, but something's bugging me."

It was quiet, too quiet. The animal chatter was missing.

Suddenly, from behind, full of stealth, a predator struck at full speed knocking Brian to the ground. His breath expelled forcefully. Her carrier came free of his hand.

Frantic, he scrambled trying to get back to his feet. He only succeeded at spinning on the ground, with the predator over him gaining control.

The pepper spray he carried was gone.

The Predator's hot breath was on the back of his neck. In reflex, Brian put both hands over his head. One hand ended up in the predator's mouth. Brian felt the pain.

Within moments of her carrier hitting the ground she screamed in protest.

The predator released his hand. Its breath left the back of his neck, its attention drawn to the carrier.

Her cry, demanding, was the one she used when she wanted him now.

The predator moved toward her, then stopped. Crouching low, its hindquarters were still partially on Brian's shoulder.

Brian looked up. He didn't see the pepper spray, didn't know where to look.

Having turned one hundred an eighty degrees while scrambling, he faced the carrier and saw all three predators at once. One was sniffing above her. Its head went lower with each sniff. Brian watched in horror as its head went into the carrier as it licked her. She screamed in objection. The third stood behind it and off to the side.

With its attention on her, the predator on him scooted quickly closer to the carrier getting completely off him. The one that licked her face leaned back, feet firmly planted, snarling a warning to the challenger.

He remembered Henry had told him they were independent animals, but members would travel together and fight over food.

Her cries redrew its attention. It resumed investigating, sniffing once again above the carrier.

When Brian had tried to scramble to his feet, he ended up further away from her than he would have thought possible. He went for the pistol under his arm. Quick to detect his movement, he drew the predator's attention that had licked her. He halted. Its focus on him was intent, and then it looked away, right away, when the predator leaving him scooted again to take advantage.

Both froze in place, neither gave ground.

Desperately, Brian went for the pistol.

The predator leaving Brian inched closer. The one licking her, with determined eyes raised a paw. The paw remained above its head. Then it became a blur, defending its prize; several quick cuffs went to the challenger's head.

She screamed amidst the flying fur.

Reaching the pistol, he got to his knees and fired three consecutive rounds. So close, he shot at the mass of predators in front of him. The furthest away snapped around biting the air.

Not of its own accord, the predator attacking him, laid low by the punishing blows it received jumped at the sound of the firearm; as it rose to flee the weapon, it ended up with the handle of her carrier in its mouth.

Brian's heart pounded; he fired again.

The one he hit had sat, turned its head to its hindquarters. The predator that licked her gave chase to the one with the carrier ending up along side of it, grabbing at the handle. It too got a hold of the carrier as they both ran down the path side by side starting a tug of war leaving him behind.

Brian stepped forward, took aim.

The predator sitting, now closer, turned on him. Startled, Brian emptied the pistol. It twitched with every hit slumping to the ground.

Desperately, sidestepping by, Brian reached into his pocket for the other pepper spray. Emptying the canister in one long frantic stream, he aimed high above them to go over their heads and brought it down to cover them.

The spray never reached. Out of range, they continued to carry her away.

Discarding the canister, he reloaded the pistol while running. They had already disappeared around the turn in the path heading toward the runway. He cut off the path to parallel their movement to get to the runway quicker.

By the time Brian got there, they were already on the other side close to the forest.

Without him in close pursuit they had stopped with the tug of war between them now in earnest.

Brian stopped, brought up his arm, took aim, and fired.

Missing, he moved a step forward. Now oblivious of his efforts, the tug of war continued as they parleyed for advantage. She wailed as the carrier moved back and forth. It was on the verge of going furious.

"Come on!" Concentrating, both hands went to the pistol; he held his breath, fired again.

He hit his mark. It invoked a violent reaction. The handle of the carrier broke as the one he hit went down. The opposing forces of the predators had been so violent that when the handle broke it left the carrier listing on one end of the handle at a thirty-degree angle.

At an angle, strapped in, Brian clearly saw her little arms and legs flailing in disapproval. One predator lay on the ground. The other stood with the broken handle still in its mouth, gazing at Brian.

The moment passed. Its head went back getting a better grip on the handle. It turned and headed for the forest.

Terror griped him, he broke into a dead run. He didn't want to fire the weapon, chancing hitting her, nevertheless, he emptied the clip. Bullets ricocheted at the predator's feet. It broke into a run.

Through sheer will, wishing for the rifle or another pepper spray, he had closed the gap for a moment.

Tense, hardly time, Brian tried to reload before it reached the edge. Quickly ejecting the clip, he shoved a full one in its place and got off two rounds before it disappeared. He couldn't tell if he had hit it, and emptied the clip into the trees where it had gone.

Reloading, he burst into the forest.

It wasn't there. Brian swallowed. He couldn't tell where it had gone.

"Robert!"

Chapter Twenty-Eight

"Robert!" Brian screamed again.

Forced to a stop, he knew he had to listen in order to hear.

She was there, deeper into the forest.

With renewed strength, guided by her voice, he hurried to get to her. But every time he stopped, she continued to get further away.

Reaching an open corridor through the trees, he came to a sudden stop. It sounded like she was down at the end of it. Still frightened of hitting her, he aimed the weapon toward her cry.

The discharge caused an abrupt change in the predator's direction. It turned, coming back toward him but off to his side. She wailed hard after he had fired. Instantly, he went to intercept.

As they came closer, her cries stopped.

"Robert! I'm right here!" He couldn't see them, but knew they had to be almost on top him. She needed to respond. "Robert," he called again. Five seconds went by. Unsure, he stopped, listened.

He still couldn't see her, or it. It must have spotted him and stopped. She still hadn't cried since it turned back toward him. "Robert," he said in a shortened breath, believing they were right next to him, still no response.

He fired the pistol into the air, but it resulted in neither sight nor sound. Brian turned three-hundred and sixty degrees in place scouring the area.

In desperation, "Come on, Robert, I know you're here!"

Nothing.

There was no time. He began to circle the area trying desperately to come upon them. He continued to call her name, listen, and then fire the weapon.

After three minutes of frantically covering the area, he knew he it was taking too long. What was most upsetting was she had to be right next to him and he couldn't see her. The continued absence of her cry only meant one thing; she was gone.

Time slipped away. He could do nothing but walk endlessly in search. He held his grief, counting on the hope that she lived. He would find her. In less than three hours, the sun directly overhead, he was hopelessly lost. He didn't know how to get back to the drone, but he didn't care. He wasn't giving up, even though on a rational level he knew she was gone.

In the evening, using the setting sun as a reference, he walked in the direction he believed the old airport would be. He figured the city itself encompassed a large enough area that he couldn't miss it. He would find the airport and then from there retrace his initial steps.

As Brian maintained this direction, he spotted her fuzzy toy. It hung low from a bush, which, like a marker, drew his attention. He veered, knowing the search was over, and when he got there, he fell to his knees and wept looking for her. He didn't see her, but still the pain flooded him. It was unlike anything he had ever experienced. Nothing had prepared him for this, not Henry's death, nor his lone experiment doing himself in. All along, he had held out hope.

Bent over in silent anguish, he blamed himself for not keeping her safe. When he finally opened his eyes he looked around again, further from where he was but still no carrier, or sign of her. He dug into the earth, burying the fuzzy toy.

He stayed there, hunched over until well after dark. When he stood, he knew he should leave for his own safety. But he couldn't go. He no longer feared the predator. Instead of leaving, he climbed the tree close to where he buried her toy, hoping the predator would return.

***

The sun brought its morning light. The predator had not returned. As it became light, Brian searched from the tree. It's higher vantage gave him a clear view of the ground. Nothing of her. He took his time getting out of the tree. His hand, with severe punctures, oozed. It hurt just to move his fingers, let alone grip.

In an odd way, he'd found solace during the night staying close to where he buried her toy. He knew she was gone, but somehow, someway, wanted confirmation.

Not knowing if he would ever return, though he intended to, he removed his shirt when he made it to the ground. The back of it was torn and stained, corresponding with where his back hurt as well. He ripped it into strips and tied those all around on the nearby underbrush.

Resuming the original direction, he left. Before the area was out of sight, he turned and memorized it. Taking one last look, knowing the responsibility was his and his alone, the moment overwhelmed. A loss too great, she depended entirely on him for everything. The abruptness of it all was still a shock. If he had left her on Pete's porch, she would still be alive.

He felt a fever setting in, as he blamed himself for becoming complacent. He questioned what he had been doing and thinking before they were attacked. He recognized the warning signs, but didn't comprehend them for what they were while they had screamed for his attention.

Brian found the remnants of the old city. He didn't know where he was; but picked a direction to skirt it. When he came to an area he thought looked familiar, he turned and went the direction he would have flown.

Later, he walked up to the terminal and went inside.

In her room, he took the ointment meant for her and squeezed some onto his hand and rubbed it in. His hand hurt to touch. One good thing, the ointment did not sting, and when he was done with that, he squeezed the rest of the contents onto the edge of one of her blankets. He used its length as an applicator, flipping it up over his head; then carefully pulling it from side to side, he worked it back and forth down his back, gritting his teeth the entire time.

Hungry and exhausted, he sat next to a cooler and opened it.

He recalled when the professor had told him he had an amplitude for child rearing. If the professor could see him now, he would know how wrong the profile had been.

Eventually, Brian lay on the floor and for a long time drifted in and out of a disturbed sleep.

When he woke, after sleep would return no more, he opened a new ointment and redid his hand and back. He got a shirt from its package. He knew he should eat again but that thought went away as soon as it had formed.

He fought with leaving the old airport. He wanted to continue his search. He saw no hope and through the woods on the way to the drone, he searched for any hope at all. If he found any, he would renew his search at that very moment.

Sitting in his chair in the can, Brian contemplated leaving. What was wrong was wrong, and what was right was right. It was wrong to leave. But just like finding Henry, he comprehended how impossible the task. He started the motors and with tears streaming down both cheeks blurring his vision, he took off for One-O-Seven.

***

Brian spent several days in bed fighting the fever. When awake, he grieved.

He forced himself to shower to keep the punctures clean and applied ointment until they filled in. He then let them scab over.

Gary had to wonder what was going on; Brian never spent time at the Installation.

When the fever broke, leaving him weak, but on the road to recovery, he left the house. It felt wrong staying there. If she were alive, he wouldn't be there. His need to provide for her was strongly embedded.

Brian went to the Dupe and finished the parts list. Completing it was a milestone; it should have generated some type of elation. He felt nothing by the accomplishment.

After taking a load to the hangar and telling Gary to get the rest, he drove to Pete's. Halfway up the steps he heard from inside, "Dad, Brian's here!" Then Mark ran through the door. It practically flew from its hinges. "Are you giving me a ride?"

"Are you ready for one?"

"Dad, I'm going for a ride!" Brian braced, still on the steps, expecting to be bowled over getting the usual leg hug. But Mark blew past him, heading for the cart.

"I guess you are, huh, buddy," he said, laughing, something he briefly thought he wouldn't still is capable of doing.

Pete came out just in time to see his kid climb onto the seat.

"Hey Pete," Brian said. "I didn't mean to take so long getting over." They watched Mark as he checked out the controls of the cart.

"Don't touch anything," Pete told him.

"He's not going to hurt anything," Brian said.

"You've got him excited now. We had pretty much given up on you."

"You knew I'd make it over, you shouldn't have let him do that."

"You don't know Mark; he cried when you wouldn't come. I couldn't just keep his hopes up telling him you were coming, but I never told him you weren't, just that you were busy."

"I'm ready," Mark announced, sitting tall on the seat.

"We won't be long," Brian said going to the cart. "Are you sure you're ready?"

"Yeah!"

"You guys be careful," Pete said.

Brian pulled away, watching Mark's eyes grow wide; he grabbed hold of the seat and held on.

"You're not scared, are you?"

"No, Mark's not scared."

"I didn't think so; and that's supposed to be, I'm not scared."

Brian drove, eventually ending up along the fence. It was just him and Mark and he was such the little man, a delight to observe getting his first ride.

"I have to go home," Mark said.

"Already! Why's that?"

"I have to pee."

"Oh, well, you probably didn't know this, but that's why all these trees are out here."

"Trees?"

"Yeah," Brian said, coming to a stop. "We can't go back yet, I have other planes, so let me show you."

Afterward, he drove to the Dupe where he got them hot fudge sundaes. They sat outside eating in the cart. When Brian was almost done, Mark still had plenty left to go.

"Mark, this stuff is too good to let it drip onto your shirt like that." Brian leaned over, and on closer inspection, said, "Your pants, the seat, you're even getting it on the floorboard. How did you do that?" Mark began to giggle as Brian pointed each out. "It's on your hands, all over your face. It's even in your hair. What's up with that?"

He wasn't concerned with the mess, Gary could clean the cart; and Brian would even get Mark another if he wanted it. His only concern, how could anyone let even a drop escape making it to their mouth.

When Mark finished, Brian let him steer as they made their way back to the house.

Sitting on the porch, Pete set waiting. Brian knew it had to be the first time Mark had been away without him.

When Pete saw Mark, he directed him inside where he drew a bath. While Pete was getting him out of his clothes, Mark was nonstop about his adventure. He told his dad everything, including why there were trees.

Afterward, Brian and Pete sat on the front porch while Mark played with neighbor kids a few houses down.

"Did you hear the rumor about the Installation doubling the number of people that will live here?" Pete asked.

"Yeah, you just told me."

"It sounds like they're planning to give me a couple of more kids in the next six months. If that happens, I don't know how I'll handle it. Mark can be a handful all by himself."

"Have you heard why?"

"It's the Space Center. Now that they've connected up with almost all of the ships, they need people to work there."

It was tempting to tell Pete how that had happened. But one thing would lead to another.

After a pleasant evening visiting, Brian drove to the hangar. To his surprise, he found Gary working.

"Show me what's next," Brian said, not ready to go home.

"I was just wrapping up for the night."

"That's okay. Show me what's next, and go."

"I've got everything laid out so I know where it's at. You'll mess it up."

"Well thank you mister—I am concerned about the plane—but I won't mess it up."

"Chief, I've put the whole thing together without any help. So why now? Don't get me wrong, but it wasn't easy and I don't want you screwing it up," Gary objected.

It felt odd to have Gary be so possessive over the drone. And with Gary taking pride in what he'd accomplished, Brian reverted to tack. Though he knew how astonished Gary would be if he told him what he intended to do with the drone when it was done.

"I'll take you flying tomorrow," Brian said, offering this because Gary had stopped asking for stuff from the Dupe.

He worked at the tasks Gary gave him, spending most of the night. Gary stayed and worked along side Brian, supervising the entire time.

***

Late in the morning, after a long hot shower, Brian checked his email but there was nothing from Ivan.

He had been eating from coolers for so long, at the Dupe, he selected his favorite dish of steak and potatoes. It came with corn on the cob and a side dish of salad.

When he got to the hangar, Gary was already working.

"Hey." Brian announced his presents from the hangar door. "You ready to go for that spin in the plane."

Inside the drone, Brian handed Gary one of the remotes.

"No supplies?" Gary inquired.

"We're not going anywhere. You're just flying."

Brian took off and then put Gary through his paces, after which, Brian landed lining back up with the runway.

"Go ahead, take off," he said.

It took the rest of the day and Brian's entire wherewithal to get Gary to do it correctly. But the day passed quickly as a result and he became pleased with Gary's progress.

They spent the following morning assembling solar panels to the frame on the drone. The panels interlocked, providing a smooth surface for the airflow. Each one had to be wired into the battery harness before being mounted.

In the afternoon, they were back in the drone. This time, Brian had Gary set approaches and flew over the runway, touching it.

***

Within two months, the drone was complete.

378

During this time, Gary and Brian worked inseparably, with Brian leaving the Installation only once by himself. They kept a steady schedule, except when performing Ivan's itineraries, which took them hobnobbing to many places.

Gary completed his solo flight successfully, which for him meant the drone was still in one piece when he landed.

Ivan called a meeting to announce that the Installation was doubling its personnel. To staff the facility, every child-rearer would receive two children immediately. So much for what Pete had heard. But then Ivan also confirmed the rumor saying there would be an additional two in six months. Pete would be deluged with diapers. Danny at the Research Center would have it much easier.

Pete emailed the following day to let Brian know he had to come see his new children.

Brian went. They were cute; making him miss her. Although he had never stopped thinking of her, that reminder brought her back clearer than memory alone.

Brian caught up on all his other duties as well, bringing everything up to date, save the apprenticeship. He would email Ivan soon to tell him Gary had completed it. That would make the plan for one unnecessary.

Even though he allowed himself more free time than he ever had before, he never made time to exercise. He had always looked for a consistent daily timeframe to do it and now that he could make it happen, it was always tomorrow.

***

"Gary, you can take the rest of the day off," Brian said, after they used the old drone to pull the new one from the hangar. Without a break in over two months, Brian was certain Gary would jump all over the opportunity.

"No way, Chief. You're getting ready to test the plane. I'm staying to watch." His tone said, *what are you thinking?*

"That won't be for several hours," Brian said. "It needs to charge."

"I know that, but I built it and you're not testing it without me here."

"Okay, but after that, you're going. And if you do that for me, you can have tomorrow off too. Wait. Make that the next four tomorrows."

"Make it five and I won't ever tell Ivan you started that fire."

"That's extortion, but I'll make it six if you care to join me for lunch while we're waiting."

"Six days. Really?"

"Sure, you've earned it."

"So who's extorting who here?"

Although Brian laughed, he had to be careful. He needed Gary to leave, but he didn't need to be quite so adamant about it. Six days was a steep price for a few hours alone.

When they returned from their meal, Brian opened the access panel and checked. He knew it wouldn't be fully charged, which would take a few days, but it was far enough along that it would fly. He inserted the memory unit he was instructed to dupe, which came as an attachment on the last email from Brian at the Space Station. Brian punched in the code he had received as well and waited.

Getting confirmation of the program's success, he closed the panel. He was anxious to get the drone in the air. It wouldn't be long now and Gary would leave.

"I hope it works," Gary said.

"The part I put together will. I don't know about the part you did," Brian said.

"I was only hoping because you did some of it."

"I'm hoping because you did a lot of it."

"The cart worked, didn't it?"

"Yep, but this isn't the cart," Brian said. "And we're putting that question to rest right now." He pushed the button to start the motors. Slowly, the blades began to turn.

"That's a good sign, all the motors are turning," Gary said. Brian waited while the blades got up to speed. He then taxied over the tarmac. "It's looking good, Chief." There was excitement in his voice.

When in position to takeoff, Brian didn't hesitate. Powering up, it sped down the runway. "Here we go," Brian said. Reaching airspeed, it lifted off. Immediately Brian began testing the controls to ensure they worked. It responded beautifully. Brian felt relief wash over him. "Good work, Gary. You did an excellent job. Enjoy your six days."

Gary stood there, not budging, eyes on the drone. He never could take a hint. It was time for him to go.

"I'm flying it next," Gary said.

"You don't need to fly it right now." Brian was hesitant to hand over the remote. This close, one little mistake would ruin it. Besides that, Brian was more than eager to run the next test, which he would only do after Gary was gone.

"Come on, Chief, hand it over and then I'll go."

Brian put it on autopilot, feeling control slip away.

"Make sure you use the viewer."

"I know; everything's backward when it's flying toward us." Gary turned the drone and brought it down. He flew it directly overhead. It was so close; Brian's hair blew back. With the autopilot reset, Gary handed it back, leaving it on a steady climb heading away from the Installation. "Thanks, Chief, I'll see you in six days." He could feel Gary's sense of accomplishment as he walked to the cart. It was an important moment, one he would never forget, one Henry intended Brian to experience.

Brian walked to the hangar, leaving the drone on the path Gary had set. He felt he should reward Gary with something special. But didn't know what. Gary already had everything he wanted from the Dupe.

When Brian reached the door to the hangar, he stopped and watched Gary drive away. He took a deep breath and waited until he could no longer hear the drone. Then he set it to circle, keeping it on a steady climb, letting it drift back directly overhead.

The drone that served Ivan flew at the ideal altitude. Brian would position this one five hundred feet above it.

By the time the drone was ten miles high, he had it directly overhead. He looked, but couldn't see or hear it, and he knew exactly where to look.

With it in position, Brian set the holding pattern and stepped into the hangar reaching into his pocket for his new device, which the program for duping also came with the last email. He flipped it open and turned it on. Locating the number from storage, he hit send.

The phone rang.

"Joe's pizza, this is Joe, may I help you?" Brian laughed at the Space Station.

"I'll bet it took you every bit of three months to come up with that," Brian smiled from the hangar. "I'm glad this thing works, I can hear you clearly."

"You got the plane done sooner than I thought you would."

"I know. I lost Robert. She saved my life. Predators took her." His emotions ran high; both from having his communication link back and letting Brian at the Space Station know she was gone. He almost broke down.

"I'm sorry... Robert? Is that what you named her?"

"Yes."

"What happened?"

He relived that horrific day. It was something Brian at the Space Station would understand fully, and did.

When Brian finished, Space Station Brian said, "Her name is Amy."

"Amy?"

"Remember those mummified remains?"

"Yes."

"That's Amy. It's her digitalization from when she was a baby."

"Amy. It sounds so strange."

"It's a girl's name."

"Incredible! They have different names."

"I'd have to look it up, but Robert probably has a girl's version." To Brian on earth that didn't matter. He would always remember her as Robert. He had flown back and carved 'Robert' into the tree where he buried the toy. "You know I've been waiting for your call. I have something you need to take care of."

"Great. Every time you have something for me to take care of, it turns into a major event."

"This promises to be bigger and better. But it'll take both of us to find out if it works."

***

The following morning Brian left the Installation with the pods attached to the drone. When in the air, he switched modes on the remote and set the new drone to follow. He then called Brian at the Space Station to let him know he was on his way.

Three fourths of a day later, he called again to tell Brian at the Space Station he would be on the ground in twenty minutes.

He had no more than got out of the drone and started setting the warning system when his phone rang.

"I haven't gotten the warning system set yet, but go ahead."

"I have to get your position first," Space Station Brian said. "You know this better work," he said more to himself then to Brian. "Okay, got it. Don't move from where you're at and stay on the line. I need you to tell me what you see."

"Is it safe?" There was no response. "Okay, it must be safe. I don't see anything. What am I looking for?"

"It'll take a second. And I don't know what to tell you to look for. As far as I know, nothing like this has ever been done. I've got it aimed east of you about two hundred feet, so you should be fine where you are."

"Should be?"

There was a long pause. "You see it?"

"No. Shouldn't I be running the other way, or something?"

"Don't be funny."

"Well, it might help if you told me what you're doing. Wait…" Brian standing on the sand paused.

"Describe it."

"Never mind, it's just a dust devil."

"Is it where I said to look?"

"Yes, it's next to a tree if that helps."

Brian continued to watch, realizing it wasn't a dust devil; it stayed in one place and was very clear.

"That has to be it. Tell me what it looks like."

"I don't know. A dust devil."

Another delay before Brian at the Space Station said, "Come on, keep talking. Describe it."

"What do I say? Dust devil doesn't really give the correct picture, but it's as close as I can come," Brian said. "It looks like…well, it's not moving, and there's a depression developing in the sand under it."

"Is it getting bigger, smaller?"

"It hasn't changed that I can tell."

Then it dissipated as quickly as it started.

"It's gone."

"Can you see it?"

"I just told you, it's gone."

"That's not what I meant. It isn't gone, it's just finished. It should be safe to go over there now. Let me know what you find."

"I don't know about this, and I wish you'd quit saying *should* be. You didn't tell me there would be any danger."

"I told you this has never been done before. I'm making sure you're careful."

"Sure, easy for you to say from up there, but give me a second, I'm on my way." Brian walked toward the tree. When he was closer, "I'll be…"

"You see it?"

"Part of the tree is missing. In the depression, it looks like there's a bowl."

"That's it!" The excitement clearly came over the phone. "Pick it up."

"I'm not close enough."

"Well, when you are, pick it up. It's a gift for you."

There was something moving in the bowl.

"Are you sure it's done? I see something moving."

"Excellent, that's our first little space traveler. And he's made it safely to earth. We won't need the spaceships any longer, they are obsolete."

"Don't disconnect them. It helps keep Ivan out of my hair."

"Why do you think they're still hooked up?"

When Brian made it to the depression, he bent and grabbed the bowl by the rim.

"It's a fish. I thought you were whacked when you said the ships were obsolete. How did you get this to work?"

"It's really quite simple. I used the same technology that allows you to hear my voice, with a few modifications of course."

"I'm listening."

"The signal for the fish was composed of a given wave length. The waves I used here came through three different lasers to achieve pinpoint accuracy when I transmitted them to where you are. Those signals came from different sectors in space so they would intersect one another from different angles. Each signal is super imposed with a tremendous amount of information, each carries its own set of instructions, which not only influences the atoms where they intersect, but wove them into what you're holding."

"You're a whiz. I'll bet it's a nightmare of a program."

"Somewhat."

"What made you think of it?"

"You remember that first project at the Research Center on matter transmission?"

"Of course. What a disaster?"

"This was just the next logical step from there. Instead of sending the matter to where you want to go, use the matter that's already there. It's much simpler."

"So why isn't the fish dead? You didn't use a defibrillator."

"All that took was a small charge stored in its heart; just enough to nudge it along."

Brian took a couple of steps around the rim of the hole and stooped to touch the tree where the chunk was missing from it. Other than being very smooth, it felt like a tree. As he squatted, he spotted what remained of a seagull on the edge of the depression. The base of the tree had blocked it from view.

"I don't know how this works, but there's a chunk missing out of the tree where the dust devil touched it. And there's a seagull that's half-gone. It looks like your program melted away everything it touched."

"It caught a seagull?"

"I'm telling you what I see, but I'm assuming it did. Its head and one wing are gone."

"Interesting. I'll have to see if it can identify life forms so the program doesn't collect the particles it needs from them.

"Brian," Brian said from earth, "you're smarter than I am, aren't you? I never would have figured this out."

"You made me that way, Chief."

"Amazing... You're whacked, but you aren't whacked."

"You think I'm whacked, what about you? Which reminds me, you've been getting your exercise, right?"

"We're both whacked, but at least you have my sense of humor. Now it's time for you to do something for me."

"Name it."

Later, Brian put the fish in the can. He had no idea what to feed it. Now that it had traveled through space on its own, it could take care of itself in a nice little pond somewhere after he dumped it.

Chapter Twenty-Nine

"Are you sure you want to go through with this?" Brian asked from the Space Station.

"Absolutely," Brian answered at the front door. He stood off to the side, out of the view of the camera.

"Okay, you're free and clear to wander about the Space Center, though I wish you'd reconsider. You know you don't have to rush right into this; putting it off until later is okay."

"Thanks again for your unwavering advice, but I'm ready now," Brian answered. He already had the key in the door, and when he turned it, it didn't budge. "Dang, the key doesn't work."

"What did you expect? One solution, Chief. Find a rock."

Brian took one from against the building and broke the glass. He reached through and unlocked the door, then picked up the carrying case with the memory unit and went in.

"I'm in, headed for the digitalizer now."

"Ivan should really take better care of his equipment. It's a shame all those cameras malfunctioned. I wonder what caused them to all go at once?" Brian laughed from the Space Station. "It can't be good. Someone's bound to break in and take advantage."

"Stop it."

"One last time Chief, turn around while you still can and leave."

"We've been through this a hundred times. You're sure you've got control from up there?"

"Of course I'm in control. I've been tempted on many occasions to change Ivan's menu selection at the Dupe. I haven't done it yet; so how's that for control? But can you imagine the look on Ivan's face if there were a predator on the platform? He'd pee his pants."

"Will you stop it? You're becoming sadistic."

"Well, may I remind you that the cameras no longer work; and even though you never mentioned it, there was an alarm, which, I might add, no longer works either. Now where was I? Oh yeah, he'd pee his pants, but you know what; I couldn't be that mean to a predator. Ivan would give it indigestion and the council would have to go through the trouble of getting a new chairman."

"Stop it."

"Oh, come on, Chief, you're spoiling all my fun. I get a lot of mileage out of the things I could do to that old geezer. It's my only entertainment."

"Please, I have to concentrate."

"You're no fun," he said, and disconnected.

Inside the room, Brian got everything running, and lay on the table letting it pull him into the equipment. He had wrecked the non-remastered memory unit trying to get her digitalization from the Space Center on it when he first tried to do it at home and now had to redo it. This time, the IV hit the mark.

Once out, he reset the equipment, and initialized the vaporizer. He left everything on and walked out of the room, calling the Space Station.

"It's set; tell me you're set."

"I could have turned it on for you, don't worry about my end."

"I'm on my way to the Dupe. I'll call when I'm ready."

"Some people have all the fun. I should call Ivan. Let him know what you're up to. That'd be interesting."

"You know what? You're beyond help some days," Brian said. He didn't know if Brian at the Space Station even heard through all the laughter.

"Ivan's not going to be very happy when he finds out."

"It was your idea," Brian said, entering the main aisle alongside the control room.

"Just trying to be helpful."

"Well, once we pull this off, it'll be a big help. I wish I'd thought of it."

"Well, actually you did," Space Station Brian continued to laugh.

As he went down the curved aisle, he kept thinking there should be some sort of law against teasing yourself. Some days he put up with a constant barrage.

Just before reaching the entrance to the control room, he came to an abrupt stop. "There's someone ahead of me," he said into the phone, while reaching into his pocket.

"Ivan?"

"I don't think so. He disappeared around the curvature when he saw me."

"Leave."

"I can't, he's between me and the door."

"Go out the side."

"That's a long way around," he said, but turned to head that way. Brian jumped, dropping the phone. Ivan was coming at him from behind, in bedclothes, and barefoot, with a gun pointed at him.

"It's you! It's been you all along, hasn't it?" Ivan emphasized every word. "I thought, but I didn't find anything at your house that you took from here. What's in the case?"

"It's empty."

"Open it."

Brian did, adrenalin filling his veins.

"Good, I caught you before you got anything. Drop the case." Brian dropped it. "No matter what I do, I can't keep you out of here, can I? How did you get in?" Brian didn't answer. "Fine, it doesn't matter. I've got you red-handed now. You'll never set foot in here again. I'll see that you pay for this the rest of your life."

The long barrel of the gun shook in Ivan's hand as he threatened. His eyes were wild; he looked as if he intended to shoot Brian on the spot. Brian couldn't figure out how or why Ivan had showed up. And he had showed up so quickly. Then it dawned on him; Ivan lived at the Space Center.

But what alerted him? The cameras and alarm were off.

Just then, He spotted movement behind Ivan and leaned to one side to see. Ivan turned to look; and when he did, Brian bolted for the door of the control room. Stopping, he had to pull it toward him to get through. It squeaked loudly in protest from jerking so fast and aggressively.

Unnerving, Brian didn't know what to do. This wrecked his plans. Sprinting past Ivan's desk, he turned the corner intending to dash down the hall, but stopped. Ivan could easily cut him off going down the other hall, or get a clear shot at him if he followed.

Turning down to one knee, Brian lowered himself aiming his gun at the door.

Unbelievably, through the distortion of the glass, Brian spotted Ivan coming back toward the door. Although this action confused him, because it left Ivan wide open. He knew Ivan saw him turn the corner, and he was now coming in through the door to get him. It was not an intelligent move, unless you believed your query had no weapon.

Without faltering, Brian fired. He unloaded the pistol not knowing how the glass would affect his shots.

Bursting into millions of pieces, the whole sheet dropped at once, along with Ivan to the floor.

With shots fired, his adrenaline bumped up several levels. Even though he hated to shoot, he had to prevent Ivan from shooting him. And although he started to shake because of what he had just done, a glimmer of hope rushed over him. He would be able to complete what he set out to do. It came at Ivan's expense, but was better than the alternative.

Ejecting the clip, Brian headed straight to Ivan. He stepped over the low wall which had held the glass. Chambering a round, he trained the gun on Ivan, who was face down. Brian looked, but didn't see Ivan's weapon. He must have fallen on it.

Blood pooled as it came out from under his body. Brian didn't know if Ivan was dead, but needed to be sure where the weapon was before turning his back. He felt for a pulse at Ivan's neck. Brian's own heart pounded so hard, he couldn't tell if he felt his own pulse or Ivan's. He grabbed Ivan by the shirt at the shoulder and rolled him over to get the weapon.

Brian gasped. It wasn't Ivan. It was Henry!

Staring in disbelief, raw emotion shot through him. "Henry," he said under his breath. He went from crouching to his butt falling to the floor. He had just shot Henry. Everything around him dissolved away as he tried to understand.

Brian felt helpless. Flooding his minds eye, he saw Henry clutching his arm again.

"Don't move," Ivan yelled, shattering his perplexity. Ivan had gone all the way around and now stood in the control room by his desk in the same place Brian had just been standing when he shot Henry. Barefoot, Ivan stayed away from the glass. It was hard for Brian to swing back from the emotions that gripped him, but his life depended on it. Ivan was an imminent danger. "I see you've discovered Henry's little secret. That's too bad. Toss the gun."

He did so immediately. Ivan didn't need an excuse to shoot. He flung the gun with so much force it glided down the hall.

"Who is this?" Brian asked.

"Who do you think? It's Henry," Ivan said. "He doesn't appear to be breathing. He is dead, isn't he?"

"I don't know."

"It doesn't matter. There's another one running around here. They're not too bright, but one of them came and got me when they saw you. To be quite honest, I'm tired of taking care of them. It was Henry's job to take care of them before you came along. I told him to get rid of you, because he wasn't spending adequate time at it. But what happened? Henry died, and I got stuck with you and their care."

"I take it Henry worked at the Research Center," Brian said.

"At one time, and he convinced me he had the memory duping thing all figured out. Once persuaded, I went first. I call that one Ivan Two," he said, spelling it. Brian understood then where Ivan came up with his password, Iv@n1. "He's such an idiot, wanders around here all night with the others. Henry went behind my back and tried duping himself two more times, with some minor adjustments. I keep them locked up downstairs during the day. And now that you've discovered them, everyone will find out. I can't let that happen, Brian." Ivan relayed the last hysterically.

Brian understood then why Henry had to get rid of him as his apprentice and why Henry had caught on so quickly when he explained the memory duping process. He also understood why Ivan was so adamant about the break-ins.

"Stand up, and keep your hands where I can see them. Do it slowly. Now!" Ivan screamed.

Brian heard it in his voice; Ivan intended to see him dead. This wasn't some animal hunting for food that could be easily diverted with pepper spray.

Precarious as he stood, Brian's stomach was in knots. He had just killed Henry and Ivan was crazed. He was going to die. The gun was of no use. He had thrown it too far down the aisle. He needed it; if he were going to die, he would do so fighting.

"I assume you have your cart. Get Henry; we're going for a ride."

Henry had fallen in the direction he was walking, which put Brian closer to the door than where Henry had been when Brian shot him. He bent over as if to get a grip to lift him, crouching as he prepared for flight. The glass kept Ivan where he was. Brian could be out of the line of fire in less than a second. His muscles tensed as one hand touched the floor and the other reached for Henry. He leaned. Ivan had a clear view of him all the way to the gun. Brian did not intend to go that way.

With every ounce of energy, he hurled himself past the door. Ivan fired, but Brian was already gone. Sliding on his belly, he immediately pushed up and caught stride with a hand going into his pocket for a pepper spray.

He heard the door squeak. Ivan fired; bullets whizzed by ricocheting along the outside curvature of the hall. Brian thought the broken glass would have keep Ivan from using the door. Brian turned into the wall going up against the inside curvature, breathing hard, pepper spray aimed down the hall.

"It's of no use, Brian. You have no place to go," Ivan said as he came toward him. Another shot rang out and whizzed by.

Brian dropped to the floor letting loose a small burst of pepper spray.

Ivan sneezed, and then cursed as a hail of bullets followed.

Brian canvassed the whole area in front of him, emptying the can.

Ivan sneezed several more times, further away, retreating.

Reaching into his pocket for another pepper spray, Brian began to crawl toward Ivan. He hoped it was the last thing Ivan expected him to do.

As he crawled forward, he listened. Ivan had either stopped sneezing or left. Brian could no longer hear him. If Ivan had recovered, he only got a small whiff of pepper spray and could be waiting, or he had left, in which case, he would be back. Before it became just a matter of time, Brian had to get to the exit.

Back in survival mode, there was no thought of finishing what he had started.

Because he hadn't heard the door squeak when Ivan retreated, he figured Ivan bypassed the control room. Though he could assume nothing; even though barefoot and sneezing, Ivan could have stepped over the wall where most of the glass was located.

As Brian crawled forward, his phone came into view. It had ended up closer to the wall and was now half-buried under glass. If he could get to it, he could call for help.

Brian at the Space Station could turn the front of the building into one big pit, eliminating Ivan. Or he could turn Ivan into a roach; or send a machinegun, grenades, anything to keep Ivan at bay.

When Brian reached the glass, he began to push it aside with his arm. Breaking it into small pieces, he found there were no shards or sharp edges. Ivan must have known it would not readily hinder him.

He inched forward as he cleared a path; eventually he lay across the front of the control room door.

The glass, now mounded, took too long to move. Close to his phone, Brian began crawling over the glass grinding pieces against each other and the floor. It pinpointed his location. If Ivan were in the control room, he would hear. It wouldn't take much too simply walk up from the other side and shoot. Crawling face down, Brian would never see it coming. Making it to the phone, he picked it up, turned to his side so he could see and flipped it open.

The phone was dead. Brian pushed buttons trying to get it to come back. It wouldn't work.

From where he lay, he could see the gun further down the aisle. Sitting in the open, it would be risky to try getting it. It was visible from both the control room and further down the aisle. Brian couldn't decide what to do next. Inaction pinned him in place. He couldn't just wait there for Ivan; he had to do something. But one false move, it would be over.

Determined, discarding the phone, he reached into his pocket for his last pepper spray and turned onto his back. With a pepper spray in each hand, he put one arm above the wall and sprayed across the inside of the control room.

Sitting up quickly while he continued to spray, Brian took in everything he could see at once, aiming the other can every where he looked. He didn't see Ivan. He stood, dropping the spent canister. The other canister went into his mouth. He raced for the gun. As he ran, Ivan came into view. He was waiting further down the aisle; up came his arm with the gun when he spotted Brian.

Brian dove. Bullets went by so close he could hear them screaming through the air. Hitting the floor, he scooped up his gun. Rolling to his back, he fired as he slid to the wall. By the time Brian hit the wall, which stopped him; the gun was empty of all but one shell.

Ivan hadn't waited for him just anywhere, but by an adjacent hall which he took cover down as soon as Brian aimed his weapon.

When the wall stopped him, Brian scrambled to his feet. Sprinting, he headed straight for where Ivan disappeared.

Brian ran hard. His feet pounded the floor. There would be no doubt of his approach. Ivan's gun appeared around the corner. In rapid succession, Ivan fired, spraying bullets everywhere. When the gun appeared, Brian went down feet first. Instead of shooting the last round at Ivan's arm, Brian dropped the gun letting it cling-clank against the floor. It must have sounded like sweet success as Ivan peered around the corner.

Brian fired the pepper spray, still sliding, anticipating where Ivan's head would pop out at point blank range.

Ivan crawled around gasping for air. Blindly, he searched for his gun. Instead of finding it, he ran headfirst into the wall.

Brian picked up Ivan's gun. Without saying a word, he picked up his gun too and reloaded it before holstering, and then he walked back down the aisle to retrieve his phone. There was information on it Ivan couldn't have. He crunched over the glass staring at Henry, who had lost so much blood he couldn't possibly be alive.

Brian had a difficult time coming to terms with Henry and Ivan being in cahoots with each other. They were very different people, and Brian couldn't imagine them being close friends. He never would have guessed.

"You hurt the boss man?" Ivan Two said from the control room.

The utterance sent Brian for his gun. He dropped the phone, for a second time. Aiming, he almost shot Ivan Two before he understood what was said. Ivan Two had no reaction to his defensive posturing.

Other than wearing clothes instead of pajamas, he looked identical. Even the hair was combed the same.

"The boss man will be all right; just give him some time. Sorry about Henry." It bothered him to have shot Henry, even though he understood he'd done it mistakenly.

"Okay."

With that assurance and apology, Ivan Two went his merry way, going about his usual business.

Brian picked up and pocketed the phone, then headed for the exit.

As he left, he passed the old geezer boss man, hacking up a lung, still blinded and drooling profusely on the floor.

With Ivan incapacitated, he would risk taking the time to complete what he set out to do. Once in the cart, he drove without lights. Of everything he needed to do, this was the most important. Worried, he began to debate whether he would have time.

Brian oscillated between believing Ivan would suffocate from lack of breath to fearing Ivan would recover quickly and soon try to stop him. Wallowing in what he had tossed up, Brian knew he had time. It was just a matter of how much. Compelled by this logic, he continued on his course. Trouble, he didn't want to underestimate Ivan. He could make it to a bathroom and wash. The other Henry, or Ivan Two, could be instructed to help. If that happened, he would recover quicker. He would then bring everything he had to bear down on Brian.

Though feeling insecure, Brian stepped into the cafeteria compelled to complete what he had planned.

He stepped up to the keypad to the Dupe. Because of how easy his phone had quit working, among his first selections were half-dozen new phones. It was essential from this point forward to stay in contact with the Space Station, hence the security of extras.

At the same time, he selected a shotgun, in case the need arose. He didn't intend to use it unless he had to. He knew everyone within One-O-Seven on sight, and there was no one, save maybe Ivan, whom he cared to harm. If left alone, he would leave in peace, but leave is what he intended to do. This would ensure he was able to do so. He dropped the pepper sprays into his pocket first.

Prepared, Brian set all three carriers on the floor by the platform.

Over the next thirty-five minutes, he tucked a baby away into each carrier. Each bundle was put together identically, and every one of them was female.

He brought each into the world separately, giving himself time to prepare each for travel.

It didn't take long to remove the defibrillators and get them into diapers and dressed. His experienced hands prepared them expertly.

With the last earmuff snugly in place, Brian pulled the memory unit and picked up all three carriers at once.

Feeling surreal, he sat in the cart under a starry sky with the shotgun across his lap. Peaceful, it was quiet and calm, which was in stark contrast to how his night had been going. He sat there and took the moment in hoping the peace he felt depicted their future.

As he programmed a phone, one of his precious bundles began to cry.

Brian punched the number when the phone was ready.

"Are you okay?" was the first thing he heard.

"I'm done. Are you set to undertake the last bit of business?"

"I hear one of them. Tell me what happened?"

"Ivan showed up."

"I know that. He's already reported you as a non-citizen."

"He's premature; I haven't left yet. Has anyone responded?"

"Not yet. Give it a couple of hours and they'll be all over One-O-Seven like flies. Where are you?"

"I'm at the Dupe," Brian said, starting to move the cart forward toward the hangar.

"Why are you still there? Are you staying to watch?"

"No."

"Then go. By now he has help."

"I don't think so. Ivan's not going to ask for help. Its one thing to call in a non-citizen report, quite another to air out your dirty diapers for everyone to see. He has some business to deal with before he'll get help."

"You don't have time for this. It's urgent that you leave. Wait," there was a short pause. "I'll have to call you back in a moment. There's phone chatter I need to monitor."

"Fine, I'm on my way. I'll tell you about it later," Brian said. "Don't forget the digitalization."

"I won't." Space Station Brian hung up.

Brian was surprised Ivan had reported him so soon as a non-citizen. He wouldn't have had a clue Brian planned to leave. The only conclusion Brian could draw, because of what had happened—Ivan knew Brian was gone. Ivan would have been correct, plan or no plan.

Earlier in the day, he'd emailed Ivan to let him know Gary was making the next shuttle run solo. This put One-O-Seven's drone out of Ivan's use for at least four days and possibly five.

If Ivan had any inclination of the second drone, he would be waiting at the hangar. Brian was sure Ivan didn't suspect, but stopped short and put on the infrared goggles. When the cart stopped, one of the girls fussed giving away their position.

Brian proceeded slowly. Nothing revealed itself as he drove past the hangar and continued over the tarmac to the drone, which sat on the runway ready to go. Brian had brought it down just before dark.

At the drone, he loaded the girls into the canister, which sat under the wing and then he climbed in himself. Though he couldn't stand up inside, there was room to stretch while lying. He could sit inside as well.

For proper balance, a duplicate canister sat empty on the other half of the wing.

Brian imagined the platform of the Dupe had descended by now. On it, Ivan would find a not very bright Brian. It was the last thing that needed to be done to complete the ruse, and was completed courtesy of the Space Station.

Brian knew now Ivan would be able to provide the proper care and training.

The only surprise for everyone would be that Brian had used the vaporizer, but everyone would buy it, including Ivan. Ivan had been Brian's only concern, but even he would believe because it kept his secret safe. Brian wanted everyone to believe. It didn't matter whether they thought he used the vaporizer on purpose or by accident, as long as no one came looking for him.

Before starting the motors, Brian called the Space Station.

"I'm busy, call back."

"I'm leaving. I don't know if I'll be able to hear you. I have to know, did you transmit the digitalization to the Dupe?"

"Yes," he said, and disconnected.

Brian started the motors, and took off.

Chapter Thirty

Brian slept despite the fact that the canister flexed under the wing like a humming bird visiting flowers.

When daylight reached through the nose of the canister, which danced across Brian's face, he opened his eyes. He was instantly caught between elation and *what have I done?* Both feelings stirred intently. It didn't take long before he began to smile. He had actually gone through with it and his biggest consolation—he made it out with the girls—even after Ivan found him inside the Space Center.

There would be no turning back.

On his knees, Brian unzipped the hoods of each carrier just enough to peek inside. Everybody was asleep. He scooted the floor to the back of the canister. Opening the hatch, he relieved himself. Next, he opened a cooler, took out a hot plate, and then scooted forward to the nose. Dome-shaped and faceted by framework, tempered glass formed the nose and part of the floor. When he reached the front, Brian sat right on top of the glass and began to eat. He had an excellent view and knew this could be his last ride in a drone. He wished he hadn't missed the sunrise. He took in the horizon as he ate cognizant of that fact.

Since the inception of the idea of putting a canister under the wing, which he laid out on his laptop, he liked the concept of this design. It hadn't taken long to build and he was pleased with the results.

He wanted to call the Space Station to find out what Brian there knew, but with the canister sitting just behind the propeller, there was no way to hear.

As he ate, he thought of Gary. Gary was the only flaw in his plan. Even though Ivan didn't have a clue about the new drone, Gary would put two and two together and go forward when he figured out the new drone wasn't on loan to another Installation as Brian had told him.

Ivan would be surprised when Gary came to him about the second plane. It would become his primary concern; though Ivan wouldn't believe Gary, and would see Don for independent confirmation that the parts had been run through the Dupe.

What protocol would Ivan instruct the Special Forces to follow? They wouldn't know where to begin. Brian wished he could be a bug on the wall when the crap hit the fan. Ivan would be furious. This was going to embarrass him in front of the council. They might even consider replacing him as their chair. The best-case scenario; Ivan would cover it up and no one would ever find out or come looking for him.

After breakfast, he sequenced through all of the girls, feeding by tapping their chins, changing them and preparing all for the drop.

Within the hour of getting them ready they reached their destination. Brian dropped a cooler with a chute and watched it float to the ground. If possible, he needed to avoid the trees, and brought the drone around on a slightly adjusted course for a second attempt over the small clearing. His first try hadn't missed by much.

Hitting the mark with the second, he made a wide circle and returned to the same course. When he reached the mark, Brian released all three carriers one after the other before jumping himself. All chutes opened and floated to the ground.

Once he landed he took off his chute and trotted to the closest carrier. Checking to ensure she had landed safely, he removed the chute from the carrier while she cried.

"Did that scare you? It's okay, kiddo; tell me how many younger than you who can say they've parachuted from a plane, huh? Not even Henry did that, not to mention Gary. And you're not allowed to count the other two."

Brian gathered them, relived after finding all had fared well, although none remained silent. When all three were safely with him, he took the remote and set the drone to climb to its new position above them. Next, he pulled the phone from his pocket and called the Space Station.

He stepped away a little in order to hear.

"This is Brian."

"You're too funny, like there'd be someone else that would answer."

Space Station Brian laughed. "You wouldn't know if I duped company."

"You're right, but I don't think so, you're always complaining you're going to starve. I would never understand why, if you did so," Brian said. "We're on the ground; I've been dying to know what's going on at the installation."

"There's not much to tell. Ivan got eleven planes to respond. Three planes are still en route; four are circling One-O-Seven looking for you. The other four Ivan put on standby. Based on that, I think he believes you've vaporized yourself."

"That's good."

"Yes it is. I'm all set with your coordinates. I'm sending the shelter now. It'll be about a quarter mile away."

"Which way?"

"South."

"Thanks, I'll catch you in a bit; all three of my companions are looking for assistance."

While Brian talked, he had kept a constant vigil. Flipping the phone closed, he got all three carriers and headed south.

Weaving his way through the woods, he stopped often to set the carriers down. All together they were quite a load, and getting them under motion had quieted them. He was ready to call the Space Station when he was sure he had gone further than a quarter of a mile, thinking he missed it, when he came upon a large circular clearing.

The trees were funky. A distinctive cut-off defined a circle with all the foliage inside gone. Depending on where the trees stood dictated how much of them remained. Nearby, one tree without much of a trunk had already fallen away from the center of the circle and lay on the ground. Others, with the weight of their branches all to one side, leaned away. Some of those only remained upright, caught against the trees into which they leaned.

Expecting a small shelter, Brian smiled when he saw the house. Four-stories with a glass roof, it encompassed a large area sitting at the bottom of the melted depression. The depression started out steep and had less of an incline closer to the front door.

Brian went into the depression following the incline up to the front porch. He set the carriers on the porch. He opened the door and looked inside. The room he entered was completely furnished. The scale of everything was much larger than anything that existed at the Installation. He brought the carriers inside, closed the door and left them there while he went exploring. The carpets had no sign of wear, unlike every place he had lived before.

On the second floor, he found a study, complete with a terminal sitting on a large desk. He called the Space Station.

"Do you like it?" Space Station Brian asked, without even saying hi.

"Like it? I love it. I was expecting something simple. This is elaborate. The size of this place alone is overwhelming. You must have worked on the program the whole time, it's no wonder it took so long."

"It wasn't bad; mostly detail work."

"I still can't believe you figured out how to do this."

"Did you see the water?"

"Water! Where?"

"Fourth floor."

Brian ran up the next flight of stairs. When he rounded the corner at the base of the last flight of stairs, he saw the glass ceiling. In anticipation, he began to giggle as he went up. Composed entirely of glass around him, he burst out laughing in excitement. This floor had nothing in common with anything at the Installation. A glassed foyer held an inset containing the door to the pool. He went to it

"Oh, wow! Brian, this is amazing, thanks," he said, laughter still present in his voice as he went through the door. He ripped off his shirt, shoes, pants, and waded in with nothing on. "What a nice touch. This is fabulous. The water's great too, so warm."

"Glad you like it, Chief. I was up all night. It's off to bed for me, I'll call later."

Brian got out of the water. Taking a plush towel from the stack on a table by the door, he used it to dry, and then dressed. One flight after another, he went all the way down to the first floor where the girls were located. He wanted to tell them about the pool, but all was peaceful, so Brian didn't disturb them. Instead, he got on the floor and spent the next half hour exercising, something he had put off for too long.

Afterward, lying on the carpet next to them, he felt a sense of euphoria that wouldn't go away. The luxury sent from the Space Station overwhelmed. After Robert had been taken, planning this was the only thing that had kept him sane. Every morning it gave him a *reason* to get out of bed.

Brian fell asleep where he lay.

The girls kept waking him for what seemed a constant barrage of care, but every time, Brian lay back on the floor and went to sleep after fulfilling each need.

Later the phone rang. Brian pulled it from his pocket and shut it off. Blissfully, it was the best sleep he could remember getting. It wasn't because it was continuous, but because he could lay there and keep doing it. The last time he drifted off, he was thankful he kept waking or he wouldn't have known it was the best sleep he had ever gotten.

Early the following day Brian remembered his phone. He turned it on and called the Space Station. It rang a while before he got an answer.

"What do you want?" The voice from the Space Station was groggy.

"You rang."

"Yes I did, but you didn't answer."

"I was tired. I shut the phone off."

"I called with important news and you shut your phone off. Then you have the nerve to call me when I'm asleep and I don't have enough sense but to answer."

"So turn me in to Ivan. What's up?"

"They called the search off."

"Really...!"

"Yes, really, I thought you'd want to know."

"I do, so it worked."

"It'll work until Gary comes back, but if you'd like, I can call Ivan and let him know you did in fact leave the Installation. That news would put him right back on his toes, he'd pee his pants all over again."

Brian laughed. He had just been forgiven for shutting off his phone.

"That won't be necessary. And thanks again for everything. I'm grateful. It's hard to believe I'm here."

"Glad you like it."

"Yes, it's fabulous; so much luxury. A lot more than you led me to believe," Brian said, truly appreciative.

"Enjoy it. Your terminal has everything on it that'll explain everything you need to know to understand the science behind how I got it to work. Spend a little time with it, you'll see. The walls are loaded with solar panels and battery wire. You'll never lack power. I have to use the bathroom and that's a chore to do up here," Space Station Brian said. "I'll call later. Have fun."

***

The kitchen had several appliances.

Brian didn't know what any of them were for. One, however, let out a blast of cold air when he opened it. It was full of foodstuff, but unlike the cooler with hot and cold sections, it was just cold and colder.

He called the Space Station to find out why the other stuff was included with the house. Guided over the phone, Brian prepared a hot meal on the stove. He had fun doing it, and Brian at the Space Station wanted to know how everything tasted. He kept asking for more detail no matter how in-depth Brian went.

Every room had inviting furniture. It was all so new and in much better condition than anything he had at the Installation except for the few things he had duped.

Plush, everywhere he went the carpets were soft under foot.

On the third floor, there were more bedrooms than he would ever use. Each female had a separate room already prepared, which came complete with toys, and a closet full of clothes. In his room, the bed was huge and the closet was full as well.

The bathroom off his bedroom was luxurious. The shower stall had several showerheads. When he first discovered those, he undressed immediately and turned them all on at once. He was thrilled he didn't have to go without. And it was the best set-up he had ever used.

Over the next few weeks, Brian kept adding new things to his exercise routine making it longer. He didn't bother with any set time, just did it whenever he wanted. He recorded each day what he accomplished showing a steady increase in the amount. Most days, he did the routine more than once.

The chair at his desk had more controls on it than any chair he had ever seen. It was very comfortable, and he would have been embarrassed to admit to Space Station Brian that he spent more time sleeping there than working.

Demanding, the girls always came first. He took them one at a time into the water every day. Even though they weren't old enough to splash around, he enjoyed taking them in because he knew it wouldn't be long before they would.

Each day, Brian made more discoveries within the house. The garbage disposal was a completely new concept to him. He stopped using it because it seemed wasteful to put the organics down the drain.

The supplies he had dropped remained where they were. He had tried once to pull some of it from the top of the trees. But there was so much he had brought and dropped and because the Space Station provided everything he wanted, he didn't bother again.

He piled whatever he discarded outside in one area, including diapers. Space Station Brian had the spot pegged; and all the waste they generated became useable items.

Brian found himself at the stove too often. Although he was beginning to understand the terminology in the cookbook, he was no connoisseur over the stove. His cupboards were loaded with stuff Space Station Brian sent. He always wanted to know how everything tasted. Brian wanted a break from cooking and a break from telling the Space Station how good it all was.

With the Dupe, it took longer to decide what he wanted than it did to provide it. Brian already considered cooking a waste of time, easier to just call the Space Station for his meals.

One morning, almost a month to the day they'd arrived, Brain was at the stove doing eggs over easy.

He had a kid in one arm holding the back of her head in the palm of his hand with her legs draped over both sides of his arm at the elbow. There was another crying on the floor at his feet. The third, upstairs, was presumably still sleeping. He needed to get up there to check on her.

His phone rang.

He turned the stove off and pulled the phone from his pocket. Just then, his toast popped up. He wanted to get it buttered while it was still hot so the butter would melt.

"What do you want?" he said into the phone holding it against his shoulder so he could flip the eggs.

"And a mighty fine how do you do to you too."

"If you called just to chat, I'm busy."

"No, I wanted something."

"What is it?"

"Have you picked names yet?" Brian at the Space Station had sent a book, which was loaded with a host of names. He had skimmed through some of it for the female gender.

"No, I've only glanced through it," he said tentatively, because he had had it for a while. He had already grabbed the toast and was buttering it one-handed.

"Was there any you liked?"

"I don't know. First, I have to figure out how to tell these guys apart. Right now, I've been numbering the back of their diapers. Beside that, some of the names in there I don't know how to pronounce," Brian admitted. "So how am I supposed to decide which ones to use?"

"That's your problem, not mine," Space Station Brian said. "I called to let you know the search for you is back on and I'd pick Molly, Jackie and Kelly."

"When did this happen?"

"Um, not too long ago. They're totally confused as to what's going on and are doing it as a precautionary measure. They don't know if you're out there or not. They're assigning each Installation known places you could land the drone. After that, who knows; maybe they'll perform a grid search starting at One-O-Seven. I wouldn't worry about it. You're a grain of sand on the beach."

"Molly and Kelly are fine. Jackie is too close to Jack."

"It's supposed to be."

"Well, it's what I called Robert the first time. Come up with something else. And, you know what else? You're a fine one to tell me not to worry. It's easy for you to say when you're sitting up there where no one knows you exist."

"Chief, I don't know what to tell you. I'll be glad to let you worry all you want. How does Katie sound?"

"Katie's fine. The house will be easy to spot from the air. And they won't be able to miss the supplies. Most of that stuff still hangs in the trees."

"Molly, Kelly and Katie, it is. I like those. For the house, there's camouflage netting sitting in your junk heap, get it over the house and bare area. No one will be able see you from the air then. Take a walk out to the supplies later today so I can get a fix on where they are. I'll come up with something to get rid of them."

"You have an answer for everything."

"I can't help it; too much time on my hands."

Brian laughed, "Yeah, right."

After they hung up, he sat at the kitchen table eating his eggs and toast. The butter hadn't melted as completely as he liked; and it hadn't taken Gary all that long to go see Ivan.

Ivan had thought Henry had been a bad influence over Brian. Brian wondered what Ivan would think of his influence over Gary. Cooking fish over a fire, just like Henry. All that stuff from the Dupe. And Brian never stayed at the Installation except for the last few months. Gary would have no reason to hold any of it back. Though Gary had better not mention anything about the fire where they collected aluminum...the little twit never even had the guts to ask if he could jump from the plane.

If Ivan knew how unimportant Brian felt his secret to be about Ivan Two and the two Henrys, maybe they could have struck up a deal. He could call Ivan now and threaten him with exposure if he didn't call off the search. The crusty old fart would be more than surprised. But it wasn't a good idea. As it was now, Ivan couldn't be sure if Brian existed.

After feeding the girls and exercising he went outside and began assessing how to get the netting to the top of the trees so he could spread it over the house.

He called the Space Station for an extension ladder.

That made it easy. He leaned the ladder up against the bare side of a tree, climbed up, and tied off the netting. He then moved the ladder to the next tree. He tied a piece of rope down further on the netting, climbed the ladder, and pulled it tight before tying it off and cutting the rope. He repeated that all along the tree line.

A few drops of rain started to fall as he did the work. For a while, the drops came and went. Later, the drops increased to a drizzle, but nothing serious enough to keep him from working.

He made progress until he was a fourth of the way around the circle. He called Space Station Brian.

"You're pesky today. Now what do you want?"

"You didn't send enough netting."

"The house isn't that big; there's plenty of netting."

"You're right; it's plenty to cover the house. I'm tying it off to the trees in order to get it over the house and cover the bare area. You'll need to send more."

"Ah, the trees aren't as close to the house as I thought."

While they talked, he walked over to what was once his trash heap. It was becoming a hole, as they needed more things than the waste they generated. He spotted a small furry critter scavenging through the garbage. He had never gotten this close and when the orb appeared, the critter looked up, sort of froze in place and dissipated quickly. Before the orb stopped, the critter was gone.

"This thing would make an awesome weapon. You could turn drones into rocks and drop them out of the sky like flies if any of them got too close to us."

"I suppose I could, but that would be sadistic, not to mention it would take each Installation months to replace their drone."

"Maybe, but it'd keep us safe. I'm off to put this stuff up, I'll catch you later."

He hung up and walked into the hole to get the netting. Self-conscious, he promptly got out. After seeing what happened to the critter, he would never go near the hole without ensuring Space Station Brian had no intention of using it.

Pulling netting up over one corner of the house, Brian made progress. As he worked, the drizzle turned into a steady rain.

When he finished, he looked up through the netting. It didn't look like much, and he was convinced anyone flying over would still spot the house.

He got a shovel. In the woods, he dug up a tree and transplanted it into the bare area. The rain became heavier. Already wet, he continued. His shoes became a mass of mud as he slipped and sloshed through the barren area, and then cleaned up half way decent as he traipsed through the woods in search of another tree he could handle.

Upon finishing, he laughed at what he had done. Compared to what he needed to accomplish, it was pitiful. The trees had to be much bigger in order to do any good, but it was a ton of work just doing what he had done. He quit to go inside.

He took his shoes off on the front porch. He wanted to keep the house clean and decided he'd call for a new pair. Stripping, he opened the door and set everything from his pockets on the floor.

Running upstairs, Brian took a hot shower. Afterward, it was comforting to snuggle into some dry clothes.

He brought the girls downstairs. Down pat, he began the routine of feeding them.

The night before, he had decided who was who and wrote their names on the back of their diapers.

In the downstairs rocker, he rocked Kelly as she drank a bottle.

Through the window, a flash brightened the room, followed by the crack of thunder. Kelly started to pout.

"Oh, don't be afraid, it's just a storm. This one's been brewing for a while, and you'll see plenty more."

The wind blew the curtains; rain surged in onto the floor through the small opening. It began to pour outside.

Holding Kelly, Brian went around closing the windows all the way. On this floor, he had only opened them a crack because of the predators. He hadn't seen any yet, but he was sure that was just a matter of time. There was an abundant wildlife presence that would handily support them.

More flashes, more booms, and one of the other girls started to cry.

Because of the storm, he resigned himself to the fact that he would be providing a little extra care and comfort until it passed.

A pacifier went into Kelly's mouth as he put her on the floor next to the other two. He then picked up the one crying and turned her around to read the back of her diaper. Lightning struck close by. The lights flickered in the house. Resounding, the crash came instantaneously; all four of them jumped.

"Boy, Katie! That was close. Did you feel it? I could hear the windows shake."

He sat back in the rocker and fed her next. The rain didn't let up, nor did the lightning or wind.

When she finished, he burped her, and set her on the floor next to the others.

"Molly, I have to get your bottle. You'll have to wait a sec."

The rain continued to come down hard.

In the kitchen, while he waited for the formula to warm, Brian felt his socks get wet. Looking down, he saw muddy water going past his feet as it went under the stove. The water rose around his feet.

The mess it was making on the floor frustrated him. He followed the muddy stream back to the front door where he watched it come in from under it. The amount of work it would take to clean the carpet was disappointing. He wondered if it would ever come completely clean.

Brian opened the door to see why the rain was seeping in. The knob turned hard. When the dog in the latch passed the strike plate, muddy water forcefully removed the door from his hand.

Halfway up the door, the water rushed in. His eyes widened at the sight as he tried to close the door. He made no progress against the pressure of water coming in. He had to stop. He raced through the developing slurry to the girls. The water traveled quickly beating him to them.

Grabbing one, he haphazardly stuck her under his arm; the second went up under the same arm. Buoyant, the third was no longer on the floor; in his rush to get her, he pushed her under the muddy water trying to get a hold.

After securing all three, he waded to the steps with water and mud halfway to his knees. It continued to rise.

Upstairs he deposited all three girls onto his bed. Soaked and soiled he would now have to clean the bedding. He left them, and ran back downstairs taking note of the muddy tracks he had left on the stairs.

The water, now above his knees, was still coming in.

He tried shutting the entrance again, and just barely was able to do so. He headed for the basement. Opening that door would get rid of the water downstairs.

With some force, Brian put a foot on the jamb and pulled the door toward him. Standing on tile, he braced himself into the door, grabbing the inside knob, knowing the rush was coming. The surge still swept him from his feet. He splashed onto his rear, never letting go of the knob, and was swept through the doorway pulling it shut. He ended up on the stairs, now holding the knob.

Dripping dirty water from head to toe, he got to his feet and tried the door. Standing lower, and not able to use the jamb as he had from the other side, he couldn't apply the same force. He was trapped in the basement, and the girls upstairs.

He went downstairs in search of something to open the door. Grabbing the first thing he found, he went back to the top and proceeded with a sledgehammer to swing at the door. Made of wood, water sprayed through the first hole he punched through. He punched another next to the first working his way up.

Fighting against the ever increasing surge of water which continually poured over him, he made progress. Once freed, the busted half of the door with the knob tumbled downstairs with the flow of water. He turned sideways keeping his balance and slowly got out.

While the water ran into the basement, Brian returned to the girls. He dripped muddy water all of the way up the stairs for a second time.

Stripping at the top, he left his clothes there, and went through the bedroom to the bathroom. All of the girls were crying. He flicked on the light and stepped into the shower. When he turned the water on, the light went dim; it then brightened, only to dim again.

While the water warmed at the shower Brian went back into the bedroom to get the dirtiest female first, he checked through the windows; the heavy downpour had abated, though it still rained. He got the one who had gone under, taking her to the shower.

Before stepping inside, he checked the temperature. In less than five minutes, he stepped out mostly clean himself.

Wrapping her in a towel, he laid her on the floor and took the next one into the shower. The light continued to flicker, fluctuating in brightness. The glow ebbed duller with each sequence of the cycle.

With three clean girls on the floor, he went back in and soaped down himself. He was ready to rinse when the water stopped working. Though the light was still on, its constant change in brightness was annoying. Using what dripped off the showerheads, Brian managed to remove the soap from around his eyes.

Going through the bedroom, he stopped briefly. One of the girls still cried.

"Molly, I'm sorry, I know I said it would just be a second for your bottle, and you'll have it, in another moment or two. But excuse me long enough to jump in the pool." He figured it had to be Molly; she was the only one who hadn't eaten.

All the way to the water, Brian tried to recall which baby belonged to which name. With them only in towels, he ran through all the movements he had made, but wasn't sure who was laying where when he picked them up from the muddy water. During the shower, he had stripped them and tossed their stuff into the trash. Memorizing the order he sat them down with towels, he would go through the trash. The last one out, their stuff would be on top. It was important to him to get their names right.

He toweled dry while heading back to the third floor.

At his closet, he dressed, picking out shorts and a pull over.

At the top of the stairs, he picked up his dirty clothes pinching them between his fingers and thumb holding them out as he went down the steps.

On the main floor, a layer of muck squished between his toes. Without water he didn't want to get dirty, although for his feet it was already too late.

Brian walked to the front door and deposited his soiled clothing on the floor. He remembered he had emptied his pockets there. He was glad for the extra phones upstairs, though the Space Station would eventually figure out to send another if he wasn't able to get through.

Walking to the kitchen, the main floor was beyond help.

At the stove, he grabbed Molly's formula.

Upstairs, he took who he assumed was Molly and sat in the upstairs rocker. While she ate, he programmed another phone.

Space Station Brian answered, "You again. What do you want now?"

"It's raining," Brian told him.

"You must be bored. Don't you have anything better to do than call me with a weather report? If you're not all that busy I can send a couple of more kids."

"Look, when you duped the house, it ended up at the bottom of the depression the orb makes," Brian said, very controlled. "The power's doing funny things and the water doesn't work anymore."

"I take it the rain got into the house."

"The main floor is ruined. It'll never come clean because I'm not even going to bother. Every time it rains, it'll flood. The basement has at least six feet of standing water," he said, exaggerating a little at this point.

"On a scale from one to ten, how bad is it?"

"That's a tossup. I'd say between one and two million, but maybe closer to three."

"I'll need a couple of days to work on the program." Brian could hear him tapping on the keyboard after that.

The following day, Brian brought the drone down. He wanted to see the house from the air. It took a while to descend. Using the forward camera view on the remote, he heard the drone as it approached and then flew over. He didn't see the house. He brought it back around to take another look. He spotted the house then, but it wasn't easy to pick out. Much to his surprise, the netting worked.

A few days later the power quit working altogether. Brian had to call for every need. He used the pool for baths until it turned a greenish black, which didn't take long.

Brian called the Space Station for water.

"Brian's duping service, how may I help you?" The statement was concise. Brian could tell he interrupted.

"We need water."

"I sent twenty-five gallons last night." His annoyance triggered.

"Look, you only have to push a button to give it to us. The girls and I need baths. I've got to haul it up to the third floor. So quit worrying what I'm doing with it, I'd push the button for you in a heartbeat, so push it for me. I won't carry anymore up there than I have to."

Brian heard him mutter, "I wish you could push the button for me." Then he spoke up, "My supply of organics will be depleted soon. I won't last much longer up here."

"I'm sorry there wasn't anything more, but I didn't know and there's nothing I can do about it now."

"It's something you didn't know…obviously I know that."

"If you could get the vaporizer to work…?"

"We've already been down that road. I've tried, there's no fixing it. If I could have done so, I'd already be gone. And as you know, if it doesn't work, I won't bother because when I come out of the equipment I'll still be here. You have no idea, you can't even imagine, what it was like or how it affected me when I found out I was me here and not you there."

"If I could I'd trade places with you, I would."

"Believe me, you wouldn't fair any better, but thanks." Without a gap, in what he said, he changed the subject, the frustration still evident, "Every time you call, I have to stop what I'm doing; it causes delays getting your new place done."

"That's irrational. Would you rather we die down here from lack of supplies while you program us a new place? It kind of defeats the purpose, doesn't it? But go ahead, vent all you want."

"I'm ready to push the button. Is there anything else? I need to get back to what I was doing."

"Diapers."

"You go through those like water."

"You're telling me?"

"You were ready to set out on your own without my help," Space Station Brian said. "How did you expect to survive?"

"I don't know."

"Hopefully you figure it out before I'm gone."

The Space Station's couple of days turned into more than six weeks.

Chapter Thirty-One

Fully loaded, Brian set out shortly after dawn. He called the Space Station as he closed the front door. He was glad to escape into the fresh air. The main floor smelled of rot. It had begun to permeate the whole house.

"I'm leaving."

"This'll be quite a hike," Space Station Brian said. "But you shouldn't be much longer than three quarters of the day. If you need something, anything, call me. I'll track your progress and let you know if you've lost your bearings. Be careful with that precious cargo and keep an eye out for predators."

"Believe it or not, I don't have any other plans."

Space Station Brian had sent a harness which strapped over his shoulders. Improvised, it allowed him to carry all three girls at once. Designed with one above the other, Katie and Kelly were riding on his back. Molly was in front.

He had only pocketed the necessities: a compass, his phones, the remote, and pepper sprays. He carried a shotgun, and little else.

The extra phones were newly duped for their batteries. Since loosing power at the house, the Space Station had sent him a new one every morning.

Brian had an additional piece of equipment clipped to his belt. Because of what happened to Robert, he had insisted Space Station Brian take the time to design and send a warning system. Small enough to strap to his belt, it had a range of two hundred feet, and included a viewer which would show him the direction any large animal was located in relation to where he stood.

Ahead of him lay fifteen miles of untamed territory. Unless he made good time, he would miss his regular exercise routine. He was leaving early so that wouldn't happen. He was determined to get it in when they arrived. His routine was over two hours long, and he was doing it twice a day. He had plans to take it up a notch, make it more rigorous. If he missed it today, it would be the first time he had done so since they arrived.

He didn't expect it to be a straight shot to the new place, but hoped there weren't too many places where thick undergrowth sidetracked him. Too many, and they'd spend the night outside or still be hiking after dark.

At first, he thought his exercises had helped. After several hours of avoiding anything he had to duck under or squeeze through he was tired. He stopped and called the Space Station.

"Tell me what you need and I'll have it down there for you shortly."

"Breakfast."

"What would you like?"

"The girls will have formula. I'll take whatever."

"I happen to have whatever's on the menu. It comes in a variety of flavors. Would you care to be more specific?"

"Ha, ha, just surprise me. Since we have the same taste, I'm sure I'll like whatever you pick."

"Your whatever is on the way."

"Where?"

"Due west, about seventy feet." He tuned looking for the orb, but didn't see it through the trees. "I might add you're really doing well, both time-wise and staying on track. The exercises you've been doing helped."

"Thanks. I'll call when I'm ready to set out again." Brian folded his phone and went to find breakfast.

He heard it before he could see it. When everything came into view, he didn't know why he hadn't seen the orb. It had to be large.

Three carriers sat neatly across the top of a huge table. Each carrier came complete with a formula, wipes, blankets, a change of diapers, and fresh clothes. Each carrier had an adjustable arm attached that held the formulas in place, and the formulas came pre-warmed. Brian was sure they were precisely the recommended temperature.

He put the butt of the shotgun on the ground and leaned the barrel against the table. Removing Molly, he put her in the nearest carrier and brought the bottle up to her mouth. He let go of the bottle knowing it would stay in place.

Removing the improvised harness, he pulled it up over his head and set it carefully on the ground. Manipulating Katie to her back, he then, with the straps still taut between her and Kelly, laid Kelly down in the same manner. It didn't take long before he had them both in carriers too.

He turned all three, facing them across the table, then grabbed the shotgun and walked to the other side to check out the three large plates. He sat in the chair in front of the plates.

To his right there was a switch set into the top of the table. Inscribed in the table under the switch were the words, 'Turn this on.'

Brian did so and heard a recording.

"Welcome to paradise one; you have just activated a safety barrier. Nothing can pass into where you are without being destroyed. Warning, you must turn this switch off before disembarking. Enjoy your breakfast."

Brian laughed. There was a tub of hot water with air bubbling to the surface and steam rising off the top. The pump was what he had heard as he approached. There were three shallow insets for the girls. The bubbles in them didn't have far to travel.

Next to the tub was a stack of towels. Next to the towels, a rack of clothes from which he could choose.

After eating, Brian undressed the girls, cleaned all bottoms as needed, and sat each in their own depression. Even though he knew it would be okay, he still checked the water before putting them in. Brian climbed into the big section of the tub. Water gently caressed his skin from all directions.

Finding there was a seat; he sat and stretched. After carrying the girls to this point, the water felt rejuvenating.

As Brian sat enjoying the water's massaging effect, he laughed out loud. If Ivan found him now, there would be a lot of explaining to do. Louder, his laugh thundered through the forest as he sat in the tub of hot water, safely, with three baby girls out in the middle of nowhere.

***

Before proceeding, Brian lifted the corner of the table and looked under it. He then turned off the switch.

Getting his phone, he called the Space Station.

"Brian's travel resort, how may I help you?"

"I'm on my way."

"Did you enjoy breakfast?"

"Naturally, thanks. I'm still in awe that you can do all of this. I noticed there wasn't anything half melted away this time. No depression and the grass looked like the Installation's. What did you do differently?"

"Excellent. There were some minor changes, but the batteries in your phone would long be dead before I finished explaining what those differences are."

"You're a genius. Later, okay?"

Three more times, Brian took refuge within the safety of a paradise one. Everything was the same except for the meals. Although still full from breakfast, he ate the desserts. He had called for the last safe haven just to change one of the girls and to see what was for dessert.

Toward evening, he came to a large clearing. It was unlike anything he had seen so far and called the Space Station.

"Yes." This was long, drawn out, and overly exaggerated.

"I hope I've arrived. I'm tired. I think if I sat down, I wouldn't be able to get up. I called 'cause I don't see the house."

"I never said there'd be a house."

"Oh, come on—not now! I'm not in the mood."

"Testy, testy, are we? Well keep walking and tell me what you see."

Brian stepped into the clearing. Even though there was somewhat of a cut-off, it wasn't as defined and there were no partial trees.

"There's a clearing and it's mostly grass with small trees. There's a hill in the center."

"Go to the top of the hill."

Brian stepped out and noticed the trees were all the same height. On closer inspection, the trees were all the same. They were spaced the same distance from each other too.

"This is weird. The trees look like they're all the same."

"Copy and paste. It's the only way I could get it done so quick."

"I hope they don't recognize any pattern from the air? Speaking of which, any updates on the search for us?"

"All's quiet at the Installation. I trust your stroll through the woods remained uneventful."

"Yes, it did," Brian sighed. "Somewhere along the line the kids got heavy. I just want to get them off my back and sit down. Did you take care of the other place?"

"Yes, it looks like what you're walking over now." He then consoled Brian. "I'm sorry you're tired, but you're there now and you'll like this place. It's not a house, though. It's a biosphere. You'll find it a pleasant surprise. The entrance is at the top of the hill. It's well camouflaged, so pay attention. I'm tired too. I'm calling it a night. You know where you can reach me."

They said goodbye. He closed his phone as he closed the gap to the hill.

At the top, he found the entrance right away. A glass door, it wasn't as well hidden as the Brian at the Space Station had said it would be. He opened it. The entrance led to a flight of stairs, and with no other choice, he followed them down.

When he reached the bottom, a voice, loud, asked, "Who are you?" It startled him; his eyes narrowed, still adjusting coming in from the daylight outside. The voice, so unfamiliar, evoked an uncommonly high sense of awareness. It was a woman! She stood off to the side of the room holding a knife. He couldn't help but stare; as his eyes adjusted they wandered all over her. Her chest was out of proportion to his. He got his phone, flipped it open, punching the speed dial.

"I'm Brian," he told her while waiting for an answer. Her hair was long as depicted in the drawing. However, the drawing with its large circles for her chest hadn't revealed the true nature of what he witnessed at this moment. "I'd offer a hand in greeting but I don't want to get stabbed." He heard Space Station Brian pick up. "What are you doing?" he asked.

"It's her," Space Station Brian said. The woman lowered the knife.

"Who?" Brian asked. He knew he couldn't be all that of an imposing figure with three babies strapped to him.

"Amy."

"Amy?" Brian repeated.

"How do you know my name?" Amy asked. Brian's eyes had never left her. She was beautiful. Her voice was like music. The drawing he had kept on his laptop all this time would never do her justice.

"Why would you do this?" Brian asked.

"You need help. Let me talk to her."

"No, you've gone too far." He folded the phone.

"Where are we?" she asked.

"You're on Earth."

Her eyes rolled; she seemed disappointed. He had never seen the gesture done so eloquently. His phone rang, and just then, either Kelly or Katie started to cry still on his back. He no longer felt tired.

"Who's on the cell?" she wanted to know.

"Cell?"

"Yeah, your cell phone."

"Oh, it's my worst half," he said, flipping it open.

"Please," Space Station Brian pleaded. "I have to know if she has a stash of organics. I can't last much longer without food."

Brian held the phone out. Across the room, she still held the knife; he wasn't going to take a step toward her. The baby continued to cry.

"He wants to talk to you. His name is Brian. He's at the Space Station and is dying of starvation."

Her shoulders slumped. "I suspect that's what happened to me," she said, coming forward to take the phone. He was surprised the human form could move the way she made it move. When she was close, he took in her essences. His hand tingled where she touched him taking the phone.

"This is Amy, Brian. Are you the one responsible for putting me here on Earth?"

She listened for a bit saying "Un-huh," and then she said it again, a few times. "No, there isn't." While she listened, Brian removed Molly from the harness setting her on the floor. It was the first time he had taken his eyes off her. He was removing the harness when Amy said, "Goodbye," and folded the phone.

"What'd he say?" he asked, getting Katie into his arms to quiet her.

"He said you are the responsible one, and that you are my knight in shining armor."

"Huh?"

Upon completion of A Stone's Throw Away, Sharon R. commented:

The End!!!???? Oh no!
You must let us know what happens next.
I surely do want an autographed copy of this.
Has been an excellent story. Every great story leaves you longing for more! This certainly filled the bill!"

From the Author:

First, thanks for reading. I took a lot of time to think about what to write here and have decided there's nothing I can say, it's all in your hands now. I enjoyed putting this work together for your entertainment and I hope you enjoyed. If you did, join my group: astonesthrow-away.gather.com for the latest updates on the sequel.

Because it seems counter productive to write a sequel if only a few individuals ever find out about this work, and because it's too large of a task for any one individual...maybe each of you can make this book water cooler conversation creating interest in others to read and they too can join the group.

Don't let your friends browse bookstore shelves for hours looking for a good read. You have one in your hands in search of readers. So lend your book to a friend. Once returned, lend it again.

Thanks for informing your friends that this work exist.

God Bless

Proof

Made in the USA
Charleston, SC
05 February 2013

17308735R00227